Praise for
THE INQUISITOR'S KEY
and previous BODY FARM novels by
JEFFERSON BASS

"The real deal."
Kathy Reichs

"Bass is a fresh voice in the crime novel arena."
Seattle Post-Intelligencer

"[Bass] takes the Bill Brockton series into
Steve Berry territory with this story of an ancient
mystery and a modern-day lunatic's quest to reshape
the world.... Brockton is as appealing as always,
and the story ... is clever and compelling."
Booklist

"*The Inquisitor's Key* combines medieval
history, religious conspiracy, and murder with
... authentic forensic investigation."
Huntsville Times

"[The Body Farm] is a place for terrific
thrills, chills, and other accoutrements of
mysteries. And that's a good thing."
Asbury Park Press

"[Bass] is a solid storyteller who inspires credibility
with scientific expertise.... [*The Inquisitor's
Key*] provides plenty of food for thought."
Kirkus Reviews

By Jefferson Bass

JEFFERSON BASS

THE INQUISITOR'S KEY

A BODY FARM NOVEL

HARPER

An Imprint of HarperCollinsPublishers

"Madonna and Corpse" was published as an e-book novella in May 2012 by William Morrow, an Imprint of HarperCollins Publishers.

HARPER

An Imprint of HarperCollins*Publishers*
10 East 53rd Street
New York, New York 10022-5299

Copyright © 2012 by Jefferson Bass, LLC
"Madonna and Corpse" copyright © 2012 by Jefferson Bass, LLC
ISBN 978-0-06-180706-0

First Harper premium printing: February 2013
First Harper digest printing: February 2013
First William Morrow hardcover printing: May 2012

In memory of J.W. (Bill) Jefferson

There is no yesterday nor any tomorrow, but only Now,
as it was a thousand years ago and as it will be
a thousand years hence.
MEISTER JOHANNES ECKHART, CIRCA 1300

Nothing ever happened in the past; it happened in the Now.
Nothing will ever happen in the future;
it will happen in the Now.

ECKHART TOLLE, *The Power of Now*, 1999

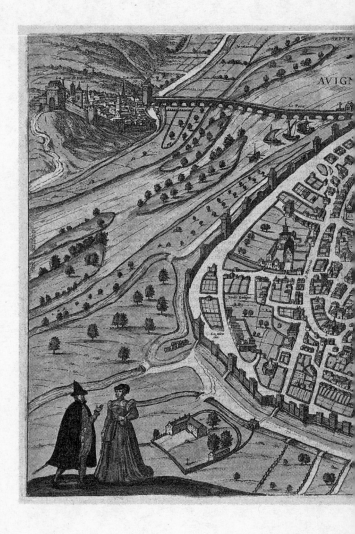

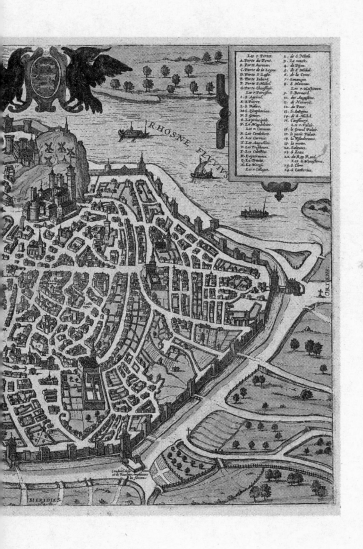

PART I

PROLOGUE

Knoxville, Tennessee
The Present

A MOCKINGBIRD TWITTERED ON a branch of a dog-wood as a middle-aged man—his hair going to salt-and-pepper, but his body fit and his movements brisk—approached a chain-link gate at the edge of a wooded hillside. The man wore a black Nomex jumpsuit, which was heavy and hot for Knoxville in June, but he'd scheduled a meeting with the university president later in the day and didn't want his street clothes reeking of human decay. Sewn to each shoulder of the jumpsuit was a patch embroidered with the words "Forensic Anthropology" and the image of a human skull, a pair of swords criss-crossed beneath it.

The gate, like the rest of the fence, was topped with shiny coils of concertina wire. Above the gate, the unblinking eye of a video camera kept constant vigil; other cameras monitored the perimeter of the fence, which enclosed three wooded acres. A large metal sign wired to the mesh of the gate proclaimed UNIVERSITY OF TENNESSEE ANTHROPOLOGY RESEARCH FACILITY. KEEP OUT. OFFICIAL USE ONLY. FOR ENTRY OR INFORMATION, CONTACT DR. BILL BROCKTON, ANTHROPOLOGY DEPARTMENT, 865-974-0010. The gate was secured by a padlock whose shackle was as thick as the man's index finger.

The man in the jumpsuit—Brockton himself—unclipped a large ring of keys from his belt, selected one, and opened the padlock. Swinging the chain-link gate outward, he proceeded to a second, inner gate, this one made of solid planks. The wooden gate, part of a high privacy fence shielding the enclosure from prying eyes, was secured by a second padlock, which was fastened to a heavy steel chain threaded through holes bored in each door of the gate. When the lock clicked open, Brockton fed one end of the chain through the hole in the board, link by clattering link, and then pushed the wooden gate inward. It opened onto a small grass clearing surrounded by locust trees, oaks, maples, dogwoods, and climbing honeysuckle vines. Stacked at one edge of the clearing, just inside the gate, were three aluminum cases, each the size and shape of a no-frills coffin. Faded shipping labels hung from the cases, along with red BIOHAZARD warnings.

Retracing his steps, Brockton exited the enclosure, returned to a white University of Tennessee pickup idling just outside the fence, and backed it through the gate and into the clearing. At the far edge of the grass, he tucked the truck between two trees and shut off the engine. Opening the camper shell and the tailgate, he slid out a sheet of plywood, pulling it across the tailgate until it was close to dropping off.

His muscles strained with the effort, for atop the plywood lay a black vinyl bag seven feet long by three feet wide, as thick and lumpy as a human body. He lowered the end of the plywood to the ground, forming a ramp, and then slid the bag down. Kneeling beside it, he tugged open the zipper—a long C-shaped zipper edging the top, one side, and the bottom of the rectangular bag—and then folded back the flap. Inside was a fresh corpse, a white male whose abundant wrinkles and sparse white hair seemed to suggest that he'd lived out his allotted threescore years and ten, maybe more. The face appeared peaceful; the old man might almost have been napping except for the unblinking eyes . . . and the blowfly that landed and walked unnoticed across one of the corneas.

From the back of the truck Brockton retrieved two thin dog tags, each stamped with the number 49-12 to signify that the corpse was the forty-ninth body donated to the research facility in the year 2012. With a pair of black zip ties, he fastened one tag to the corpse's left arm and the other to the left ankle: a seemingly insignificant act, yet one that conferred a whole new identity on the man. In his new life—his life as a corpse, a research subject, and a skeletal specimen—the man would have a new identity. His new name, his only name, would be 49-12.

Upriver, the bells of a downtown church began

to toll noon as Brockton lay 49-12's hands across his chest. The anthropologist looked up, listening, then smiled slightly. Peering into the vacant eyes of the corpse, he plucked a line of poetry from some dusty corner of memory. "Never send to know for whom the bell tolls," he advised 49-12. "It tolls for thee."

At that moment, the cell phone on Brockton's belt chimed. "And for me," he added.

A BELL JETRANGER helicopter skimmed low across a wooded ridge and dropped toward a river junction, the confluence where the Holston and the French Broad joined to form the emerald-green headwaters of the Tennessee. Beneath the right-hand skid of the chopper, a rusting railroad trestle spanned the narrow mouth of the French Broad. Just ahead, at Downtown Island Airport, a small runway paralleled the first straightaway of the Tennessee, and a single-engine plane idled at the threshold, preparing for takeoff. The helicopter pilot keyed his radio. "Downtown Island traffic, JetRanger Three Whiskey Tango is crossing the field westbound at one thousand, landing at the Body Farm."

"Three Whiskey Tango, this is Downtown Island. Did you say landing at the Body Farm, over?"

"Roger that."

"Three Whiskey Tango, are you aware that the Body Farm is a restricted facility?"

"Downtown Island, we're a Tennessee Bureau of Investigation aircraft. I reckon they won't mind."

Two miles west of the airstrip, the modest skyline of downtown Knoxville sprawled above the right-hand riverbank. The skyline was defined by two twenty-five-story office towers built by a pair of brothers who began as bankers and ended as swindlers; a wedge-shaped pyramid of a hotel, Marriott-by-way-of-Mayan; a thirty-foot orange basketball forever swishing through the forty-foot hoop atop the Women's Basketball Hall of Fame; and a seventy-five-foot globe of golden glass balanced on a two-hundred-foot steel tower like a golf ball on a tee—the Sunsphere, a relic of a provincial world's fair orchestrated by the swindling banker brothers in 1982.

The epicenter of Knoxville, though—its beating heart if not its financial or architectural nucleus— lay another mile downriver: the massive oval of Neyland Stadium, home and shrine to the University of Tennessee Volunteers. During home games against the Florida Gators or the Alabama Crimson Tide, the stadium roared and rattled with the fervor of 102,000 rabid fans. Beneath the stadium, in a grimy building wedged under the stands, was the university's Anthropology Department, home to twenty professors, a hundred graduate students, and thousands of human skeletons.

A mile beyond the stadium, the TBI helicopter crossed to the river's hilly, wooded left bank. Easing below the treetops, it touched down just outside the fence of the Body Farm. Brockton emerged from the research facility's entrance. Fighting the blast of the rotor wash, he wrestled the wooden gate into place and locked it, followed by the outer fence. Then he ducked under the spinning blades and clambered into the cockpit. As he swung the door shut, the turbine spooled up and the chopper vaulted upward, buffeting the fence and shredding oak leaves as it climbed. The pilot banked so steeply that Brockton found himself looking straight down at the naked form of 49-12, and he realized with a queasy smile that if his harness should fail and the door fly open at this moment, he would deliver his own fresh corpse to the Body Farm. But luck and latches held, and the chopper leveled off and scurried upriver with the anthropologist strapped safely aboard.

The GPS screen on the instrument panel displayed a map and a course heading, but the pilot didn't need either. He simply aimed for the plume of smoke twenty miles to the east.

The plume marked the smoldering remnants of an airplane hangar, and the charred remains of a dead undercover agent.

Paris, France
March 18, 1314

JACQUES FOURNIER HAS three advantages over most of the spectators filling the square of Notre Dame. He's uncommonly tall, so he's able to see over everyone else; he's uncommonly stocky, so he's able to push his way through the throng; and he's uncommonly dressed—in the white cassock and black scapular of a Cistercian monk—so he benefits from grudging deference as he nudges his way toward the cathedral. If someone moves to protest or shove back, he makes the sign of the cross, and that generally settles the matter. Nudge by nudge, foot by foot, cross by cross, Fournier edges toward the front of the cathedral, where a platform has been built for this morning's spectacle. The cathedral's façade is shadowed, backlit by the rising sun, but the massive rose window—fired from within by sunbeams slanting through the nave—blazes red and gold.

A murmur of excitement stirs the crowd, and a shout sweeps across the plaza like rolling thunder: "They're coming! They're coming!"

To a chorus of cheers and jeers, a chevron of royal guards pushes through the square leading four shackled men. The men are France's most famous prisoners: the last and most illustrious of the Knights Templar, the warrior-monks who acquired staggering wealth and power during the Crusades. For more than a century, the Templars were highly valued by both the king and the pope. Escorting pilgrims to the Holy Land, the Templars provided safe passage and carried letters of credit—less appealing to bandits than gold or silver—and, upon arriving in Jerusalem, cashed in the credit for currency from their vaults on the Temple Mount. But when the Holy Land was lost to Saladin and his Muslim hordes, the Templars began falling from favor. And seven years ago, in 1307, King Philip the Fair arrested hundreds of the knights, charging them with acts of heresy and perversion. "God is not pleased," the arrest warrant began—a phrase Fournier finds applicable to many situations and many people. "We have enemies of the faith in the kingdom."

The shackled prisoners are led up the steps and onto the platform just as Fournier reaches its base. The first is Jacques de Molay, Grand Master of the Order of the Knights Templar. A tall, silver-haired seventy-year-old, de Molay appears gaunt and haggard—seven years of captivity have taken their toll—but he walks with as much dignity as chains, weakness, and advanced age allow. Behind him shuffles Geoffrey de Charney, the Templars' chief commander in Normandy, followed by Hugues de Peraud and Godefroi de Gonneville. After the prisoners and guards have mounted the stage, one of the cathedral doors opens and a procession of sumptuously robed clergymen emerges: the high-ranking officials who have decided the Templars' fates. At their head is William, archbishop of Sens, who serves also as Inquisitor of France and as the king's own confessor. The archbishop is followed by Cardinal Arnold Novelli—Fournier's own Uncle Arnold. Three years ago, when he was made cardinal, Uncle Arnold handpicked Jacques to succeed him as head of Fontfroide Abbey, a remarkable opportunity and honor. Three weeks ago, a missive bearing Cardinal Novelli's wax seal arrived at Fontfroide, inviting Jacques to journey to Paris for the sentencing: "an event," the cardinal wrote, "that cannot fail to reinforce your zeal for protecting the faith." And indeed, the young abbot already feels a surge of inspiration as he surveys the solemn clerics, the chained heretics, and the mighty façade of Notre Dame.

The cathedral occupies the eastern end of the Île de la Cité, the slender island at the center of the river Seine. The island's western end is dominated by the royal palace and gardens, and this division of the island into two halves—God's half and the king's—is pleasing and instructive, Fournier thinks. *Render unto Caesar that which is Caesar's*, he reminds himself, *and unto God that which is God's*. Evenly ballasted by church and state, the boat-shaped isle maintains an even keel, at least most of the time. Occasionally the balance of power on the island shifts to one end or the other, causing France itself to tip precariously. But not today; today, king and cardinals alike agree that the Templars must be punished, for the good of the kingdom and the salvation of their souls.

As the watery late-winter sun rises above the twin bell towers, the archbishop steps forward. Quieting the crowd, he reads the Templars' names and the charges against them. "Having confessed to these crimes fully and freely," he tells the four, "you are hereby sentenced to perpetual imprisonment. May Almighty God have mercy on your souls." The crowd roars, some in approval, some in protest.

De Molay, the old Grand Master, steps to the front of the scaffold and raises his hands for silence. After a scattering of whistles and catcalls, the noise subsides. "Listen to me, and hear me well," de Molay calls out, his voice thin but strong. "We have indeed confessed to these terrible crimes." He pauses to let those words sink in, and the archbishop bows his mitred head gravely. Then de Molay shouts, "But those confessions were false—forced from us by torture!" Geoffrey de Charney steps forward, nodding and shouting that what de Molay says is true; meanwhile, the other two prisoners shrink back, distancing themselves from de Molay and de Charney. At the other end of the platform, the archbishop of Sens, Cardinal Novelli, and the other clerics huddle in consternation; then the archbishop hurries to the captain of the guards, whispering urgently and pointing at de Molay. "The Order of the Knights Templar is holy and pure," de Molay cries as the soldiers converge on him. "Our sin was not heresy—our sin was weakness! We betrayed the Order! We signed false confessions! These clerics are the real traitors to God!" A blow from one of the guards knocks the old man to his knees, and the crowd surges forward, on the brink of mayhem. As the soldiers drag the prisoners from the scaffold and force their way back to the prison, swords and lances at the ready, Fournier feels a mixture of outrage and sadness: outrage at de Molay's brazenness; sadness for Uncle Arnold and the other holy men, publicly denounced by a lying heretic!

WORD OF DE Molay's outburst is relayed to the palace. King Philip—taking a late breakfast—roars his rage, rakes the dishes to the floor, and roundly cudgels the unfortunate messenger. Next, he swiftly convenes a council of civil and church lawyers. The lawyers, no fools, assure the king that a relapsed heretic—what better proof of heresy, after all, than *denying* one's heresy?—can be executed immediately, without further trial or appeal. With equal parts fury and satisfaction, the king decrees that de Molay and de Charney will die before the sun sets.

The news spreads across the island, and out to the rest of Paris, like wildfire. Within the hour, boats begin delivering bundles of kindling to the place of execution: the Île aux Juifs—the tiny Isle of the Jews, a stone's throw upstream from the royal palace—where countless unbelievers have been executed over the years.

And so it is that six hours after the dramatic scene in the cathedral square, Fournier is jostling and nudging and sign-of-the-crossing his way forward once more, this time toward the western end of the Île de la Cité—the king's end of the island—to see de Molay and de Charney put to the torch. Fournier bulls and blesses his way to a choice viewing spot on the shore and sizes up the stack of firewood accumulating across the narrow divide of water. There's fuel enough to incinerate ten heretics, he judges, let alone two.

Fournier's assessment is based on more than a little experience with heretic burnings. Happily, he was a theology student here four years before, when King Philip burned fifty-four Templars for the same shocking crimes as de Molay and de Charney: spitting on the cross, denouncing Christ, worshiping a pagan idol, and performing acts of sexual depravity. Burning the fifty-four Templars consumed two full days and a veritable forest worth of wood; this immolation should require only an hour, or perhaps two, if the fire is kept small to prolong the pain.

Satisfied that the fuel is more than adequate for the task, the young abbot turns in a slow circle and studies his fellow spectators. They're a mangy and flea-bitten lot, most of them—*enemies of the faith*, thinks Fournier, *or unreliable friends, at best*—but a few arm's lengths to his right, he notices a cluster of other clerics. They're Dominicans, judging by their habits: a handful of novices; two friars who appear to be about his own age, possibly younger; and an older man, seemingly the group's leader. The older man is talking—lecturing, more like it—about heresy in general and the Inquisition in particular. That's not terribly surprising, since the Dominicans are the pope's chosen order for detecting and uprooting heresy. But there's something about the man's easy confidence that Fournier finds grating.

He edges closer, listening to the older man's comments with keen interest, a critical ear, and rising irritation. Fournier's no Dominican, but he's taken a keen interest in the Inquisition since his arrival at Fontfroide. Geographically, the center of the Inquisition—Toulouse—is near Fournier's abbey; theologically, the spirit of the Inquisition is close to Fournier's stern and austere heart. During the past year, in fact, he's spent weeks in Toulouse, observing and admiring the work of Bernard Gui, the devout Dominican whose masterful wielding of physical pain, theological cunning, and abject terror has broken hundreds of heretics during his seven years as Chief Inquisitor. Fournier wonders if Gui is here today, but he doubts that the Inquisitor's busy schedule allows him time to travel from Toulouse to Paris, even for such a worthy cause.

Suddenly, from the knot of Dominicans, he hears Gui's name spoken aloud, as if the older friar has somehow been reading his thoughts. The man is speaking in Latin so that the rabble around him cannot understand, but his words are clear to Fournier. The Dominican is criticizing Gui—and not just criticizing him, but mocking him: mocking a brother friar, and the Chief Inquisitor at that. "He has the fierceness of a bull," the man says with a smile. "The intelligence of a bull, too."

Fournier pushes sideways, further closing the distance between himself and the Dominican. The movement catches the eye of the friar, and when he meets Fournier's gaze, Fournier calls to him in Latin: "Would you dare to say such things about Bernard if he were here to listen?"

The older man registers mild surprise, but not the contrition and fear that Fournier expected from him. "My words will reach his ears soon enough, I feel certain," he says to the hulking young Cistercian. "When you relay them, be sure to tell Brother Bernard who spoke them: Johannes Eckhart, master and chair of Dominican theology here at the University of Paris." He bows, with a slight smile and a sideways tilt to his head—is he mocking Fournier now?—and then turns his back on the indignant abbot.

"God is not pleased," Fournier mutters beneath his breath. He considers pushing through the half-dozen people who stand between them, considers teaching the old man a lesson in respect. Suddenly a shout ripples up the shore, like a bow wave from the boat that is making its way upstream toward the Isle of the Jews, making its way toward the towering stake and the stacks of wood.

The boat, rowed by eight men, carries half a dozen of the king's guards, as well as Jacques de Molay and Geoffrey de Charney. One of the guards raises a flaming torch high overhead, and the mob roars.

THE PYRE BURNS until midnight. The two Templars are long since incinerated, but the crowd lingers, loath to leave until every stick of wood is consumed.

When the flames finally gutter and die, the Order of the Knights Templar has been extinguished. But hanging in the air, like the lingering smoke and the scent of charred flesh, is the dying cry of Grand Master Jacques de Molay: "I summon the king and the pope to meet me before God!"

CHAPTER 1

Sevierville, Tennessee
The Present

I HEARD A CLICK in my headset, followed by the voice of the TBI pilot. "Dr. Brockton, you okay back there?"

"I'm still kinda puckered from that takeoff," I answered, "but yeah, I'm fine."

He laughed. "I'll go easier on the landing."

He circled the plume of smoke, which rose from the ruins of a house. Fifty yards away was what might have been an airstrip except for the fact that it was hemmed in by houses. I pointed at the ribbon of asphalt. "What's up with that? Looks like they accidentally put a runway smack-dab in the middle of a neighborhood."

"They did, but not by accident," the pilot said. "This is Smoky Mountain Airpark. A subdivision for aviation nuts. Instead of a garage, every house has its own airplane hangar."

A small fleet of vehicles ringed the smoldering hangar and half-burned house we landed beside. In addition to the helicopter, I counted four fire trucks—two of them still spraying water on the house—plus three Sevier County Sheriff's Office cruisers and four unmarked cars, which I supposed were TBI vehicles.

I was only half right, I learned when four investigators met me halfway between the helicopter and the house.

"Good to see you again, Doc," shouted Steve Morgan over the ebbing noise of the turbine and the rotor wash. Steve had majored in anthropology, but he'd been working for the TBI for about ten years now, and he was the one who'd called to ask if I could take a quick look at a death scene. "Where's your assistant? Miranda? I thought you two were joined at the ileum."

"She's in France for the summer," I yelled. "Left a couple days ago. On a dig with some fancy French archaeologist." Whatever expression my face was showing, it made him laugh.

"Doc, do you know Dave Pendergrast, from our Sevier County office?"

"I didn't, but I do now. Good to meet you." I shook Pendergrast's hand.

"This is Special Agent Craig Drucker, of the FBI," Steve went on. He turned and nodded toward a man striding toward us from the ruined building. "And Special Agent Robert Stone of the Drug Enforcement Administration."

I smiled. "No need to introduce me to this guy," I said. "Rocky Stone and I go way back. Last time we worked together was that big meth-lab explosion that killed a couple guys up in Scott County. That was, what, three, four years ago, Rocky?"

"Ha. More like six or eight." He grinned. "My oldest kid was being born while you were piecing those two bodies together." I smiled, remembering how antsy Rocky had been to get to the hospital to see his wife and the baby, and how proud he'd been the next day when I dropped by the maternity ward to see them. "Thanks for coming on such short notice," Rocky said. "Sorry we kept you in the dark on the ride over."

"Hey, I'm not complaining," I assured him. "I'll do just about anything for a helicopter ride."

The subdivision wasn't just an aviation nut's dream; it was also, the DEA agent explained, a drug runner's dream. "For the past year," Rocky said, "we've been investigating a smuggling ring based in Colombia. They've been flying cocaine into small airports all over the Southeast, changing the drop point every time. But this place is perfect as a more permanent base—a clandestine hub, I guess you could call it. No control tower, very little traffic, virtually no risk of detection. You land whenever you've got a shipment, taxi the plane into your own private hangar, lock the door, and unload in complete privacy. This operation could have run without a hitch for years."

"So what happened?" I asked, nodding at the smoking ruins. "Turf war? A raid that got too hot to handle?"

"I wish," Rocky said. "One of our undercover agents had infiltrated the operation. What's left of him is there, in what's left of the hangar. We've got an arson investigator coming, but we'd like you to examine the body. See if he died during the fire or died *before* the fire. We need to know if it was an accident or a homicide."

"Dr. Garcia's the medical examiner," I pointed out. "He's got primary jurisdiction here." Dr. Edelberto Garcia—Eddie—served as ME for Knoxville, Knox County, and several surrounding counties.

"Actually, we called Dr. Garcia just before we called you. He says if the body's rotten or burned, you're the guy to look at it."

"That's damned decent of Eddie," I joked, "letting me have all the good ones." All four agents smiled.

"The scary thing is," Rocky said, "the Doc's not being sarcastic. He actually means it."

The truth was, Rocky was right. I actually did.

THE DEAD AGENT was Maurice Watson, alias "Perry Hutchinson," whom the DEA had planted as the manager of the airpark. Six months before, working through the drug smugglers' distributors in Atlanta, Hutchinson had offered them a sweet deal: a house, a hangar, and a key to the gas pump in exchange for a small cut of the profits.

"They brought in the first load two weeks ago," said Rocky. "It was small—just a test run. Smooth as silk. They were planning another run next week. A big load. We were all set to come down on them. But somebody got spooked—or got tipped off." He shook his head grimly. "You ready to take a look?"

"Sure. Let's go."

The intense heat of the fire had reduced the hangar to scorched brick walls and sagging steel roof trusses silhouetted against blue sky and gray smoke. Entering through a side door, I found myself sloshing through an inch of muck—a slimy mixture of water, ash, soot, and petrochemicals—and I was grateful that I'd put on my waterproof boots before delivering corpse 49-12 to the Body Farm.

Occupying one side of the hangar was a blackened Ford pickup; on the other side was a scorched plane, a V-tailed Beechcraft Bonanza; and tucked between them was a riding lawn mower, its gas cap removed. Lying on the floor next to the mower, faceup in the muck, was the corpse, its facial features all but obliterated, its left hand still clutching a five-gallon gasoline can. The heat of the fire had shrunk the flexor muscles of the arm, locking the man's fingers around the handle in what was, quite literally, a death grip. "So, looks like an accident," Stone said. "Might even have *been* an accident."

"Mighty convenient accident," I said, "the way the fire just happened to break out so close to so much gasoline."

"Damned convenient," Rocky agreed.

I knelt beside the body. "I assume he's not carrying his DEA badge," I said, "but have you checked him for other identification? What was his undercover name? Hutchinson?"

Rocky nodded. "He's got the Hutchinson driver's license. Can you get a DNA sample so we can be sure? Or did the heat . . . ? Is the DNA . . . ?"

I finished the question for him. "Is the DNA cooked? Probably not. The femur is pretty well insulated by the muscles of the thigh, and most of that tissue's still there, so we can probably get a good DNA sample. But the dental records might be quicker and easier. Can you get me those?" Tugging on a pair of gloves and kneeling beside the corpse, I opened the mouth. "Agent Stone? Unless your man had just come from a barroom brawl, he wasn't refueling his lawn mower when he died." Leaning back so Rocky could get a better view, I showed him the teeth. All eight incisors had been snapped off at the roots.

"Shit," Rocky muttered. "That doesn't look like something the fire did."

"No way," I told him. "See how the teeth are folded backward into the mouth? That's called a 'hinge fracture,' and it means somebody swung something at him—a baseball bat or a steel pipe or the butt of a rifle—and caught him square on the mouth." I studied the face with my eyes, and then with my fingertips, pressing and squeezing in order to feel the bones through the burned flesh. From there I worked my way down the entire body. When I finally got down to the feet, I looked up at Rocky. "I'll X-ray the body when I get it back to the Regional Forensic Center," I said, "but I can tell you already he's got multiple fractures. Half a dozen, at least. I hate to say it, Rocky, but somebody broke your man, bone by bone, before they killed him."

Stone's eyes had gone narrow and cold, and his jaw muscles pulsed rhythmically, forming knots the size of walnuts. "Damn those bastards to hell," he said. "How long will it take you to do the exam?"

"The exam itself, half a day," I said. "But I've got to get the tissue off the bones to do it right. And that'll take a couple weeks—we'll put him out at the Body Farm and let Mother Nature clean him off."

He grimaced. "Isn't there any other way? Something more respectful? More dignified?"

I shook my head. "I could dismember him, put him in kettles, and cook him down. That'd be a little faster. But it seems less respectful, to my way of thinking. And an aggressive defense attorney would claim that I damaged the bones in taking him apart."

He sighed. "All right, do it the way you think is best. Just find everything—*everything*—so we can nail these scum-sucking bastards." He looked at the vehicles. "Thank God we got the fire out so fast. If the gas tanks had gone up, I doubt there'd've been any of him left for you to look at."

"Wait. Wait." I looked up, my gaze swiveling from his face to the blackened vehicles. "You're saying there's still unburned gas in here?" He nodded. "In the truck *and* in the airplane?"

"Yup. The truck holds twenty-six gallons; the plane holds ninety."

"There's almost a hundred gallons of high-octane aviation fuel sitting right over our heads? We shouldn't even be in here, should we?"

Stone shrugged. "Fire's out."

"There might be an ember somewhere in that plane. One of the tanks might fail. The roof could collapse. A spark from—"

I was interrupted by a metallic clatter—the clatter of metal punching through metal—and a neat round hole suddenly appeared in the side of the airplane.

"Shots! Shots! Take cover!" yelled one of the agents. Another bullet slammed into the plane, this time into the wing, and a thin stream of pale blue liquid began dribbling from the wing and pooling atop the muck.

"Jesus, that's avgas," said Stone. "We gotta get outta here." He hoisted me to my feet and began pulling me toward the door. All around us, agents and deputies were scrambling, staring and pointing in various directions, drawing weapons. Another bullet chipped a cinder block and ricocheted off in a shower of sparks. A flame bloomed at the base of the far wall. From there it followed a finger of gas, a finger beckoning it toward the center of the hangar, toward the leaking airplane.

I tore free of Stone's grasp and ran back toward the plane. Behind me, I heard him shouting, "Doc, come back! Get out!"

A wall of flame had engulfed the far wing of the plane by the time I reached the dead agent. Grabbing his feet—the closest things to me—I tucked them under my arms and dragged him behind me like a sleigh, slipping and staggering as I hauled him through the muck. I'd almost made it to the door when the plane exploded, and a fist of fire slammed into my back and knocked me flat.

ROCKY STONE HELPED me carry the body of his dead agent to the most secluded corner of the Body Farm and lay him at the foot of a big oak. Unzipping the body bag, I tugged it free, fastened ID tags on the left arm and left ankle, and then draped the bag over the corpse.

"You broke half a dozen procedures and every rule of common sense, going back for him like that," Stone said. "And I am incredibly grateful. If you hadn't gotten him out, we wouldn't have a prayer of making a murder case."

"I wish the shooter hadn't gotten away."

"You and me both, Doc. He was only a couple hundred yards away—up on that low ridge—but by the time any of our guys got there, he was gone." Stone knelt and laid a DEA medallion on top of the bag. Closing his eyes, he said a few silent words, then stood. "So, you say it'll take about two weeks to get us a report?"

"More or less. More if it turns cool, less if it gets really hot. Once the bugs and I have cleaned him off, I'll take photos of all the fractures." I had already documented them, or at least most of them, with X-rays, which I took with a portable machine at the loading dock of the Forensic Center. But if the case came to trial, the prosecutors would need crisp photos to corroborate the fuzzy X-ray images.

Normally I'd have delegated the cleanup to my graduate assistant, Miranda Lovelady, who ran the bone lab and did much of the legwork at the Body Farm. Miranda had left for France only three days before, but already I was feeling her absence. I missed her help, and I missed her camaraderie. At the moment, though, I was relieved she hadn't been with me in Sevierville. I'd narrowly escaped being incinerated; in fact, the hair on the back of my head was singed, and if I'd been wearing my usual outfit—jeans and a cotton shirt—instead of the Nomex jumpsuit, my clothes would surely have caught fire. *Thank God Miranda wasn't there*, I thought.

She'd left on short notice, under circumstances that remained slightly mysterious to me. A week earlier, she'd received an urgent e-mail and then a phone call from a French archaeologist, Stefan Beauvoir, asking her to come help with a hastily arranged excavation. The site was a medieval palace dating from the thirteen hundreds—practically prehistoric by American standards, but nearly modern for Europe.

I'd hesitated before saying I could spare her; after all, during half a decade as my graduate assistant, she'd made herself indispensable. I valued and respected Miranda's intelligence and forensic expertise. But it went deeper than that, I had to admit: She was as important to me personally as she was professionally. In some ways, I felt closer to Miranda than to anyone else on earth, even my own son. If you took DNA out of the equation, Miranda was my next of kin. I felt certain that the bone lab and the Body Farm could limp along without Miranda for six weeks, but I wasn't sure *I* could manage that long.

"Excuse me, Doc?" Rocky's voice seemed to come from far away, not so much interrupting my thoughts as awakening me from some dream. "So if we're done here, I guess I'll be taking off. The TBI's gonna think we've hijacked their chopper."

"Sorry," I said. "Didn't mean to check out on you there. Hang on—I'll walk you out and lock up."

I bent to straighten one corner of the body bag, and as I did, my cell phone began bleating. Fishing the phone from the pocket of the jumpsuit, I glanced at the display. I didn't recognize the number; it started with 330, an area code I didn't know, and it looked longer than a phone number should be. I stared dumbly for a moment before I realized why. It was a foreign call, and 33 was the country code—the code, I suddenly remembered, for France. *Miranda!* I flipped open the phone, but in my excitement, I fumbled it, and it fell onto my foot and skittered beneath the body bag. Flinging aside the bag, I rooted for the phone, which had lodged—ironically and absurdly—beside the dead man's left ear. I had just laid hold of it when it fell silent. "*Damn* it," I muttered. I punched the "send" button, only to be told by a robotic voice that my call "cannot be completed as dialed," doubtless because it was an overseas number. "Damn damn *damn*," I muttered, but just as I finished the third *damn*, the phone rang again, displaying the same number.

This time, I did not drop it. "Hello? Miranda? How are you?"

"Ah, no, sorry, it is not Miranda." The voice was a man's, accented in French. "This is Stefan Beauvoir. The archaeologist Miranda is helping. She wanted me to call you."

My internal alarms began to shriek. "What's wrong? Has something happened to Miranda? Tell me."

"The doctor says it is—*merde*, how do you say it?—the rupture of the appendicitis?"

"Miranda's got a ruptured appendix?"

"*Oui*, yes, a ruptured appendix. She asked me to call and say, please, can you come?"

"Can I come? What, to France?"

"*Oui*. Please, can you come to France? To Avignon?" *Ah-veen-YOHN.* I didn't like the sound of it. "She is having the surgery now, and she will be very grateful if you can come."

"Doesn't she want someone from her family?"

"Ah, but it is not possible. I call her mother and her sister. Neither one has a passport. So she thinks next of you, and asks if you can please come quickly."

"Of course. I'll be there as soon as I can. I'll get on a plane this afternoon."

"*Bon*, good. You can fly into Avignon, but the flights are better if you come to Lyon or Marseilles. Marseilles is one hour by car."

Racing down the path and out the gate, I frantically flagged down the TBI chopper, which was quivering on its landing skids, transitioning toward flight. Stone took off his headset, scrambled out of the helicopter, and hurried over to me.

"Doc, is something wrong?"

"Can you guys give me a ride? I need to get someplace fast."

"Where?"

"France."

SIXTY SECONDS LATER, we were airborne again, this time with me in the right front seat. "Does this thing have turbo?" I asked the pilot. By way of an answer, he rolled the helicopter into a 90-degree bank.

"Holy shit," I heard Stone squawk from the back.

Skimming low across the river, the chopper hurtled toward Neyland Stadium. "I don't know where you can land," I said, scanning the vicinity of the stadium. "The parking lots all look pretty full."

The pilot grinned. "I think I see a spot that might just be big enough." Swooping low over the towering scoreboard, we plunged straight into the bowl of the stadium.

"Touchdown," Stone deadpanned as we thumped into the south end zone.

MY SECRETARY SCARCELY glanced up as I dashed past her desk and into my office. "Peggy," I called out, yanking down the zipper of the greasy, sooty jumpsuit. "I need you to do some airline research for me, please." Yanking off my boots and the jumpsuit, I tossed them in a corner.

"For that conference in Seattle next month? I booked your tickets last week, remember? Nonrefundable." Her typing hadn't even slowed.

"Peggy, stop typing. Listen. I need to fly to France. Marseilles. Like, ten minutes ago." On the other side of the doorway, her keyboard fell silent. "It's Miranda," I went on, pulling on the clothes I'd intended to wear to my meeting with the president. "Ruptured appendix. She's going in for surgery right now." Rummaging in my closet, I dug out my "go" bag, a duffel I kept packed and at the ready, and slung it over my shoulder.

"Oh, my Lord," she gasped. "Poor thing."

By then I was already headed for the staircase, my shirttail still untucked, my shoes and socks in one hand. "I'm off to the airport," I yelled over my shoulder. "Call me once you book it." As the steel fire door slammed shut behind me, I thought I heard her say something else, but by then I was halfway down the steps.

It wasn't until the helicopter was lifting off from the goal line that I realized what she'd said. The realization came when I saw her dash onto the field, wildly waving her arms, clutching my laptop in one hand and a small blue booklet in the other: my passport.

Twenty-two minutes and thirty-three hundred dollars later, my passport in one hand and my bag in the other, I boarded a United flight for Dulles airport in Washington, D.C. From Dulles, Lufthansa would take me to Frankfurt, Germany, and finally to Marseilles, where Beauvoir had promised to pick me up.

By the time I boarded at Dulles, I felt sure Miranda was out of surgery, but my half-dozen phone calls got no answer or return message. The silence was terrifying.

As the aircraft climbed out of Washington and wheeled toward the Atlantic, the ten-thousand-foot chime sounded, reminding me of the church bell I'd heard tolling a few hours before. *Please*, I prayed, though I could not have said to whom or what I prayed. *Please not for Miranda.*

CHAPTER 2

Marseilles, France
The Present

THE CUSTOMS AGENT DIDN'T bother to look up as he took my passport and reached for the inked stamp. "Is the purpose of your visit business or pleasure, Monsieur Brockton?" His flat tone suggested that he was already profoundly bored with me, even before I spoke.

I hesitated, uncertain how to respond. "Pleasure" didn't seem to fit the urgent nature of the trip, but if I said "business," that might open the door to more questions, or to the need for a work visa. "Uh, pleasure," I finally said. He looked up with a frown, as if he disapproved of pleasure, or of my limited enthusiasm. Then, with a slight sniff, he whacked the stamp down onto the page and flipped my passport back onto the counter.

As I emerged through the glass doors of the international terminal into the outer lobby, I scanned the crowd, searching for the face of a French archaeologist who appeared to be searching for the face of an American anthropologist. What would a French archaeologist look like? Angular and arrogant, sporting a black beret, an unfiltered cigarette, and a pencil mustache? In my anxiety over Miranda, I hadn't thought to ask Stefan how I'd recognize him, and he'd neither volunteered that information nor inquired about my own appearance.

I was midway through my second scan of the throng when, over the general din of foreign words and exotic accents, I heard a laugh—a familiar female laugh. My head snapped back to the right, to the cluster of faces I'd just rescanned, and there stood Miranda, arms spread wide, grinning broadly and shaking her head as if to say, "Unbelievable! You looked right past me! Twice!" I dropped my bag in astonishment; my hands flew to my chest, over my heart, as relief and happiness flooded me. Miranda was here, and she was all right. In fact, she looked better than all right, she looked fabulous: strong, healthy, excited, even radiant. What she did not look like was someone who'd just gotten out of emergency surgery for a ruptured appendix.

Miranda ran to me and flung her arms around my neck. "Thank you, *thank you*, for dropping everything and racing over here. I am *so glad* to see you!" She squeezed me tightly.

"Be careful," I said. "You'll rip out your stitches. Doesn't that hurt like hell? Why aren't you still in a hospital bed? How can you look so good so soon after surgery?"

She laughed again, a musical, pealing laugh like

carillon bells. "So many questions, so little time! I'm fine. Doesn't hurt a bit. I don't actually have stitches." I pulled back and stared at her, more confused than ever. She laughed again. "You're the victim of a slight deception. But don't worry; it's for a good cause, and you'll be glad you came." I shot her a glance—one loaded with questions and blame, which she clearly comprehended—but she just shook her head. "All will be revealed in the fullness of time. After we get to Avignon. Meanwhile, meet Stefan." She turned toward the line of faces, and a slight, bookish-looking man, forty or so, stepped forward, limping slightly—not one of the French traits I'd imagined. I extended my hand, and he shook it weakly. "Stefan Beauvoir, Bill Brockton." Suddenly Stefan took me by the shoulders and kissed me on both cheeks. I'd known that cheek kissing was a common French custom, but in my imagination only men and women greeted one another this way; I'd somehow overlooked the fact that men kissed other men. I preferred the American handshake. *Strongly* preferred the American handshake.

Stefan cast a dubious eye on the yellow L.L. Bean duffel I was carrying. "Where is the rest of your baggage?"

"This is it," I said. "I didn't have time to pack. Besides, I didn't think I'd be staying long." He shrugged and smiled. It was a slight, cryptic smile, as enigmatic as the Mona Lisa's but a bit more coy, as if he enjoyed prolonging my suspense.

It was lucky my bag was small, because Stefan's car—a Fiat Punto—was built for midgets. The engine was proportionately tiny, too. A few miles north of the airport, the car slowed to a crawl as the road angled up a narrow valley between rocky hills. When we finally topped out, we'd left the coastal plain for the rolling farmland of southern Provence.

Miranda kept deflecting my questions, promising to explain everything once we were in Avignon, but with each deflection I found myself growing edgier. Now that my panic about her health had been resolved, I resented being manipulated—tricked and scared into coming—and I hated being kept in the dark. "It's not a good idea to talk in the car," Stefan finally interjected when I launched another inquiry. "We might have bugs."

"He means it might be bugged," Miranda explained.

"I knew what he meant," I snapped.

"Ouch," she said.

"Sorry," I grumbled. "I'm tired from the trip—I can never sleep on planes. And somebody tried to barbecue me yesterday. So I'm kinda cranky at the moment."

"*Barbecue* you?" She sounded slightly concerned but mostly amused.

"Barbecue," I repeated. "What's the French word? *Flambé?*" I told them the story, and ended by leaning forward, putting my scorched head between the front seats.

Miranda rubbed the stubble. "Wow, that's crispy. I'd say you just used up another one of your nine lives."

Stefan took a glance, then looked in the rearview mirror. "Is there any possibility that the barbecue chef—the guy who was shooting at you—followed you to France?"

The thought had not occurred to me before. "Why? Is someone tailing us?" I turned and looked out the rear window and saw half a dozen cars behind us on the busy highway. How would we know if one of them was following us? "I doubt that the guy shooting at me had any idea who I was. And he certainly wouldn't have any way of connecting me to you, and to Avignon." But despite my confident words, Stefan's question had planted a seed of doubt in my mind, and it was already germinating into anxiety.

"I'm sure you're right," Miranda said. "And I know you're exhausted. And of course you have a right to know what's going on here. Please trust us and be patient a little longer. Relax and enjoy the countryside."

I tried. But with Stefan's eyes darting to the mirrors again and again, my jangled nerves refused to settle. "You still seem worried that we're being followed," I finally said. "Do you think someone is tailing *you*?"

"*Non*," Stefan said curtly.

"There might have been a car following us in Avignon this morning," Miranda added. "But Stefan managed to lose it before we got out of the city."

Stefan held up a hand for silence. The farther we drove, the louder the silence became.

An hour after leaving Marseilles, we crossed the Rhône—a beautiful river, almost as lovely as the Tennessee—and then Stefan abruptly whipped off the highway and onto a two-lane road. As soon as he'd made the turn, he and Miranda checked behind us again, then shared a look of relief at the emptiness of the road. Through tiny villages and past farmhouses and barns, the road followed the river upstream. After a few miles, we turned onto another highway that took us eastward, to another bridge spanning the river. On the far bank stood a low hill ringed by an ancient wall and crowned by tiled rooftops and massive stone towers, all glowing in the golden light of Provence.

"Beautiful," I said.

"Avignon," Stefan announced. "City of the popes. Once the richest and most powerful city in Europe."

CHAPTER 3

STEFAN THREADED THE FIAT through a portal in the ancient wall and into the old part of the city, navigating between stone buildings that were already old by the time the *Mayflower* set sail from England. Crooking to the left, the street burrowed into an underground parking garage carved deep beneath the hill. Stefan spiraled up several ramps, parking on the topmost level near a long pedestrian tunnel. Emerging at the end of the tunnel, we blinked and squinted our way into dazzling daylight.

We had surfaced on a large plaza, a couple of hundred feet wide but several times that long. Fronting the plaza, looming above it, was an immense castle, its high stone walls punctuated by even higher towers. "Le Palais des Papes," Stefan said. "The Palace of the Popes."

The façade of the palace was easily twice the

length of a football field, the stone walls were forty
or fifty feet high, and the towers at the corners—one
of them within spitting distance of the cathedral—
soared high above the walls. With its crenellated
battlements, the structure looked designed to with-
stand a military siege. "*Palace* of the Popes? Looks
more like *Fortress* of the Popes."

"A mighty fortress is our God," Miranda quipped.

Slightly to the left of the highest, most formidable tower of the palace rose a more graceful, less
militant spire, this one topped by a twenty-foot gold
statue of a woman wearing a tiara of stars. "Who's
the gilded lady with the stars in her crown?"

"The Virgin Mary, of course," Stefan said.
"That's Avignon Cathedral. The house of God."

"How come God's house is so much smaller than
the pope's palace?"

My question drew a smile from Miranda.

From across the river, the palace had appeared
immense but also fanciful—Euro Disney, or maybe
PopeLand. Up close, though, it loomed over the
square, hulking and intimidating. I didn't know a
lot about Catholicism, but I associated it with saints
and stained glass. This, though, was not the architecture of inspiration and aspiration; this was the
architecture of subjugation and domination.

We entered the palace by way of an imposing
central gate, a portal through which a steady stream
of tourists flowed. Once inside, we stepped behind
a large display and ducked down a cordoned-off
staircase. It led deep into the palace, to a vast chamber whose darkness seemed to clutch at the narrow
beam of Stefan's flashlight.

The beam brought us to an iron grille made of bars thicker than my thumbs, fastened with a hefty padlock. Stefan retrieved a pair of keys from a cord around his neck—keys that made me think of Saint Peter, the heavenly gatekeeper. Leaning against the grille, Stefan wrestled it open on groaning hinges, then motioned us inside and closed the gate behind us. He stooped to the floor and flicked a switch in a long cord that stretched somewhere into the darkness, and a string of dim bulbs, jury-rigged to the damp wall, revealed a crumbling stone staircase that descended through a rough-hewn tunnel.

Reaching awkwardly back through the gate, Stefan replaced the lock and clicked it shut behind us, locking us in, then led us forward. As we edged down the steep, uneven steps, we seemed to be descending not merely into the depths of the papal palace, but through the layers of time itself: one century deep, two centuries, three, four, five, six centuries into the past.

The stairs ended in a short horizontal hallway; at its far end, another padlocked gate of heavy iron guarded the entrance to a cavelike room whose dimensions I couldn't discern for the darkness. This gate was even heavier than the first, and it took Stefan and Miranda both to tug it open. Inside the chamber, stout stone pillars and Gothic arches supported a low, vaulted ceiling. A lone bulb—the last in the string of lights rigged in the stairway—illuminated a small arc of the rough floor and the nearest pair of columns. Stefan turned to study my face as I surveyed the room. "Probably too far from the dining hall to be the wine cellar," I said. "Was this a crypt? A dungeon?"

He shook his head and smiled, evidently pleased that I'd guessed wrong. "*La chambre du trésor*," he answered. "The treasure room."

"And was the treasure room half empty or half full?" I was joking, but he took it seriously.

"Totally full. *Complètement.* This room was overflowing with gold and silver and jewels. Millions', maybe billions' worth."

"Hmm. I never really thought about the net worth of the pope," I said.

"The pope did, for sure," he shot back. "The popes of Avignon were richer and more powerful than any of Europe's kings or emperors. Charlemagne ruled half of Europe. The popes ruled *all* of Europe. *Tout entier.*"

"But they didn't exactly rule," I pointed out. "Not the way Charlemagne did."

"*Non?*" He cocked his head, lifting an eyebrow. "Tell me, how was it different?"

"Well, the popes didn't have an army."

"Bool-shit," he scoffed. "Who were the Crusaders and the Knights Templar if not the pope's warriors? They were sent to the Middle East to add the Holy Land to the empire of the Holy Father. *L'impérialisme*, plain and simple."

"You're putting a mighty cynical spin on the Church," I said.

"*Mon Dieu*, just look at this place where we are working. The biggest Gothic palace in Europe. The epicenter of money and power."

I flashed back to the skyline I'd seen as we approached Avignon from across the Rhône. "Okay," I conceded, "maybe you have a point."

"Oh, hell, don't encourage him, Dr. B.," Miranda squawked. "He'll pontificate all day. Pun intended."

Ignoring her protest, Stefan resumed. "Go; sell everything you have, and give the money to the poor—that's what Jesus said. The popes said, 'Give the money to *us*.'"

"I take it you don't approve," I said drily.

He shrugged and smiled cynically. "*Au contraire, mon ami*. I approve completely. And gratefully." He swept his arm in a wide, encompassing arc. "I owe my career to the popes. They and their faithful flocks—pious, hardworking sheep—created the world's greatest art and architecture. I would be foolish and ungrateful if I did not approve."

Miranda was right; once he got wound up, it was tough to wind him down, and I was fast approaching my limit. "I'm thinking you didn't bring me here just to talk about the glory and the greed of the medieval popes," I said. "So cut to the chase. What the hell is going on here? And why all the cloak-and-dagger stuff?"

"Come," he said, and walked toward the center of the treasure chamber. As I followed him into the darkness, my eyes gradually adjusted, and I saw that a makeshift screen had been rigged between two of the pillars by hanging a blue plastic tarp, a jarring contrast with the ancient stonework. Stefan held one end of the curtain aside for me, and I stepped behind it into the blackness.

Stefan flipped another switch on an electrical

cord, and a pair of halogen work lights flashed on. My eyes squinted shut against the blinding glare; when they opened, I saw that part of the room's back wall had collapsed—a roughly semicircular section, head high and an arm span wide. The stones had been stacked in the corner of the room, the rubble excavated, and the opening shored up with rough timber framing. "I thought you were an archaeologist," I quipped. "This looks like a job for a stonemason."

Stefan pointed to the right. Along the side wall was a long table covered by a white sheet. On the white sheet was a complete human skeleton, laid out in anatomical order.

The bones looked old; their color was a cross between gray putty and red-orange caramel, with darker, greasy stains here and there. Wordlessly Stefan offered me a pair of latex gloves. I put them on and picked up the skull, my favorite place to start.

The bones were definitely a man's—the strong brow ridge above the eyes told me that, as did the big bump at the base of the skull, the external occipital protuberance: small and subtle in women, prominent in men. The nasal opening was broad, but the face itself was comparatively narrow, framed by prominent zygomatics—cheekbones—that gave it an angular, aristocratic appearance.

Cradling the skull upside down in my left palm, I studied the upper teeth and the roof of the mouth. Two molars and a canine tooth were missing, and several others had cavities. The presence of all four wisdom teeth, plus the complete fusion of the sutures—the seams—in the upper palate, confirmed that the man was an adult. Turning the skull right side up, I examined the cranial sutures, the zigzag joints in the top of the skull. In young adults, the sutures are dark and prominent, almost like irregular zipper teeth. This man's, by contrast, were smooth and fading, almost obliterated. Although cranial sutures can give only a rough indication of age, the smoothness of these suggested that this man was my age, mid-fifties, or older—maybe a decade or more older. The spine seemed to bear this out, too; the vertebrae were beginning to develop the ragged bony fringe known as osteoarthritic lipping, which is one of the skeletal signs of aging. This man's spine, I realized with an unexpected, ironic smile, probably looked a lot like my own.

It was when I looked at the ribs that I felt a familiar spike of adrenaline, the rush that always came when I got hooked on a forensic case. On the right side of the rib cage, everything was normal, but on the left side, the eleventh and twelfth ribs—the lowermost, "floating" ribs, which attach to the spine but not to the sternum—looked slightly truncated. I picked them up and inspected their distal ends, which curve around the sides of the lower chest but don't wrap all the way to the front. Normally they're tipped with cartilage, though these were too old and clean for that. But when I compared them with the matching ribs from the right side, the difference between them was dramatic. The tips of the right ribs were smooth and rounded, but the ends of the left ribs were flat and jagged. The ends of these two ribs appeared to have been sheared off by a sharp blade.

I looked up at Miranda and Stefan. "Unless this guy fell on his own sword, I'd say he was stabbed to death."

"But wait, there's more," Miranda said, eyes shining. "Look at the extremities."

I scanned the right arm, the one closest to me. I noticed nothing amiss until I got to the distal end of the forearm. Near the wrist both bones, the radius and the ulna, were gouged on their medial surfaces, as if a knife had been forced between them. I felt a slight tingling, which intensified when I inspected the left forearm and found similar gouges there.

"Now the feet," she said. I almost missed it: more gouge marks, these between the metatarsals, the bones at mid foot.

Wheels were turning in my mind, but they were turning slowly—bogged down partly by fatigue but also by disbelief at what I was seeing, or what it meant. "Okay, so what's the story? Where'd this guy come from? And why all the secrecy about a skeleton that's six or seven centuries old?"

She looked at Stefan. "Now?"

He nodded. "*Oui.* Now."

Miranda stepped forward and lifted the flap of overhanging sheet from the front of the table. Tucked on the floor beneath was a box two feet long by a foot or so square. The box was stone, but it had roughly the same shape as thousands of corrugated cardboard boxes stashed beneath the football stadium in Knoxville—boxes I myself had carefully packed with the bones of the Anthropology Department's skeletal collection. "A stone ossuary?" She nodded. "The bones were in this ossuary, sealed inside the wall?" She nodded again.

"The wall collapsed," Stefan explained. "Vibrations from a jackhammer outside. When they saw something inside, that's when they called me. And that's when I called Miranda."

"This was wrapped around the ossuary," she added, lifting a tangle of crumbling cord from inside the ossuary. Near one end of the cord was an irregular disk of soft gray metal—lead—stamped with what appeared to be tiny likenesses of two men's heads. I shot a questioning look at her.

Stefan answered. "Those figures are Saint Peter and Saint Paul. That's a papal seal."

"You're saying those bones were put there by one of the popes?" He nodded. "Why would a pope seal up a skeleton and hide it in a wall?" I asked. "Was this a rival? Somebody he killed to get the papal crown?"

"*Non*. Not if the inscription is true."

"Inscription?"

He pointed, and for the first time I noticed a flat, rectangular panel propped against one end of the ossuary. It was the lid, made of the same pale, soft stone as the box. Miranda hoisted it from the floor and laid it at one end of the table.

Two images were chiseled into the lid—images that sent chills up my middle-aged, incipiently arthritic spine. One was a lamb. The other was a cross.

Suddenly all the secrecy and skittishness made sense. This would be the find of the century—no, this would be the greatest archaeological find of all time—if these were indeed the bones of the Lamb of God, the crucified Christ.

"So," he said, "perhaps you can understand why we didn't want to tell you over the phone, or by e-mail. Too big. Too risky. And now that you know, you have a choice. Do you want to stay and help us study it, help us figure out if the inscription is true? Help us figure out if it's Jesus?" Something about the way he put it—"help us"—hit a nerve. I wrote it off as jet lag, until he added, "You could be third author on our publications." Third author? That was a role to which only first-year graduate students aspired. And the phrase "our publications" implied a cozy possessiveness on Stefan's part—not just of the bones, but also of Miranda—that I didn't like. I opened my mouth to say no, but Miranda didn't give me time.

"Come on, Dr. B," she coaxed, "say yes. It's the chance of a lifetime. And there's nobody in the world who's better qualified to examine these bones than you." I hesitated, but then Miranda gave me a pleading smile and clasped her hands, beseeching, and my resistance crumbled. *Oh, what the hell, why not?* I thought. *You've come all this way, and it's an interesting question.* What finally tipped the scales was another thought that hit me out of the blue. *And maybe it's not a bad idea to hang out here till Rocky Stone rounds up those drug runners.*

"I'd have to be back in Tennessee in a week," I said. "Two, at the most." Miranda beamed and bowed gratefully; Stefan smiled thinly.

"No problem," he said. "I'm sure Miranda and I can finish everything after you go home."

Suddenly he froze, holding a finger to his lips for silence and laying his other hand on Miranda's arm. He turned toward the staircase, listening intently, and I strained to hear what had alarmed him. At first I heard nothing, but then came the faint clatter of metal on metal: a padlock rattling as it was inspected and tugged? the upper gate shifting from an exploratory shove? At that moment the room went pitch-black. Miranda gasped, and Stefan gave a low *sshh*. In the darkness, I felt a hand—Miranda's hand—clutch mine. Finally, after an intense, interminable silence, I heard the rhythmic thud of footsteps.

Or was it the pounding of my heart?

Footsteps, I hoped, because soon the sound faded away.

"YOU REALLY THINK someone was trying to get in?" I asked as we made our way up the dark, uneven stairs by flashlight. "Maybe it was just one of the guards. Turning out the lights because he thought nobody was using them."

"Guards," Stefan scoffed. "What guards? There is one guard on duty, at the main gate. His job is to keep tourists from sneaking in without buying tickets."

"Okay, who has access to this part of the palace?"

"Dozens of people," he fretted as he reached through the gate and fumbled to open the padlock. "Maintenance workers. Tour guides. Docents. But it's dark and dirty down here, so everybody avoids it." Finally I heard the lock click open.

"*Almost* everybody," I corrected. "So who knows what's in the treasure room?"

He shook his head, then pushed the iron grille open. "Nobody, really. Just the three of us. My boss—a petty bureaucrat—knows I found some bones, but he has no idea how important they are. And he's not inquisitive."

"Well, *somebody's* inquisitive," I pointed out. "Maybe we need a security camera to find out who. Or maybe we should move the bones someplace more secure." He frowned, and didn't reply; instead, he heaved the gate shut with a clang, then snapped the lock back into place.

We'd left the treasure chamber only minutes after we'd heard the furtive sounds above us. Stefan was clearly jumpy, and I was exhausted, so we'd decided to stop for the day and resume in the morning.

"Let me play devil's advocate about the bones," I said as we recrossed the cavernous cellar, or dungeon, or whatever it was, by flashlight. "How could that possibly be the skeleton of Jesus?"

"Sshh," cautioned Stefan.

I lowered my voice to a murmur. "First off, Jesus died at thirty-three," I went on. "This guy's way older than that. Come on, you saw the arthritic changes in the vertebrae, Miranda." We reached the bigger staircase, which would restore us to the world of light and air.

"Maybe he just put a lot of wear and tear on his spine," she countered. "A carpenter? Back in the days before Black and Decker? That's heavy lifting, man. Bad for the back. Remember the skeleton from that slave cemetery in Memphis? We know the guy died at forty, plus or minus, but his spine looked sixty."

"But his cranial sutures didn't," I pointed out. "They were still very rugged. This guy's look like they've been sealed and spackled. He's older than I am; I'd bet my belt sander on it."

She laughed, but there was no time for a retort because by then we'd reached the top of the staircase, stepped around the velvet cordon, and rejoined the tourists. The maneuver made me feel like one of the costumed characters at Disney World, who cross the Magic Kingdom in underground tunnels, then pop out of concealed openings in the shrubbery when it's time to work the crowd.

Leaving the palace, we crossed the plaza and headed back through the tunnel to the parking garage. Except for us, the corridor was empty, so I renewed the debate. "Call me Doubting Thomas," I persisted, "but what about the Resurrection? If these are the bones of Jesus, he didn't rise from the dead."

"Ha," chuckled Stefan. "That would make things interesting for the Church, wouldn't it? They would have to change the story a little bit." He sounded gleeful at the prospect. "Maybe the pope hid the bones so he wouldn't have to explain them."

"Why not just destroy them?" I asked. "Get rid of the evidence altogether? That'd be a lot safer."

"Too powerful," he said. "Imagine, if you are the pope, having the bones of Christ. What a secret to possess! The ultimate knowledge, the ultimate forbidden fruit, you see?" He pressed the button of his keyless remote, and the Fiat beeped a few slots away, its lights flashing in the gloom of the garage.

"I don't see why the bones of Jesus would pose a huge problem," Miranda mused. "You could argue that he rose from the dead, lived another twenty or thirty years, and then died of natural causes, right? That still allows for the Resurrection."

"Could be," I conceded grudgingly as I folded into the tiny backseat. "But there's that whole 'ascended into heaven' bit, too—isn't that like the Resurrection, Part B?"

"Hairsplitting," she said, with a definitive slam of the door. "How many bones can dance on the head of a pin? Come on, let's get you settled at Lumani, then grab some grub."

STEFAN HAD LEASED an apartment near the Palace of the Popes for the summer, and Miranda was staying in a modern, charmless hotel a block from the palace. That hotel was fully booked now, though, as was every other hotel near the palace—a month-long theater festival was about to fill Avignon with throngs of tourists—so they'd been forced to look farther afield for my lodgings. Within the narrow circumference of old Avignon, luckily, no place was terribly far afield.

The Fiat spiraled down through the underground garage and out past the city wall, and Stefan turned onto a road that circled the wall like a moat. To our right were the wall's stone ramparts; to our left, the green waters of the Rhône. Halfway around the perimeter, we re-entered the old city and doubled back, this time hemmed tightly between the wall's inner face and the press of densely packed houses, their stone and stucco façades crowding the narrowest sidewalk I'd ever seen. We pulled up in front of a three-story structure that offered only one tiny, round window—scarcely more than a porthole—at street level, though the upper levels each had several large windows. An arched wooden door, painted emerald green, was set into the wall to the left of the porthole, but the door was locked, and didn't look like a gateway to hospitality, at least not to my bleary eyes. Stefan rapped sharply on the door, waited a bit, and then rapped again, harder. Miranda, meanwhile, wandered farther up the street, stopping at a vine-draped opening in the wall that was secured by a pair of barn-style doors, also emerald green. "I think this is the entrance," she called. "Here's a sign, and a doorbell." She pressed the button, and deep within the building I heard a faint buzz.

The sign, partly hidden by the vines, consisted of three repetitions of the word "Lumani" cut from a thick plate of steel and bolted to the wall, one atop the other. The vines hung halfway down the doors, an irregular fringe that varied between chest and head high. The tendrils reminded me of kudzu, the fast-growing Tennessee vine that, given half a chance and half a week, could swallow trees, barns, even slow-moving cows. Inside, I heard footsteps approaching the doors, then the rattle of a key in the lock. I suspected I was about to be greeted by an eccentric, crabby old Frenchwoman in bathrobe and slippers.

The left-hand door swung open, and the crabby old Frenchwoman turned out to be a lovely woman, possibly fifty, with wavy brown hair, warm brown eyes, and an even warmer smile. "Ah, *bonjour*. Hello, and welcome to Lumani," she said. "I am Elisabeth." An elfin-looking man with sparkling eyes and a short fringe of gray hair rounded a corner and joined her. "And this is my husband, Jean." The final sound of his name—the *-on* of *zhon*—lodged in her nose rather than emerging through her lips, and I was reminded that French pronunciation was a mystery I would never master. "Please, please to come inside."

Miranda, Stefan, and I ducked beneath the curtain of vines, followed my hosts down a short driveway, and stepped into a place of enchantment: a huge, enclosed garden courtyard complete with an arbor, hammocks, a gurgling fountain, large plane trees, and an immense metal mobile hanging from a cable rigged to one of the trees.

"What a lovely place!" exclaimed Miranda, turning in a slow circle to take it all in. Jean offered to show us around, while Elisabeth went to pour drinks—wine for everyone else, orange juice for me.

Lumani was like a cozy private gallery. The walls were covered with abstract paintings, and the garden and indoor spaces were full of sculptures, large and small. "The art is beautiful," I said. "Are the artists local? From Avignon?"

"I made the sculptures," Jean said shyly; then, with obvious pride, he added, "The paintings are by Elisabeth."

Elisabeth emerged with the tray of drinks. I'd requested orange juice, but what she'd brought me was a deep red. Was it cranberry? Not my favorite, but I took a polite sip. Surprisingly, it *was* orange juice, freshly squeezed with a hint of pulp, but a richer flavor than regular orange juice—as if even the fruit in Avignon spoke with an exotic accent. "Delicious," I said.

"*Merci. Oui,* it's very special," she said. "*L'orange sanguine.* Do you say 'bloody orange'?"

Miranda grinned. "Blood orange," she said, arching her eyebrows. "How appropriate."

After we finished our drinks, Jean took me upstairs to my room. It was a third-floor aerie—I was practically nesting in one of the plane trees—with a bird's-eye view of the garden. In the distance, beyond Jean and Elisabeth's smaller, separate house, sprawled a jumble of tiled rooftops and spiky church spires. One of the spires, silhouetted against the sky a few blocks away, was unlike any I'd seen before: an open iron frame, its cluster of bells completely exposed. It was a bare-bones skeleton of a steeple, I realized; exactly my kind of steeple.

I pointed. "That church steeple—is it being restored?"

He followed my gaze. "Ah, *non,*" he said. "That is the design. It's built that way for the mistral."

"The what?"

"The mistral. Strong wind from the northwest. The tower is open so it doesn't fight against the wind. The wind blows through, instead of pushing it down." I liked the steeple even more now; its spare skeletal beauty was born of function.

As I leaned on the sill, lingering over the view, I noticed Miranda looking up, waving. "I'm jealous," she called. "I wish *I* had a room overlooking the Garden of Eden."

"Come visit anytime," I said. "Just watch out for snakes. And don't eat the apples."

"SORRY, MIRANDA. WHAT?" I hadn't heard the question. My brain was empty but my mouth was full. Blissfully full.

"I know carbon-14 dating's pretty good," she repeated, "but how close can it get? How precisely can it nail the age of the bones?"

"Pretty damn close," I finally answered. "*Man,* that's good."

I was finishing a bowl of lamb stew—my second bowl of lamb stew—at Pace é Salute, a Corsican restaurant near Lumani that Jean and Elisabeth had recommended. Its name translated as "Peace and Good Health," both of which I regarded as fine things, but neither could compete with the honeyed lamb stew, made with tender chunks of lamb and a rich sauce of honey, garlic, citrus, and savory broth.

Suddenly Miranda's question triggered a faint memory—faint but recent, something that had occurred as I was preparing to board my flight from Knoxville to Dulles. Was it really possible that only eighteen hours had passed since my secretary, Peggy, had dashed out to the helicopter with my computer and my passport? Reaching into the inner pocket of the jacket I'd been wearing for the past four thousand miles, I pulled out a letter she'd tucked into my passport—a letter marked "Urgent" that had arrived in the morning's mail. "I'm glad you said that," I told Miranda. "I would have forgotten this until the next time I went to the dry cleaner's. And that might've been years."

The envelope was postmarked Charlotte, North Carolina. Smoothing the letter, I scanned it again, because I'd given it only a cursory glance on the plane. "You're not the only one interested in C-14 dating. So is the Institute for Biblical Science."

"The Institute for Biblical Science?" Miranda's eyebrows shot up. "Isn't that a contradiction in terms?"

"Not necessarily," I said, "though in practice, yeah, science often takes a backseat to the Bible."

"And they're writing to ask your advice about C-14 dating? I'm surprised they're not writing to heap fire and brimstone on you. You've taken some fierce swings at creationism from time to time."

"Not fierce," I said. "Just factual. Okay, maybe a little fierce, too. I don't get a lot of fan mail from the fundamentalists." Putting on my reading glasses—a recent, annoying necessity—I read aloud. "'Dear Dr. Brockton: I'm writing to ask your opinion on the accuracy of carbon-14 dating. Our Institute is initiating a study of artifacts from the Holy Land, and we would very much appreciate your thoughts on the precision and reliability of C-14 dating for establishing the age of artifacts, as well as human and animal bones. I would also appreciate any insights you have on the feasibility of extracting and sequencing genetic material from bone specimens. We would be happy to hire you as a consultant on this project, although—as you might expect—our budget is limited. Please contact me at your earliest opportunity to discuss this exciting project. Best regards, Dr. Adam Newman, Ph.D., Scientific Director, Institute for Biblical Science.'"

I folded the letter and reached for the envelope, but Stefan held out his hand. "Permit me?" I handed him the page. He read it quickly, then handed it back with a look of disdain. "Do what you want, but I advise you to stay away from them. Crazies. If you work with them, it will damage your reputation."

Miranda leaned forward on her elbows. "What makes you say that?"

"A colleague of mine did some excavation at Qumran," he said. "The place where the Dead Sea Scrolls were found. Someone from this place—this so-called institute—didn't like a journal article she published. They attacked her work, tried to destroy her credibility. They even made threats against her. Very unpleasant."

"Thanks for the heads-up," I said, stuffing the letter back in my jacket.

"But we digress," Miranda reminded me. "C-14?"

"Oh, right." I spooned another dollop of sauce from the bowl. "*Yum.* If—and mind you, this strikes me as a mighty big if—if the bones from the Palace of the Popes are two thousand years old, the C-14 report will say something like 'two thousand BP plus or minus one hundred.' That means 'two thousand years before the present, with a one-hundred-year margin of uncertainty either way.' Wiggle room, in other words. So the two-thousand-year-old bones could be as old as twenty-one hundred years or as young as nineteen hundred."

"Actually," Stefan said, "we should be able to get

closer than a hundred years. If it's a good sample, an AMS test—accelerator mass spectrometry—can tell us the age plus or minus forty years."

"Wowzer," Miranda marveled. "I'm used to time-since-death estimates of days or weeks, not millennia. How does it *do* that?" It was one of Miranda's favorite multipurpose utterances; sometimes it meant "Explain, please," but sometimes—in response to, say, a 3-D laser hologram or a fiery sunset—it meant simply "That's amazing!"

Stefan laid down the Corsican grilled cheese sandwich he'd been nibbling on, and he smiled the smile of a man who loves hearing himself explain things. "The machine, the spectrometer, counts the carbon atoms in the sample," he said, "and it calculates the ratio of three different isotopes— three different forms of carbon. The ratio of those isotopes is like a signature . . ." He trailed off, frowning, then held up a finger, recalibrating his explanation, and resumed. "*Non*, the ratio is like a time stamp—the time stamp on an e-mail or a security-camera photo—that we can match to the ratio in the atmosphere at any point in time."

"Call me dense," Miranda persisted, "but how do you know what the ratio in the air *was* two thousand years ago?"

"Ah," he beamed, "because the rings in trees have recorded the ratio in the air, year by year. And we have analyzed tree rings all the way back to ten thousand years ago."

"We have?" Miranda arched her eyebrows. "We, you and I? Or we, you and other people?"

Stefan's eyes narrowed in annoyance. "We, the

scientific community," he said testily. I dabbed at my mouth with my napkin, hiding my smile. "So when we find which tree ring has the same ratio as the bones, *voilà*, we know that the man died the same year the tree ring was formed."

"I like it," Miranda said. "An atomic stopwatch. A wood-burning atomic stopwatch. And it's really that accurate, that reliable?"

"*Oui*, sure. You know the Shroud of Turin, the so-called burial cloth of Jesus?" Miranda and I both nodded. "You remember when the fabric from it was carbon-dated?"

"I remember that," I said, "but Miranda was probably still in diapers. Wasn't that, like, twenty years ago?"

"It was in 1988," Stefan preened.

"I'll have you know I was wearing big-girl pants in 1988," Miranda said. "But I was too busy watching *Sesame Street* to tune in to the Vatican News Network."

"So," Stefan began, warming up for another mini-lecture. "Millions of people believe the Shroud of Turin is two thousand years old, *oui*?" *God*, I thought, *he does love to hear himself talk*. Was it just his smugness I objected to? Or was I jealous of him at some level—resentful of his tightness with Miranda, afraid he was taking my place in her esteem? Whatever the reason, I was starting to wish I hadn't agreed to stay on and help the two of them. "But it was seen for the first time," he went on, "the first time we can be sure of, anyway, here in France, in 1357. The C-14 samples were cut—"

"Wait, wait," Miranda interrupted. "The Shroud

of Turin started out as the Shroud of France? No kidding?"

"No kidding," he said impatiently. "It was first shown in the village of Lirey, near Paris, in 1357. But the believers say *non*, the Shroud is much older than 1357. So finally, in 1988, the Vatican allows scientists to make a C-14 test. A small bit of the cloth is cut from one corner"—he made a snipping motion with his fingers—"and pieces are sent to three different laboratories. And *voilà*, all three labs say the same thing: The Shroud is from the fourteenth century." He smiled wickedly as he pointed at me. "Ha! From the same century as Bill!" Miranda giggled, and my face flushed.

I pushed back from the table. "You know what, guys? Ancient relic that I am, I'm really beat," I said.

"Oh come on, Dr. B," Miranda cajoled, looking contrite. "It was a joke. Don't leave."

I waved off any further conversation. "It's okay. Stay; enjoy your dessert. I can find my way back from here."

That much was true—I had no trouble finding my way back. It was finding my way forward that seemed difficult at the moment.

CHAPTER 4

I PEERED OVER MIRANDA'S shoulder at the screen of her laptop. "Okay," I said, "push the button. Let's see what the verdict is."

It was nearly noon, though no speck of sunlight could penetrate the depths of the palace's subterranean subtreasury. We'd spent the morning taking measurements of the bones, a task that was tedious, time-consuming, and therefore welcome: a convenient excuse to ignore how awkwardly dinner had ended.

Miranda had keyed dozens of measurements into her laptop, and was running ForDisc, software we'd developed at UT to compare unknown bones with our forensic data bank, which included thousands of skeletons whose sex, race, and stature were known. Might ForDisc shed light on the racial and geographic origin of our John Doe—or Jesus Doe?

Miranda scrolled the cursor and clicked. "Gee,

here's a shocker," she said. "It's a dude." I laughed; given the robustness of the skull and the narrowness of the pelvis, there'd been no doubt in my mind that the skeleton was male. "Hmm," she mused. "You measured the stature directly, right?"

"I did—head to heel—and added a bit to make up for the missing cartilage."

"And what'd you get?"

"About one hundred sixty-six centimeters; five five."

"*Hmm*," she repeated. "ForDisc puts him at one hundred seventy-five centimeters—nearly five nine."

"That's odd. *Really* odd." Could my tape measure be off—by four full inches? I stepped back and took another look at the skeleton. Suddenly I was struck by how unusual the proportions were—an anomaly I'd registered subconsciously but had failed to appreciate fully. "Look how long of limb and short of trunk he is," I said to Miranda and Stefan. "This guy was like a human stork." ForDisc estimated stature by extrapolating from femur and tibia length, and normally that formula was quite accurate. But the formula was fooled by a leggy guy like this—a reminder that it's the exceptions and outliers that make life interesting and keep science challenging.

The software was also handicapped by the age—or rather the youth—of its data. ForDisc knew nineteenth- and twentieth-century skeletons well—especially modern white Americans—but ancient bones were terra incognita to it. And so, like us, ForDisc didn't know if our guy was first century or fourteenth, if he was Palestinian or Parisian.

"Well, rats," said Miranda. "I want a ForDisc

upgrade. One that has time-travel and crystal-ball features."

I was disappointed, too, but Stefan seemed unfazed. "No problem. Let's get the samples for the C-14 test. That's the big question anyway: How old are the bones—seven hundred years or two thousand?" He turned to me. "Do you prefer to be a dentist or a bone surgeon? I brought a saw if you want to cut a cross section from the femur."

"Dentist," I said. "Pulling teeth is easier. Besides, it doesn't fill the air with bone dust. Or with plague spores. What if this guy had the plague—wasn't there an epidemic here in the fourteenth century?" Miranda nodded. "So shouldn't we be worried? Shouldn't we be wearing masks?"

"Yes, but no," said Miranda. "It *was* really bad here. An infected ship anchored at Marseilles in January of 1348, and the rats swam ashore. Plague hit Avignon two weeks later. Within a matter of months, two-thirds of the people were dead— twenty, thirty thousand people. Corpses rotting in the streets, choking the river."

"Terrible," I said. "Must have been terrifying, too."

"A lot of people blamed the Jews," she went on. "All over Europe, Jews were driven from cities. Entire Jewish settlements were massacred. Horrific. But here, the pope at the time of the plague— Clement the Sixth—defended the Jews, said they *weren't* to blame. He even offered them refuge."

"That took guts," I said. "The townspeople could've turned on him."

"No kidding," she agreed. "What's the old

saying? 'The friend of my scapegoat is my scape-goat'? But plague doesn't make hibernating time-bomb endospores the way some other bacteria do."

"And you know this how?" I pressed.

"I studied up on the way over last week—journal articles on plague were my in-flight entertain-ment." Despite my lingering annoyance about the unpleasant turn the dinner-table conversation had taken, I gave her a grudging half smile for that. "In London," she added, "a team of scientists is trying to reconstruct the entire DNA sequence of the plague bacterium. They're getting snippets from known plague victims—bones from a fourteenth-century plague cemetery—but they're having a hard time piecing the genome together. Bottom line? Plague doesn't survive for centuries, and this guy's not contagious."

"Okay, okay, I'm convinced. But I'd still rather pull a tooth than butcher a bone."

"Let's send a molar," Stefan suggested.

Holding the mandible with my left hand, I gripped one of the eighteen-year molars, a wisdom tooth, pinching it firmly between my right thumb and forefinger. I wiggled it gently and felt a slight grating as the tooth wobbled in the dry socket. Wiggling a bit harder, I began to tug, and with a rasp and a faint crunch, it pulled free of the jaw. "What do you think?" I asked, holding out the tooth for Miranda and Stefan to inspect. "First century or fourteenth?"

Miranda weighed in first. "I say it's him. With a capital *H*: *Him*."

"Jesus? Really?" I pointed toward the fringe of

osteoarthritis on the spine. "But he's ancient," I reminded her. "*My* age; maybe older."

"Nah, not older," she shot back. "Just harder working. Wore out his spine."

"You surprise me, Miranda. I had you pegged as a doubter."

She shrugged. "Sometimes I like to play the long shot. Makes life more interesting."

I looked at Stefan. "What about you? How do you vote?"

He shrugged, looking bored. "Oh, of course it would be interesting if Miranda was right, but that's unlikely. I think probably fourteenth century." He said it in a monotone, but his eyes flickered, and I wondered if he was more hopeful than he was admitting.

I reached for the Ziploc bag, but Miranda stopped me before I could drop the molar in. "Wait. No fair. You haven't said what *you* think."

"Rats. You know how I hate to go out on a limb." I held up the molar and studied it. It was a dull grayish brown nearly down to the roots; the gum line had receded during the man's life. A large cavity had burrowed into the center of the tooth's crown. Could this stained, decaying tooth really be from the man whom millions around the world revered as the Son of God? "It's clear to me now," I finally said, "that this guy died six months ago, and that all this is an elaborate hoax to cover up a modern-day murder." I nearly dropped the tooth when Miranda punched me on the arm, hard. She had a sneaky right cross that way; it wasn't the first time she'd popped me when she thought I was being insolent.

"You're no fun," she said, but her eyes were smiling—maybe at my silliness, maybe at finding an excuse to punch me—and it felt as if we'd finally gotten out of the minefield of last night's prickly conversation and back onto safe, comfortable ground again.

I tipped the tooth into the small bag. Stefan took the bag from me and was about to seal it when I stopped him. "Should we send them two? The lab said 'one or two teeth,' didn't they?"

"I think one is enough," he said, "but okay, if you want to send two." I picked up the mandible again and grasped another molar. "Wait," he said. I looked up from the jaw. "Not another molar."

"Why not?"

"No reason. Call it a crazy Frenchman's superstition. This time . . . a canine."

"Okay. I mean, *oui, monsieur*, you're the boss." I shifted my grip to a canine, one of the fanglike "dogteeth." This one was pegged tightly into its socket; the snug fit and the tooth's tapered shape made it harder to pull, and I was forced to use pliers. The tooth came free, but the root snapped off in the jaw, giving the tooth an oddly flattened base. I balanced the tooth upright on the table briefly, just for fun, and then slid it into the bag, where it settled against the molar with a slight click.

"So where's the C-14 lab?" I asked. "In Paris?"

"*Non, mon ami*. Guess again."

"Oxford? That's one of the places that tested the Shroud of Turin, right?"

"Wrong again. I think you will not guess. We send the teeth to Miami."

"Miami? *Florida?* Why on earth?"

"Because the world's biggest C-14 lab is there. Beta Analytic. They have offices in Europe—and Asia and Australia—but they're just offices. The only lab is in Miami. They have two AMS systems and fifty-two liquid scintillation counters."

"What's a liquid scintillation counter?" Before he could answer, I waved my hand. "Never mind—I don't need to know. How long does it take? A week? A month?"

"*Pas du tout*—not at all! Days. One or two days, after they get the sample. Last year I sent them a goat bone from a first-century site in Turkey. Four days later, *voilà*, I get the results."

"That's faster than I can grade a batch of test papers," I said. "Must be expensive."

"Not so bad. This will cost eight hundred euros. Twelve hundred U.S. dollars. Sure, it's a lot. But if these are the bones of Christ, that's a small price to pay to find out, *n'est-ce pas?*"

"Jesus!" Miranda exclaimed, then laughed at her unintended double entendre. "Just imagine—if the Virgin Mary on toast can fetch thirty thousand bucks . . ."

"Excuse me?" I felt a step behind her in the conversation. "The Virgin Mary? *Toast?* What *are* you talking about?"

"The Sacred Sandwich." Now I was two steps behind. "Don't you pay *any* attention to the world outside the Body Farm?" She rolled her eyes happily; one of her great joys in life was giving me grief. "Some lady in Florida takes a bite out of her grilled cheese sandwich and then she notices the BVM—"

"The what?" Three steps.

"The BVM—the Blessed Virgin Mary. A portrait of Mary's face was scorched into the bread. So the woman seals the sammy in Tupperware and keeps it on her nightstand for ten years. Then she sells it on eBay. Some online casino buys it for thirty grand."

"That's so bizarre," I said, "on so many levels." A host of questions popped into my mind: White or whole wheat? Why Tupperware rather than a Baggie? Didn't Mary mold? But I decided there was no future—no worthwhile future, at least—in delving further into the Sacred Sandwich. "I am amazed, and know not what to say."

"I say, 'Praise the Lord and pass the pickles,'" she cracked. "Anyhow, if somebody will pay thirty K for the BVM on loaf bread, think what the bones of Jesus might fetch. Not, of course, that you'd sell him on eBay, right, Stefan?"

"*Non*, never." He smiled ironically. "People who shop on eBay can afford a sandwich *sacré*, maybe, but not the bones of God."

IT WAS A juxtaposition of ancient and modern, in more ways than one.

Avignon's hospital was a complex of concrete-and-glass buildings located several miles outside the stone wall ringing the city. The contrast between the medieval city and the new suburbs was more than just striking; it was deeply disorienting, given how far back into the past I'd traveled in the space of twenty-four hours. Sure, the battering ram of modernity had smashed through the city's ramparts; in addition to ancient buildings, the walls encircled cars, computers, even a few Segways. But those were trivial, fleeting artifacts; they seemed to skim the city's surface like water bugs on a pond, without penetrating its depths or altering its medieval essence. Outside the walls, though, Avignon was not so different from Knoxville, and this hospital could have been transplanted to any suburb in the United States without looking out of place.

A deeper, more interesting juxtaposition, though, was the one about to transpire within the hospital—specifically, in the Clinique Radiologique, where we were bringing the skull for a CT scan: ancient bones, twenty-first-century technology.

"You know there's no compelling scientific reason for this," Miranda pointed out, not for the first time.

"Sure there is," I repeated.

"Is not," she said. "Admit it. We're burning time and X-rays just for fun."

"O ye of little curiosity," I countered. "O thou scoffer; vile, mocking spirit. We are gathered together in the spirit of scientific inquiry." I held the boxed skull aloft as I walked, as if I were a priest and the skull some sacred relic—which, after all, it might actually be. "Besides, don't you want to know what he looked like?"

"Sure I do. I think it'll be . . . *fun.*"

I shook my head, exasperated and amused. She was stubborn. And she was right, of course: what fun, to get a forensic facial reconstruction of what might be—almost certainly wasn't, but yet *might* be—the face of Jesus, a face that I had arranged for a forensic artist to "sculpt," in virtual clay, on a 3-D scan of the skull.

Stefan had persuaded a friend in the hospital's Radiology Department to do the scan. We'd parked at a loading dock behind one of the hospital's two low towers and threaded a maze of service corridors. After enough turns to make me wish I'd left a trail of bread crumbs behind—the hospital was nearly as labyrinthine as the palace, though a lot better lit—we entered a wide public corridor and followed signs that even I had no trouble translating from the French: RADIOLOGIE.

Stefan's friend turned out to be an attractive young woman named Giselle, whose name tag identified her as a MANIPULATRICE ERM, which appeared to mean she was an X-ray tech. She led us to a room containing a large, doughnut-shaped CT scanner, and turned to me. *"Monsieur, s'il vous plaît."* Please, sir. My French was getting better by the minute, I said to myself, but I unsaid it a panicked instant later, when she added, *"Mettez-le ici."* Seeing my blank look, she pointed to the box under my arm, then to the machine's scanning bed. I nodded sheepishly. Removing the skull carefully, I set it on the pillow Giselle offered, then rolled up the towel I'd used as padding in the box and wrapped it around the base of the skull to stabilize it. After a final check to make sure the mandible was correctly articulated at the jaw's hinge points, I nodded at Giselle, and she led us through a doorway and into a control room. As I watched through thick windows whose glass contained lead—less elegant but more protective than the leaded windows of Avignon's chapels—the bed of the scanner moved in and out of the opening in the scanning head. Slice by slice, X-rays cut through the bone, and the differing densities they encountered registered on the screen; line by line, a detailed picture of the skull materialized on the screen. When it was done, Giselle slowly rotated and inspected it, making sure the entire skull had been imaged. The detail was astonishing; so was the ease with which the *manipulatrice* could manipulate the image: removing the top of the skull, for instance, to show the floor of the cranial vault, or slicing open the tiny caverns of the frontal sinus. As she effortlessly explored the hidden, inmost structural secrets of the skull, I found myself marveling, Miranda-like, *How does it* do *that?*

JOE MULLINS WAS three thousand miles to the west of France, but ten minutes after Giselle scanned the skull in Avignon, Joe was looking at it in Alexandria, Virginia.

Joe was a forensic artist at the National Center for Missing and Exploited Children, a mouthful of a name that he mercifully shortened to the acronym NCMEC, pronounced "nickmeck." After a traditional fine arts training in painting and drawing, Joe had taken an unusual detour. He'd traded in his paintbrushes and palette knives for a computer and a 3-D digitizing probe; he'd forsaken blank canvases for bare skulls—unknown skulls on which he sculpted faces in virtual clay. By restoring faces to skulls, Joe could help police and citizens identify unknown crime victims.

I'd worked with Joe on a prior case, one involving boys who'd been beaten to death at a reform school in Florida, but the Avignon case was different from the reform-school case in a multitude of ways. For one, we already knew the identity, or at least the supposed identity: Jesus of Nazareth. But was it, really? ForDisc hadn't been able to shed much light, but perhaps Joe's facial reconstruction—based on the skull's shape and the artist's subtle eye—could tell us whether our man had been a first-century Jew from Palestine.

Joe wasn't looking at the actual skull, of course. After the CT scan, Giselle and Miranda had uploaded a massive file containing the 3-D image of the skull and sent it to a file-sharing Web site—a cyberspace crossroads, of sorts—called Dropbox. Joe had then gone to Dropbox and downloaded the file, and, as the French would say, *voilà*.

The case clearly didn't involve a missing or exploited child, so Joe couldn't do the reconstruction on NCMEC time. But he was willing to do it as a moonlight gig, a side job, and when I'd first e-mailed to ask if he'd be able to do it—and do it fast—he'd promised that if we got the scan to him by Friday afternoon, he'd have it waiting for us first thing Monday.

My phone warbled. "Hey, Doc, I've got him up on my screen," Joe said. "What can you tell me about this guy?"

"Not much, Joe." I didn't want to muddy the water by telling him what the ossuary inscription claimed. "Adult male; maybe in his fifties or sixties. Could be European but might be Middle Eastern."

"Geez, Doc, that doesn't narrow it down much."

"Hey, I didn't include African or Asian or Native American," I said. "Give me at least a little credit."

"Okay, I give you a little credit. Very, very little."

"You sound just like Miranda, my assistant. *Way* too uppity."

He laughed. "This Miranda, she sounds pretty smart. She single, by any chance?"

Sheesh, I thought. "Take a number," I said.

CHAPTER 5

"SHALL WE FIND SOME fishing poles," I joked, "and see what we can catch from the end of this fancy pier?"

Miranda, Stefan, and I were standing on the ancient stone bridge that stretched halfway across the Rhône. After we left the hospital's Radiology Department, Stefan had headed for Lumani, skirting the city wall—the fastest way to cross old Avignon was to detour around it—but as we'd passed under the bridge, I'd admired the four graceful arches. In response, Stefan had whipped the car off the road, parked, and led us up through a tower and onto the bridge, or what was left of it.

"No fishing," he said in response to my question. "You don't want to eat anything that comes out of the Rhône."

I peered down at the emerald water. "Looks pretty clean to me," I said, leaning over the metal rail for a better view.

"Be careful," he cautioned. "That railing isn't strong. See, a piece of it is missing." He pointed to a nearby gap in the rail, cordoned off by orange plastic safety mesh. "The river is full of industrial chemicals," he went on. "Terrible toxins and carcinogens. Not just in the water; the sediment in the bottom of the river is full of them, too."

"Okay, I take your point," I said. "I won't fish, I won't swim, and I won't eat the mud. It's still a pretty river, though." He made a grimace of disagreement.

A few paces farther out on the span, Miranda hummed a few bars of music, then began twirling, singing in French, "*Sur le pont d'Avignon, l'on y danse, l'on y danse*"; a moment later Stefan chimed in, trailing a line behind, turning the song into a round. Miranda and I had never sung together at all, I realized with a pang, much less sung rounds. Halfway through the verse, Miranda lost her place in the lyrics, falling into sync with Stefan for the last two lines.

"Crap," she laughed. "I mean *merde*. I can't sing rounds worth a damn. I lack the courage of my melodic convictions."

"What's the song?" I asked. "How do you know it?"

"It's about dancing on this bridge, the *pont* of Avignon. My mom used to sing it to me as a lullaby." She smiled at the memory.

"It has lots of silly verses," Stefan added. "You dance, I dance, we all dance. The girls dance, the boys dance. The dolls dance, the soldiers dance. Frogs. Gorillas."

"Frogs and gorillas? My mom never mentioned those," Miranda said. "She just sang the first verse over and over. No wonder it put me to sleep—it was *so boring*! Matter of fact, I could use a nap right now." She faked a yawn.

Halfway along the bridge was a small stone building, ancient and showing its age badly. The front of the building partially blocked the bridge; the back, though, jutted above the river, supported by an extension of one of the bridge pilings. "Nice fishing shack," I observed.

"The chapel of Saint Bénézet," said Stefan.

"Saint who?"

"Bénézet," said Miranda. "The kid that built the bridge."

"*This* bridge?" She nodded. "It was built by a kid?"

"Yep. Maybe a teenager. Hard to be sure. 'A young shepherd boy' is how most of the stories put it. I read up on it after Stefan brought me here." Suddenly I was less excited about the bridge, now that I knew I was retracing an outing they'd made together. But Miranda went on. "The kid's minding his flock, minding his business, and suddenly he has a vision, or an angel swoops down, or some such. God tells him to build a bridge over the Rhône, right here. So Bénézet goes and relays this message to the bishop of Avignon. The bishop says, 'Yeah, sure, kid—'"

"Wait," I interrupted. "Really? The bishop says, 'Yeah, sure, kid'?"

She cut her eyes at me. "What, you're thinking the bishop says, 'Forsooth, callow youth, thou pullest my leg'?"

"Okay, smarty, I guess 'Yeah, sure, kid' is more like it."

"Anyhow," she resumed. "So then the bishop says—and I'm paraphrasing, mind you—'Okay, junior, if you want me to believe that God sent you, you gotta prove it. See that huge stone over there? Thirty men can't lift that stone. If you can, I'll believe you; if you can't, go back to the farm and quit wasting my time.' So the kid—"

"Young Bénézet?"

"Our boy Benny. Benny goes over and hoists it with his pinky—"

"With his *pinky*?"

She rolled her eyes in exasperation. "So maybe he uses *both* pinkies. The point, Dr. Hairsplitter, is that Benny hoists the giant rock, plunks it in the river, and *voilà*, the bridge building has commenced. Seven years later, while the bridge is still going up, Benny goes down—dies, at age twenty-five, plus or minus."

"Of overwork?"

She shrugged. "Overwork. Underfeeding. A surfeit of saintliness. Who knows? The historical record is vague on cause of death."

"But that's why the bridge only goes halfway across the river."

"Not at all. When Bénézet dies, it's far enough along that other, lesser mortals can finish it. But maybe their workmanship wasn't as miraculous as his, because after four or five centuries, most of the arches collapsed during floods and wars. *Anyhow.* Bénézet's body was entombed in this sweet little chapel they built on the bridge to commemorate him."

"Is it still here?"

"*Duh.* If you keep walking another twenty feet, you'll smack into it."

"Not the chapel, smart-ass, the body. Is it still here in the chapel?"

"*Non,*" said Stefan, who had kept quiet for what was—for him—a remarkably long time. "During the French Revolution it was moved to a convent outside the city to protect it."

I couldn't resist a joke, though I feared it would trigger another round of pedantry. "Even corpses got guillotined during the Revolution?"

"The revolutionaries considered religion an institution of tyranny," he began, and my fears were confirmed. "All over France, they destroyed churches, religious statues, other symbols of oppression."

God save us from oppressors, I prayed. *And from pedants.*

"*But,*" Miranda interrupted, snatching back the reins of the narrative, "here's some trivia you'll find interesting. He was an Incorruptible."

"Excuse me?"

"Bénézet. He was an Incorruptible." She stopped and nodded at the stone chapel, whose stout wooden door faced the bridge. "Bénézet's body, lying here for centuries, did not decompose. Leading one of the popes, in the sixteen hundreds, to proclaim Bénézet one of the Incorruptibles."

"The Incorruptibles." I sounded it out slowly, savoring the syllables and the meaning. "Sounds like a band of crime-fighting comic-book superheroes waging war on bribery and embezzlement. 'Holy hedge fund, Miranda—someone on Wall Street is making insider trades! This looks like a job for the Incorruptibles!'"

She groaned, as I'd figured she would, and as I'd hoped she would. But she was right: I *was* intrigued to learn that Saint Bénézet was an Incorruptible—someone whose corpse did not decay. Catholics considered incorruptibility a sign of sainthood, but I looked at it through the lens of science. A few years back, I'd examined the body of a young woman—a pregnant young woman—who'd been killed and hidden in a cave for thirty years. The cave's cool, damp conditions turned her soft tissue into a substance called adipocere—sometimes called "grave wax"—and the transformation was so complete, she might almost have come from a wax museum rather than a crime scene. In the morgue, I'd paused to admire her lovely features, and then I'd sprayed her body with hot water, watching with wonder as her prettiness and her half-formed baby melted away, dissolving like some sweet sad dream in the heat of a summer's day.

I thought of her—that lovely murdered young woman who had spent three decades as an Incorruptible—as I stood on the ancient bridge beside an antique chapel where a shepherd-turned-engineer had lain in state for centuries.

According to Stefan, the move to the convent for safekeeping had not agreed with Bénézet. Some years after the French Revolution, the nuns to whom he'd been entrusted opened the saint's coffin, the better to revere his perfectly preserved remains. Imagine their disappointment to discover that the miracle—like the man himself—had expired, and his mortal coil had shuffled off silently, unheralded by angelic fanfare or human notice.

HUMAN NOTICE: WE seemed to be attracting it. As I leaned recklessly on the tubular steel rail of the Bénézet bridge once more, watching a long, slender canal boat slip beneath the outermost arch, Miranda laid her hand on my arm. "Don't look now," she murmured, "but someone's stalking us."

"Where?" Trying to look casual and touristy, I raised my eyes, pointing to the fortress on the river's far shore, as if calling Miranda's attention to it.

She looked in that direction, smiling and saying, just loudly enough for Stefan and me to hear, "Downstream about a hundred yards. Edge of the parking lot. There's a red-and-blue sign. Guy in a floppy hat standing behind it, propping binoculars on top. Don't look yet."

I swiveled slowly, with only a passing glance at the spot she'd indicated, and gazed upward at the cathedral and the papal palace, which loomed above us on the rock. "You're right," I said. "That's the biggest pair of binoculars I've ever seen. And they're pointing right at us."

"*Merde*," Stefan muttered a moment later. "Now he has a camera. A big telephoto lens." He raised his arm, hitched up the cuff of his sleeve, and made a show of checking his watch. "*Allons-y.* Let's go. Turn your backs and cross to the other railing, so he can't see us. Then let's get the hell out of here."

Hugging the far side of the bridge, we hurried back along the span. This time there was no singing or dancing. As we exited the tower and scurried to the car, I asked, "Did either of you get a good look?"

"*Non.*"

"'Fraid not," Miranda said. "White guy with tan hat and black binoculars. That narrows it down to about, what, a zillion people?"

I recalled Stefan's nervousness as we'd driven from Marseilles to Avignon, and again when we'd heard noises near the treasure chamber. I'd been inclined to dismiss it as excessive paranoia—that, or Stefan's exaggerated sense of importance—but now I was re-evaluating. "Have you seen someone watching you before now?"

"*Oui,*" he said. "Nothing as obvious as binoculars and a camera, but yes, I think so."

"When did it start?"

He shrugged. "A few days ago."

"Maybe the day before you got here," Miranda added. "Remember, Stefan? You got that phone call when we were having lunch, but then the caller hung up without saying anything?"

"Ah, *oui*. And then you thought someone was following us back to the Palais . . ."

"But when we turned around, he ducked down an alley and disappeared," she finished. "So now I'm questioning everything, everybody. The guy behind me at the café this morning—did he smile because he thought I was cute, or was he just pretending to flirt so he could study me? The woman in the hotel lobby—was she really reading that newspaper? Hell, now that I'm feeling paranoid, even *you* seem kinda sinister, Dr. B, you know?"

I knew, and I made a mental note to make a phone call to Tennessee as soon as I was alone.

"STONE HERE."

"Rocky, it's Bill Brockton." I backed into a doorway in a narrow street that was just around the corner from Miranda's hotel. She'd gone to her room to catch up on her e-mail for an hour, and Stefan had headed off to an electronics store to buy a motion detector and alarm for the treasure chamber. I was on my own until seven, when I'd arranged to fetch Miranda for dinner.

"Doc? I thought you were in France," said Stone. "Did you just make that up so you could get the extra helicopter ride?"

"No, I *am* in France. Rocky, I need to know if there's a chance—any chance at all—that one of your drug smugglers might have followed me here?"

The line was silent for a moment. "Are you serious, Doc?"

"Unfortunately, yes," I said. "I realize it's unlikely, but I need to know. Somebody's watching us—me, Miranda, and this French archaeologist we're working with."

"Are you sure? What happened? Exactly?"

"We just caught someone watching us through binoculars from about a hundred yards away. Then he traded the binoculars for a camera with a really long lens."

"You're sure he wasn't just sightseeing? Taking in the scenery?"

"Come on, Rocky. Howitzer-sized binoculars,

followed by a foot-long telephoto? What would *you* think if you saw that kind of optical artillery aimed at you?"

"I'd probably think, 'Oh shit,'" he acknowledged.

"So. Any chance your bad guys have tailed me to France?"

"I doubt it," he said . . . but his tone was hedging. He sighed. "The truth is, I can't completely rule it out. We've got a bad leak somewhere, Doc. I don't know where, but we've just had another operation compromised. So yeah, it's possible they know we called you in. If they do, they know you'd be important at a trial. I'm sorry, Doc. I was gonna call you soon—you're on my list, but I'm up to my ass in alligators, and I've got half a dozen undercover operatives I'm trying to pull in before it's too late."

"I understand," I said. "I'll let you get back to it. Good luck, Rocky."

"Thanks, Doc. I'll call you as soon as I know anything. Meanwhile, watch your back."

Suddenly, just as the call ended, I felt myself falling, toppling straight back. Reflexively I yelled; an answering shriek sounded in my ear as I thudded into someone and we landed in a tangle of arms and legs. A moment later, I was helping an irate Frenchwoman to her feet—a woman whose door I'd been leaning against at the moment she opened it. Mortified by my clumsiness—and by my inability to say anything but "*pardon, pardon*" by way of apology—I slunk down the street and around the nearest corner.

But it's not paranoia, I finally consoled myself, *if they really are out to get you.*

CHAPTER 6

"**OKAY, YOU CAN OPEN** your eyes now," I said.

She did, and she squealed with delight. "Oh, *sweet*—a fancy hotel named after *moi*!"

"We're having dinner here."

"Cool! That's so . . . *boss*, Boss."

We were standing, Miranda and I, in front of the Hotel La Mirande, an elegant little jewel box tucked into the dead-end street behind the Palace of the Popes. I'd stumbled upon La Mirande only forty-five minutes before, shortly after I'd stumbled upon the slightly bruised, very irate Frenchwoman.

I had never stayed in a place this fancy, and surely never would—the rooms started at eight hundred dollars a night—but how could I pass up a chance to take Miranda to a swanky restaurant that bore her name? Besides, Stefan was occupied procuring the motion detector and alarm for the treasure chamber. A quiet dinner seemed like a good chance to catch up with Miranda—and to learn more about her prior history with this pretentious pedant who might soon be the world's most famous archaeologist.

I pulled a glossy brochure from my pocket. "Here, this gives a little background about your establishment."

She took a look and laughed. "Ooh, architectural erotica—my favorite kind. Listen: 'This timeless refuge offers a dreamy, relaxing, and authentic experience in a refined, eighteenth-century décor. . . . Behind its stunning façade, La Mirande exudes the sweet way of life of yesteryear.'" She surveyed the exterior, an elegant neoclassical composition in butter-colored stone, its windows capped with gargoyles and angels, gods and goddesses, sunbursts and swirls of cake frosting in stone. "Stunning façade indeed," she concurred. "The façade," she added, "is from the seventeen hundreds, but parts of the building date back to the early thirteen hundreds, when a cardinal—a nephew of Pope Clement the Fifth—built his palace on the site." She was enjoying this, and that pleased me. "Come on, let's go inside and show them what chic cosmopolites we are."

If the hotel's exterior was quietly elegant, its interior was almost intoxicating in its richness. Crystal chandeliers and sconces glittered everywhere; paintings and statues and flowers filled the spaces, set against backdrops of gilded wallpaper, brocaded drapes, rich paneling, sumptuous sofas and chairs. An interior courtyard was set with candlelit dining tables; so was a lush outdoor garden that offered spectacular views of the floodlit walls of the Palace of the Popes. Miranda flitted from space to space, statue to statue, ruffle to flourish, her face beaming. "This place is *so excellent*," she exclaimed. "You could probably pay my assistantship for a year for what dinner's gonna cost, but *wowzer*, Dr. B, how *gorgeous*." She laughed, a fountain of delight. "I know money can't buy happiness, but *damn*, it sure can open doors to places that make me smile."

We ate in one such place, a linen-draped, candlelit table in a corner of the hotel's garden. Fairy lights twinkled in the trees around us; above us soared the graceful windows of the papal chapel, flanked by a pair of massive towers.

We were midway through dinner—duck breast for me, "line-caught sea bass" for her—before I worked up the nerve to go on my own fishing expedition and angle for details about Stefan. When I wasn't busy bristling at his pretentiousness, I had realized, I was fretting about something else. I'd seen the way he looked at her, heard the way she spoke to him. They shared a familiarity that went beyond collegiality; a familiarity that might be, or might have once been, intimacy. *It's none of my business*, I scolded myself, but that didn't stop me from casting the lure. "Stefan's quite a character," I said casually. "Remind me how you know him?"

She didn't exactly take the bait—her gimlet look told me she knew she was being cross-examined—but she answered the question anyway. "Remember when I did the dig in Guatemala, the summer after my first year of graduate school?" I nodded. "He was a crew leader. I worked under him."

I raised my eyebrows at the phrase "worked

under him." I expected her to roll her eyes at that and fire back one of her signature smart-ass retorts. Instead, she turned crimson and looked down at her fish, swimming in butter and seaweed sauce. "Sorry, Miranda. I didn't mean to embarrass you. I was joking, or meant to be. I think. I hope."

She looked up, slightly defiant but also vulnerable. "It's okay. I had it coming, after the way I've let Stefan be a jerk to you. I did get involved with him in Guatemala, and I shouldn't have. I was a kid, and he was my boss. *And* he was married, though he said that didn't really matter, because the French don't mind infidelity—'We approve of extramarital affairs,' he said. Exact quote. *He* approved, turns out, but his wife didn't."

"And you know this how?"

"Because she came to Guatemala. A birthday surprise. A *big* surprise. When she found me in his tent, she came at me with fingernails and teeth."

"Ah. That would imply a certain level of disapproval."

"She took the next flight home and promptly divorced him." She took a deep draw from her glass of red wine. "I'm also embarrassed that I still feel awkward about it. It's been five years. It shouldn't still bother me."

"Says who?"

"Myself. My inner critic. My friends who have hookups and don't think twice about it, who act as if sharing a bed with somebody's no different from sharing a taxi or a park bench. I've just never been able to be that nonchalant about the whole sex thing." She spun the stem of the glass between her fingers; the wine swirled up the sides, then sheeted back down. "I feel guilty about Stefan's marriage, too. If not for me, he might still be married."

"Maybe. But maybe miserably married. As it is, he seems like a fairly happy guy. Pompous, but happy." She smiled. "Anyhow, if she hadn't caught him with you, she'd have caught him with someone else, don't you think?"

"Oh, probably. Much as I'd like to believe I'm something special, I probably wasn't Stefan's only . . . extracurricular activity."

"Sounds like he had his sales pitch down pretty well. 'Ah, *chérie*, I am ze Frenchman. I must, how you say, *cherchez la femme. Non? Oui!*'" She laughed at the parody, and I felt doubly glad—glad to make her laugh, and glad to do it by skewering Stefan. "But you know what, Miranda?" I caught and held her eyes; she looked back skittishly. "Even if Stefan's a womanizing jerk, that doesn't mean you're wrong about the other thing. You *are* something special. You're lovely, you're smart, you're strong and brave and spirited. You're amazing."

She raised her wineglass in my direction. "I'll drink to that," she said, smiling . . . but the smile looked wistful. When she set down the glass, her fingers lingered on the stem, and I felt a powerful urge to reach across the table and squeeze her hand. But would the gesture be one of friendship and empathy, or something more complicated, something more like Stefan's overtures? I hesitated, and while I did, she let go of the glass and took her hand off the table.

I retreated to safer, more neutral ground. "Before the year you went to Guatemala, how'd you spend your summers? Other trips abroad?"

"Are you kidding? I worked my butt off. I had summer jobs from the time I was twelve. Babysitting. Mowing yards. I taught swimming a couple years. Spent three summers as a lifeguard."

"City pool? Country club?"

"Nah, the real deal. Daytona."

"Daytona Beach? Lifeguarding on the ocean?" She nodded. "Ever save a life?"

She smiled briefly. "Yeah. I did. I saved a life." She looked away, somewhere into the past, then looked at me again. "But I lost one, too." I waited, very still, hoping she'd go on. "My second summer, there was a girl—eleven, maybe twelve; she still had a kid body, and still had a kid's innocence and exuberance. It hadn't gotten complicated for her yet, the way things get for girls when they hit puberty, you know? Anyhow, she was bodysurfing on this gorgeous, gorgeous day." I felt a rush of dread for the girl. "The waves were perfect—sweet little breakers, three, maybe four feet. That girl was having such a great time, just flinging herself into those waves with total abandon, riding them all the way in. She'd stagger up out of the foam with a suit full of sand and this huge, dazed grin on her face. Made me happy just to watch her. Then along comes this big-ass wave, twice the size of the others she's been riding."

"Oh no! What happened?"

"I can still see it so clearly. The top of the wave is just starting to curl when it gets to her. The wave lifts her up, and up—this twig of a girl, halfway up a mountain of water—and then it comes crashing down. I mean, that wave just *explodes* with her inside it."

"God, how awful."

"I see her tumbling, flipping end over end, then she smashes into the sand headfirst, like a post being pounded by a pile driver. When I got to her she was facedown, underwater, being pulled out by the undertow. I was sure she was dead, or worse—paralyzed, a quad." I felt nearly sick just hearing about it. "But she *wasn't*. Amazingly, she wasn't. Her forehead looked like somebody'd taken a cheese grater to it, but once I got the water out of her lungs, she came to and she was okay. Coughing and crying, but okay." In the candlelight, diamonds sparkled at the corners of Miranda's eyes and then rolled down her cheeks. She wiped her eyes on her napkin, then blew her nose into it with a trumpeting honk. Then she laughed. "Miranda Lovelady: You can dress her up, but you can't take her out."

I felt as if I'd just ridden a roller coaster. "Wow. How come you never told me that story before?"

"We've never talked swimming before."

"So that was, what, ten years or so ago?" She nodded. "Whatever happened to the girl? Have you stayed in touch with her?"

She shook her head. "Couldn't. Didn't know how. As soon as she came to, her parents yanked me off her, scooped her up, and skedaddled—straight to the ER, probably. Never asked my name or even said thank you. Too freaked out to be polite, I guess." She shrugged. "Doesn't matter. I'm still the one who saved her. Funny—I like to imagine I'm that girl's hero; that she thinks of me as some sort of guardian angel watching over her. God knows, girls need all the watching over they can get." She said it sadly, and I wondered if Miranda wished *she'd* gotten more watching over and guarding.

"You're *my* hero, Miranda. You make me proud."

"Thanks, Dr. B. Sometimes I make *me* proud, too. I did the right thing that time." She looked away again. "Not so much the next time. The next summer. It was a guy that time—an adult. He got into a rip current, got carried out. By the time I saw him, he was out past the surf line. He didn't know what to do, and he panicked; he was flailing, struggling to get back toward shore. Wrong thing to do. You can't beat a rip current head-on; can't outswim it. You've got to turn ninety degrees, swim parallel to the shore, till the current lets you go." She paused, took a breath, then another. "*His* mistake was, he tried to fight it. *My* mistake was, I hesitated." She shook her head, still angry at herself. "He was a big guy—taller than you, and stocky; I'd noticed him when he waded in—and when he got into trouble I hesitated, just *sat* there, because I was afraid he'd overpower me, take me down with him. Finally I grabbed a torpedo float and started swimming, but by then it was too late. He went under when I was halfway there; washed up two days later and a mile south, minus his eyes and his lips and his fingers and toes." She drained her wineglass. "That's still on my shame list, written in indelible ink. Thing is, I'm not sure I could've gotten to him in time even if I'd dived right in. But I'll never know. Because at the crucial moment, I hesitated. God, I've wished a million times for a do-over, you know?"

"I do," I said. "I've got a few of those, too. Who doesn't? But from where I sit, Miranda, I see you do the right thing all the time, again and again." I made her look at me. "Once upon a time, when I was wishing hard for a do-over, someone older and wiser told me that life's a river. It's not Daytona Beach, where the same water keeps washing up on the same damn spot again and again; it's a fast-flowing river. That guy's death? That happened way upstream, Miranda. Trying to swim back to that spot is like swimming against a rip current. Remember that girl you saved. You've spent all these years being her guardian angel. Let her return the favor. I bet she'd loan you some of that innocence and exuberance if you asked."

She looked away as she parsed what I'd said, looking for any trace of insincerity or condescension, I imagined. Finding none—for there was none to be found—she smiled. This time, if there was wistfulness or poignancy in her smile, I couldn't see it. And I was looking mighty close.

The candles were burning down and the night was getting cool by the time we left La Mirande. I wished I had a jacket to wrap around her shoulders; I considered wrapping an arm around her, but there was something fragile, something . . . *sacred*, somehow, in the air around us, and I didn't want to risk disturbing it.

Thank you, I said silently to the universe, or to God, or to the river of life. *Thank you.*

THE NEXT MORNING, Stefan—low on sleep and high on irritation—was still struggling to install and debug the motion detector. I offered to help, though the offer was neither sincere nor particularly useful, given my ineptness with electronics. Blessedly, Stefan declined and actually shooed us away, which meant that I had Miranda to myself again. When we emerged from the palace onto the plaza, I felt almost giddy with freedom—a middle-aged schoolboy playing hooky. "What shall we do, Miss Miranda?"

"Let's pretend we're tourists," she said. We dashed to Lumani. We arrived there in search of a guidebook; we departed with not only a guidebook but also a car: In a gesture of remarkable trust and generosity, Jean and Elisabeth loaned us their car, so—ensconced in an aging Peugeot and armed with a tattered English-language guide to Provence—we set out. Gingerly, for it had been years since I'd driven a car with a clutch, I eased us into the street and along the base of the ancient wall, which bristled with watchtowers every fifty yards. I checked the mirror often to see if we were being followed. Unless an eleven-year-old girl on a bicycle had been trained as an assassin, we were in the clear.

We started with a detour through the town across the river, Villeneuve-les-Avignon. *Villeneuve* meant "New Town," Miranda translated; it was a name that had been accurate once upon a time, but that time was a thousand years gone. During the thirteen hundreds, Villeneuve, which was not so tightly cramped as Avignon, became a wealthy suburb of the papal city, and fifteen cardinals built palaces there, though none, as far as we could see, had survived. What *had* survived were two monumental structures: a 130-foot tower that once controlled the western end of Saint Bénézet's Bridge, back when the bridge spanned the entire river; and a massive fortress that encircled the town's hilltop. Both the tower and the fortress had been built to send a clear message to the uppity people of Avignon: The pope might hold the keys to heaven, but the king's earthly army could break open the city gates on an hour's notice, if papal push ever came to sovereign shove.

From Villeneuve we took narrow country roads, Miranda navigating with the guidebook and a large-scale Michelin map on her lap. As the tires sang on the asphalt, my heart hummed along, and I felt lighter and freer than I had since my arrival. Ten miles or so north of Avignon, Miranda pointed to a ruined fortress on a hilltop. "Châteauneuf-du-Pape," she announced. "It translates as 'New Castle of the Pope.'"

"All these ancient places with modern-sounding names," I commented. "I guess five hundred years from now, people will say the same thing about New York, huh?" I threaded my way up through the village and parked beside the ruins. The structure had been built in the early thirteen hundreds, according to the guidebook, and had survived the ravages of time and the elements for six centuries. Unfortunately, it had not survived the ravages of Hitler's soldiers. During World War Two, German troops filled the castle with dynamite and blew it up, destroying all but an L-shaped section of wall and tower.

Clambering along the edge of the ruins, we had a good view of the broad plain below, which was filled as far as the eye could see with vineyards, the neat rows of vines lined with river rocks. "The rocks capture the heat of the sun," Miranda read, "to keep the vines warm at night." Both the castle and the vineyards were the legacy of Pope John XXII, the second of the Avignon popes. "He was well known for his love of wine," she went on, "and also for his sour disposition." She laughed. "After he drank it, I guess it turned to vinegar in his soul."

As we made our way back to the car, I noticed a stone staircase burrowing into the hillside, ending at a door set deep in the foundations of the fortress. I nudged Miranda and nodded down toward the doorway. "Pope John's wine cellar?"

"Looks more like Pope John's dungeon to me." She was right. The steps were narrow, steep, and crumbling; the arch of the doorway was low; the door itself was recessed a couple of feet into the thick stonework. "Holy heretics, Batman," she muttered. "This place feels haunted. Let's get out of here."

As the Peugeot clattered and corkscrewed back down through the town, Miranda announced, "I'm starving. How about lunch?"

"Sure. Can you make it back to Avignon?"

"I can make it back to that little café we passed two seconds ago. Look, there's a parking place. On the right. Here, here, *here*." I whipped the car into the spot, forgetting to push in the clutch, and we lurched to a stop as the engine stalled. "Smooth, Dr. B."

"Thanks. Anybody ever tell you you're bossy?"

"Nobody who valued life and limb," she said, and I laughed.

The café, La Maisouneta—"Provençal dialect for 'The Little House,' I think," Miranda said—was as humble and homey as La Mirande had been elegant and expensive. The handful of other customers seemed to be locals, not tourists: a rumpled young couple with a toddler crawling beneath the tables; a stocky older woman, her hair in curlers; a middle-aged man in paint-spattered coveralls. The menu was scrawled on a blackboard behind the counter, but most of the dishes on it were unavailable, the hostess informed Miranda. Lunchtime was just ending, and the kitchen had run out of everything except salad and something called *reblochon*, a traditional local dish consisting of melted white cheese with a potato on the side. "White on white," I muttered. "Sounds terrific."

It *was* terrific, in fact. The dish had been baked until the top of the cheese was golden brown and crispy, and it was garnished with crunchy bits of salty ham. It was, I decided, nearly as special as my first night's feast of Corsican lamb stew.

Then again, maybe it wasn't the food that was special; maybe what was special was stumbling across this hole-in-the-wall café on a steep cobblestone street in an ancient town, sitting across a stained checkerboard tablecloth from Miranda. She was speaking, but I had no idea what she was saying; instead, as I watched her mouth move, I was thinking what a lovely woman she was; I was wishing I weren't her boss; wishing I were twenty years younger. Suddenly she stopped talking, stared at me, and waved her hands like semaphore flags.

"Sorry, what?"

"I knew it," she sighed. "You had that lost-in-space look on your face. Where'd you go?" Hope and terror surged in me—*Should I tell her? Has she guessed?*—but she shook her head. "Doesn't matter. So, I was just saying that the Romans crucified thousands of people, but only one set of crucified remains has ever been definitively identified. Found in an ossuary in Jerusalem in 1968. Totally a fluke. One of the heels still had a nail in it; the nail had hit a knot in the wood, and it bent, so when the body was taken down, the nail yanked out a chunk of wood."

I chewed on the information while chewing on a bite of cheese-slathered potato. "When did you study up on crucifixion?"

"Right after Stefan showed me the bones." I regretted my question; I didn't want Stefan sharing the café table with us, even figuratively. Luckily, he merited only a passing mention. "It was uncommon to nail people to the cross," she went on. "Rope was more common."

"Rope?"

"Sure. You just tie the wrists to the crossbar." She spread her arms wide, her hands slightly above shoulder height, tilting her head sideways and slightly down, though not enough to hide the playful smile on her face. "Asphyxiation's the cause of death, right, if you're hanging on a cross by your arms for hours?" I nodded, feeling a bit short of breath myself. Miranda made even crucifixion look miraculously fetching. *Get a grip, Brockton*, I scolded inwardly.

"So . . . uh . . ." I struggled to put together a sentence. "Do you think the gouge marks in our bones are fake, then? Made by a medieval-relic forger who didn't know that nails weren't generally used in crucifixions?"

She shrugged. "Maybe. But then again, what good's a fake relic if nobody knows about it? The point of relics—the cynical point, at least—was to attract pilgrims. Not a lot of pilgrims visited the pope's treasure chamber, I'm thinking. Besides, they'd've needed X-ray vision to see it. Makes no sense." Just then she got a text message. When she read it, she frowned. "Well, crap. Stefan says he needs me to help him test the motion sensor."

I suppressed a sigh. He had elbowed his way to the lunch table after all.

We'd planned to finish our day another twenty miles north, at the city of Orange, whose immense Roman amphitheater was already a millennium old when the cornerstone was laid at the Palace of the Popes. But Miranda felt obliged to help Stefan. And the truth was, my heart wasn't really in playing tourist. Except for my delight in having Miranda to myself, I was just killing time—drumming my fingers on the stage sets of history—while waiting to hear from Joe Mullins. Waiting to see the face of the man whose bones had been entombed in a wall seven centuries before.

Would it be the face of a medieval murder victim—or the face of Jesus of Nazareth?

CHAPTER 7

**Châteauneuf-du-Pape
1327**

A FAINT SHEEN OF perspiration bedews the forehead
and fleshy upper lip of Jacques Fournier—Cardinal
Jacques Fournier, for the past week now—as he's
ushered into the pope's chambers. The journey
from Avignon to the countryside castle has taken
an entire sweltering day, but a papal summons is
a mark of high favor, and a private audience is a
rare privilege, especially for a young, freshly hatted
cardinal.

Pope John XXII hunches on a wooden throne by a
window that overlooks vineyards—*his* vineyards—
spreading across the wide valley. His desiccated,
dyspeptic face is crosshatched with wrinkles, and
the liver-spotted hands clutching the arms of the
chair bear an unsettling resemblance to the carved
talons that serve as the throne's four feet. A papal
claw slithers forward by an inch, and Fournier

kneels—no easy task for a man of his bulk—to kiss the Fisherman's Ring on the old man's bony third finger. Despite his conspicuous contempt for earthly luxuries, the young cardinal's eyes linger on the massive gold signet. John XXII's monogram is simple yet regal, and the embossed image of Saint Peter hauling a net aboard a small wooden boat portrays to perfection the hard, humble work of fishing for the souls of men.

"Rise, my son," the pope rasps, "for there is work to be done." Fournier lumbers to his feet, puffing with the effort, and inclines his head to listen. "Your zeal for the purity of the faith is exemplary. Your inquisition rid us of the Cathar heretics in Montaillou, and we are most grateful."

"Your Holiness honors me beyond all deserving," Fournier murmurs. "I pray that we have seen the last of the Cathars. But we must remain vigilant."

"Quite so, Jacques, quite so. And not just against the Cathars. The Father of Lies sows seeds of evil everywhere. This is why I have elevated you and brought you to the papal court. We must guard Christ's holy church against those who would destroy it from within."

"It is my privilege as well as my duty, Holy Father."

The pope moves his hands to the lap of his silk robe and twists the gold ring. "How closely have you followed the problem with the Franciscans?"

Fournier inclines his head, his plump sausage-fingers interlaced. "I know that one faction, the Spirituals, preach that our Lord and his followers lived in poverty," he says. "And that we should all do likewise."

"They're happy to live in housing they say belongs to me," snaps the pontiff. "Happy to consume food and wine they say belongs to me. And happiest of all to denounce me for possessing these things that sustain their lives of precious purity." He is sputtering with anger, spraying drops of spittle that sparkle in the slanting afternoon light.

Fournier shakes his head sadly. "They do Your Holiness an injustice. And now . . . but perhaps it is not my place to speak of it."

"To speak of what?" The aged head snaps up, the eyes blazing.

"One hears . . . *reports*, Holy Father."

"What kind of reports?"

"The Franciscans' minister general, Michael of Cesena, grows bolder. He openly calls Your Holiness a hypocrite, a hedonist, and a heretic." The pope's fingers scrabble at the arms of the chair. "Forgive me if I speak too frankly," Fournier continues, "but now Michael is said to be conspiring with Louis of Bavaria to destroy you. Their goal is to put a Franciscan on the papal throne. Perhaps none other than Michael himself."

"Spawn of the Devil," the old man rages. "Sons of Satan. They must be brought to heel."

"Louis might prove difficult to rein in, but would Your Holiness consider summoning Michael to Avignon for . . . questioning?" The pope's glittering eyes bore into Fournier's; the cardinal bows deferentially. "I stand ready, of course, to serve in any capacity you think helpful."

The pope nods. "Bring them here." Reaching into a pocket of his cassock, he rummages ineffectually. "There are cells beneath us," he rasps. "Also in the bishop's palace in Avignon." Finally he extracts a pair of keys and hands them to Fournier. *Not quite the keys to heaven,* thinks Fournier, *but the papal dungeon is a starting place.*

He takes the keys and takes his leave. On his way out, though, he hesitates, then turns. "Your Holiness, I beg your pardon. My conscience would trouble me if I did not mention another matter. I'm also hearing disturbing reports from the archbishop of Cologne."

"Do Michael and the Franciscans foment trouble in Cologne, too?"

"No, Holy Father, not Michael; someone else. Someone far more subtle, and perhaps far more sinister. He does not bother to criticize you, Holy Father. This man dares to criticize God Himself."

CHAPTER 8

"I HAVE AN IDEA for you," Elisabeth said, setting my morning glass of blood orange juice on the table in Lumani's garden. "For your—how do you say it?—zhondo?"

"I'm not sure I understand," I said. "For my what?"

"Your zhondo. Your dead man with no name. Your mysterious bones."

"Oh, my John Doe." I smiled, but I was puzzled and concerned. How did she know about the bones? I'd been careful not to discuss the case with Elisabeth and Jean, given Stefan's skittishness and my new paranoia. "Did Stefan or Miranda tell you about him?"

"*Non, pas du tout.* Not at all. It's simple to guess. I look you up on Google after you arrive. I do this to learn about every guest. Most of the time, I find nothing. But you—you are a famous bone detective!"

"Not so famous."

"Ah, *monsieur*, you are wrong. Too humble. So. A bone detective comes all the way to Avignon. *Pourquoi?* Because someone has found mysterious bones, *oui*? You and your friends, you arrive wearing badges from the Palais des Papes that day. So I think, *ah*, they are working at the Palais; this is where the mysterious bones are found. You see? Simple."

I couldn't help laughing. "Elisabeth, you're a better detective than plenty of police officers I know." She seemed to like that, but she wasn't finished yet, apparently, because she raised her index finger and wagged it at me. "So, mysterious bones at the Palais. *Oui? Oui.*" She nodded, pleased to have answered her own question. "Whose bones? Someone from the time of the popes. Someone important. Someone whose death the pope needs to hide, *oui? Oui.*"

"Are you really an innkeeper and artist, Elisabeth? Or are you an undercover cop?"

She laughed. "Artists, we have big imagination."

"And you can imagine who this John Doe is?"

She looked self-conscious for the first time. "Maybe yes, maybe no. But there is a mystery in Avignon at the time of the popes. An important man comes here. He has powerful enemies. And he disappears."

I was starting to get intrigued. "And who was this important man?"

She smiled, happy to have me on the hook, and then drew a deep breath and launched into her story. "In the early thirteen hundreds," she began, "there was a popular and powerful preacher in Germany, a Dominican friar named Eckhart. *Jean*. John. Johannes, in German. You have heard of him? Meister Johannes Eckhart?" She cocked her head and lifted her eyebrows.

"I've heard the name, but I don't know anything about him," I admitted. "Tell me."

"*Ah.* Well, he was brilliant. My cousin is a Dominican, and he tells me about this. Eckhart was a great . . . *théologien*?"

"Theologian. It's the same word in English."

"*Ah, bon.* Eckhart studied in Cologne with Albertus Magnus—Albert the Great—*and* with Thomas Aquinas, the two most brilliant men of the time. Then he taught theology in Paris. *But*"—she raised a finger for emphasis—"he was also a great preacher. Very much loved. The Dominicans were the best preachers. They took the message out to the people."

"The evangelists," I said, nodding. "So what happened? You said he had powerful enemies?"

"Yes. One is the archbishop of Cologne. He is jealous because he is not so popular like Eckhart. So. He accuses Eckhart of heresy. *Ah*, but Eckhart fights back. He appeals directly to the pope, Pope John Twenty-Two. And in 1327—Eckhart has sixty-six years at this time—he walks from Cologne to Avignon, eight hundred kilometers, to make a defense."

"At age sixty-six, he walked eight hundred kilometers? That's five hundred miles."

"He was a strong man. But his enemies were more strong, sad to say. The man who led the case against him here was *le Cardinal Blanc*—the White Cardinal."

"But . . ." I felt silly asking. "Weren't *all* the cardinals white in those days?"

She furrowed her brow, then laughed. *"Ah, non,* not the skin. The robe. He always wore the white robe of the Cistercian monks. Even after he became a cardinal. Even after he became the pope."

"Wait. The White Cardinal became the pope? Which pope was he?"

"Benedict Twelve," she said. "Before he was pope, his name was Fournier. Jacques Fournier. He was brought here by Pope John Twenty-Two to be the *police théologique.*"

"You mean to punish heretics? Like the Inquisition?"

"Exactement. He adored to be the Inquisitor. He protected the back of the pope. And when John Twenty-Two died, *voilà, le Cardinal Blanc* became the new pope, Benedict Twelve. He was the one who built the Palais des Papes. Before, the pope was in the bishop's house. Then he tears that down and builds the fortress."

"But while he was a cardinal, he was Eckhart's enemy?" She nodded gravely. "The cardinal who was the pope's guard dog?" Another nod. "That *is* a powerful enemy."

A third and final nod. "You see? Eckhart comes to Avignon in 1327 to make his defense. And he is never seen again."

"I DON'T KNOW if this Eckhart is *our* guy," I whispered, "but he's sure an *intriguing* guy."

Miranda nodded without glancing up from the

screen of her laptop. We were sitting in Avignon's library—a spectacular library, housed in a former cardinal's palace—beneath a gilded, coffered ceiling in the main reading room, which had once been the grand audience hall. When I'd mentioned Elisabeth's theory about Meister Eckhart, Miranda had taken the idea and run with it, straight to the library's reference desk.

Now I was skimming an English-language book on Eckhart's life and teachings, which a helpful young librarian, Philippe, had found on the shelves. Meanwhile Miranda was combing Web sites and archival materials about Avignon's cemeteries and death records, looking for any references to Eckhart's death or grave. "The date of his death is unknown," she murmured. "So is his burial site. Like Elisabeth said, he came here—in 1327 or 1328—to defend himself against charges of heresy. Then, poof, he drops off the radar screen. No mention of him until March 1329, when John Twenty-Two issued a papal bull, a pronouncement, condemning a bunch of Eckhart's teachings. According to the bull, Eckhart took them all back—get this—*before he died.*"

"Sure *sounds* like bull," I said.

"Indeed. But the point is, we know he was dead by March 1329."

I went back to my book. The more I read, the more I liked this Eckhart. I didn't understand a lot of what he said, but he seemed smart, genuine, and passionate about what he believed. He criticized those who asked God for personal favors, or who prayed "thy will be done" but then complained if things didn't work out the way they wanted. And he had a sense of humor—not a quality I generally associated with monks and theologians. "My Lord told me a joke," Eckhart wrote, "and seeing Him laugh has done more for me than any scripture I will ever read." He could even be a bit cheeky. "Listen," I said. "He writes, 'God is not good, or else he could do better.' No wonder the theology police put him under surveillance—he's giving the Big Guy a bad grade."

Miranda looked thoughtful. "Maybe," she said. "Or maybe he's playing with language—*good, better, best*? God's not merely good, because good's only so-so? Maybe he means God can't be anything but best?"

I shrugged. "Dunno. This is why I study bones, not philosophy." The most striking thing about Eckhart, though, was how fresh, how modern, some of his insights sounded. "Get this," I told Miranda. "He wrote, 'If the only prayer you ever say in your entire life is "thank you," it will be enough.' I like that. Then there's, 'The more we have, the less we own.' Or how about this: 'The price of inaction is far greater than the cost of making a mistake'?"

She flinched. "Ouch. Too bad they didn't stress that one in lifeguard training—I might've gotten off my ass sooner and saved that dude from drowning."

I kicked myself for having jabbed her sore spot. "Sorry. I take it back. Here, remember this one instead: 'Do exactly what you would do if you felt most secure.' Good advice, right? Be your best self? Sounds like something Dr. Phil might say."

She snorted. "What do you know about Dr. Phil? Have you *ever* read or heard anything he's said?"

She had me there. "Okay, okay. It sounds like something I *imagine* a New Age self-help guru might say." I flipped a page. "So does this, in a brainier way: 'There exists only the present instant . . . a Now which always and without end is itself new. There is no yesterday nor any tomorrow, but only Now, as it was a thousand years ago and as it will be a thousand years hence.' Isn't that a Zen-like, New Agey thing for a Catholic friar to be saying seven centuries ago?"

She smiled. "Very Zen. Very Tolle."

"Very what?"

"Not what, who: Tolle. *Eckhart* Tolle, in fact— he's another big self-help guru. His books have sold zillions of copies. *And* . . . Hmm, hang on. . . ." Her keyboard clattered with rapid strokes. "*In*-teresting. According to this bio, Eckhart Tolle, darling of the yoga set, was originally named *Ulrich* Tolle. He changed his first name to Eckhart 'as a tribute to a wise medieval philosopher and theologian.' *This* wise medieval philosopher and theologian, I'm thinking. Tolle's huge, very New Age." She scrolled down the screen of her laptop. "His blockbuster book's called *The Power of Now*, and it's all about living in the present moment. How did your medieval monk describe it—as the eternal Now? Here's the modern guru's spin on that: 'Nothing ever happened in the past,' writes Tolle; "it happened in the Now. Nothing will ever happen in the future; it will happen in the Now.' Same idea, slightly different words."

"Hmm," I said. "So how come the modern guru gets rich and famous, and the medieval monk gets hauled in on a heresy charge and then vanishes, maybe gets murdered?"

She shrugged. "Timing is everything. I guess the masses weren't ready for Now until . . . you know . . . *now*."

I couldn't help smiling. "Touché, but not true," I told her. "Meister Eckhart was an incredibly popular preacher. *Too* popular. He was brought down by jealous rivals." I shook my head. "Why is so much scheming and backstabbing—and front stabbing, for that matter—done in the name of God?"

"Duh," she said. "Don't pretend to be a dumbass. You know perfectly well why." I *didn't* know perfectly well why, but I suspected she was about to *tell* me why. "People and their gods are just like people and their dogs."

"Huh?" This time I felt myself six conversational and logical steps behind Miranda.

"You know how people and their dogs resemble one another? Crabby little ladies with snappish little Pekinese? Beefy bubbas with waddling bulldogs? Same thing with theology. Someone who's bighearted, like your man the Meister, sees God as benevolent. A cruel, vindictive jerk, on the other hand, imagines God as harsh and vengeful. See? At the end of either leash—the dog leash or the God leash—there's really just a mirror."

The images—God on a leash, God as a narcissistic reflection—were shockingly irreverent. But she had a point, in an editorial-cartoon kind of way. Miranda almost always had a point.

* * *

IT WAS NEARLY midnight Sunday; I should have been sleeping, but after tossing and turning for two hours, I gave up, got up, and got dressed.

Outside, a fierce wind was roaring across the rooftops. What had Jean called it? The mistral. The mistral was roaring, and the bells in the skeletal iron steeple of the Carmelite church tolled each time the gusts peaked. The moon was full, and the lashing branches outside my window cast shadows that twisted and writhed on my bed, beckoning me outside for some reason. Tiptoeing down the stairs, I unlocked the inn's rattling wooden gate—the wind nearly tore it from my grasp—and set out into the gale.

Avignon was a maze of narrow, crooked streets, but it was a small maze—barely a mile wide, according to the map I'd studied—so even if I got lost, I couldn't get terribly lost. Besides, Lumani faced the stone ramparts that ringed the city; to find my way home, all I'd need to do was find and follow the wall. If I walked an extra half mile, so what? The ancient city was beautiful, and the exercise would do me good.

Leaving Lumani, I turned left and followed the wall westward, toward the rocky hill where the Palace of the Popes and the cathedral perched. The streets were empty at this hour, and the city itself was largely shuttered and silent. The only noise came from the wind: the surging, surflike mistral churning across roof tiles and seething through the shredded leaves of plane trees.

I'd not gone far—ten minutes' easy walk, a scant

half mile—when the street butted into another stone wall, even higher than the ancient ramparts: Saint Anne's Prison, a historical marker informed me, though it was no longer in use. Moonlight cascaded down the rock wall like water sheeting down the face of a cliff. The surface was rough, pockmarked with deep, shadowed craters, which I stepped closer to examine. From waist level up to a height of eight or ten feet, rectangular niches had been gouged into the blocks, and these niches—a hundred or more—were filled with objects: photos, figurines, crucifixes, trinkets, talismans. I puzzled over it, and suddenly I realized what I was seeing. Family and friends of the men inside the prison had filled the niches with mementos and relics.

A half block farther, I came upon a stone chapel tucked against the prison wall; a historical marker identified it as the Chapel of the Pénitents Noirs. The Pénitents Noirs—the Black Penitents— belonged to a religious society that revered John the Baptist; this particular group of them had banded together in the fifteen hundreds to minister to the prison's inmates as their own way of doing penance. The chapel was small and simple, with the exception of an ornate relief panel above the doorway. The panel, carved in stone, measured eight or ten feet wide by at least fifteen feet high. Most of it was filled with angels, clouds, and rays of sunlight, or rays of heavenly glory; at the center, two hovering angels held some sort of serving tray between them in the sky. By the pale light of the moon, as the mistral roared overhead, I saw that the angels were serving up the severed head of the Baptist: a grisly reminder that martyrs—their bodies and bones—occupied a prominent and powerful place in the faith of medieval Catholics. More mementos and relics.

Zigging and zagging through the labyrinthine streets, I made my way toward what I hoped was the Palace of the Popes. Sure enough, above a nearby rooftop loomed a massive tower, fifteen stories high. The battlements at the top overhung the tower's wall slightly; moonlight streamed down through narrow slits in the overhangs, streaking the stones of the wall. The slits, I realized as I reached the tower's base and peered up, would allow boiling oil to be poured down onto attackers—or, at the moment, down onto me. *So much for turning the other cheek*, I mused.

The buttressed foundations seemed to grow like stony roots from the rock. A cobblestone pedestrian alley, carved deep into the rock, wound upward along the base of the palace here. Threading my way through the tight passage and passing beneath the thick arch of a flying buttress, I emerged into the great square fronted by the Palace of the Popes.

I found myself at the southeastern corner of the palace, far from the main entrance, and at the opposite end from the cathedral. The walls gleamed silvery white in the moonlight, with deep shadows delineating the arches and overhangs and arrow slits in the masonry. As I studied the details, a shaft of light at the base of the wall caught my eye. A small wooden door at the corner of the palace opened, and a man in black emerged, closing and locking the door behind him. He started across the square, and his walk—a loping gait with a slight limp—looked familiar. "Stefan?" I was only thirty feet from him, but the rushing wind swept my words away, so I called again, louder. "Stefan!" He whirled, scanning the square, coiling into a crouch as if to run. "Stefan, it's Bill Brockton," I yelled, waving both arms. He uncoiled and met me halfway.

"*Mon Dieu*, Bill, *quelle surprise*. What are you doing here at the middle of night?"

"I couldn't sleep," I said. "The wind, I guess— rattling the rooftops and rattling me. So I decided to take a walk, see the city by moonlight. What are *you* doing here at this time of night?"

He rolled his eyes. "A rah," he said.

"Excuse me? What's a 'rah'?"

"A rodent. A big mouse."

"Oh, a *rat*," I said, remembering that the French tended to swallow the ends of their words.

He looked impatient. "*Oui*, a rah-*t*." The way he emphasized the *t* this time, it almost sounded as if he'd spat it at me. "I finally got the motion detector working correctly," he went on. "I have it linked to my computer, and something set it off a few min-utes ago. So I came quickly. But it was just a big rat, eating a sandwich I left in the corner of the *trésor-erie* at lunch today. *Quelle peste!*"

"Better a rat than a thief, though," I offered. "And at least you know the alarm works."

"*Bien sûr!* Of course. But now I'm on the edge, so it's difficult to sleep."

"You're welcome to join me on a walk, if you want."

He seemed surprised by the offer. "*Oui, pourquoi pas?* Midnight in the city of the popes. I will be your tour guide."

Damn, I thought. *Be careful what you wish for.*

Stefan gestured at the façade of the palace. The tour was beginning. "This part closest to us," he announced, "is the 'new palace,' built by Clement the Sixth between 1342 and 1352."

"He was the pope who protected the Jews during the plague?"

"*Exactement.*"

"Busy guy."

"*Oui.* So, the big windows at this end of the building? The audience hall, where he held court. Above is his private chapel. Chapel—ha! It's bigger than the cathedral! You know what Clement said about being pope?" I shook my head, as he'd hoped I would. "Clement said none of his predecessors knew how to be pope."

"What did he mean?"

"He meant that none of the others knew how to throw such big parties. He was also called 'Clement the Magnificent.' When he was crowned as pope, he gave a feast for three thousand people. He served one thousand sheep, nine hundred goats, a hundred cows, a hundred calves, and sixty pigs."

"Goodness. That's, what, ten, twenty pounds of meat for every person?"

"Ah, but there is more. Much more. Ten thousand chickens. Fourteen hundred geese. Three hundred fish—"

"Only three hundred?"

He stretched his arms wide—"Pike, very big

fish"—then transformed the gesture into a shrug. "But also, Catholics eat a lot of fish, so maybe it was not considered a delicacy." He held up a finger. "Plus fifty thousand cheeses. And for dessert? Fifty thousand tarts."

"That's not possible. Surely somebody exaggerated."

"*Non, non, pas du tout*. We have the book of accounts. It records what they bought, and how much it cost."

"How much did it cost?"

"More than I will earn in my entire life. But it was a smart investment. It made him a favorite with the people who mattered—kings and queens and dukes. And, of course, with his cardinals and bishops, who sent him money they collected in their churches." Turning away from the palace, he pointed to a building on the opposite side of the square. "Do you know this building?" I shook my head. "It's just as important as the palace."

"What is it?"

"The papal mint."

"Mint, as in money?"

He nodded. "The popes coined their own money, and they built this mint here. They made gold florins in the mint, then stored them in the treasury in the palace."

"The popes had their own mint? That seems ironic, since Jesus chased the money changers out of the temple in Jerusalem."

"If you look for inconsistencies, you will find a million. The popes had armies. They had mistresses. They had children. They poisoned their rivals. They lived like kings and emperors; *better* than kings and emperors."

"And nobody objected?"

"Oh, sure," he said. "Some of the Franciscans—founded by Saint Francis of Assisi—they were very critical. They said monks and priests and popes should live in poverty, like Jesus. Pope John the Twenty-Second didn't like that. He condemned the most outspoken ones. He had many Franciscans—monks, even nuns—burned at the stake."

By now we'd reached the upper end of the square, where the palace sat cheek by jowl with the cathedral. Here the square lay well below the palace and the cathedral, and an immense staircase led up to a broad terrace in front of the church. The terrace held an immense crucifix, surrounded by statues of angels and weeping followers; high above it, atop the bell tower of the cathedral, the large gilded statue of Mary gazed down on her crucified son, her arms stretched downward as if in appeal.

Stefan pointed to our left, the northern end of the square, which was bordered by a large, elegant building. "Speaking of wealth, here's one of the *livrées*."

"The what?" The word he'd said rhymed with *eBay*, but I knew that wasn't right.

"*Livrées*. The cardinals' palaces." The building was immense—twice the size of the White House, maybe three times. "There were more than twenty *livrées* here and across the river in Villeneuve. Today, only two *livrées* are still standing in Avignon. This one, the Petit Palais—the Little Palace—is now a museum. Beautiful medieval paintings inside. The other one is the *bibliothèque*, the public library. You have seen it, *oui*?" I nodded. "Come. I have two other places to show you on our moonlight tour of the city of the popes."

We recrossed the palace square, and then another narrow plaza; after a few more turns, Stefan stopped on a narrow street and pointed to the entrance of an old building. I read the sign above the door—THÉÂTRE DES HALLES—and turned to him with a puzzled look. "A theater. So?"

"*Non, non.* Well, okay, *oui*, a theater. But read the other sign. The small one, beside the door." On the wall was a historic plaque like the one I'd seen on the old prison. Beneath the French inscription was an English translation: *Here, in the 14th century, stood a church where Petrarch first saw his Laura.* Stefan studied me. "You know Petrarch?"

I sensed another lecture coming. "Famous poet and philosopher, if my ancient memory serves." Stefan nodded. "Somehow I'd thought Petrarch was Italian, not French."

"*Oui, tous les deux.* Both. His family was Italian, but they moved to France. He lived in Avignon for years."

"That must have been exciting for a poet."

"Yes and no," he said. "He found his muse here—this Laura." He gestured at the plaque, as if it were the woman herself. "But Avignon? Petrarch hated it. Despised it. He called it a sewer, called it Babylon. Called the papacy 'the whore of Babylon.'"

"Strong words."

"Some of his words were even stronger. 'Prostitutes swarm on the papal beds,' he wrote. He accused the pope and his entourage of rape, of incest, of orgies."

"So why did he stay in such an evil place? He couldn't leave Laura?"

Stefan smiled. "Perhaps. But also, he was nursing at the breast of the whore of Babylon."

"Excuse me?"

"He was the private chaplain to one of the Italian cardinals. The pope's money supported Petrarch while he composed love poems and attacked the papacy." Stefan glanced at his watch. "Come."

After several twists and turns, we started down yet another narrow street, Rue Saint-Agricol. He stopped in front of an arched opening between two small shops and pointed. A narrow vaulted passage, almost a tunnel, led through the walls, passing beneath the upper stories of a building, and then opened into a small courtyard. Within the court-yard were several large cloth umbrellas and café tables. I looked at him, puzzled; what was he show-ing me?

"Here. The last stop on our midnight tour." He led me farther into the courtyard. The back wall of the courtyard was formed by the side of an ancient stone building forty or fifty feet high. Arches in the wall showed traces of former glory: the outlines of tall Gothic windows whose stained glass was long since gone and whose stone tracery had been filled in centuries ago. "This building was once the chapel of the Knights Templar. You know about the Templars?"

"A little. Not much more than you said the other day, the day I arrived. The Templars escorted pilgrims to the Holy Land during the time of the Crusades, right?" He nodded. "And fought the Muslims." Another nod. "And they made Dan Brown a zillionaire a few years ago."

His brow furrowed. "Dan Brown?"

"He wrote *The Da Vinci Code*."

"Ah, *oui*." He snorted. "The book that says Jesus and Mary Magdalene made a baby, and the Templars guard their descendants. Crazy bool-shit. The Templars were destroyed by the king and the pope seven hundred years ago. King Philip owed them a lot of money. Instead of paying back the money, he accused them of heresy, locked them up, and took all their money and property. He made Pope Clement his accomplice."

"Clement? The Magnificent? I hate to hear that. I was starting to like the Magnificent."

"*Non*, *non*, not that Clement. The previous one— Clement the Fifth. Clement the Fifth was the first French pope, the first Avignon pope. He was the marionette—the puppet, I think you say—of King Philip. The king forced Clement to abolish the order and excommunicate the Templars, even though they had done nothing wrong. Shameful."

"Too bad," I said. "Clement the Magnificent sounds like a better guy than Clement the Puppet. No wonder he got a better nickname." Stefan walked to the heavy wooden door of the chapel and began tugging at the handle. "Stefan! What are you doing?"

"It's okay," he said. "I have a key. The owner is a friend of mine." He opened the door and stepped inside. "Come on, don't you want to see?"

I followed him through the doorway, expecting an empty, ruined shell. But in the opposite wall, three of the soaring leaded-glass windows remained intact; moonlight poured through them, illuminating an astonishing sight. The chapel's high, vaulted interior was filled with tiers of modern, auditorium-style seats on elevated risers. The seats faced what had once been the altar; in its place now was a small stage. Over the stage and directly over our heads as well, gleaming metal trusses held clusters of high-intensity spotlights.

Stefan laughed at my obvious confusion. "Not what you thought, huh? It's a theater and conference center now. It's all set up now for the festival. The Avignon Theater Festival starts in two weeks. There are theaters all over the city—fifty, maybe even a hundred small theaters. There will be a thousand performances in Avignon during the three weeks of the festival. Performances all day, all evening, sometimes even all night. One year, in the courtyard at the Palace of the Popes, I watched a ballet that started at sunset and finished at sunrise the next morning. Crazy. Exhausting. Also *magnifique*." He gestured at the stage in the chapel. "Someone should write a special drama for this place," he went on. "Something about religion and money and power. A deadly combination, don't you think?"

"Certainly for the Templars," I agreed.

We left the chapel; he locked the door behind us, and we returned through the narrow passageway to Rue Saint-Agricol. He pointed me toward Lumani and stood at the opening. When I looked back from the corner, he was still there, watching and waving good night as I turned down another corner of the maze.

When I reached the inn and crawled into bed, my mind finally spiraling toward sleep, I thought about Stefan's account of the Templars; about the dangers of mixing religion with money and power; about Avignon's long history of drama. The modern theater festival surely paled in comparison to the real-life pageants and power plays enacted here centuries earlier by popes and peasants, kings and cardinals, painters and poets. And a man who appeared to have been nailed to a cross seven centuries ago. Or was it twenty centuries ago?

All the world's a stage, I thought drowsily. *All of Avignon's a stage.*

The tune of Miranda's childhood lullaby entered my sleepy head. *Sur le pont d'Avignon.* How did it go? I couldn't recall the words so I substituted new ones, the only words I could think of that fit the half-remembered tune carrying me down, down, deep into sleep.

Avignon, Avignon. All roads lead to Avignon. Avignon, Avignon . . .

CHAPTER 9

**Avignon
1328**

AVIGNON, AVIGNON. WHY DID he come to Avignon?

For the old man who is groaning on the rack, the road has led inexorably to Avignon, and to this agonizing moment, but why? Because, he reminds himself, it is God's will. There is no moment but this moment; no reality but this pain; no will but God's will.

He gasps as the lever swings again, the taut ropes creak under the added strain, and the ratchet clicks into the next cog in the gear. He has been on the rack for an hour now, and each quiet, metallic click of the ratchet, as the jailer lifts the lever that turns the gear, brings the excruciating certainty that this time, surely, his limbs will be torn from their sockets.

A rotund figure, cloaked in white, stands beside the jailer and leans over the old man. The robe is topped by a conical white hood; within its dark interior, the eyes burn like coals. "I put you to the question once more. Tell me the truth. Where did you learn these errors?"

"What errors?" gasps the old man. "Tell me, Fournier."

The hooded figure draws an angry breath. "There are no names here. Only you, heretic, and I, Inquisitor."

"You want the truth? Here is the truth: You are Jacques Fournier, a shoemaker's son turned cardinal, and you are afraid, or you would not be hiding beneath that hood. But does the hood change your voice, alter your fears and your weaknesses? Does your beloved white robe hide the belt of fat that your gluttony has fastened around your belly? Will these ropes sunder the name Eckhart when they tear apart my body?"

"Insolence will not save you. Insolence to this holy office only confirms that you are indeed a heretic. You have preached that God is not an intelligent being. Who taught you that heresy?"

"God taught me that, Fournier. God is not a being; God is *more* than a being. God is everything."

"You understand nothing of God."

"Of course not. If I could understand God, he would not be truly God. God is as far above my intelligence, Fournier, as you are below it."

The Inquisitor pushes the jailer away from the lever and seizes it himself, then leans into it with his considerable weight. It is an action Fournier has imagined performing a thousand times or more these past fourteen years—ever since the day the two Templar heretics were burned on the Isle of the Jews. Ever since the day Eckhart dared to criticize inquisitors, prompting young Fournier to fume *God is not pleased*. The ratchet clicks once, clicks twice, as the older, heavier Fournier forces the lever and turns the gear. The body of the aged man on the rack reaches a breaking point; tendons tear, and he screams before losing consciousness.

When he comes to, he is crumpled on the cold stone floor of a low-vaulted cell, which is tucked into the foundations of a building that is formidable on the outside, palatial on the inside.

TWO FLOORS ABOVE the crumpled old man, the Inquisitor sits in a carved chair in a marbled audience hall. Atop the white robe he has draped a red shawl, and he has exchanged the Inquisitor's hood for the broad-brimmed red hat that marks him as a cardinal, a Prince of the Church. Facing him, on a throne, slumps His Holiness, Pope John XXII, who croaks out a question. "Are you sure of this, Jacques?"

"Quite sure, Holy Father. I have put him to the question several times."

"You mean . . . ?"

"Yes, Your Holiness. Today I nearly tore him apart, yet he clung defiantly to his heresies. You've read his defense; he accuses his critics of 'ignorance and stupidity.' He is as arrogant and proud as Lucifer himself."

The pontiff sighs, or wheezes. "We had hoped you'd be able to correct his understanding. Your success in rooting out the Cathar heretics in Montaillou was remarkable."

"The Cathar heretics in Montaillou were simpletons, Holy Father. Shepherds and shopkeepers. Consider the woman Beatrice. She didn't consider it a sin to have carnal relations with a priest, because it brought them both pleasure—and besides, her husband gave her permission. Idiots, all of them."

The pope waves his hand impatiently. "Yes, yes; I've read the transcript of her confession. Hers and hundreds of others. You were very thorough in your pursuit of heresy. And *quite* exhaustive in your record keeping." Fournier feels a flash of anger; is the pontiff mocking him now? The old man sighs before continuing. "So in view of your prior success with heretics, we had hoped you could bring Eckhart to heel."

"Eckhart is no country bumpkin," snaps the cardinal. "Some compare him with Aquinas. He has a quick wit and a dangerous mind. And he delights in spinning circles around those who are less nimble."

"Has he spun circles around you, Jacques?"

The plump cardinal gives the shriveled pontiff a mirthless smile. "It's hard to spin circles when one is stretched on the rack."

"Will he ever confess his errors and submit himself to correction, do you think?"

"Never, Holiness. He's old, arrogant, and stubborn."

"A pity. Well, do what you must to keep him from leading more people astray. Still, it would be good if he could be brought to repentance before he dies."

Fournier smiles a broader, more genuine, more sinister smile. "I pray without ceasing that he will die in a state of grace, Holy Father."

CHAPTER 10

**Siena, Italy
1328**

SIMONE MARTINI LEANS FORWARD and stares into
the eyes of Jesus, frowning. The Savior's face is
scarcely a foot away, and Simone's not sure he likes
what he sees. Can these really be the eyes of the
Son of the Almighty? If so, shouldn't they be larger,
wiser, more . . . *godlike*, somehow?

"Not bad," says a voice, so unexpected and
startling that Simone jerks upright, whacks his
head on a ceiling beam, and nearly topples off the
scaffold—a twenty-foot fall to a stone floor, which
would surely smash his skull like a ripe melon. His
surprise and dizziness swiftly give way to pain and
to anger. Who has dared to interrupt him at this
delicate moment, as he's making the final repair to
the fresco? Didn't he give strict instructions that he
was not to be disturbed? The paint must be applied
before the plaster dries; otherwise it won't bond

properly and the fresco will be ruined. Truth be told, Simone had been on the verge of laying down his paintbrush, satisfied with the Savior's eyes after all. Still, he finds the intrusion doubly infuriating: His order was ignored, and now a bump on his head hurts like the devil. Rubbing the rising knot, he looks down to see which of his assistants has just earned a thumping.

But it's not an assistant. Simone can't see the man's features—the hood of a cloak shrouds the face in shadow—but Simone knows his half-dozen apprentices by their shape and stance, and this stooped, stumpy creature isn't one of them. "The face is quite good," the stranger adds. "But the hands are too small and the fingers are *much* too short." Simone can hardly believe his ears. Who is this rude fellow, and how dare he criticize the work of Siena's most respected painter? "If you're depicting Christ giving a blessing, the right hand must be more prominent; the first two fingers must be long and slender." *Insolence!* thinks Simone. *Insufferable insolence!* Quivering with rage, he scampers down the scaffold and draws back his fist.

The little stranger removes his hood, and Simone gasps. "Master Giotto!"

Giotto di Bondoni, the best artist in Tuscany—and therefore the best in the world—springs into an old man's parody of a fighter's crouch. Then he laughs, steps forward, and flings his arms around Simone in a hug. When he releases him, he steps back and surveys the immense fresco, which covers an entire wall of Siena's Palazzo Pubblico, the city's center of government. Originally painted by

Simone in 1315, the fresco depicts the Virgin Mary surrounded by saints and—above her, at the top of the painting—Jesus, raising his right hand in benediction. During a storm a few weeks ago, a leak in the roof damaged a bit of the painting. Had the rivulets appeared a few inches lower—streaking Christ's cheeks, rather than discoloring his hair—the change would have been hailed as a miracle: "Behold! The Savior weeps!" Instead, it was dismissed as water damage, requiring a big scaffold and a small repair.

The old master makes a sweeping gesture that encompasses the entire fresco. "Not bad," he says again, this time in a voice whose warmth and admiration are unmistakable. "Not bad at all, especially for a plaster boy who was always slow."

Now it's Simone's turn to laugh. "I wasn't slow—just overworked. You were too cheap to hire enough helpers."

"Cheap? *Cheap?* Are you kidding? Do you know what I got paid for those frescoes in Padua? Nothing. Less than nothing. Three years I worked like a dog in that chapel, and that bastard Scrovegni paid me a pittance. You know what I had to do to make ends meet? I'm ashamed to tell you, Simone. I made copies of Duccio's paintings and signed his name—pretended they were *his* work!—because Duccio fetched better prices than I did back then. And that's not the worst of it. Once, when I needed money to buy more pigments, I put greasy pig bones in gilded boxes and sold them as relics of saints." Simone is shocked; he opens his mouth to ask a question, but Giotto waves him off. "I don't want to talk about it. It's too degrading." He makes a face of distaste. "And the Scrovegnis rich as kings. You know how they made their money, yes?" Simone shrugs; he'd heard the rumors, of course, swapped by gossiping assistants as they mixed plaster or ground pigments, but he's not sure how much he's supposed to know. And besides, he doesn't want to deprive Master Giotto of the pleasure of telling the story. "Usury," Giotto hisses. "Lending money at ruinous rates. Worse than the Jews, that family. Ever read Dante's *Inferno*?" Simone shakes his head. "Dante puts Scrovegni's father in the seventh circle of Hell for usury. I'd put Scrovegni the younger in the eighth circle, for fraud. Usurers, liars, and thieves, the whole family."

Giotto spits—right on the floor of the public palace, the most beautiful building in Siena!—then looks again at the fresco, and beams. "Ah, but this is wonderful, Simone. Huge, too—*almost* as big as my *Last Judgment* in the Scrovegni chapel." He turns to Simone and looks his former apprentice up and down. "How old are you now?"

"Forty-four, Master Giotto."

"Amazing. You were a beardless boy when you mixed plaster for me in Scrovegni's chapel."

"That was twenty-five years ago, master."

"Amazing," he repeats. "Just think, Simone—if you're already painting so big and so well at forty-four, what will you be doing at sixty-two, when you're as old as I am?"

"I'll be studying the things you're painting at eighty," the younger man answers, "despairing of ever catching up."

"Nonsense." Giotto shakes his head and rolls his eyes, but Simone can tell by the half-suppressed smile that the compliment is appreciated. "I hear you married into a family of painters. Memmo's daughter—what's her name?"

"Giovanna."

"Ah, yes. I remember her as a pretty little girl. And do you and Giovanna have a brood, a passel of little Martinis?"

"Not yet," says Simone, wishing that Giotto had not broached this subject, a source of sadness between him and Giovanna.

"A man as handsome as you should make many babies, Simone. Look at me—I am the ugliest man in Florence, but I have six children. Do you wish to know my secret?" Simone nods, miserable but polite. "The darkness."

"The darkness? How do you mean?"

"In the darkness, Simone, I am as handsome as any man!" The old painter laughs at his joke. "Now clean your brushes and come with me. We're dining with your father-in-law. I've just seen his frescoes in San Gimignano, and I want to know how he did it."

"Did what, Master Giotto?"

"Got paid to paint men and women—*naked* men and women!—bathing together, going to *bed* together! On the walls in the palace of government! A man can bear to paint only so many martyrs and virgins. Let us move to San Gimignano, Simone—or better yet, to Avignon; that's where the money is now—and let us start a new fashion of painting there. Courtesans, concubines, and lusty country wenches. Get me those commissions, my boy, and I will pay you ten times more than I paid you to mix plaster."

Simone laughs. "At that rate, Master Giotto, I would still starve."

CHAPTER 11

Avignon
The Present

I'D BEEN UP SINCE 5 A.M., despite the fact that I'd been wandering the streets with Stefan until one, and I was obsessively checking my e-mail inbox every five minutes. I'd hoped Joe might send me a picture of his facial reconstruction by now. It was 8 A.M. in Avignon, which made it 2 A.M. for Joe; I couldn't imagine he was still up and working.

I'd just decided to head downstairs for a croissant when my computer chirped to announce a new e-mail. My heart began to thump when I saw that it was from Joe. I opened it eagerly but there was no message, only a small icon indicating that an image file was attached. I clicked on the attachment, and with maddening, line-by-line slowness the mask-like image of a clay face materialized on the screen. Joe had done it; he'd restored a face to the skull from the Palace of the Popes.

As I studied the features, I had the eerie feeling that I knew the guy, or at least that I'd seen him before. Was it just that I'd seen Joe's work before? Facial reconstructions, especially when done by the same forensic artist, do share similarities: "white female #7"; "black male #4." Was that the reason this face looked familiar? I turned away, looked out the window to clear my mind, and then directed my gaze at the screen again.

Again I felt the tingle of unexpected familiarity. Who *was* this guy, and why did I think I knew him? It wasn't simply that this was another generic white male, similar to a hundred other reconstructions I'd seen. This face was distinctive, the face of a unique individual: long and narrow, with prominent cheekbones and a slightly crooked nose, perhaps broken once in a fight. I'd noticed the general features when I'd examined the skull, but they were more pronounced now that Joe had fleshed out the bones.

Suddenly a synapse in my sleep-deprived brain fired. Pulse racing, I fired off a message to Joe: *got it. great work—thanks. are you still there?*

yes, came his answer a few seconds later.

can you do a couple of quick tweaks?

A pause. *what sort of tweaks?*

can you give him long hair? and a mustache and beard? oh, and maybe smooth out some of the wrinkles, take 10 years off him?

As I waited for his response, I feared he might balk.

so, you want me to give him rogaine & botox—er, claytox, right, doc?

right, joe.

no problem.

I breathed a sigh of relief, then sent another message: *not to sound pushy, but how long will that take?*

depends. you want it fast, or want it good?

I smiled. *start with fast*, I wrote back. *if i need good, I'll beg you for that tomorrow.*

good answer. fast is lots easier for me right now—just got a new case I need to jump on. give me twenty minutes. i'll tinker with it and shoot you a revision ASAP.

Twenty minutes was going to drive me crazy, so I went downstairs to grab breakfast. In my nervousness, I wolfed down three croissants and a dozen strawberries. Just as I reached the top of the stairs and opened the door of my room, I heard the chime of a new message arriving.

how's this? was written above the revised image.

How was it? It was astonishing.

If Joe's facial reconstruction was accurate, the bones of Avignon belonged to a guy who was a dead ringer for the man on the Shroud of Turin.

CHAPTER 12

Turin, Italy
The Present

"WHAT'D YOU THINK," SHE whispered, "that they were gonna open the drapes, pull it down off the wall, and let you lay it out on the floor?"

Miranda and I were kneeling—kneeling and bickering—in a corner of the Duomo di Torino, Turin Cathedral, where we'd journeyed after seeing the face Joe Mullins had sculpted on the Avignon skull. Miranda had tried to talk me out of the trip, a seven-hour drive, insisting that nothing short of a direct order from the pope himself would get us a glimpse of the Shroud. But I'd refused to be deterred; somehow I'd convinced myself that if I showed a photo of Joe's facial reconstruction to someone in authority—the senior priest? a bishop? an archbishop?—he'd be so astonished by the re- semblance that he'd happily arrange for me to com- pare the images side by side.

There was another reason I'd pushed for the trip, though I'd not mentioned it to Miranda. Rocky Stone had phoned shortly after I received the facial reconstruction. "Doc, I've got good news and bad news," he'd told me. "The good news is, I know who the shooter in Sevierville was—a Colombian named Cesar Morales. The bad news is, he got off a plane in Amsterdam an hour ago." Morales was in Amsterdam to negotiate a drug shipment, Stone believed. "But I can't guarantee he's not looking for you, too," he'd added. "I've contacted Interpol," he went on, "so the police in the Netherlands and France will be looking for him. But I want you to be careful. Lay low. Get out of town for a day or two, if you can." What he said next had surprised and moved me. "I'm on the next flight for Amsterdam," Rocky had added. "I'll be there tomorrow morning . . . and I won't stop looking till I find him."

An hour after Rocky's unsettling call, I borrowed Jean and Elisabeth's car again—this time I was putting some serious mileage on the venerable Peugeot—and Miranda and I had raced up the flat belly of France to the foothills of the Alps, then angled eastward and careened through mountain passes and granite tunnels before finally looping down into the Po River Valley and the grimy sprawl of Turin.

Turin Cathedral was tucked inconspicuously at the edge of a paved plaza, flanked by the ruins of an ancient Roman gate and city wall. I might have overlooked the church entirely if not for the tall, freestanding bell tower beside it. I was surprised at what a small, drab building held the Christian world's most famous relic. Turning to Miranda, I'd joked, "I'm reminded of my friend Sybil's comment when she saw the Grand Canyon. 'I thought it'd be bigger,' was all Syb said."

"I've had that same thought on a few occasions," Miranda had answered with a sly grin as we crossed the threshold.

Inside, too, the cathedral was spare and austere: plain wooden benches, unadorned columns and plaster walls, a stone floor inlaid with octagons of white and gray, linked by small squares of red.

The Shroud was housed in a side chapel at the front of the nave, on the left side of the building. In front of the relic was a simple kneeling rail eight or ten feet long, and—between the rail and the Shroud—a wall of glass stretching from floor to ceiling. Within the glassed-in chapel, the Shroud was mounted above a long white altar garnished with woven thorn vines—reminders of the barbed crown placed on Jesus's head before he was crucified. A black curtain, the width of the chapel, hid the relic completely from view; a poster-size enlargement of the face on the Shroud—a ghostly gray negative, which was more dramatic than the faint, reddish-brown image the cloth actually bore—was suspended above the altar. The poster was a consolation prize, of sorts, for those of us whose pilgrimage to Turin was thwarted by the black curtain.

Still kneeling, I unfolded the two prints I'd brought with me. One was a normal, positive print of the face Joe had made; the other was a negative image, which Miranda had created by Photoshopping Joe's file. The likeness between the images I held in my hand and the poster behind the glass wall was uncanny, especially when I compared the Photoshopped negative with the poster.

Unfortunately, no one in authority had been astonished by the images we'd brought, because no one in authority was anywhere to be found. Except for one other pilgrim—a stout woman who knelt beside me and cast disapproving glances as we whispered—the only person we'd managed to find in the cathedral was an ancient woman selling Holy Shroud bookmarks, postcards, posters, books, and other mementos at the tiny gift shop at the rear of the nave.

"It's almost closing time," I whispered. "Maybe we'll have better luck in the morning."

Sssshhhh, came an annoyed hiss from the woman on my left. She was German; I knew this not from the accent of her *sssshhhh*, but from the wording on the prayer card she'd chosen to kneel before. A Shroud-inspired prayer had been printed in seven different languages and posted on the railing for the convenience of the faithful. Between angry glances our way, the woman at my elbow was muttering the German prayer in a guttural growl.

"They get a zillion requests a year to see the Shroud, touch the Shroud, cut a tiny snippet of the Shroud," Miranda whispered on. She'd dropped her voice so low it was barely audible; she was all but breathing the words into my ear, and I found the intimacy of the communication both unsettling and exhilarating. "You think your request is special.

So does everybody else—the parents of the dying kid, the nun who's had a vision, the physicist who's thought of a new way to authenticate the image on the cloth. Everybody thinks they're special. And everybody *is*. So the priest or the bishop or whoever has to treat everyone as if *no* one is special."

"I know, I know," I whispered back. "But I thought it was worth a try. I thought maybe . . ." I shrugged.

"I know what you thought. You thought maybe you could convince him your case was extra special. *Especially* special." I couldn't help laughing—she knew me so well.

Ssshhh!

"Yeah, right," I conceded. "My specialness and two euros will get me a cup of cappuccino."

"More like four," she corrected.

"Four euros? Six bucks? For something I don't even like?"

"That's your own fault. It's never too late to grow, expand your horizons."

"Yeah, well, show me the Shroud of Turin and I'll drink all the cappuccino you want."

"Really?"

"Really."

"Tenured, full professor's word of honor?"

"Word of honor."

"Prepare to chug some caffeine with your humble pie," she said, looking mischievous.

SSSSHHHH!!!!! The angry shush filled the nave. The German lurched to her feet and stormed out, the accusatory echoes of her clogs ricocheting like gunshots.

* * *

LAID OUT FLAT in the hallway of the Hotel Diplomatic, where Miranda and I had booked rooms for the night, the Shroud of Turin ran half the length of the corridor. The tips of the toes practically touched the elevator; the other end of the image stretched to a window overlooking a noisy Turin street. What filled the floor was not, of course, the sacred relic itself; rather, it was a full-length, life-size, high-resolution photographic print of the entire Shroud, all 14.3 feet of it, plus another six inches of border at each end.

The print had arrived rolled like a scroll, tightly packed in a cardboard shipping tube. To flatten it, we'd briefly rerolled it the opposite way, inside out; that had mostly tamed the curl, though we'd had to anchor the corners with our shoes.

On my hands and knees, studying the face, I looked up at Miranda. "Come on, you gotta tell me. Where'd you really get this? It did *not* 'miraculously appear' at the front desk."

"Sure it did," she chirped. "Okay, with a little help from Holy Shroud Guild dot org."

"A Web site?"

She nodded. "A Web site with an online gift shop. Through the miracles of Google, AmEx, and FedEx, I ordered it yesterday morning, right before we left Avignon on this wild-goose chase. I had the image file—a *huge* file—sent to a blueprint shop here, and I got them to deliver it to the hotel."

"I take it back," I marveled. "It *did* 'miraculously appear.' So how much does a full-length, high-res, special-delivery print of the Holy Shroud go for these days?"

"About a week's pay," she said. I whistled, but she cut me off. "A week of *my* pay, not yours. That's actually dirt cheap, as miracles go."

I turned my attention once more to the image on the replica of the Shroud. The body apparently had been laid faceup on the linen, with the feet at one end and seven or eight feet of fabric extending beyond the head. That part was then doubled back and folded down over the face, torso, and legs. The front and back images linked at the top of the head—an odd, hinged effect, rather like Siamese twins conjoined at the crown of the skull. Judging by the photo, the Shroud's linen fabric was a stained and dingy ivory color; the image of the man was a faint reddish brown, with brighter red splotches and trickles here and there—in places consistent with wounds from scourging, crucifixion, and lacerations from a crown of thorns.

The color and faintness of the image surprised me. Most news articles and Web sites about the Shroud showed an eerie black-and-white face, like the large poster hanging in the cathedral. Those versions looked like photographic negatives, because they *were* negatives: dramatic, high-contrast images in which the linen backdrop appeared dark gray, the eye sockets looked dark gray, the eyelids a lighter shade of gray, and—lightest of all, in the photo-negative versions—the cheekbones, eyebrows, nose, mustache, and beard. The scroll Miranda and I were studying on the hotel floor, on the other hand, was a positive print, one that faithfully reproduced the actual image on the Shroud. In our copy, as in the real McCoy, the highest points were darkest, as if a damp cloth had been pressed onto a face and body coated with reddish-brown dust.

Studying the man's face, I found myself distracted by his hair. "Hmm," I said.

"What?"

"Well, I don't get it. He's lying on his back, right?"

"So they say. So it seems."

"Then how come his hair looks like it's hanging straight down, the way it would if he were standing up?"

"Hmm, indeed," Miranda echoed. "Good question."

"And another thing," I continued. "What's with these bright red stains all over the body—the wrists, the feet, the side, the back, the forehead?"

"Duh. They're the wounds of Christ, dummy. From the nails, the scourging, the crown of thorns, the spear in the side. Remember?"

"Duh yourself," I retorted. "I do remember the wounds of Christ. But there shouldn't be blood on them. He wouldn't have kept bleeding after he was dead. Besides, he's too perfect."

"How do you mean, perfect? He's a bloody mess, Dr. B."

"Exactly. He's the *perfect* bloody mess." She looked at me as if I'd gone over the edge. "Take that trickle of blood on the head." A red squiggle, three inches long by a half inch wide, meandered down the forehead from just below the hairline to the medial end of the right eyebrow. Along the way, it broadened in three spots, as if it had seeped into lines in the forehead.

Miranda knelt and scrutinized it. "From the crown of thorns. What about it?"

"According to the Bible, the crown of thorns was put on his head before he was crucified. Before he carried the cross through the streets of Jerusalem. Before he hung there for hours. In all that time and all that trauma, that neat little ribbon of blood doesn't get smudged by a flood of sweat? Doesn't get smeared as the body's wrestled down from the cross and lugged to the tomb? Doesn't get washed away as they're cleaning the body for burial? They're burying him with sweet-smelling spices and wrapping him in this fancy piece of linen, right? Why wouldn't they bother to wipe the blood off the face while they were at it?"

"I take your point," she conceded.

"And look at that foot," I went on. "That nice bloody sole is flat against the cloth, the knee bent the way it is on every Jesus on every crucifix you ever saw. Think about all those dead guys on the ground at the Body Farm—does one knee bend artfully like that? No way—their feet flop out to the sides."

Miranda nodded slowly. "It pains me to say it, but you might actually be right." I smiled; she enjoyed the game of pretending I was slow-witted. "In fact, if you look at this forensically, the whole thing starts to seem totally staged—as if somebody was working from a checklist: Crown of thorns? Check. Spear wound? Check. Nail holes? Check. Scourge marks? Check." Miranda was on a roll. But suddenly she clutched my arm and gasped. "Oh, my God."

"What?!?"

"I just had an idea, Dr. B. A brilliant, awful idea. Millions of people believe the Shroud is a holy relic, right? But what if it's exactly the opposite?"

"The opposite of a holy relic? What do you mean?"

She took a deep breath before heading down this new trail. "Let's assume, for the moment, that those C-14 tests back in 1988 were right—that the Shroud is only seven centuries old. In that case, it's a fake, right?" I nodded. "But what if it's a fourteenth-century *not*-fake?"

"Huh?" I stared at her, utterly confused.

"What if it's medieval but also genuine, Dr. B? What if all the bloodstains, all the wounds, *are* real?" She pointed at the image, moving her hand up and down as if she were doing a scan. "What if this piece of cloth documents actual trauma, but *fourteenth-century* trauma? Not the scourging and crucifixion of Jesus, but the scourging and crucifixion of a guy in Avignon—a guy killed specifically to create . . . *this*!" Her hand stopped scanning; her finger pointed accusingly at the face. "This could be the world's first snuff film. A snuff Shroud. Created expressly, deliberately, in order to document the very murder it depicts."

The idea was startling; stunning, even. Could she possibly be right? Could the Shroud depict a deliberately staged fourteenth-century murder? And could the bones of Avignon—our "zhondo," as Elisabeth called him—be the bones of the victim?

I looked at the image again in this new light. Yes,

it looked like our zhondo's face. But not our zhondo's stature. I had a tape measure in my overnight bag, but for starters, I lay down on the floor alongside the Shroud, side by side with the man's image. "So, who's taller?"

"He is. He's got a couple inches on you, maybe more. How tall are you?"

"Five-ten."

"So he's a six-footer," she said. "That's pretty damn tall, whether he was first century or fourteenth. Most guys back then were, like, five feet, five five, right?"

She was right. During the twentieth century, the average stature of adult males had increased by six inches or more—in developed countries, though not in Third World countries—as a result of better diet and health care. "Yeah, little bitty guys," I agreed. "I've seen suits of armor my twelve-year-old grandson couldn't fit into." My heart sank as I realized the implications. "Damn. It's not our zhondo, is it, Miranda? Can't be."

"'Fraid not," she said. "This guy's half a head taller than our guy. Sorry, Dr. B; I know the facial reconstruction got you all excited about connecting the dots."

"Oh well," I said breezily. "It was an interesting possibility. But so's your snuff-Shroud theory. Wouldn't that be ironic, if somebody was killed to make a 'holy' relic? Anyhow, we've still got a medieval murder on our hands in Avignon, right?" I nodded at the Shroud. "And now maybe we've got *two* medieval murder cases. Twice the bodies, twice the fun, right?"

She didn't find my little pep talk any more convincing than I did.

Slipping my shoes back on, I rolled up the Shroud and tucked it under my arm. "I'm pooped," I said, heading for my room, which was at the end of the hall—right where the foot of the Shroud had been moments before. "Sorry I brought you on a wild-goose chase." I stepped through the doorway.

"Dr. B?" I stopped and leaned my head back into the hallway, just far enough to see her smiling at me. "Just for the record? I love chasing wild geese. Good night, Dr. B. Sleep well."

I HAD A dream, and in my dream, I went back to the chapel in Turin Cathedral; went back to make one final attempt to see the Shroud.

As I walked down the center aisle, I saw a man dressed as a high priest—a bishop or cardinal, perhaps even a pope—behind the chapel's glass wall. The black curtain hiding the Shroud had been opened, and I hurried forward, eager to see the relic at last. But above the altar, behind the curtain, was nothing but a blank wall.

Astonished, I stared at the priest. Beside him, in the shadows, stood another man. This man, his face in shadow, was holding a small bundle, which I recognized as the Shroud, folded like a bedsheet. The man handed something to the priest; it was a thick bundle of money, I realized. The priest bowed, and the man disappeared through a dark doorway in the back of the chapel. Then the priest turned and saw me. He pointed a finger at me, and then reached for a golden cord hanging from the ceiling. He pulled the cord, and a heavy black drape slid shut, hiding not only the blank wall and the empty altar, but the entire chapel from my view.

CHAPTER 13

I AWOKE AT DAYBREAK, disturbed by the dream, and trudged back to the cathedral, where again I was confronted by the maddening curtain that shrouded the Shroud. Was it possible that my dream was actually true—that the wall behind the black drape was indeed blank? Could the Shroud be elsewhere—locked in an underground Vatican vault for safekeeping? Rented out to some devout billionaire who paid a fortune to possess it during the long intervals between public exhibitions?

Leaning forward, I studied the glass wall that separated me from the artifact I'd hoped to see. The thickness of the glass was hard to gauge, but I assumed it was at least an inch thick, maybe more—possibly bulletproof; at any rate, surely Brockton-proof. *There must be a back door into that chapel*, I thought. *A way in, so the pope can open the magic curtain every decade or two . . . or the cleaning lady can dust it once a month.* Could I bribe the cleaning lady?

Jimmy the door with a credit card or a paper clip? Suddenly I laughed—was I really fantasizing about breaking into a heavily protected chapel in order to scrutinize what was probably a fake relic? I took one last wistful look, then headed out in search of a café.

The café's barista was a pretty brunette with immense brown eyes and a microscopic English vocabulary. After several fruitless, awkward attempts to request hot tea, I stammered out the words "*caffè crema*," which I guessed to be Italian for "coffee with cream." She smiled and nodded, and I congratulated myself on my suave Italian.

I uncongratulated myself two minutes later, when she handed me a thimble-size vessel containing what looked—and *tasted*—like soft-serve mocha ice cream. It was 8 A.M., far too early for ice cream. The barista looked my way, saw my confusion, and hurried over, cocking her head to punctuate the question in her eyes. I took another taste, and she beamed when I shrugged and smiled and trotted out the only other Italian word I knew: "*Magnifico!*"

Suddenly a dusty file drawer in my memory flew open. *Magnifico:* One of my all-time favorite graduate students used to say that a lot—and her name sprang to the tip of my chilled tongue and from there into the café, right out loud: "Emily Craig!" Years before, Emily had written an article that had *something* to do with the Shroud of Turin, though I couldn't quite dredge up the details from that file drawer in my mind. Emily was now the forensic anthropologist for the Commonwealth of Kentucky, and we kept in touch across the mountains between

Knoxville and Frankfort. Did I have Emily's number in my phone? I did! I hit "send" to place the call.

She answered on the sixth ring, just as I'd expected the call to roll to voice mail. "Hello?"

"Emily? Hi, it's Bill Brockton."

"Who?"

Perhaps we'd not kept in touch quite as well as I'd imagined. "Bill Brockton."

"Bill *who*? Oh . . . Dr. *B*? Uh . . . okay. Yeah. Hi. Give me, uh, give me just a second here."

Her speech was slow and thick. Was it possible that she'd been drinking? At 8 A.M.? "Am I catching you at a bad time, Emily?"

"Well, since you ask, *yeah*. I don't know what time it is where you are, but where I am, it's two in the morning."

"Oh, crap, Emily, I'm so sorry. It's eight here—I'm in Italy—and I was so interested in what I'm calling about, I didn't even think about the time difference. Go back to sleep. I'll call you again at a reasonable hour."

"Hell, I'm awake now," she said, "and you've got me all intrigued. If you hang up now, I'll just lie awake all night wondering why you called. So spill it."

"Okay. If I'm remembering right, a few years ago you wrote a journal article that had something to do with the Shroud of Turin."

"A few years ago?" She gave a groggy laugh. "Try fifteen years ago. Maybe more. I was still in the Ph.D. program at the time, so let's see, that would have been 1994 or '95. It was in the *Journal of Imaging Science and Technology*. Probably not on your regular reading list."

"Can you give me the skinny on that article? Like, an abstract of the abstract?"

"Sure, more or less." There was a pause. "Wait. Did you say you're in Italy?"

"I did."

"Where in Italy?"

"Three guesses."

"You're in Turin? My God, are you looking at the Shroud?"

"Ha. I wish. I'm definitely, damnably *not* looking at the Shroud. *Everybody's* not looking at the Shroud; it's under wraps until 2025, they say. But I *am* looking, or at least have been looking, and will be looking again, at a full-size, high-resolution photo of it."

"No offense, but wouldn't it have been easier and cheaper and smarter to just have that sent to Knoxville?"

"Long story," I said. "Yeah, it would've. But I was in France, so Italy was right next door. Sort of. Anyhow, that article you wrote—didn't it have something to do with your prior career as a medical illustrator? Or am I imagining that?"

"No, that's right. Very good. Okay, here's the story. One afternoon at UT, I was sitting in a lecture by Randy Bresee—"

"Randy Bresee—textile scientist?"

"Exactly. I was taking his course on textile forensics. And that particular day, he showed slides of the Shroud of Turin. He called it 'the greatest unsolved textile mystery of all time.'"

"What did he mean?"

"He meant the mystery of how the image was put

on the cloth. Part of the mystique of the Shroud is that supposedly there's no way to reproduce that image with any technique known to man. 'Not made with hands' is how the church puts it, I think."

"What's so special about it, besides the subject matter?"

"The image is so faint, so superficial—it's only on the surface of the fibers, not soaked in. It's barely there at *all*. No brushstrokes; no snow fencing."

"Snow fencing?"

"If you brush paint or pigment on fabric—even a really, really light coat—it piles up on one side of the fibers," she explained, "like snow drifting against a fence. Tough to avoid that. Then there's the way the image jumps out at you when you look at the photo negative of it. More lifelike than the positive, but more ghostly, too. So it really *is* an interesting mystery."

"Especially for an artist-turned-detective, like you."

"Absolutely. Anyhow, sitting there in that classroom that day, seeing the slides and hearing about this mystery, I got cold chills—I thought I might even throw up—because all of a sudden I *knew*. At the end of the class, I went up and said to Randy, 'I know how they did it.' He laughed and said, 'Yeah, right.' So I went home that night, got my friend Tyler to come over and pose for me, and I did it."

"Did what, exactly?"

"I made an image of Tyler, on fabric, that had all the characteristics of the Shroud. It was on a linen handkerchief. It had no brushstrokes, it didn't soak into the fibers, and when I took a photograph and looked at the negative, it had that same 3-D effect and that same ghostly look."

"That's amazing," I said. "So sitting in a UT classroom one afternoon, you solved a mystery that was six hundred and fifty years old? How'd you do it—and why didn't I pay more attention at the time?"

I could practically hear her shrug. "It wasn't a murder case. And I was just a lowly student."

"One thing I don't get, Emily. I stayed up late last night researching the Shroud on the Internet, and everything I read—even recent stuff, with science in it—still claims there's no way to duplicate that image. Have you ever sent your article to the people who say that?"

"Ha." It wasn't really a laugh. "I sent that article all over the place. I even demonstrated the technique, on camera, to a History Channel crew that was filming a documentary about the Shroud. The Shroudies—that's what I call the die-hard believers—were incredibly hostile. I got hate mail: letters saying I was doomed to hell, letters calling me a Christ killer, letters threatening my life. So yeah, I'd say I described my work to some of the people who say that. And they were none too happy."

"How'd you do it, Emily? Tell me about the technique."

"Simple. Incredibly simple. Dust transfer. Medical illustrators use it all the time. *I* used it all the time, when I was a medical illustrator. You create the image on one surface, using charcoal or red ochre or—"

"Red ochre?"

"A pigment. Ferrous oxide—rust, basically. Ochre's found in clays all over the world, in various shades. Red ochre—the *best* red ochre—comes from southern France."

The hairs on the back of my neck twitched. "Southern France?"

"Yeah, somewhere down around Provence; I forget where. It was used in the cave paintings in France and Spain—fifteen, twenty, thirty thousand years ago. Dust transfer, too. Those paintings weren't actually paintings; they were illustrations. They'd sketch the outlines of the figures—horses or bulls or whatever—with a burned stick, then rub on red ochre to add color."

I'd thought I was excited when I first dialed Emily's number; now, I was beside myself. I felt my hands shaking as I cradled the phone to my ear with one hand and took notes with the other. "And that's how you made the image of your friend Tyler? You just rubbed dust onto the handkerchief?"

"Ah, no. It was a little more complicated than that. No snow fencing allowed, remember? So I added a step. I used a soft brush, dipped in dry, red-ochre powder, to dab an image of Tyler's face onto a piece of newsprint. No outlines, just shading with dust; heavy in the high spots—the bridge of the nose, the eyebrows, and so on—and light in the low spots. I dabbed very gently, from different directions, so there wouldn't be any strokes. Once I had a dense, smooth image, I laid the handkerchief on top and rubbed it with the back of a wooden spoon."

"Like doing a brass rubbing?"

"Sort of, but much less pressure. So the cloth picked up only trace amounts of the pigment."

"It wasn't too faint to be seen?"

"You'd be surprised. It takes only a tiny, tiny bit of red ochre to stain the fabric. If you get it on your clothes, it's tough to get out."

"So you don't have any trouble believing that an image created in this way could survive for hundreds of years?"

"Hell, I don't have any trouble believing it could survive for *thousands* of years. Some of those cave paintings have been on the walls for thirty thousand years. The fabric of the Shroud, on the other hand: *That* I'm not so sure about. And if I remember right, Randy Bresee seemed doubtful that a piece of first-century linen could hold up this long."

"But in either case—first century or fourteenth—you're sure it's a fake."

"Define *fake*. I'm sure it's an illustration, Dr. B—I'd stake my life on that. I think it was created during the Middle Ages. And I've got a pretty good idea who did it. But *fake*? That implies fraud or deception. And there's a chance—a small chance, at least—that it wasn't created to defraud or deceive."

"I'm afraid I'm not following you, Emily."

"Okay, this might sound far-fetched," she said, "but just consider this scenario for a second. What if the Shroud was created in the spirit of an autopsy photo? Back in the days before photography existed. What if it was an attempt to capture a moment, to document exactly how Jesus looked when he was taken down from the cross?"

I hadn't expected this wrinkle in the Shroud. "But you just said you thought it was made in the Middle Ages. So how could it capture a moment that happened fourteen centuries before?"

She sighed. "Okay, here's where it gets far-fetched. Suppose there was an earlier Shroud, one that *did* date back to the first century. Suppose that this original Shroud gradually starts to fade and crumble. Finally, suppose that in the thirteen hundreds, a brilliant artist is commissioned to make an exact copy, to preserve the image for another thousand years."

"Suppose pigs can fly," I said. "You're right; that sounds far-fetched. If there *was* an ancient, authentic, first-century Shroud that got copied in the thirteen hundreds, what happened to it? Wouldn't somebody have saved it, even if it was in shreds? I can't imagine commissioning a copy but trashing the original."

"It's a stretch, I grant you," she conceded. "I came up with it as a way to mesh faith with facts—the radiocarbon dating, the presence of iron oxide in the image, the good condition of the linen. It worked, sort of, for a while. Before I floated that idea, none of the Shroudies would give me the time of day."

"And after?"

"After, one of the Shroudie Web sites actually posted my article. Briefly. But I still got hate mail and threatening phone calls."

"I admire your efforts to reconcile religion and science," I said. "But I'm not convinced. Remember Occam's razor?"

"How could I forget? You drummed it into our

heads over and over. 'The simplest explanation that fits the facts is usually correct,' right?"

"Exactly. So what's the simplest explanation for an image of Jesus that first surfaces in the Middle Ages—the heyday of fake relics—on fabric that C-14 labs tell us is fourteenth century? I can't help thinking it's a fake, created to attract pilgrims to Lirey, the French village where it appeared in 1357."

"I know, fakery fits the facts." She sighed. "And yeah, it's a lot simpler than my scenario."

"Can I circle back to something? You said you think you know who made the Shroud. Who?"

"Ah. My money's on Giotto di Bondoni," she said at once. "Brilliant artist. Crucial, crucial figure in the transition from medieval art to the Renaissance. Giotto's people look real, three-dimensional, not flat and stylized like medieval icons. Late twelve hundreds, early thirteen hundreds, so the timing's right. The style's right, too."

"How so?"

"One, the guy on the Shroud is long and thin, and Giotto's figures tend to be long in the face and in the body. Two, religious art was his bread and butter, but Giotto himself was a skeptic. Three, he was a notorious prankster. Think about it: If you're a religious artist *and* a religious skeptic, what would be the ultimate prank? How about faking the burial shroud of Jesus—and getting away with it? Be tough to top that, wouldn't it?"

"But wait—if it's a prank, doesn't that contradict your autopsy-illustration theory?"

"I'm not head over heels in love with that theory.

I offered it as an olive branch to the Shroudies. And they clubbed me over the head with it."

"So if Giotto wasn't copying an earlier Shroud—if he did it as a prank, or a fake, or whatever—then it's not a likeness of Jesus, or of *anybody*, for that matter. He could just make up any old face, right? He wouldn't have needed a human model." I was asking for two reasons: I needed to lay my Avignon hypothesis to rest once and for all, and I was still intrigued by Miranda's snuff-film theory—a theory that resembled Emily's autopsy-photo idea, but with a sinister twist.

"Occam's razor, Dr. B. Giotto was an artist. Artists use models. Of course there was a model."

"But the guy in the painting—"

"It's not a painting," she interrupted. "It's an illustration."

"Okay, okay, the guy in the *illustration:* Would his dimensions, his stature, match the stature of the model?"

"Absolutely, if the artist was doing a life-size illustration," she said. "A good artist can draw exactly to scale. When I was a medical illustrator, I did it all the time."

Exactly to scale: The words sliced through my Avignon theory like a razor, parting and crumbling the hypothesis like ancient, fragile linen.

AN HOUR LATER, I was sprinting up the staircase of the Hotel Diplomatic and pounding on Miranda's door. "Miranda, Miranda, *wake up!*" I drummed again, louder, hoping she hadn't sallied forth in search of coffee and breakfast.

"Jeez, what the *hell*? Just a second." A moment later the door was opened by a bleary-eyed Miranda, wearing only a long T-shirt. "What's wrong?"

"Nothing's wrong," I said. She glared, plucking twists of toilet paper from her ears. "Sorry, I thought for sure you'd be up already."

"Man, I'd *just* gotten to sleep," she grumbled. "Be grateful you got a room on the back side of the building. Away from the sirens and car alarms that blared all night long." She pressed her palms against her eyes. "So, what's up—besides you, early bird?"

"This," I said, stepping aside to show her the Shroud, which I'd unrolled in the hallway again.

"I'm thinking Housekeeping's gonna do some damage when they run the vacuum cleaner over that," she said, but I could see her curiosity awakening.

"I just talked to Emily Craig."

"Emily? In Kentucky?" I nodded. "Just now?"

"Maybe an hour ago."

"Betcha woke *her* up, too, didn't you?"

"Well, yeah. I did wake her up. But that's not the point."

"Might've been the point to Emily. Are you about to tell me what *you* think the point is?"

"I am. Emily was explaining how the Shroud could've been made. A dust-transfer illustration— like a cave painting, or a brass rubbing." Miranda nodded, rubbing sleep from her eyes. "She thinks the Shroud was made by a medieval artist named Giotto. Giotto was—"

She fluttered a hand in the air. "Yeah, yeah, Giotto and I go way back. I minored in art history."

She pondered. "Okay, stylistically, Giotto seems plausible."

"But *Giotto's* not the point, either," I said.

She sighed. "Anybody ever mention that you take a long damn time to get to the point?"

"I'm getting there, I'm getting there. So Emily's going on about how a good artist can draw to scale. *Exactly to scale.* Which is just rubbing my nose in the fact that the Shroud guy isn't our Avignon guy. Can't be."

"Because our Avignon guy's six inches too short."

"Right. The Shroud guy is ten percent taller. But then, after I hung up, I thought, *hmm.*"

"Don't tell me, let me guess. The *hmm*—that's the point."

"Exactly the point, Miss Smarty-Pants. Because after I thought, *hmm*, I thought, *If he can draw exactly to scale, maybe he can scale it up, too. Why not larger than life?* So I found a copy shop. Hey, you know the Italian word for 'photocopy'?" She shook her head wearily. "*Fotocopia.* Isn't that great? Anyhow, I found a *fotocopia* shop. Look."

I knelt and laid a photocopy over the face on the Shroud. It was a full-frontal image of the Avignon skull. I'd taken the CT scan to the *fotocopia* shop, enlarged it to 110 percent of actual size, and printed it on clear Mylar film. When I moved out of the way, Miranda gasped. "Oh, my God, it *is* him—the fit's *perfect* now!"

I couldn't help preening. "See? The *hmm* was important, right?"

"No shit, Sherlock. Very important."

The effect created by the overlay was almost like

X-ray vision; almost as if we were looking through the face on the Shroud and seeing the bones beneath. I'd used this technique, facial superimposition, in several cases over the years: superimposing photographs of missing persons onto skulls that turned up, seeing if the face fit the skull. Most times the fit was terrible—the eyes floated out beyond the edges of the skull, or the nose hovered in the middle of the teeth, or the skull's chin was twice as wide as the one in the photo—but sometimes, like now, everything on the face aligned with everything on the skull.

In a court of law, facial superimposition couldn't be used to prove an identification; it could be used only to exclude one—to say "No, that face can't possibly fit that skull." If the Shroud face hadn't aligned with the Avignon skull—the scaled-up skull—I'd have concluded once and for all that the portrait in Turin and the bones in France belonged to different men. But this was a better fit than I could have imagined, and Emily Craig's confident assertion—that a good artist can draw exactly to scale—no longer struck me as artistic license, as illustrator's exaggeration.

I fetched my tape measure, and Miranda and I took measurements from the Shroud to compare with those from the bones. We couldn't get as many measurements as I'd hoped, because the Shroud's image was vague, the landmarks tough to pinpoint. It was like examining a newspaper photo through a magnifying glass: the closer you look, the less you see. Still, the few solid measurements we managed to get—overall stature, femur length, nasal breadth, nasal length—fit well, once we scaled up the bone measurements. Even the skeleton's leggy, storklike proportions—the short trunk and long limbs—were accurately rendered on the Shroud. "Everything's the same, just ten percent bigger," Miranda said. "Why do you suppose he did that?"

I shrugged. "Maybe he wanted it to look more impressive."

She laughed. "Maybe he was getting paid by the foot."

I laughed, too. "We can probably never prove it, but I feel sure. This guy on the Shroud is our guy from the palace."

"But who *is* our guy?" she said. "Is it Eckhart, or is it Jesus?"

"That, Miranda, is the million-dollar question."

CHAPTER 14

"*IN*-TER-ESTING." MIRANDA WAS SCROLLING down the screen of her iPad as the car careened through a curve near the Mont Blanc Tunnel on our drive back to Avignon.

"How can you read on these roads without getting carsick? I'd've thrown up before we got out of Turin if I tried that."

"It's a gift," she said. "I have many. Now shut up and drive. And listen. Three interest items about the Shroud. Interest item number one: In the 1990s, a prominent microscopist named Walter McCrone found red ochre in the image on the Shroud—and vermilion pigment in the so-called bloodstains."

"That would explain why those are bright red," I said. "I was gonna circle back to that at some point. Since when is dried blood cherry red? Every death scene I see, dried blood's almost black."

"Right. The point is, this microscopist McCrone seems to support Emily's position. Interest item number two: When the Shroud first surfaced in Lirey, France, a bishop in a nearby town got suspicious. He poked around, asked a lot of questions, and eventually wrote to Avignon to warn the pope that it was a fake—'cunningly painted,' he said—created to draw pilgrims to Lirey. What's the catchphrase these days? 'Faith-based tourism'? Ha. This sounds like a case of *fake*-based tourism."

"Did this sleuth of a bishop happen to finger Giotto as the cunning painter?"

"He did not," she said, "but I'm glad you asked, because that brings us to interest item number three. In June of 2011, an Italian art historian, one Luciano Buso, announced that he'd found an artist's signature—guess whose?—hidden in the Shroud. Somewhere around the face, supposedly." She unfastened her seat belt, and the car began beeping in alarm. She clambered out of her seat, squeezing her way into the back.

"What are you *doing*?"

"Getting the Shroud." She wormed her way back to the front, belted in, and began unrolling the giant print. One end of it flopped halfway across the windshield, and I nearly ran off the road before I managed to bat it away.

"Are you crazy? There are so many better reasons to die than this." I pulled onto the shoulder and parked.

"Sorry; it got away from me for a second there." She hopped out of the car, laid the print on the hood, and unrolled it as far as the face. "Come help me look." She pored over the image, squinting and frowning. "I don't see a *damn* thing that looks like 'Giotto.' Do you?"

"No," I said, "but that swirly bit around the eye looks kinda like a doggie."

She retrieved her iPad from the floorboard and did further searching. "Okay, here's the picture this art historian gave to the media. A close-up of the neck, showing the signature." She enlarged the picture and studied the screen. "Hmm." Then she studied our immense, high-resolution print again. "*Hmmmmm.*"

"*Hmmmmm,* what? I'm assuming the *hmmmmm* is important."

She showed me the screen. "In his print, just above that double wrinkle in the neck, can you kinda-sorta see a *potential* 'Giotto'?"

I was surprised by what I saw. "Yeah, I kinda-sorta *can.* It's grainy, but I see something that could be a lowercase cursive *g* and a couple round bits that might be *o*'s."

She stared at the mammoth print. "But now look at ours. Notice anything funny?"

"It's really different. I see blotches and splotches, but everything looks all vague and random."

"I think he's cranked up the contrast a lot in his picture. Not in the whole image; just in that part of the neck. Looks like he's Photoshopped it to highlight what he wants us to see." Then she groaned loudly. "Oh, good *grief.*"

"Now what?"

"Look. On the actual Shroud, the forehead blood—the artful, crown-of-thorns trickle of blood—is above the right eye." Then she pointed to the iPad. "But in this art-detective's version, it's above the left. He's flopped it, left to right." She growled in annoyance. "No fair. Shit, Dr. B, if I played image doctor for a day or two, I could probably make it say 'Miranda rocks!' somewhere in there." She rolled up the scroll, shaking her head in disgust. "Come on, let's go. What a gyp."

"Too bad," I said. "I was hoping this Giotto story might help Emily Craig's work finally get the attention it deserves."

We hadn't gone more than a few miles before Miranda simmered down and resumed the quest for interest items. "During the early Middle Ages, there were supposedly dozens of 'true shrouds' rattling around—more than forty, according to one guy who's researched this. But none of those showed an image of Jesus; they were just strips of cloth. It wasn't until . . ."—she paused to scroll—" . . . 1203 that there was a record of a shroud with an image. But it just showed the face, not the whole bod."

"Where was it?"

"That one turned up in Constantinople," she said, "which was the crossroads of the relics trade."

"How come?" I asked.

"How come it turned up?"

"No, how come Constantinople was the crossroads of the relics trade?"

"Ah. Because of Saint Helena."

"And what's she the patron saint of?"

"Of relics, looks like. Helena was the mother of Constantine—the Roman emperor who finally gave the seal of approval to Christianity. She was quite the pack rat when it came to relics. She made a pilgrimage to the Holy Land and brought back a boatload of 'em. A true cross or two, three crowns of thorns, the Holy Sponge—"

"The Holy *what*?"

"Sponge. The Holy Sponge. A Roman soldier stuck a sponge on a stick and gave Jesus a drink up on the cross. Holy Nails."

"Wait, go back. The sponge? Really? Jesus dies a horrible death, his friends and family are devastated, but as they're pulling him off the cross and hauling him away, somebody stops and goes, 'Say, soldier, can I have that sponge?'"

"So the story goes. Where was I? Oh, Holy Nails—*lots* of Holy Nails. At least thirty Holy Nails, scattered all over Europe." She scrolled down the screen, then hooted. "Wow. The Holy Stairs: twenty-eight marble steps—I'm not making this up—from the palace of Pontius Pilate, the Roman governor. The steps Jesus stood on, supposedly, when Pilate washed his weaselly hands of the whole affair."

"So after the grieving disciples snag the Holy Sponge and pry out the Holy Nails, they swing by the governor's palace and pinch an entire staircase?"

"I'm just telling you what it says. Quit interrupting. There's more, so much more in the realm of relics. Feathers from the wings of the Angel Gabriel, plucked or molted when he swooped down to tell Mary she was pregnant. Vials of Mary's breast milk."

"Gag."

"Six Holy Foreskins."

"*Whose* six Holy Foreskins?"

"Jesus's, of course."

"He had six of them? Or was the One True Penis snipped six times?"

She shrugged. "Maybe the rabbi was a rookie." She consulted the screen again. "The body of Mary Magdalene—three Mary Magdalenes, actually, in three different places. The tail of the donkey on which Jesus rode to Jerusalem on Palm Sunday. A few heads of John the Baptist. A tear Jesus shed."

"A tear? One of the 'Jesus wept' tears, from when Lazarus died?" She nodded. "And somebody just happened to be standing by with an airtight container?" I shook my head. "Twelve disciples? Jesus would've needed hundreds—*thousands*—to trail along behind him and scoop up everything he ever touched for all this stuff to be real. What a racket."

"Well, yes and no," she said, surprising me.

"How no?"

"People venerate relics everywhere, always. Relics can be props—they can dramatize and validate the religion's story; visual aids. But they can also be considered talismans, with magical powers—the power to heal the sick, raise the dead, protect a city against invading armies. People crave relics—beautiful ones, like the Shroud, or even cheesy ones like the Sacred Sandwich." I remembered what I'd seen on my midnight walk—mementos stuffed in the moonlit niches of a prison wall, and the nearby carving of John the Baptist's severed head—and it gave her argument the ring of truth.

"So, circling back," I said. "Whatever happened to that shroud from 1203—the one with the image?"

"Oh, that," she said. "It vanished in the sack of Constantinople a year later. In all the raping and pillaging."

"Who raped and pillaged Constantinople?"

"The Crusaders."

"The *Christian* Crusaders? Raping and pillaging the crossroads of Christianity?"

"Depends," she answered, "on how you define 'Christian.'"

Just then the ring of my phone sounded—a startling noise high in the Alps, miles from any city. I snatched it from the console, narrowly missing a road sign as I sneaked a glance at the display. *Private number.* "Hello?"

"Hello, is this Dr. Bill Brockton?"

"Yes, it is."

"Dr. Brockton, my name is Dr. Adam Newman. I'm the scientific director of the Institute for Biblical Science, in Charlotte, North Carolina."

"Ah, yes," I said. "I got your letter a few days ago."

"Are you going to be able to help us with our project? We're very anxious to get to work, and we're very much hoping you're interested."

I hesitated. I'd been dubious when I first read the letter, and Stefan's report had only confirmed my uneasiness. But I didn't want to be offensive. "I'm sorry, but I'm afraid I won't be able to help you with that, Dr. Newman."

"I think you'd find it a fascinating opportunity," he said. "If you'll let me tell you more about it, I think you might reconsider."

"Even if I wanted to, I couldn't take it on right now," I said. "I'm out of the country. I'm in France."

"France?" There was a silence, and I thought I'd lost the call. "Well, *gracious,* lucky you. What part of France?" Something about his hearty tone sounded false, but before I could decide how—or whether—to answer the question, the world went dark, we plunged into the Mont Blanc Tunnel, and Dr. Adam Newman was gone.

CHAPTER 15

AFTER DROPPING MIRANDA OFF, I eased the Peugeot through Lumani's wooden gate just in time to see Elisabeth arranging purple stalks of lavender in a tall vase on one of the garden tables. She waved and nodded. "Ah, *bonjour*. You are back so soon. How was your trip? Did you see the famous Shroud?"

"No, we didn't. It was impossible."

"Ah, *quel dommage*—too bad."

"It's okay. It was a useful trip. We bought a copy of the Shroud. A life-size photograph. For three hundred dollars."

She gasped, and as she drew in her breath, she exclaimed, "Ah!" I'd never heard anyone do that before—speaking while inhaling. The intake of breath somehow invested the "ah" with a little more wonder and a *lot* more charm. "*Mon Dieu.* For so much money, I hope it has the power to make miracles."

"Well, I didn't fall asleep and crash your car in the mountains, so maybe it does have miraculous powers."

"Caffeine," she said. "Caffeine has these powers, too. Do you want a coffee?"

"No coffee, thanks. But I'd love a cup of tea, if you don't mind." She turned toward the kitchen. "Oh, Elisabeth, before I forget. You're an artist. Did you study art history, too?"

"Only a little."

"I have a friend—she's an anthropologist and an artist—who thinks that the Shroud of Turin was made by Giotto."

"A painting by Giotto?" She wrinkled her forehead and frowned. "No, I don't think so. The picture, the image, is too *maigre* . . . what is the English word? . . . thin? Not the man, but the picture. It is like a ghost, almost not there. Paint would be more strong."

"You're right," I agreed. "Not paint. Dust. Pigment. Red ochre. Like a cave painting." I pretended to sprinkle powder into my palm, then puffed it onto an imaginary surface.

"Ah!" There it was again, the charming, breathtaking "ah." Just hearing it made me smile. "Red ochre. I think it is possible."

"Do you know if Giotto ever worked in Avignon?"

She shrugged. "*Pfft*. I don't know. *Peut-être*— maybe. Artists came from all over Europe to paint at the *palais*. Also at the *livrées* of the cardinals.

There were many walls to decorate, and much money to collect. Artists come to money like flies come to honey."

I laughed. "I thought all artists were poor and starving."

"*Most* artists are starving. But if the pope likes you, you will never go hungry."

WHEN ELISABETH RETURNED with my tea, she was balancing the cup on a pair of books: a lavish coffee-table art book about Giotto, and a smaller book, which she opened once I lifted the cup from it. "*Vies des Artists*," she said. "*The Lives of the Artists.* By Vasari. You know Vasari?" I shook my head. "Giorgio Vasari. Italian. Sixteenth century. He made architecture, but also biography and history."

"A regular Renaissance man," I punned, then worried that the joke wouldn't translate.

She laughed. "*Ah, bon.*" She checked the smaller book's contents, then flipped to a chapter. "So. Vasari writes this about Giotto. He says, 'When Clement Five became pope and brought the papal court to Avignon, Giotto came with him. And while he was here, he made many beautiful pictures and frescoes, which pleased the pope and the entire court very much. And so, when the work was all finished, the pope sent him back to Florence with love, and with many gifts. Giotto was rich and honored and famous.' You see," she said with a smile, "I told you: If the pope likes you, you don't starve."

"Ah," I said.

CHAPTER 16

I MADE IT TO the library an hour before closing time. Neither of Elisabeth's books showed paintings from Giotto's Avignon period, but I felt sure the library would have a more comprehensive book. And I was glad to have another occasion to visit the former cardinal's palace, which was now a palace of books.

The building was fronted by a square courtyard, which was open to the street but was flanked on its other three sides by a magnificent stone building in the shape of a low, wide U. The two wings seemed like later additions to the building's massive central core; that part was three stories high—three very tall stories of pale, putty-colored stone, topped by crenellations. Unlike the battlements atop the Palace of the Popes, the crenellations here appeared merely decorative; the building was large, but not fortified, and the immense leaded-glass windows in its façade would have posed no barrier to attack.

I entered through a large glass door at the center of the building. Directly inside was a foyer with a massive stone staircase leading upward. One floor up, I entered the main reading room—once a cardinal's banquet hall, it now served up a feast of books—and made for the reference desk. There I found the helpful librarian Philippe on duty again. He smiled at me in recognition. "*Bonjour, monsieur.* Are you back for more research on Eckhart?"

"Not this time," I answered. "Art history this time. Do you have any books on the artist Giotto? An Italian painter. Giotto di . . ." I floundered for the last name.

"Di Bondoni. But of course. *Magnifique.* Come." He led me down the long wall of the great room, to a section where oversized art books were shelved. They were arranged alphabetically, and midway along the wall, we came to *G.* Philippe pulled out two books—a thin one and a fat one—then reshelved the thin one. "That one is no good," he said dismissively. "Everything in that one is also in this one. And more." He handed me the fat book; it was two inches thick, a foot high, eighteen inches wide, and ten pounds heavy. The text was in French, but I figured that didn't matter much; I was interested in the pictures.

"Thank you," I said to the young man. "This is such a beautiful library. Is it okay if I take this upstairs to the mezzanine?"

"Sure. I prefer the mezzanine also. Very tranquil, and the view is the best."

I lugged the book up another flight of stone stairs, emerging onto the balcony that overlooked the grand hall. I could easily imagine five hundred guests—cardinals, bishops, wealthy merchants, dukes and duchesses, and other lords and ladies. Twenty feet below me, where the banquet tables would have been set with gilded china, sparkling crystal, and platters of food, row upon row of shelves now marched across the tiled floor. Twenty feet above me were the timbered squares of the coffered ceiling, whose main joists measured at least eighteen inches square.

I was headed for one of the balcony's wooden study tables when I spotted a chair tucked into a deep recess beneath a leaded-glass window. I settled into the cozy niche, imagining myself living and working in such opulence: a visiting scholar, perhaps, or the personal physician to his eminence the Cardinal, stealing a few moments in this out-of-the-way nook to peruse an illuminated manuscript from his prized collection.

Soon I forgot sumptuous surroundings; all my attention was riveted on Giotto's paintings, especially a series of frescoes in a jewel box of a chapel in Padua, Italy. The chapel, belonging to the wealthy Scrovegni family, couldn't have held a hundred people, but every square inch of the walls was covered with frescoes—more than fifty of them—depicting themes and scenes from the Bible, including numerous episodes in the lives of Mary and Jesus. The images were overwhelming in their number and richness; the little church reminded me of the Sistine Chapel, except that the paintings were smaller and closer to eye level. What refined and devout people the Scrovegnis must have been to commission such glorious art.

Finally I looked up from the paintings, rubbed my eyes, and then flipped to the index. I ran my eyes down the *A* section, toward the bottom, to see which pages featured Giotto's Avignon paintings. I found no entry for Avignon. Puzzled, I lugged the book downstairs to the reference desk and showed the index to Philippe. "There's nothing in this book about Avignon. Do you have another book on Giotto? One that shows what he painted while he was here?"

"Here?" He looked puzzled.

"Yes, here. In Avignon. This city." I smiled. He frowned. "Pope Clement the Fifth brought him here," I explained, proud of my knowledge. "He painted beautiful pictures and frescoes here, then he went back to Florence, more famous and beloved than ever."

His frown deepened. "Monsieur Giotto did not paint here. He never even visited here."

"But he did. I read it in an art history book."

"What book?"

"*The Lives of the Artists.* By . . . Vasari?"

"Ah, *oui*, Vasari." He laughed. "He just made up that stuff about Avignon."

"What?"

"Yeah, it's pure fiction. Vasari does that all the time. He tells great stories about famous painters and poets, but half of them are made up. Invented."

This was a twist I hadn't expected—another wrinkle in the Shroud, or at least in my theory that the Avignon bones were intimately tied to the Turin Shroud. I thanked him and began walking away, disappointed. Then a thought occurred to me, and I turned back toward Philippe. "Are there any famous fresco painters who *did* come to Avignon?"

"Ah, *oui*. The one who did the beautiful frescoes in the Palais des Papes. He is the neighbor of Giotto."

"Excuse me?"

"Come." I followed him to the oversized art books again, and he led me once more to the *G* section. "You are finished with Giotto?" I handed him the tome, and he tucked it into its slot on the shelf, but not before sliding out an adjacent volume, a much slimmer one. I noticed the word "Avignon" in the book's title—an encouraging sign. "See," Philippe said, smiling. "Giovanetti. Giotto's closest neighbor on the bookshelf." He translated the title for me: *"An Italian Painter at the Court of Avignon."*

"Sounds perfect. I'll take it."

I returned to my window nook on the mezzanine and buried myself in the book. Most of the images showed frescoes in the papal palace—frescoes I hadn't seen, since my forays had been confined to the subtreasury and the dark staircases leading to it. Giovanetti and his apprentices had painted three chapels in the palace, as well as the pope's private study. Unlike the religious murals in the chapels, those in the pope's private study showed scenes of French country life: a stag hunt, the deer portrayed at the very moment it was caught by the hounds; a rectangular pool where men fished with nets and with lines; a pair of gentlemen hunting with falcons. Despite the passage of nearly seven centuries—and obvious signs of damage—the frescoes remained vibrant. But were they the work of the same hand that had created the Shroud? I studied the faces, looking for similarities in features or style. But just as with the image on the Shroud itself, the harder I looked, the less I could see with certainty.

Immersed in art and uncertainty, I was slow to notice the electronic warble reverberating through the cavernous stone chamber. Someone's cell phone was ringing. Frowning, I scanned the balcony and the reading room for the culprit; that's when I noticed several faces frowning at me. *I* was the culprit. Embarrassed, I scurried to the staircase and checked the display; it read *Tennessee Bureau of Investigation.* "Hello, this is Bill Brockton," I said in a low voice that I hoped would carry through the phone but not throughout the stone building.

"Dr. Brockton? Is that you? I can barely hear you."

"Yes, it's me," I said, a bit louder, cupping my hand around the phone to muffle the sound, which tended to echo in the stone stairwell.

"Doc, it's Steve Morgan at the TBI."

"Steve. How are you? I hope you're calling to say that the TBI and the DEA have rounded up that whole drug ring. I know Rocky was hot on the heels of one of them in Amsterdam." The phone fell silent. "Steve? Did I lose you?"

"No. No, I'm here. I hate to say it, but I've got bad news, Doc."

"What's wrong? Are you okay?"

"Yeah, I'm okay. It's not me; it's Rocky. He . . . he was killed last night, Doc."

"What?"

"In Amsterdam," he went on. "Morales, the guy

Rocky tracked to Amsterdam? He and Rocky shot each other. Both dead."

I sat down on the stairs. "Oh, God," I said. "You're sure?"

"Yeah. I've got photos from the scene."

"Damn it. *Damn* it. Does his wife know yet?"

"I just left the house. She's mighty torn up."

"Oh, dear God. Bless her heart. And those two kids. I . . ." My head was swirling with grief and guilt. "Steve, he went to Amsterdam because of me. He was trying to make sure I was safe."

"He was doing his job, Doc. The DEA was running a dangerous operation, and it got compromised. He couldn't trust anybody else. You're not the only reason he went. He had people working undercover in Amsterdam, and he needed to reel them in. It's not your fault."

"I wish I could believe that."

"Believe it, Doc. Not your fault." In the background, I heard another phone ringing, and I heard Steve answer it, then speak tersely, though I couldn't make out the words. "Doc, I gotta go," he said when he came back on the line. "I know he was a friend of yours. I'm really, really sorry."

"Yeah. Yeah, me, too. He was a good man. I . . . thanks for the call, Steve. Be careful out there." My left arm dropped to my side; the phone slipped from my fingers and fell to the floor, bouncing down two of the stone steps before clattering to a stop. I left it there.

Years before, I had lost a wife to cancer. More recently—just as I'd emerged from my cave of grief—a woman I'd begun to love had been murdered. And now Rocky Stone, a good man, a dedicated cop, a devoted husband and father. At the moment, my heart felt like a graveyard full of tombstones.

I don't know how long I sat there, staring unseeing at the stone steps. After a few seconds or many minutes, I felt a hand on my shoulder and a voice asked, in Irish-accented English, "Are you all right, lad?" I looked up. Standing before me, two steps down, was a silver-haired priest. He was *dressed* like a priest, at any rate—the black pants and shirt with the white clerical collar—but he didn't *look* like a priest, or at least like any priest I'd ever seen. I guessed him to be ten years older than I was, but he had the physique of a man half his age: tall, broad shouldered, flat stomached. His shirt was short sleeved, and it strained to contain his chest and his biceps. He leaned closer, looked into my eyes, and asked again, "Are you all right? Anything I can do to help you?"

I took a deep breath to steady myself, then another. "Thank you, but no." Another breath, which came in very raggedly. I forced it out between pursed lips, as if I were blowing out birthday candles. Rocky Stone was what, forty-four? Forty-eight? "It's kind of you to offer, though. I just got some bad news. It blindsided me."

He kept his left hand on my shoulder and extended his right, which held my cell phone. "I'm thinking this was the bearer of bad tidings; would I be right about that, lad?" I nodded, taking it from him. "I got a phone call like that once," he said. "Long ago. Changed my life. It's been an interest-

ing life, and lots of it's been good. But I'd give anything not to have gotten that call, you know?"

I nodded again, intrigued now, or maybe just
desperate to be distracted from my own sadness.
"Do you mind my asking what your bad-news call
was?"

"Ah. No, lad, I don't mind. Part of me penance is
tellin' it." I looked up, puzzled. "It was bad news that
I had a hand in bringin' about, see?" I didn't see, but
he seemed to be diving into deep inner waters, so
I waited for whatever it was that he felt bound by
penance to tell. "I was twenty-two when the Troubles began. A young hothead livin' at home with
me mum in Banbridge, not far from Belfast. I had
no job, no goals, and nothing better to do than to
brood and rage, and blame everything that I hated
about my life on the British Army and the Protestants. So I joined the Provisional IRA. I didn't actually do much; I suppose *I* was provisional. Mostly
spouted off a lot, in front of me mum and my little
brother, Jimmy."

He paused a moment before continuing.
"Jimmy was sixteen, and he looked up to me more
than he should've. 'Rivers of blood,' I liked to say,
'that's the only thing can wash the devils out of
Northern Ireland.' And while I was talking such
stuff, Jimmy was listening. Jimmy was *believin'*. So
Jimmy joined up. He didn't even tell me. Jimmy
wasn't a talker—Jimmy was a doer. Nothing provisional about Jimmy. Jimmy planted a culvert
bomb under one of the roads into town—that was
our version of the IEDs that maim so many soldiers in Iraq these days. But the bomb went off

prematurely. It wasn't a British Army vehicle that Jimmy's bomb blew up; it was a school bus. Three kids died; seventeen were injured. Some of them lost arms, legs, eyes."

He stared out the window of the stairwell, as if watching the story unfold. "The army hunted Jimmy for weeks; it was hard for him to find food or shelter because the one thing all sides agreed on— Protestants, Catholics, Loyalists, Brits—was what a terrible thing young Jimmy Halloran had done. They finally found him in a barn on the coast at Mill Bay, alone and weak with hunger. He wouldn't give up; I'm not sure they gave him a real chance, but even if they did, he wouldn't have taken it. He wounded three soldiers during the gun battle. It took six bullets to bring him down. And you know the last thing he said?" His voice had gotten thick, and as I glanced up, I saw him wiping his eyes before he resumed. "Sorry, lad. Tellin' it brings it all back. Jimmy's dying words, said the officer who phoned with the news, were *my* very own words: 'Rivers of blood.' God forgive me." He crossed himself, and breathed out a sadness that came from deep in his core. "So you can see why I might feel the need to do a bit of penance."

"I'm sorry, Father," I said. "That's a heartbreaking story."

"Ah, the heart—not as easily broken as we think it is, lad. Bruises often but rarely breaks, truth be told. Now, how about we go and get you something for that freshly bruised heart of yours, eh? Maybe a dram of brandy or a pint of Guinness to revive you?"

"Thanks. But I don't drink."

"What's that?"

"I don't drink."

"What? Not a drop?"

"Not if it's alcohol."

"Well, then, it's a piss-poor priest you'd have made, lad." I looked up, startled, and his eyes—red rimmed—were now twinkling. "No alcohol? You've got no aptitude for the priesthood. No vocation, no calling." To my surprise, I found myself smiling at his cheeky irreverence. "Well, no matter—I've got vocation enough for the both of us. Come along, if you like; I'll have the brandy *and* the Guinness, and you can have coffee, or tea, or broccoli juice, or whatever other wretched beverage American teetotalers consume instead of nectar from heaven."

He reached out a hand; to my surprise, I took it and let him haul me to my feet. As he headed down the staircase toward the library's exit, he turned and looked over his shoulder. "Coming, lad? I'm Michael Halloran, by the by."

I started down the steps after him, abandoning the Giovanetti book in the window alcove where I'd left it. "Do you serve a parish here in Avignon, Father Halloran?"

"You can call me Father Mike. Or just plain Mike. Or anything else, except Father Halloran."

"I'll go with Father Mike," I said. "Friendly, but respectful."

"Once I've had a drop or two, you can drop the 'Father,' if you're wanting to respect me a bit less."

I laughed. I was surprised to feel so relaxed with a priest; ever since my wife's death, I'd had little use for organized religion or its foot soldiers. "I suspect you're good at your work, Father Mike."

"Devilishly."

He held the exit door for me and we emerged, blinking, into the building's courtyard. "Oh, you never answered. Do you serve a parish here in Avignon?"

"No, but it might not be such a bad posting," he said. "I'm just here on holliers."

"Excuse me?"

"Holliers. Holiday. Seeing how the other half lived, seven hundred years ago."

"Half? More like the other one-millionth of one percent."

"Arithmetic was never me strong suit, lad. Is there something I can call you besides 'lad'?"

"Oh, sorry. Of course. I'm Bill. Bill Brockton."

"A fine, honest-sounding name. And what brings you to Avignon, Bill Brockton?" He nodded at the impressive façade of the former cardinal's palace. "And to this humble little parson's cottage? Are you on holliers, too?"

"Not exactly. I'm an anthropologist. I'm here to look at some bones."

"Bones? What sort of bones?"

"Just some old bones found at the Palace of the Popes."

"A pope's bones?"

"I don't think so."

"A papal mistress, perhaps. Clement the Sixth had a niece he was mighty fond of—that's what he called her in public, at least. Or possibly a pope's bastard son."

"You *do* look on the bright side, don't you, Father Mike?" He laughed. "I don't know who it is. Realistically, probably never will. All I know for sure is that the bones are very old, and the guy died a very painful death."

"Must've had his finger in the till, then. The popes didn't take kindly to that." He pointed up the street. "So, Bill Brockton, I just happen to know that there's a pub two blocks yonder way. Shall we wend our way thither, for my heavenly nectar and your hellish excuse for a beverage?"

"AH, ME, THAT'S a shame," he said, when I told him about Rocky.

"I feel at least partly responsible," I added, explaining my involvement in Rocky's case. "I need to figure out some way to help his wife and kids."

"Heavens, can it be? Are you an honorable man, Bill Brockton? I don't see many of your ilk these days. My parish has seven honorable men in it." He frowned. "No, make that six."

"It's a small parish?"

"Oh, goodness no. We have two hundred people at Sunday-morning Mass. But only a handful of those are honorable men. One in fifteen or twenty: It's the universal wheat-to-chaff ratio for men, I'm sorry to say. In women, it's higher. I'd say as many as one woman in three is honorable."

"For such a cheerful fellow, you're mighty cynical, Father Mike."

"Call me crazy. Call me observant. Call me

whenever there's beer on tap." He hoisted his mug and took an appreciative swig of Guinness.

"So, you seem like a down-to-earth priest, Father Mike. Can I ask you something?" He nodded, licking froth off his upper lip. "When you look around Avignon at all the signs of wealth and excess and greed—the popes filling their coffers with gold, the cardinals building grand palaces like the library—how do you account for it? How do you reconcile it with the teachings of Jesus, who preached the virtues of poverty and humility?"

"I don't reconcile it. I can't. It's not reconcilable; it just *is*. Or *was*. Things are better now, I think. Not perfect, but better. I think the clergy's less obsessed with money and power and more interested in spirituality. I hope so, anyhow. The medieval Church was a product of its times, just as the early Church was, and just as the modern church is. You know, we like to call the Church 'the bride of Christ.' Well, she's like any other bride: Sometimes she's an angel, and sometimes she's a bitch." His words drew a shocked laugh from me. "The church is just people, Bill Brockton. Capable of beauty and nobility, but also capable of duplicity and depravity. The bravest, noblest church work I've ever seen—work that raised up villagers and brought down a dictator in Latin America—was led by a priest I knew. After he was killed, I learned he was also a pedophile. Sometimes the Church enables us to do our worst; more often, I hope, it ennobles us to be our best."

His openness was refreshing. So was his willingness to hang on to the church's ideals despite its failings.

"You seem to have a bit more air in your tires now, Bill Brockton. Is that true?"

I smiled. "Actually, it is."

"Then I'll be leaving now. I've got a sacred mission to attend to."

"A mission? I thought you were on—what's the word?—holliers?"

"And so I am. But Dublin is playing Manchester on the telly in ten minutes. It'd be a sin to miss the start of the match." He fished in his pocket and pulled out a pen. "I happen to know you've got a mobile." He smiled. "If you'll give me your number, I'll call you before I leave town. I'd enjoy another chat, Bill Brockton."

To my surprise, I realized I would, too. *Perhaps,* I thought, *I've been underestimating men of the cloth.*

CHAPTER 17

Avignon
1328

"YOUR HOLINESS?"

"Come in, Jacques. I have not seen you these past three days. Where have you been?"

"I've been dealing with Eckhart. Your Holiness, I . . . There is a problem. With Eckhart."

"I am well aware of it," the pope says drily. "We discuss it often, do we not? The papal crown is not so heavy, and I am not so feeble, that I have already forgotten how diligently you strive to show him the errors of his teachings."

The White Cardinal—heretic hound Fournier—reaches a plump hand into his robe and retrieves a handkerchief to mop his brow. Despite the autumn chill already settling into the stones of the building, his forehead glistens with beads of sudden sweat.

"There is, Holy Father, a new problem."

"What is it? Have you allowed him to escape,

as you did the Franciscan devil Michael, after I dragged Michael here for you to break? How could Eckhart escape, too? You told me Eckhart could no longer walk."

Fournier folds the handkerchief, makes another pass. "Eckhart has not escaped. Eckhart has died."

The pope's ancient eyes look sharply at the man who is his protégé and doctrinal enforcer. "This preacher was already too popular with the people, Jacques. Have you now made a martyr of him?"

The handkerchief is hopelessly inadequate to soak up the rivulets of sweat coursing down the cardinal's face. "He was old and frail, Holiness. In his sixties."

"I'm eighty-five," the pope croaks. "Do not insult me, insolent boy." Fournier is nearing fifty—hasn't been a boy for more than thirty years—but he's old enough and wise enough not to quibble over terminology, especially in the midst of a scolding that makes him feel like a slow-witted pupil. "Eckhart walked here from Cologne—five hundred miles on foot—to answer the charges against him. He was not a frail man. Not when he arrived."

Fournier slides his tongue over his lips, back and forth, a nervous habit that looks vaguely obscene. "Perhaps the rigors of the journey took a delayed toll on him."

"Perhaps the rigors of your questioning proved too much for mortal flesh," the old man replies. "Your zeal is commendable, but your measures can be excessive."

"How can one go too far to protect the purity of the faith, Your Holiness?"

"By mistaking anger for righteousness, and rigidity for strength. I remember a woman you burned in Montaillou, two years after I made you bishop. Do you?" How could Fournier forget her, that stubborn, stupid shrew who refused to break for him? But he simply nods slightly, hoping to deflect the conversation. "Remind me why you burned her?"

"She refused to take the oath, Your Holiness. I begged her, again and again. I gave her many chances."

"You burned her because she would not swear to tell the truth?"

"She would not." Irked now, Fournier can't resist the urge to justify himself. "And as you know, the oath is required of all who are called before the Inquisition."

"Was anyone else burned for refusing to take it?"

"No one else refused, Holiness."

"Then perhaps no one else knew the teachings of our Lord as well as she did. Jesus said, 'Do not swear, either by heaven or by earth or even by your own head, but simply say yes or no.' Did he not?" Fournier inclines his head ever so slightly. "Tell me, Jacques, why was this a burning offense, this peasant woman's refusal to swear an oath?"

Why were half a hundred Templars burned in Paris, Fournier thinks, *and four Franciscan monks in Marseilles?* But he dares not voice those questions. Instead, he responds, "She defied the holy office of the Inquisition."

"She defied *you*, Jacques, and it enraged you." The old man studies the clenched jaw and flashing eyes of his middle-aged protégé. "Cardinal Fournier, I speak now as your spiritual father. Make confession, admit to the sin of pride, and do whatever penance your confessor requires."

Fournier kneels, his face livid. "Yes, Your Holiness."

"So Eckhart is dead. Died on the rack, I suppose." Fournier does not correct the supposition; does not admit that he has broken one of the Inquisitor's fundamental rules: Shed no blood. Instead, he makes a show of rising from his knees. The old man shakes a clawlike hand, dismissing his own question. "No matter. But we must not allow our foes to use his death against us."

Fournier nods. "Your Holiness is wise, as always. I will see to it." Bowing once more, he turns to leave the audience chamber, the hem of his white cassock gliding an inch above the gritty floor, remaining—as ever—unsullied.

"Jacques?"

He stops, looks over his shoulder. "Yes, Holiness?"

"Did Eckhart die in a state of grace?"

"Yes, Holy Father. At the end—the very end—he confessed his sins, renounced his erroneous teachings, and prayed for forgiveness. It was inspiring to see him saved." The papal head nods, or perhaps it simply dodders. Either way, Fournier chooses to interpret the gesture as a benediction, and he leaves before the pontiff can call him back.

Descending the narrow staircase to the cells where prisoners are chained, the cardinal replays the scene once more in his mind. Only a few hours have passed, but already he has seen the scene a hundred times, exactly as he sees it again now:

Eckhart is no longer fit for the rack—his arms and legs too badly damaged by months of torture. Despite obvious agony, the man has refused to yield; has remained stubbornly, damnably unrepentant. "Perhaps my thoughts are mistaken," he groans, "but my heart is pure. My heart loves God completely. I cannot be a heretic."

"Are you so perfect?" Fournier demands. "Unblemished? The very lamb of God? So be it." He sends the jailer to summon a carpenter, and he orders the startled carpenter to fashion a wooden cross in the cell, and to fetch rope, spikes, and a hammer. The carpenter complies, quaking in fear, then flees. Reluctantly, the jailer ties the heretic to the cross and helps wrestle it upright, leaning against the wall, but then he, too, retreats from the cell.

Eckhart's breathing is scarcely more than a whisper now, scarcely enough to keep him alive. Minute by minute, as he hangs from his arms and his chest sinks, he is inexorably suffocating. "I can still save you," Fournier tells him, pressing the tip of a spike against the soft flesh of Eckhart's left wrist. "Confess your sins, renounce your heresies, and beg forgiveness."

"I have no sins," Eckhart gasps. "I have no heresies. I am at one with God."

The iron spike rings as the hammer smashes into it— once, twice, three times.

The three-part sequence—demand, refusal, the ring of hammer upon spike—is repeated at the other wrist, and then at the feet.

Incredibly, Eckhart continues to breathe, if a rasping death rattle can be called breath.

"You have only a moment left," Fournier tells him. "Repent, and reconcile with God."

"How can we be reconciled?" the old man murmurs, sparking a flame of hope in Fournier. "How can we be reconciled, when we are already one? God and I are one."

"Arrogant liar." Reaching into a sleeve of his robe, Fournier takes out a dagger. "Die and be damned." He thrusts the blade beneath the ribs of the man who, just a year earlier—just before he walked five hundred miles to defend himself at the court of the Holy Father—had been Europe's most prominent preacher.

CHAPTER 18

STEFAN WAS LEANING AGAINST the wall at the southwest corner of the palace, waiting beside the door where he'd made his midnight exit a few nights before. As we approached, he dropped a cigarette to the cobblestones and ground it out, then took the lanyard from around his neck and unlocked the door. The key to the palace fascinated me: It was made of silver, or perhaps steel; its head was cut with an elaborate pattern of filigreed scrollwork; branching symmetrically from two sides of the cylindrical shaft were stubby bars of varying lengths—bars that resembled ribs jutting from a spine. Never had the term "skeleton key" seemed so descriptive.

"So. You wish to see frescoes by Giovanetti?"

"Please," I said. "Giotto has an alibi, so Giovanetti's our new prime suspect."

Stefan rolled his eyes. "Now you think *Giovanetti*

made the snuff movie?" Miranda had filled him in on the trip to Turin, the short-lived Giotto theory, and my conviction that the bones of Avignon were linked to the Shroud of Turin. Was there a hint of scorn in Stefan's voice when he asked about Giovanetti?

"He's worth a look," I said, trying to keep my irritation under control. "Giotto never left Italy. The bones were in France—and the Shroud first surfaced in France. So geographically, at least, Giovanetti fits the facts." Stefan looked annoyed but took us inside.

He led us through a labyrinth of passages and stairways I'd not seen before—how long had it taken him to learn his way around the sprawling, soaring maze of the palace?—and stopped before a locked door near the top of one of the towers. This door, too, answered to the master key, and Stefan ushered us into a room that took my breath away. Every square inch of the plastered walls and ceiling vaults was covered with vivid images: people and landscapes and buildings, scene upon scene, all set against a background of deep blue.

"Oh, my," breathed Miranda.

"Beautiful," I said.

"*Oui*, not bad. This is the chapel of Saint Martial. In the third century, the pope sent him to France. They say he converted many people and made many miracles." He pointed to specific panels, one by one. "Healing the sick. Raising the dead. Casting out devils." The last of the ceiling panels showed an old man kneeling before a handsome, haloed saint; flapping overhead, on batlike wings, was a scaly brown demon that two angels were shooing away. "One legend," Stefan went on, "is that Saint Valérie of Limoges—a martyr, beheaded for her faith—walked to Saint Martial carrying her head in her hands, so he could perform the last rites for her."

Miranda scanned the walls and ceiling. "I don't see a headless woman on the hoof. I guess she's off-screen, digging her own grave."

"You're twisted," I said. "You know that?" She nodded happily.

My eye was drawn to an area where the fresco was badly damaged. The bright, vivid images were absent altogether or were reduced to faint outlines. Looking closer, I saw that a layer of plaster a half inch or so thick was missing in these areas. "What caused all the damage? Water?"

"*Non*. Soldiers. During the nineteenth century, the palace was used as a military barracks. The soldiers chiseled out the faces and sold them."

I scanned the frescoes, and sure enough, virtually all the missing images were faces. One panel showed Jesus flanked by four followers. The four followers' faces were gone, but Jesus remained unscathed. *Pious vandals*, I wondered, *or just superstitious?*

I walked closer to inspect the damaged figures. Faintly traced on the base coat of plaster—the layer exposed when the surface had been pried off—was the black outline of a woman's face: a face that fit perfectly with the undamaged body. I turned to Stefan. "Why is the outline of her face still visible? Did that bleed through the layer of wet plaster?"

"Ah, *non*. That's a charcoal sketch. A study. The artist draws the scene on the rough wall, then puts on a layer of smooth plaster. He paints the scene while the plaster is still fresh—that's why it's called 'fresco.' The paint soaks in, and *voilà*, it becomes part of the plaster. Over time the colors can fade, but the paint cannot peel off. Except with a chisel."

"How did the artist remember all the details, after the sketch was covered with wet plaster?"

Stefan looked at the ceiling, or beyond, lifting the palms of his hands. "A miracle."

"So, Boss, what's the verdict?" Miranda finally asked. "You think Giovanetti's our guy? Did he do the Shroud?"

I took another look at Jesus, then rescanned the entire room, floor to ceiling. "This is beautiful," I said. "Giovanetti was a great painter." Finally I shook my head. "But the *style's* not right. His people are . . . I don't know . . . too *pretty*. Too delicate. They don't have the heft, the fleshiness, the *power* that the figure on the Shroud does." I sighed. "That's my two cents' worth, anyhow."

"Agreed," said Miranda. "Too bad, though. Seemed like a great theory. Stefan, what do you think?"

"I think you are chasing smoke." He checked his watch. "*Merde*," he cursed, "I must go now. I have a stupid meeting with a petty bureaucrat."

Miranda laughed. "But how do you *really* feel about him? And who is this charmer?"

"*Pfft*." His meeting, he said, was with the city official who had jurisdiction over the palace. "I tell him I need to move the bones, and he says no, and no, and no," he fumed. "I keep saying, 'Someone's going to steal them, and then you will be sorry,' but he won't listen. He is even too cheap to pay for the motion detector—I had to buy it with my own money. *Fou. Idiot.*" He shook his head in disgust. "*Allons-y.* Let's go."

He led us out by way of a different door, which—like every door in the palace, seemingly—yielded to his master key. This door opened onto a cavernous banquet hall, which was filled with display cases and milling tourists. Frowning at the tourists, Stefan pointed us toward the far end of the hall, where a doorway led to the main exit.

Miranda ducked through the doorway, and I was just about to, when I stopped dead in my tracks. There on the wall at the end of the banquet hall—on plaster the color of old linen—was the face of Jesus, larger than life. The eyes were piercing; the nose was long and slightly crooked, as if it might have been broken once in a fight; the first two fingers of the right hand, uplifted in a gesture of blessing, were long and thin.

"Miranda—wait! Come back!" She wheeled and hurried toward me, her face full of concern. I pointed; when she saw the picture, her eyes widened and her jaw dropped.

I read the plaque on the wall. The picture was a preliminary study for a fresco, it explained, like the sketch I'd seen upstairs. But this wasn't a crude outline in charcoal; this was a finely detailed work of art, rendered in the same reddish-brown hue—and the same sure, powerful style—as the face on the Shroud of Turin.

The portrait was the handiwork of another Italian artist, one who—unlike the stylistically promising Giotto—actually *did* work in Avignon at the time of the popes. He was known by three names.

Simone Martini.

Simone of Siena.

Master Simone.

CHAPTER 19

Avignon
1328

"MASTER SIMONE, HURRY! PLEASE hurry! If we're caught, this will happen to *us*." The nervous jailer leans backward slowly, easing his head through the doorway of the cell just far enough into the hallway to look and listen. He sees and hears nothing, but when he straightens and turns his attention into the cell, he pleads again, "*Hurry*."

His eagerness to leave is inspired by more than just fear of detection. The scene set before him is like something from one of his nightmares—and in fact, after this night, it will *become* one of his nightmares, destined to haunt him for the remaining seven years of his life.

Six oil lamps flicker on the cold stone floor, their wicks sputtering at odd, startling intervals as they're struck by droplets from the damp ceiling. All around the small cell, the lamps cast shadows of

Simone at work. As he bends, straightens, shifts his feet, moves his arms, the shadows jump and writhe, like demons performing a macabre dance around the dead man stretched at the center of the cell.

Despite the jailer's entreaties, Simone cannot, will not be rushed; such a remarkable subject demands his full attention and best work. The corpse—an older man, but robust, or a ravaged, ruined version of robust—lies faceup on the stone floor. He is nude, but Simone has modestly crossed the hands above the genitals. The artist is fascinated and horrified by the wounds, the very stigmata of Christ. The punctures in the wrists and feet are fringed by ragged flesh and crusty blood; the knife wound in the side is sharply edged, but the blood and serum from it are smeared down the torso, hip, and leg. A crude wooden cross leans against the back wall of the cell and it, too, bears bloody stigmata.

Simone never expected such an opportunity when he arrived in Avignon. He came simply to test the patronage waters at the papal court—to see if French clerics might consider loosening their purse strings for an Italian painter. But a painter can kiss the hands of prospective patrons only so many times before his lips and his spirit grow chafed. Once that happens, he needs to work, whether there's money in it or not. So having had his fill of Avignon's splendor, Simone sought out its squalor, making the rounds of its prisons, hospitals, and cemeteries, concluding each polite inquiry by pressing a florin discreetly into the welcoming palm of a jailer or nurse or gravedigger.

It's not that Simone is morbid; far from it—no

one loves life more than Simone of Siena! But it's always a good idea to study and sketch a corpse or two, if opportunity presents itself. In a religious painter's line of work, the quick outnumber the dead, but not by so wide a margin as one might suppose. There's a steady market for martyr paintings, of course, but the real money is in dead and dying Christs: A painter who's quick with his brush and smooth with his tongue can feed a family of ten solely with commissions for crucifixion paintings. It's crucial, therefore, to master death and dying, but where to find the examples? Living models—thieves and prostitutes and beggars, who'll pose for a pittance or a porridge—are far easier to come by than dead ones. Far more troublesome, too, though: the living wheedle and whine and fidget, while the dead demand no fee or food. Corpses hold stock-still, no matter how many hours the sitting lasts. On the other hand, if the sitting stretches too long, the stench becomes distracting, especially in summer. Ripeness is a virtue in fruits, women, and opportunities, Simone has learned, but not in corpses. *This* corpse, though— freshly dead, laid out on a cold stone floor in late fall—this corpse is a godsend.

The trip to Avignon came up unexpectedly in the midst of a chapel commission in Tuscany. Simone had spent months drawing the sinopia studies on the rough walls; finally every scene was sketched, and all that was needed was the duke's final approval. That would surely be a mere formality— after all, each scene featured at least one family member in a prominent position, a flattering light.

The Virgin Mary bore a striking resemblance to milady the duchess; Joseph, to the duke himself; the baby Jesus, to the duke's squalling brat and heir; John the Baptist, to the duke's younger brother; and so on and so on, down to the final feebleminded cousin, portrayed as a simple shepherd. The sketches done, Simone had ground his pigments, made new brushes, set up his worktable, and asked permission to mix plaster and proceed. But fate had intervened: His honor the duke had galloped off into the night, narrowly escaping an assassination, and was now rumored to be hiding in Rome, or perhaps Naples, or possibly Venice by now. The chapel project had ground to a halt for god knows how long.

So when the invitation came to accompany a musician friend to Avignon—Avignon, which Master Giotto claimed would be the new promised land for artists—only a fool would have refused, and Simone was no fool. He and the musician, a mischievous flute-player, set off through the Susa Valley, paying a larcenous toll at the Savoy Gate, the monumental arch guarding access to the Alps. They'd followed, in reverse, the tortuous route taken by Charlemagne's troops five centuries before, and by Hannibal's lumbering war elephants ten centuries before that.

The ancient alpine route was well traveled but not easy. Winding along foaming rivers, skirting the faces of looming glaciers, the road was often blocked by rock or ice, occasionally cut by landslides; the June weather alternated between mild sunshine, fierce rainstorms, and occasional brief blizzards. If not for the help of a band of monks crossing from Turin to Grenoble, Simone and his friend might never have completed the crossing. But complete it they did, and as they followed the Rhône down to the arches of the beautiful bridge and the bustling papal city on the hill, Provence had wrapped her warm arms around Simone like a sweet lover, and he'd found Avignon to be quite fetching.

Also quite chaotic. If ever a modern-day Babel existed, surely it was Avignon. The official language of the church was Latin, but with French cardinals and courtiers, Roman emissaries, German and English theologians, aimless Spaniards in varying degrees of drunkenness, and the Provençal natives jabbering in their own ancestral dialect, it was not uncommon to hear half a dozen languages within the space of a block, and to understand none of them. Fortunately, a city so brimming with languages was also brimming with translators, so Simone found ways to communicate.

He spent his first few days sketching faces and buildings in the city's main squares and churches, but then—inspired by the chance sighting of a cart bearing a body to a graveyard—he decided to cast his net in different waters: the waters of the Styx, river of death. Simone liked knowing that he was swimming against the current, and he smiled as he thought of a passage of scripture he was deliberately turning on its head. The day of Christ's Resurrection, when His grieving followers went to visit His tomb, an angel had asked them, "Why do you seek the living among the dead?" Here in bustling, booming Avignon, Simone set about to seek the dead among the living.

His initial inquiries, at charnel houses and hospitals and apothecaries, were met with suspicion and incredulity, not surprisingly. After all, why would any artist in his right mind want to draw corpses when he could paint pretty women instead—chaste virgins or, better yet, lovely madonnas, baring ripe breasts to suckle holy infants? But gradually, as he persisted in his rounds and deployed his charm and his coins, nuns and priests and gravediggers began to trust and like the crazy painter. Fortune smiled on him during his second week in Avignon: A stonemason fell from a scaffold in the nave of a church, breaking his neck when he hit the floor. The sketches of his corpse would surely be useful references for some future painting of the death of Lazarus or the murder of Abel. Two days after the mason's fall, a child was trampled by a runaway horse—not ideal, the mangled little body, yet still potentially helpful if Simone is someday commissioned to depict, say, King Herod's Slaughter of the Innocents.

But this latest find—a robust man killed by crucifixion!—this, for a fresco painter, was manna from heaven. Simone had profusely thanked both God and the jailer for this unique opportunity. To God, he expressed his thanks in prayers; to the jailer, in florins.

Now, studying the corpse in the warm glow of the flickering lamps, he marvels at how poorly the crucified Christ is always portrayed. In every representation Simone has ever seen—and ever done—the wounds look contrived, even silly, with their spurting fountains of blood, and the flesh and bone lack any semblance of sinew or substance. For the first time, Simone Martini feels a sense of obligation and duty—not to the sacred subject matter of some scene he's being paid to paint, but to the human subject himself, this dead man offering himself so freely to the hungry gaze of the artist. "This is my body," the man seems to be saying, "which is broken for you. Feast your eyes upon it." And so Simone does, devouring the visual banquet of legs, belly, chest, face, and ignoring the jailer's panicked pleas for haste.

Simone's first drawings of the corpse are quick and crude—a flurry of fast, flowing lines he makes without even lifting the charcoal, without even taking his eyes off the body to inspect his work. Despite their swiftness and spareness, the sketches capture the essence of the lifeless form: the long, sad face; the strong sinews, now gone slack; the tangibility and carnality of the corpse. Next he makes detailed drawings of individual structures—fingers, feet, nose, eyes, ears—cramming pages full of body parts, like macabre still lifes of some thoroughly dismembered corpse. Finally, having gotten to know the dead man in all his particulars, he draws the entire body with great care. Except that what he draws is not, in fact, the body; what he draws is light and shadow—but no, he draws even less than that. His charcoal pencils cannot draw light, they can only sketch darkness: shades of shadows, ranging from the watery gray of dawn to the soft, utter blackness of velvet. And such magic

Simone can work with shadows! Curving a shadow around an oval of blank white, he can create the illusion of roundness and of highlight: the illusion of an egg, or a forehead, or a breast. And from two simple elements—shadow and not-shadow—he now conjures flesh, blood, hair, fingernails, even mortality and mournfulness. Seeing this magic unfold, the jailer is bewitched, finally forgets his fears, and watches in rapt silence.

At last, just as the first paleness of dawn begins showing through the narrow slits that pretend to provide air and light to the prisoners' cells, Simone tucks the remaining stubs of charcoal into his cloak, rolls the sheaves of drawings, and nods his readiness to leave. After making sure the way is clear, the jailer leads him out. He is about to close the door when the painter stops him, speaking for the first time since entering the cell and beholding the dead man on the floor. "What can you tell me about him? What crime did he commit to merit such a death?"

The jailer—a man who has witnessed, and who has inflicted, more than a few deaths in his service to the Church—fixes the painter with a long look. Answering questions—especially troubling questions—was not part of the bargain he made with the Italian. He shakes his head and withdraws through the stone archway, and the door groans on its hinges. But just before it closes completely, he puts his lips to the narrow gap. "They claim he preached words from the Devil," he says, "but I heard him speak only with kindness and faith. I'm a simple man; I don't pretend to understand the arguments of these churchmen. But his crime, I think, was to put them to shame by his faith and his goodness. I do believe he was a holy man—the only holy man I've seen in my twenty years among cardinals and popes. His sin, I think, was to be free of sin."

"You make him sound like Christ reincarnated."

"I don't expect him to rise from the grave, Master Simone. But if he does, the bastards will find a reason to kill him again."

The vertical strip of shadow narrows, darkening into a thin black line, and then it is gone, displaced by oak planks and iron hardware. The opening into the darkness has closed, at least for now. Simone Martini—altered in ways he will not understand for years, if ever—turns from the realm of shadow and illusion and death, resuming his place in the world of life and breath, light and color.

CHAPTER 20

Avignon
The Present

LIGHT AND COLOR FILLED the square, a leafy park that was jammed this Sunday morning with tables of bright fabrics, fresh flowers, watercolor paintings, and Provençal delicacies—cheeses, wine, honey, olive oil, strawberries, raspberries. Miranda was auditioning samples of cheese and wine—wine tasting at 10 A.M.—to round out our picnic basket. Stefan had offered to meet us here and take us on a field trip to the Pont du Gard, an ancient aqueduct that was one of Rome's finest feats of engineering. I wasn't looking forward to having him along, but I was excited about the aqueduct. "Listen to this," I said, glancing up from the guidebook. "The aqueduct is sixteen stories high and fifteen hundred feet long, but it drops only one inch from one end to the other. Can you imagine building with that kind of precision two thousand years ago?"

"*Mmm*." Miranda smacked her lips. "I can imagine eating my weight in this goat cheese."

"It carried forty-four million gallons of water a day. Isn't that something?"

"You really are in touch with your inner nerd, you know that?"

"Where's Stefan? He was supposed to be here half an hour ago, wasn't he?"

"Forty-five minutes."

"Try his cell phone, will you?"

"I have. Twice. My call went straight to voice mail."

"Try it again. Maybe he's over at the palace."

"Oh, I'm *sure* he's at the palace," she groused. "Which is why he's not getting my calls. A nuclear blast couldn't get through those walls, let alone a cell phone signal."

"Then let's just go over there," I suggested. "Seems silly to sit here and wait for him. Either he forgot about the plan, or he got sidetracked by something."

I hoisted the backpack over one shoulder—Miranda had managed to cram a hefty load of lunch treats into it—and we headed for the palace, a ten-minute walk away. As we approached, Miranda phoned again, but once more the call went to Stefan's voice mail.

At the palace's main entrance, we flashed our badges, ducked behind a cordon, and threaded our way down the staircases that led to the base of the treasury tower. "I assume he's locked the gate behind him," I fretted. "Do you think he'll hear us if we yell?"

"I've got a pretty good set of lungs," she said. "The last guy who grabbed me in a parking garage got a perforated eardrum to go along with his scratches and bruises."

Surprisingly, though, Stefan hadn't locked the gate; he hadn't even bothered to close it. "He must be expecting us," I said. "Either that, or he's getting really careless."

"If he was expecting us, he should've left the lights on," Miranda grumbled. She flipped open her cell phone to wake up the display screen, and used the light to scan the wall for the switch.

"Ingenious," I said. "You're so resourceful."

"Hey, I grew up watching *MacGyver*. I can make a computer out of matchsticks and paper clips."

"Really?" Even by the faint glow of the phone, I could see her eyes roll. "Oh. You were being sarcastic."

"Not sarcastic. Only hyperbolic."

"Miranda, if you hope to have *any* success in academia, you've got to stop exaggerating. If I've told you once, I've told you—"

"Yeah, yeah, a billion times," she interrupted. "The same number of times you've told me that joke. *Damn* it, where's the switch?" She yelped as a spark split the darkness, followed by the feeble glow of bulbs trailing down the staircase like luminous bread crumbs.

I'd expected the subtreasury to be brightly lit by the work lights, but it wasn't. Miranda looked worried as we stepped into the gloom. "Stefan?" No answer. "Stefan, are you in here?" Silence. "Come on, Stefan, this isn't funny. If you're in here, come on out. You're creeping me out." The only sound I heard was Miranda's breathing, which had turned fast and ragged.

"Let's turn on the work lights," I suggested, as much to distract Miranda as anything else. "Can you find the switches for those?"

She opened her cell phone again and disappeared behind one of the support pillars; a moment later, my eyelids and pupils clamped down against the glare of the halogen bulbs.

The lights only underscored the emptiness of the room. Miranda looked at me; wordlessly, we headed for the blue tarp that curtained off the excavation area. I ducked around one end of the tarp, Miranda around the other. Our eyes automatically swiveled to the same spot. The table was empty; the bones were gone.

"I feel sick," Miranda said. "Whatever's going on, it's not good."

"Maybe not," I conceded, "but let's try not to panic. Let's look around a little more, then go outside and try to reach Stefan again." She nodded, chewing her lip.

I studied the table where we'd laid out the bones in anatomical order. The white sheet was still in place; a few small smudges and stains confirmed that yes, this was where the bones had lain. I lifted the fabric that overhung the table and stooped to peer beneath it. "The ossuary's gone, too," she predicted, and she was right. "Goddamn it," she said, but there was no heat behind the curse, just weariness. "I should have known."

"Known what?"

"Known better. Known something would go wrong. Known that Stefan was working an angle. Known that he was still the same guy who cheats on his wife, shafts his colleagues, or does some other damn selfish thing that's gonna blow up in our faces and make *us* the collateral damage, the civilian casualties, the friendly-fire deaths." I considered trotting out my exaggeration joke yet again, but it dawned on me that Miranda might not be exaggerating this time. "He's taken the bones and skipped town," she said. "I just know it. They're probably on eBay right now."

"They won't be on eBay," I said, "but they sure aren't here, and I don't see a helpful note explaining why. Let's lock up and see if we can find out what the hell's going on."

We switched off the work lights, climbed the stairs, and switched off the dim string of bulbs in the stairwell. By the faint light of Miranda's phone, I wrestled the heavy gate shut, then hit a problem. "I don't see the lock," I told Miranda.

She brought the phone closer, playing its bluish-white glow over the hasp and then the nearby bars. "Hmm." She widened her search, sweeping the light horizontally across the entire gate at waist height, then in progressively lower tracks at each horizontal crossbar. When she reached the level of the floor, she grunted, then said softly, "Oh, shit." I bent to look at whatever she'd seen.

The padlock—the industrial-strength lock with the inch-thick shackle of hardened steel—had been cut in half.

"NOW WHAT?" ASKED Miranda.

We'd voiced our concerns to the ranking security officer at the palace; he took notes and promised to investigate, but he didn't seem nearly as worried as Miranda and I were. After that, we'd gone to the police station, but the entrance was locked. A notice taped to the glass door announced FERMÉ—JOUR FÉRIÉ. OUVERT LUNDI. "Damn," said Miranda. "Closed. Religious holiday. Open Monday."

"Swell," I said. "It'd be a great day to rob a bank, if we weren't otherwise occupied." I hesitated. "Do you . . . happen to have a key to Stefan's apartment?"

She punched me in the shoulder. "*No,* I don't happen to have a key to his apartment, but thanks for the vote of confidence. I came to work, not to get laid." She drew a deep breath and exhaled slowly. "Sorry; my issue, not yours. It was a reasonable question. But the answer's still no. I don't have a key."

"Do you know where it is?"

"What, the key?"

"No, Einstein, the apartment," I said.

"Ah. Actually, I do know where the apartment is. Stefan invited me for dinner the first night. I think I can find it again. It's not far from the palace, and it's got a balcony with a view of the palace and cathedral. If we stand at the front of the cathedral, I bet I can spot his balcony, and then we can figure out how to get to his building."

Fueled by fear, we hurried back to the main plaza and scurried up the staircase to the cathedral, positioning ourselves directly in front of an immense crucifix. Shading her eyes against the late-morning sun, Miranda scanned the skyline. "I wish I hadn't had that third glass of wine that night," she said. "The view of the palace and the cathedral was great. I remember that much, but not much more than that." She frowned, shaking her head. "*Damn it. Why didn't I pay more attention?*"

I couldn't resist the opening. "Hmm, maybe because you were delirious from appendicitis?" Her elbow caught me just beneath the ribs. "*Youch!* Now it's *my* appendix that's exploding. Come on, you know you deserved that."

"Yeah, I know. Sorry—I'm taking out my guilt on you. It's less painful that way." She gave me another token jab. "See? I feel better already."

"So, the night of the winefest, you went out on the balcony. Were you standing? Perching on stools? Sitting on a stone balustrade?" She shrugged. "Doing handstands on a metal railing?"

"*Yes!*" she suddenly shouted, grabbing my arm. "That's it—a metal railing. A cheap-ass, flimsy metal railing. One of the damn welds broke when I leaned on it. I almost fell off, from five stories up. Dogs would've been licking my brains off the sidewalk. Only thing that kept me from falling was a windsock I managed to grab." She shook her head. "*That's* why I didn't go to bed with Stefan that night, even though I was looped and he was trying to put the moves on me. I thought, *You bastard, you let me lean on this cheap-ass, flimsy railing that could've killed me. You're still the same thoughtless, selfish sonofabitch you were last time I saw you.* It's true, Dr. B—*plus ça change, plus c'est la même chose.*"

"Huh?"

"Old French saying. 'The more things change, the more they stay the same.'"

"I prefer Eckhart's warning about the price of inaction," I said. "Come on, let's look for a fifth-story

balcony with a cheap-ass, flimsy metal railing." Together we studied the buildings that overlooked the
plaza, the palace, and the cathedral.

"It was a block or two away," she said. "Maybe
three. I remember rooftops between Stefan's place
and the palace." Suddenly she smacked herself in
the forehead. "Jesus, Mary, and Joseph, what a
dumb-ass. I took a picture from the balcony with
my iPhone." She fished out the phone and whisked
her finger across the screen, scrolling through her
photos. "Here it is!" She performed a magician-
like maneuver with her fingertips, and the view
zoomed in, enlarging the details at the center of the
photo. The image was small—not even the size of
a postcard—but it was crisp enough to show three
sets of tiled rooftops, a cluster of chimneys, and a
thicket of television aerials between the lens and the
spot where we were standing. I studied the photo,
looking for distinctive features that would help me
lock in on the balcony. "*Got* it," she said, squeezing
my arm again, then pointing. "The modern building? The one with the ugly TV antennas on top?"

"I see it."

"One floor from the top, slightly left of center.
See that red and blue and yellow thing? That's the
wind sock that saved my life."

"Let's go," I said.

She didn't answer. She was already halfway down
the stairs.

WE TOOK TWO wrong turns in the maze of streets to
the west of the palace, but within twenty minutes

we were standing before the glass-doored entrance to Stefan's building. The doors were locked—not surprising—but I'd given no thought to what we'd do once we found the place.

"Now what?" I said.

She scanned the sidewalks on either side of the street, then pointed to a shoe store that was two doors down. "Come on. Have you got some money?"

"This is your idea of a plan? To buy shoes?"

"Watch and learn."

Five minutes and ten euros later, we walked out of the shoe store, laden with shopping bags filled with shoe boxes. Empty shoe boxes. The clerk had stared at us as if we were crazy, but buying a dozen boxes was a lot cheaper than buying a dozen pairs of shoes. Our hands conspicuously full, we loitered in front of a women's clothing boutique next to the apartment entrance, pretending to window-shop. A saleswoman smiled and beckoned to us from inside—our bags marked us as big spenders—but Miranda fended her off with a slight shake of the head. The woman's smile faded, and her expression shifted to disappointment, then suspicion. Suddenly Miranda hissed, "*Now!*"

A middle-aged man had just emerged from the apartments, and the door was swinging shut behind him. "*Monsieur, monsieur, s'il vous plaît,*" Miranda called. The man looked our way, and—seeing an attractive young woman struggling with an armful of packages and a faceful of smile—he caught the door and held it. Miranda sashayed inside with a "*Merci beaucoup,*" trailing feminine mystique and me in her wake.

We tucked our shopping bags behind a potted palm tree in a corner of the lobby and called the elevator. When we got off on Stefan's floor, Miranda turned right. Walking slowly, she studied the doors on the far side of the hallway—the side facing the palace. She hesitated in front of a door marked 407, then moved on.

"Don't you remember which one is his?"

"*Sshh.*"

"Wasn't his balcony the third from the end?"

"*SSHH!*" She sounded scarily like the German woman in Turin Cathedral.

Three doors from the end, at 405, she stopped and nodded, pointing at a small, half-peeled decal on the door. With the knuckle of her index finger, she rapped three times, then pressed her ear to the wood and listened. Wordlessly she shook her head. She knocked again, louder this time, and once more she listened. Nothing. She reached for the knob and slowly, slowly tried it. To my surprise, the door opened and we stepped inside.

The apartment was a mess: dirty dishes in the sink and on the kitchen counters, clothes everywhere, mail and stacks of papers strewn on every horizontal surface that wasn't occupied by dishes. My first thought was that the place had been ransacked, but my second thought—considering that ransackers don't tend to smear food on plates and silverware—was that Stefan was a terrible slob. "Not exactly a neat freak," I observed. "Was it like this the night you were here?"

"No, it was neater than this." Miranda surveyed the carnage in the kitchen. "I think that plate there—the one with the dried hummus and moldy pita bread?—I think that was mine. And I'm pretty sure that's my wineglass; it has my lipstick on it."

I refrained—barely—from asking, *Since when do you wear lipstick?*

It was in the bedroom that my mental pendulum swung back to my first thought. Having lived alone for years now, I knew what bachelor clutter looked like: dirty clothes strewn on the floor; clean clothes piled on the dresser and bed. Mostly I kept a handle on my housekeeping, though occasionally the clutter got out of hand. But Stefan's bedroom was beyond cluttered; Stefan's bedroom was a study in chaos. All the drawers of the dresser hung open, empty or nearly so; shoes, sweaters, even spare linens had been pulled from the closet floor and shelf; the overstuffed armchair in one corner of the room lay on its side, the fabric lining on its underside in tatters. "Somebody's been here looking for something," I said, feeling a chill run up my spine.

"I've got a bad feeling about this, boss," Miranda murmured.

"Call Stefan's phone again."

"I've already called a dozen times. I called just before we went in the shoe store."

"I know, but we weren't in here when you did. I'm sure he's not going to answer. I want to know if his phone's in here."

"Ah. Good idea." She hit the redial button, and through her speaker, I heard his phone beginning to ring. Unless the ringer was off or the battery was dead, his phone wasn't here.

After five or six rings, I expected to hear a voice

mail coming faintly through the speaker. What I heard instead electrified me. There was a click, then silence: The call had been accepted, but whoever took it didn't speak. Miranda's eyes, big as saucers, met mine. "Hello?" she said. "Stefan?" No response. "Who is this?" she demanded. "Where is Stefan?" There was a long silence on the other end of the line, and then a click, and the screen flashed the message *Call ended*.

"TAKE A RIGHT here," I said. "I think it's in this block."

"Where are we going, and why?" Miranda was edgy, and I didn't blame her.

"A few nights ago—it was the night before we went to Turin—I couldn't sleep, so I went for a walk. It was late, around midnight. I bumped into Stefan. He was coming out of the palace."

"At *midnight*?"

"Yeah. We walked around for, I don't know, half an hour or so." Just ahead, on the left, I spotted the passageway leading from the Rue Saint-Agricol. "He brought me here." I led her through the corridor and into the courtyard. "This used to be the chapel of the Knights Templar. Stefan had a key—funny, Stefan seems to have keys to everything—and he took me inside. He was kinda dragging his heels when we left." Suddenly I remembered. "When *I* left. I walked away, but he didn't—he hung around here, and I wondered if maybe he was waiting for somebody else to show up. He acted anxious to get rid of me, you know? And he stayed behind after he shooed me away."

"Jesus, why didn't you tell me this sooner?"

"The truth?"

"Please."

"I wondered if maybe he was meeting you. A moonlight rendezvous in the chapel of the Templars." She didn't say anything, but I noticed the muscles of her jaw working. Reluctantly, I reached for the black iron knob, hoping that it would not turn in my hand. But it did. The chapel's heavy wooden door swung inward, and Miranda and I stepped inside.

The air was cool in the stone interior—cool, pungent, and coppery. It was a mixture of smells I knew only too well. "Maybe you'd better wait outside," I told Miranda.

"Hell, no." I knew there was no point arguing with her.

A maroon velvet drape separated the entryway from the soaring, vaulted space of the chapel itself. As I held the curtain aside, Miranda stepped through, and I followed half a step behind.

She gasped and reached back for me, her fingers digging into my arm. Then she turned and buried her face in my chest.

Congealing on the stone floor was a pool of blood, already black at its rim, still red at the center. High overhead was the arched metal truss that supported the theater lights. Suspended horizontally from a cable and pulley at the center of the truss was a short wooden beam. And nailed to that beam—like some modern-day minimalist crucifix—was the nude body of Stefan Beauvoir.

PART II

The Second Coming

Turning and turning in the widening gyre
The falcon cannot hear the falconer;
Things fall apart; the centre cannot hold;
Mere anarchy is loosed upon the world,
The blood-dimmed tide is loosed, and everywhere
The ceremony of innocence is drowned;
The best lack all conviction, while the worst
Are full of passionate intensity.

Surely some revelation is at hand;
Surely the Second Coming is at hand.
The Second Coming! Hardly are those words out
When a vast image out of Spiritus Mundi
Troubles my sight: somewhere in sands of the desert
A shape with lion body and the head of a man,
A gaze blank and pitiless as the sun,
Is moving its slow thighs, while all about it
Reel shadows of the indignant desert birds.
The darkness drops again; but now I know
That twenty centuries of stony sleep
Were vexed to nightmare by a rocking cradle,
And what rough beast, its hour come round at last,
Slouches towards Bethlehem to be born?

—WILLIAM BUTLER YEATS

CHAPTER 21

FOR A LAW-ENFORCEMENT AGENCY that had locked its doors and taken a holiday, the French Police Nationale now responded with impressive speed and force. Barely five minutes after Miranda had dragged a startled French passerby into the gruesome chapel—a desperate measure, but that's what it took to persuade him we had a true emergency—I heard the two-note clarinet warble of a French siren. It was soon joined by another, then a third, then a fourth. The cacophonous quartet crescendoed and then died as the caravan of police cars screeched to a halt in the narrow street outside. Eight uniformed officers charged toward us through the passageway and across the courtyard. Miranda and the passerby waved them into the chapel as I held the door. When they saw Stefan's body hanging in midair, his face a mask of agony, two of the officers crossed themselves; one, a close-cropped young man who couldn't have been a day over twenty, staggered back to the doorway and vomited, barely missing my shoes.

A wiry, forty-something man with the crisp bearing of a former soldier took charge, ordering two of his underlings to cordon off the area. It wasn't hard to do; they simply taped off the ten-foot-wide mouth of the corridor that led to the street. The words stretched across the opening were in French—ZONE INTERDITE—POLICE TECHNIQUE ET SCIENTIFIQUE—but the yellow-and-black tape spoke the universal language of crime scenes.

Talking in rapid-fire French with the man who'd placed the emergency call, the officer in charge—Sergeant Henri Petitjean, according to the ID bar on his chest—divided his attention (that is to say, his piercing glare) between the shell-shocked man, Miranda, and me. The unfortunate Passerby, who had probably been anticipating a leisurely Sunday-morning *café au lait* and baguette, was doing a lot of exasperated shrugging and indignant pointing—the shrugging at the policeman, the pointing at us; eventually, he gave a dismissive wave of his hand and turned to leave. In a flash, the policeman spun him around, pinned him to the wall, and made it crystal clear that he was not going *anywhere* except to one of the courtyard café tables, where he ordered the shaken man to sit.

The soldierly sergeant turned to us. "*Monsieur et madame. Parlez-vous français?*"

I knew enough French to know that he was asking if we spoke French. I also knew enough to say, "*Non, pardon. Anglais?*"

He glared at me, then turned his hawkish eyes on Miranda. *"Madame?"*

Miranda gave a regretful head shake. "Only a little bit. *Seulement un petit peu. Nous sommes américains."*

"Ah. Americans. *Quel dommage."* Too bad for him, or too bad for us? He touched the radio transmitter on his shoulder and spoke rapidly into it. I could make out almost nothing of what he said, except for French-sounding versions of *homicide* and *crucifixion*. Amid the hissing, crackling reply, I heard *"Crucifixion?"* He touched the transmitter again and repeated it. *"Oui, crucifixion."* The same question came over his receiver again. This time he practically smashed the transmit button. *"Oui! Crucifixion, crucifixion, cru-ci-FIX-ion!"* This time his meaning got through; I heard the dispatcher's *"Merde! Mon Dieu!"*—"Shit! My God!"—and then, after a pause, what sounded like the English words "day cart." This response seemed to satisfy the officer. He grunted by way of a sign-off and then led Miranda and me to another of the café tables, some distance from the glowering Frenchman whose morning we'd ruined, and motioned for us to sit. He posted one of the officers beside the French pedestrian and posted another, the vomiter, near our table. The queasy young man had regained his composure by now, but his face remained ashen, and the muscle at the corner of his right eye was pulsing as if it were hooked to an electrode.

It wasn't long before a forensic team—equipped with white biohazard suits, cameras, and evidence kits—arrived and entered the chapel. Not far behind them came a plainclothes officer, whom I took to be a detective. He looked to be about my age; his wavy black hair was going to gray, as were his bushy, tufted eyebrows. His brown eyes were deeply recessed beneath a prominent brow ridge. His complexion was the slightly sallow olive tone of Mediterranean peoples, and under his eyes were deep lines and dark circles, almost blue-black. His shirt cuffs and collar were frayed, his black pants had faded to a dull charcoal, and his shoes were badly scuffed.

The detective and the uniformed sergeant conferred in low tones beside the chapel door; at one point the detective paused and leaned backward, peering around the sergeant to study Miranda and me, then straightened and continued the murmured conversation. After several minutes of this, he and the officer entered the chapel.

The detective spoke briefly with the disgruntled civilian who'd gotten roped into the drama, then allowed the man to leave. Casting a final baleful glance in our direction, the man ducked under the crime-scene tape and vanished.

"Good morning," said the detective, nodding first at Miranda, then at me. "You two found the body, yes? I need to ask you some questions." His English was crisp and fluent, with a hint of a British accent. "My name is Inspector René Descartes." He took out a notepad and flipped it open, then uncapped a pen and began to write.

"Like the philosopher?" asked Miranda. "The Descartes who said, 'I think, therefore I am'?"

"Yes, that one. We are related—by blood, or by wishful thinking. 'I think I am a relative, therefore I *am* a relative.'" Miranda managed a slight, strained smile before he continued. "Tell me what happened. But first, your names, and spell them, please." We did; his eyebrows lifted slightly when Miranda said "Lovelady," but he didn't comment. "You're both Americans?" We nodded. "Are you traveling together?"

"Yes," said Miranda, at the very moment that I said, "No." The pen hovered above the notepad. Descartes looked up, his gaze lighting first on Miranda, then swiveling to me, before returning to Miranda again. She flushed slightly. "We're working together," she explained.

"But she got here before I did," I added.

"I see," he said in a neutral tone. "Mr. . . ." He checked his notepad. "Mr. Brockton, would you please wait here? Have a seat. Make yourself comfortable." *Sure*, I thought. *Comfortable—no problem. Stefan's dead, and this guy's bound to consider us suspects. Very comfortable.* "Mademoiselle Lovelady, would you come with me, please?"

He led her to a table in the farthest corner of the courtyard, offering her a chair before taking one himself. He drew his chair close to hers, possibly so they could speak more privately but more likely so she would feel off balance, unsettled by the intrusion into her personal space—a favorite interrogation technique, I knew, of homicide investigators.

He interviewed Miranda for what seemed an eternity—more than an hour, in any case, for I'm sure I heard a bell toll eleven, and later counted twelve. *It tolls for thee, Stefan,* I thought. Finally he brought Miranda back and motioned for me to follow him. Miranda's eyes were wet and red rimmed. I offered her my handkerchief, but she shook her head and wiped her eyes with the back of her hand. I gave her shoulder a quick squeeze, then followed the inspector to the distant corner.

"I'm sorry this takes so long," he began. "As you can imagine, this is a very unusual crime. And a very disturbing one."

"Yes, of course," I said. "A good murder investigation takes time."

He smiled. "Mademoiselle tells me you know a lot about murder investigations. In fact, I am somewhat familiar with your career. One of our big French newspapers, *Le Monde*, published a story about the Body Farm a few years ago. I still have it in my files. Very interesting work. Someday, if I visit the United States, I would like to see your research facility."

"Certainly." I took out my wallet and fished out a business card. "Just let us know when you're coming." He took the card and read the front, then flipped it over and studied the back. "What are these lines and markings? It looks like a small measuring scale."

"Exactly," I said. "If I'm taking pictures at a death scene and need to show the size of a bone, I've always got one of these, even if I don't have a ruler or tape measure."

He nodded. "Very useful. Very clever." He flipped a page in the notebook, which was half filled now with notes from his interview of Miranda. "So, please, Dr. Brockton"—I took it as a good sign that he'd promoted me from "Mr." to "Dr."—"tell me about the events of this morning. Start at the beginning. Take all the time you need."

He took copious notes as I talked, interrupting occasionally to ask me to slow down a bit, or to reword a phrase he didn't fully understand, or to clarify a point.

He bore down on me when I told how Miranda and I had looked around Stefan's apartment. "Why did you go there?"

"We were looking for him. He wasn't at the palace; we hoped we'd find him at home."

"Why didn't you just call him?"

"We did. Many times. I'm surprised Miranda didn't tell you that." His eyes flickered almost imperceptibly, which I took to mean that she *had* told him, and that he was simply cross-checking our stories. "We also went to the police station, but we couldn't get in. There's probably a security-camera video of us knocking on the door, right?" He shrugged. "Anyhow, by that time, we were really worried about him. Looking at his apartment seemed like the only thing we could do."

"But you went inside the apartment. I have to say, that was unfortunate. That looks suspicious. Why did you do that?"

"We were worried," I repeated, "and the door was open. We were afraid he might be sick, or hurt."

"Did he seem unhealthy to you, the last time you saw him?"

"No. But people get sick without warning; people die without warning. I had a friend who was forty-six—my friend Tim, a strong, athletic guy—who had a stroke one day out of the blue, dropped dead instantly. I knew a healthy young woman, a television reporter, who dropped dead in the middle of her nightly news broadcast. Another friend of mine slipped and hit her head on the bathroom floor; she lay there for two days before she came out of her coma and managed to call an ambulance."

"Remind me not to become your friend," he said. "It sounds very bad for the health."

"*Touché*, Inspector." I smiled. "The point is, unexpected things happen. If we'd known Stefan was dead, we wouldn't have gone in. And if we were his killers, we *certainly* wouldn't have left fingerprints on the doors and light switches and who knows where else. I know better than to contaminate a crime scene, Inspector. We just didn't know it *was* a crime scene."

He wasted no time pouncing on that. "What makes you say that the apartment is a crime scene?"

"Drawers were dumped out, Inspector. Furniture was cut open. If it's not a crime scene, it's the messiest apartment in France. Before we saw his apartment, I was just worried; after we saw it, I was sure something bad had happened. That's when I thought to come here, to the chapel. If we hadn't gone into his apartment, the murder wouldn't even have been discovered yet."

He was still frowning. "But why did you think to come here, to the Templar chapel? How did you know he would be here?"

"I *didn't* know he'd be here. But I thought it was worth looking."

"Why? What made you think that?"

"I'm not sure. For one thing, I suppose this was

the only place that I knew Stefan had some sort of . . . *connection* to, besides his apartment and the Palace of the Popes. But that's not all. This place seemed important to him for some reason. He brought me here one night last week—I couldn't sleep, so I went out for a walk. It was very late—almost midnight—but I ran into Stefan on the street. We walked around for a while, and he brought me here, showed me the chapel, took me inside. He had a key; said he was friends with the owner. It was strange, though. Almost like he was letting me in on a secret."

"What secret, Dr. Brockton?"

I shook my head. "I wish I knew. I just got the feeling that this place was more than an old building to Stefan." I picked at my memories and intuitions a bit deeper. "There was something about the way he was behaving," I finally managed. "When we first got here, it was almost like he was checking the place out—he looked up and down the street very carefully before he led me through the passageway, and he checked the courtyard before we went inside the chapel. And then, when we left, he sent me away, but he stayed behind. It was almost like he was eager to get rid of me." A realization finally crystallized. "Almost like he was expecting someone else to show up very soon."

He leaned forward, his gaze intensifying. "Any idea who he was expecting?"

"None. Sorry. I wish I did."

He leaned back, obviously disappointed, and studied his notes. Then he rubbed his eyes and took a deep breath, followed by another. "Inspector? Are you okay?"

He gave his head a shake, blinked hard, and raised his bushy eyebrows high, as if to open his eyes as wide as possible. "I'm just a little tired," he said. "I put in some long hours on a case recently. An art forger who committed suicide." He suppressed a yawn. "Tell me about Mademoiselle Lovelady."

The request caught me by surprise. "Miranda? She's great. Smart as hell. Hardworking. Strong-minded. Funny. Spunky."

"Spunky? What is *spunky*?"

"It's slang. It means feisty. Brave. Tough."

"Ah. In French, we say *plein de cran*. 'Full of guts.'"

"Oh, yes, gutsy. Miranda is very gutsy."

"Do you trust her, this gutsy assistant?"

"Miranda? Completely. I'd trust her with my life."

Descartes flipped back through his notes, twirling his pen between his fingers. He had just looked up to ask another question when his cell phone rang. Excusing himself, he stood up and walked toward the mouth of the passageway to take the call. He was gone for several minutes. When he returned, he sat, looked me square in the eyes, and said, "Your assistant—what was her relationship with Monsieur Beauvoir?"

The question caught me off guard, and Descartes would have to have been blind not to notice. "Fine, I think. He asked her to come help with this excavation, so he clearly thought well of her. She came, so I assume she thought well of him, too."

"Do you know why they thought so well of one another? And for how long a time?" *Crap*, I thought, *not this*.

"I think they met six or eight years ago. When she was an undergraduate student. Miranda was on a dig in Guatemala that Stefan organized."

He chewed absentmindedly on the end of a fingernail, still eyeing me closely. "Did you know that they were lovers?"

There, the shoe had dropped; I had known that question was coming. "It wasn't any of my business if they had a personal relationship."

He shrugged. "But did you know?"

"Yes. She told me shortly after I got here. She felt awkward about it."

"Awkward about telling you? Or awkward about being lovers with him?"

"Both, I guess. But it was very brief, and it happened a long time ago, Inspector. I think *lovers* is too strong a word. It was a quick fling at a field school. It happens all the time."

"All the time?" He raised his eyebrows and tilted his head slightly.

I flushed at the innuendo. "Not all the time, but it happens. It doesn't necessarily mean very much. I thought the French were very tolerant about casual love affairs."

"Sometimes. Not when one of the lovers ends up crucified. Tell me, was she angry with Monsieur Beauvoir? Resentful?"

"Resentful? About what?"

"About anything. About what happened in Guatemala. About what happened—or what *didn't* happen—in Avignon." Good God, did he actually think Miranda might have nailed Stefan to that beam?

"Look, Inspector, Miranda and I have worked together for six years. I never heard her mention this guy until she told me she was coming here. If she were burning with rage for years—or longing for love—I think I'd have heard about it."

He shrugged again, and I found the gesture annoying; it might simply mean "Who knows?" but it might also mean "What the hell do you know?" "Do you know where Mademoiselle Lovelady was last night?"

I returned the shrug. "I assume she was in her hotel room."

"And do you know where Monsieur Beauvoir was last night?"

I flung up my hands in exasperation. "Well, if I were *guessing*," I said sarcastically, "which is all I can do, I'd *guess* that for the first part of the night, he was in his apartment, and for the rest of the night, he was here in the chapel dying."

He smiled slightly, ironically. "Actually, he was in Mademoiselle Lovelady's hotel room until almost midnight." His words felt like a punch in the gut. He studied my reaction. "You seem surprised."

"I . . . Yes. I'm surprised. But as I said, whatever personal relationship they might have had—or might *not* have had—it's none of my business."

"I disagree, Dr. Brockton. Normally, no. But now—with Monsieur Beauvoir hanging there in the chapel—I think it is very much your business. You are involved, in some way, with a murder. You are swept up in the tide of events. You do not have the luxury of detachment."

His words were confirmed by a sinking feeling

in my gut. Somehow, for reasons I could not begin to fathom, I had turned a fateful corner in the labyrinthine streets of Avignon, and I wasn't at all sure I could find my way out of the maze again.

"Excuse me? Dr. Brockton?" His voice sounded faraway; I felt as if I were swimming up from deep water to reach it, and I had the impression he'd called my name more than once.

"I'm sorry. Yes?"

"Dr. Brockton, where were *you* last night?"

"*Me?*" I stared at him in astonishment. He nodded. "I was in my hotel room."

"The same hotel as mademoiselle?"

"No. A different one. A little inn near the ramparts. It's called Lumani."

"Ah, *oui*, Lumani. You found a beautiful place to stay."

"Actually, Stefan found it for me. I think he knows the owners. *Knew* the owners."

"Docteur, were *you* angry with Monsieur Beauvoir?"

"Why on earth would I be angry with him?"

"Perhaps you were jealous of his attentions to your assistant."

"Oh, please," I said. "I wasn't. But even if I was, I certainly wouldn't kill anyone over something like that. Besides, I didn't even know that he went to see Miranda last night until you told me just now."

"Perhaps you were angry that he tricked you into coming to Avignon. That was very manipulative, *non*?"

"It was, and I didn't like it. But once I found out the reason for the trick, I understood."

"And what, exactly, was the reason for this trick?"

"Didn't Miranda explain it to you?"

"She did give me her explanation. Now I'm asking for your explanation."

"She and Stefan had uncovered some very old bones in the Palace of the Popes," I said. "The ossuary—the bone box—was engraved with an inscription that might cause big news." He said nothing; simply waited. "The inscription claimed that the ossuary contained the bones of Jesus Christ. If that inscription proves to be true, this is the most sensational find of the past two thousand years."

He stopped writing. "But how can you prove whether they are real or fake? You can't use DNA testing, I think. Because you don't have DNA from Jesus to compare."

"Exactly," I agreed. "But some people would argue with you. Some people think you could get DNA from the bloodstains on the Shroud of Turin. I don't think so; I don't think the Shroud is authentic—I think it's a clever medieval forgery—and I don't think the stains on it are really blood." I decided to see if Inspector Descartes had any sense of humor. "On the other hand, if the Holy Sponge is authentic, it might contain traces of Holy Spittle, along with some DNA."

"The Holy Sponge? Please, what is this Holy Sponge?"

I explained.

"*Incroyable*," he said, shaking his head in disbelief.

"What would really help," I went on, "would be dental records: X-rays of the Holy Teeth."

The inspector stared at me as if I were insane, then—when he realized I was joking—he laughed.

"I like that," he said. "*Oui*, X-rays of the Holy Teeth would be very helpful."

"Oh!" My joke had reminded me of something serious. "We sent two of the teeth to a laboratory for carbon-14 dating, to see how old they are. We should get the results any day now. I'm guessing the teeth are only seven hundred years old, but if the lab says they're two thousand years old, the bones suddenly become much more interesting."

"What bones?"

"What do you mean, 'what bones'? The bones I've just been talking about, Inspector."

He repeated the question. "*What* bones?" He held out his upturned hands. His empty hands. Now I understood his meaning. "Where are these special bones?"

"I have no idea, Inspector. But I think if you find the bones, you'll find the killer. What's the French expression that means 'Look for the woman'? *Cherchez la femme?*" He nodded. "How would you say 'Look for the skeleton'?"

"*Cherchez le squelette.*" The word sounded almost like "skillet." "Of course we will search for the skeleton. But I don't understand, Docteur. Why all the secrecy? Why not just tell the world that you found these bones and explain that you need to do more tests to know if they are Jesus?"

"You want the truth?"

"Of course I want the truth. I always *only* want the truth." For a moment I feared that I'd angered him, but he didn't look mad; only intense. "Come." He stood abruptly, beckoning to me to follow him. He led me into the chapel, where the forensic technicians seemed to be looking for the controls of the electrical winch that had hoisted Stefan into the air. Descartes studied the suspended body; then his gaze shifted to the fresco on the wall behind it, the wall above the altar. The painting showed a rosy-cheeked cherub hovering in the sky, beaming, as if delighted by the body hanging a few feet away. The detective shook his head slightly. "I don't believe in angels or miracles or Holy Sponges, Docteur. But I do believe in the truth. *La vérité*." A weary look clouded his eyes, and I wondered if he was thinking about the dead art-forger again. "I just have difficulty to find it sometimes."

"How would you say it, Inspector—'*Cherchez la vérité*'?"

He smiled slightly. "*Oui. Exactement.* So yes, please, tell me the truth about why Monsieur Beauvoir was so secretive."

"This is just my opinion," I stressed, "but I think Stefan wanted to keep it a secret because he was afraid someone else would take credit for the find; someone else would get the glory—some bureaucrat at the palace or the Ministry of Culture or wherever. I think he wanted all the glory for himself. Stefan wanted to be the one in the spotlight."

I heard the whine of an electric motor. Overhead, the beam twitched and Stefan's body jerked as the cable spool began to turn. As the wire unwound, the beam descended, slowly spinning in the glare of the theater lights.

Stefan had gotten his wish. He had taken center stage, and he was in the spotlight.

CHAPTER 22

MIRANDA WAS QUIET ON the walk back to her hotel, which was fine by me.

She looked tired and sad. I felt tired and sad, too; also confused and unsettled. I was shocked and puzzled by Stefan's murder, but I wasn't traumatized by it; he was a colleague, true, but I'd barely known him, so finding his body had been almost like stumbling upon a murdered stranger. No, my confusion and distress had more to do with Miranda. Was there something going on between her and Stefan after all? Had she lied to me about that? If she had, what else had she lied to me about? And was Descartes right—had his murder, and our involvement, made Miranda's private life my business?

Perhaps it had, I concluded reluctantly. I was wrestling with what to say when I looked up and noticed where we were. Ambling on automatic pilot, we'd reached the Palace of the Popes. Miranda stared bleakly at the stone façade; silent tears sprang from her eyes and rolled down her face. "God, I hate this place," she whispered fiercely, not so much to me as to herself, or perhaps to the palace. "I thought I'd died and gone to heaven, or at least to Disney, when I first saw it. The glory and the glamour, I totally fell for it, you know?" She laughed bitterly. "I was too dazzled to see that Stefan was just playing me. Probably using me to get to you—wanting to add your forensic heft to the project to give it more credibility. It never occurred to me to suspect him of that. I only suspected him of wanting to get into my pants again."

It was, I supposed after my initial shock, as good an opening as any to the conversation we needed to have. "And did you want him to?"

"No. Well, maybe. But not really." She shook her head. "God, what a mess. Would you let me just talk for a while? Can you just listen, and not interrupt, and try not to judge me?" She took my arm and led me to a bench at the edge of the plaza. "I hadn't thought about Stefan for years; I really hadn't. So when he first got in touch with me about this, I barely even remembered who he was. He had to say his name twice, and add 'in France.' But after that, it was like this seed started to germinate—ha, shades of Zeus and Leda; the seed of unfinished business, somehow. Digging around in the Palace of the Popes sounded cool, and so did a paid junket to France. But I got this nervous, hopeful feeling, too; this hope that maybe we could somehow get rid of some of the scar tissue we'd created six years ago, when Stefan's wife showed up and I left Guatemala in disgrace." I nodded; I wasn't entirely sure I understood, but I'd been instructed not to interrupt, and I wanted her to know I was listening.

"So as soon as I get here, Stefan starts talking about how glad he is to be working with me again. How sorry he is about what happened in Guatemala. How grateful he is to have a chance to become real colleagues. I tried not to make too much of it; it sounded good, but I couldn't help wondering if he was working me a bit, trying to get into my pants again. And he did make a pass at me that night on his balcony, but I turned him down, just like I told you. But what I *didn't* tell you about that night is, I didn't burn the bridge completely. I was willing to consider the possibility that there actually could be something there—something genuine with Stefan—after all."

I nodded, biting my tongue to keep from asking if Stefan had given her reason to hope for more. It was almost as though she'd read my mind, though. "He kept dropping hints along those lines," she went on. "Talking about what an opportunity this find was. How we could publish off it for years. How it could open all sorts of doors for us. Turns out death's door was the only one, huh?" She took another deep breath. "There's another thing I haven't told you. Stefan came to my hotel room last night."

I broke the no-interruptions rule. "I know."

She looked miserable. "How?"

"Descartes told me."

"Shit. I'm sorry you didn't hear it from me first." She looked down at the cobblestones. "About ten o'clock last night, Stefan calls me, says he's on his way home from dinner and can he swing by for a minute and talk to me about something. I say okay. He shows up at my room with a bottle of wine, and he's all funny and charming, and I let him talk me into having some wine with him. A couple glasses in, I'm feeling relaxed and happy, and then he starts kissing me. And this time, I'm not planning on turning him down. But then he starts whispering stuff in my ear about how he wants to run away with me. How we can get out of the rat race of academia. Live somewhere beautiful and exotic. Travel the world. Write novels, raise orchids, do whatever the hell we want. At first I just figure he's trying to sweet-talk me, but he keeps on and on, so finally I ask him what the hell he's talking about—it makes no sense to me; it sounds crazy and juvenile. So then he gets defensive and mad. He gets up and storms out."

"That's it? That's all that happened?"

"Almost; not quite. As he's walking out the door, he turns and says, 'You have no idea what I'm offering you, Miranda. The door's opening tonight. Right now. I'm stepping through it. I'd love for you to go with me.' He stands there looking at me, just . . . *waiting*. Then he shakes his head, steps into the hall, and shuts the door behind him. And then he's gone."

"Let me get this straight. He wanted you to leave the hotel with him, right then, at midnight, to seize some golden opportunity?"

"I think he did. I keep turning and turning those words over in my mind, and that's where I end up every time."

"Did you tell Descartes this?"

"Yes. I don't know how seriously he took me. Or whether he even believes me."

Suddenly I felt dizzy, almost sick. "If you'd gone with Stefan, you might have ended up hanging in that chapel with him. Nailed to the back side of that beam."

"Yeah."

CHAPTER 23

THE MISTRAL HAD COME roaring back at nightfall, churning through the leaves of the trees in Lumani's garden. I tossed and turned for hours, chasing sleep without catching it—like a donkey forever pursuing a carrot suspended just beyond its nose. I was finally getting my first taste of it when I heard a tapping at my door, so light it was all but drowned out by the wind. I sat up in bed, instantly on full alert. "Hello? Who's there?"

"It's me, Dr. B."

"Miranda? Are you okay?"

"Yes. Sort of. Not really."

Switching on the bedside lamp, I scrambled out from under the covers, fumbled with the lock, and opened the door in my T-shirt and surgical scrub pants. Even by the low light spilling from my room, I could see how ravaged her face looked. "You look like hell."

Normally, this would have prompted a smart-ass response, but she simply nodded and crumpled against my chest. I wrapped my arms around her and patted her back. "I'm sorry," I said. "Do you want to talk about it?" She shook her head. "Do you want to go get some coffee or something to eat? If we can find someplace that's open?" She shook her head again.

"I just don't think I can be by myself. Can I come in?"

"Of course." The room wasn't designed for company; the only places to sit were the bed and a narrow wooden chair in the corner. I nodded toward the chair. "Do you want to sit down?"

"Don't take this the wrong way," she said, "but what I'd really like is to just sleep. I've been tossing and turning for hours, but I got really creeped out in that hotel room. I could still smell Stefan's cigarettes and cologne in there; still feel his presence." She drew a deep breath, then blew it out through pursed lips. "I just so desperately want to sleep. Would you mind if I slept here with you?"

"Miranda, I'm not sure that's such a good idea."

"Maybe not, and I'm sorry to ask, but I really don't want to be alone." Her eyes looked sad and weary. "Just sleep. I promise. Please? I need a friend right now, not a boss."

Five minutes later I was sharing my bed with Miranda, and I knew there'd be no sleep for me. I was lying on the far side of the bed, on the edge of the mattress, my thoughts and emotions swirling. I focused on my breathing, making it as regular as possible. Three seconds a breath. *In-in-in. Out-out-out. In-in-in. Out-out-out.*

The covers rustled, the mattress shifted slightly, and I felt Miranda press against me. She spooned up behind me, her knees tucked into the bends of my legs, her chest and belly against my back. She wrapped one arm around my shoulder and laid a hand on my chest. She patted my heart—*tha-thump, tha-thump, tha-thump*—and I swear, it beat in time with her touch. Gradually her body went slack and her breath grew deep. With each breath in, her belly swelled against me; with each exhalation, the hair on the back of my neck stirred.

Her body twitched slightly—a dream, or some neural synapse firing at random—and she took a deeper breath, then settled more closely against my back. Despite the bizarre and bloody events of the past twenty-four hours, the feeling of her body snugged against mine gave me a profound sense of well-being and comfort. A line from Meister Eckhart popped into my head: "If the only prayer you ever say is 'Thank you,' it will be enough." Lying there with Miranda spooned up behind me—alive, unhurt, and important to me in ways that I didn't understand fully, or perhaps was afraid to face—I prayed again: *Thank you. Thank you. Thank you.*

CHAPTER 24

WHEN I WOKE, SHE was gone. On the nightstand, I found a note in Miranda's small, neat script. It said, "Thank you, thank you, thank you." Underneath the thanks, these words: "A souvenir. Maybe it doesn't mean anything, but maybe it's important." I tucked the note—an odd souvenir, I thought, or at least an odd inscription—in the drawer of the desk.

A few minutes later, as I was brushing windblown leaves off a chair in the garden, Jean appeared, a cordless phone in his hand. "A call for you."

Inspector Descartes was on the line. "I have something interesting to show you," he said. "Can you come to my office?"

"Yes, of course. I was just about to have breakfast. Tea, toast, and strawberries in the garden. Can I eat first, or do I need to come right away?"

"You can eat first," he said, then, "or . . . I could come there. We could talk over breakfast."

"I'll ask Jean—"

"I'll be there in ten minutes," he said, and the phone went dead in my hand.

DESCARTES TOOK HIS coffee black and concentrated: a small shot of espresso so dense he could almost have eaten it with a fork. Turning one of the lounge chairs by the fountain to face the sun, he set his espresso and a plate full of strawberries on a small table, then settled into the cushions, loosened his tie, rolled up his sleeves, and slipped on a pair of wraparound sunglasses. "Ahhh," he grunted happily. If not for the threadbare dress clothes, he might have been settling in for a day of Riviera sunbathing.

I sat in an adjoining chair with my cup of tea, now cold, along with two pieces of crusty toast slathered with cherry preserves. I sat without eating, waiting to see what he wanted to show me. He was in no hurry. His breathing grew slow and deep, and I wondered if he was going to sleep. "Inspector, you wanted to show me something?"

"Mmm? Ah, *oui*, of course." I was glad I'd asked. "Yes, it's right here." He patted his shirt pocket, then pulled out a folded sheet of paper. With almost maddening slowness he unfolded it and peered at it, then handed it over. "Yes, I thought you might find it interesting."

It took a moment for the name on the letterhead to sink in, but once it did, my adrenaline surged, and my eyes raced down the page.

"We found it in the office of his apartment," he said. "We almost missed it. It was in his fax machine. It's the report—"

"I know, I know," I interrupted. "Good God." I reread it, just to be sure I hadn't misunderstood. "Or maybe I should say 'Jesus Christ' instead." What I held in my shaking hands was the report from Beta Analytic, the Miami lab where we'd sent the teeth for C-14 dating. The figures practically leaped from the page: "1,950 +/- 30." According to the lab, the teeth—the teeth I'd pulled from the skull in the ossuary—dated back to the year A.D. 62, plus or minus thirty years: the century in which Jesus had lived and died. "So they might be the bones of Christ after all." My mind was racing as fast as my pulse. "You said you found this in his fax machine. Had it been faxed to him, or had *he* faxed it to someone else?"

He smiled. "You would make a good detective, Docteur. The answer, I believe, is both. We looked at the machine's archive, the log, I think you call it. He got a fax from Miami around eight P.M. on Saturday. Right after that, between nine and nine thirty, he sent three faxes."

"Three? Did the first two fail?"

"No. All three went through. They were to three different places. Rome, London, and the United States."

"Damnation," I said. "I think Miranda was right—I think Stefan was up to no good. He made such a big deal about keeping the bones secret, but the minute he got the lab results, he ran to the fax machine. Have you tracked the numbers yet?"

"We're working on it." He frowned. "There's some bureaucracy we have to go through to get the records."

"Do you know where in the United States?"

"Ah, *oui*. The city is Charlotte."

"Charlotte?" I was stunned. "My God. Some guy in Charlotte got in touch with me a week ago. Asked if I would examine some bones and artifacts from the first century."

Descartes sat up straight, no longer sunbathing. "Who is this guy? Where do we find him?"

"His name"— I rummaged through my mental trash bin— "is Newman. Dr. Adam Newman. Director of the Institute for Something-or-other. Ah: the Institute for Biblical Science."

He took out his notepad and wrote down the name. "You know this place, this institute? It's a serious scientific institution?"

I shook my head. "I'd never heard of them." Suddenly I made a connection. "But *Stefan* had heard of them. I showed him the letter they sent me. He warned me to stay away from them—said they were religious nuts, and if they disagreed with my work, they'd try to damage my reputation."

"Interesting," Descartes mused, "that Monsieur Beauvoir knew more about this American group than you did."

"You think that's who he faxed in Charlotte about the bones?"

"*Peut-être.* Maybe so. It's a good place to start."

"What about the London and Rome faxes? Who was he faxing there?"

He shrugged. "Other people he wanted to know about the age of the bones. But which people, and why? *Sais pas*—don't know." He selected a crimson strawberry from the plate and popped it into his

mouth. He chewed slowly, as if testing the strawberry, and an appreciative smile dawned across his
face. "Ah, *délicieuse*," he breathed. "The food and
wine in Provence are so wonderful. If I weren't
living on a policeman's salary, I would love it here."
He cast a swift, wistful look around the garden and
at the lovely buildings. Then, to my astonishment,
he took a croissant from the platter, wrapped it in a
napkin, and slipped it into his jacket pocket. Seeing
the expression on my face, he raised his eyebrows.
Was he inviting me to tease him? Daring me to
challenge him? I did neither, and after a pause he
continued. "Perhaps, Docteur, you can help us find
out who he was faxing. If you are willing."

"Me? Help how? Does it require me to do anything illegal, immoral, or dangerous?"

"Illegal, no. Immoral, also no." He smiled. "Sorry
if that disappoints you."

"You didn't say it's not dangerous, Inspector. I'm
guessing that means it is?"

He held out a hand and waggled it. "Perhaps."

"Does 'perhaps' mean 'definitely'?"

"You can say no, of course."

"You think someone killed Stefan for the bones?"

"Unless someone killed him for screwing your
assistant."

I hadn't expected that. I felt the blood rush to my
face, and I realized that I might have just stepped
into a trap. Did Descartes still consider me a suspect? If so, had my reaction just raised his suspi-
cions, made me look guilty? I was too angry to
care. "Look, Inspector, I know what you think—
Miranda's personal life is fair game. Fine; you do

your job. But if you want me to help you dig up dirt on Miranda, the answer's no; you're on your own."

He seemed surprised by my reaction. "No, *pas du tout*—not at all. I was being ironic. I forgot you were sensitive about that." Was he being sincere? There was no way to tell. "Of course the murder is about the bones. Immediately after he gets this report"— with his right index finger he pointed to the paper in my hands—"he faxes it to three people." He held up the finger. "A few hours after that, he's dead." He held up his other index finger, then brought the two fingers together. "They are connected. How?" He tapped his temple. "I think he tries to sell the bones. I think he has three potential buyers—three fishes on the line. And one of the fishes kills him."

"So, *cherchez le squelette*," I reminded him. "Find the skeleton, you'll find the killer."

"Maybe." He drained his cup and studied the sludge in the bottom. "Yes, maybe he takes the bones to a rendezvous at the chapel, and the buyer kills him and takes the bones." I nodded; that was my guess about what had happened. "But I think not." I looked at him in surprise. "Kill him, yes; shoot him—*bang!*—and take the bones, sure, it makes sense. But crucify him? Why? Why kill him in a way that's risky to get caught? A way that's slow and painful? Maybe to try to get information from him. Torture him into talking. You see?" I nodded; there was logic to that. He held up the finger yet again. "Also, why search his apartment, if you already have what you want?"

"Maybe to make sure there's no evidence at the apartment, no paper trail for the police to follow?"

"*Non*," he scoffed. "Whoever searched that apartment wasn't looking for a piece of paper. He was looking for the bones. Of this I feel certain."

"So what do you do now, Inspector?"

"I ask you to contact the three fishes."

"Me? Why?"

"To offer the bones for sale."

"But I don't *have* the bones," I pointed out.

"A minor complication," he said, smiling. "You pretend to have them." Suddenly the "dangerous" part of his request was becoming clear.

"Why don't *you* pretend to have them, Inspector?"

He laughed. "Ah, *oui*. I will send this fax to the three fishes: '*Bonjour, monsieur*, if you still want the bones of Jesus, bring ten thousand euros to my office at the police station tomorrow morning.' Like that?"

"No, not like that. Go undercover. Cops do it all the time."

"I would make a terrible undercover officer," he said. "I cannot act. My acting smells like shit. Besides, perhaps the killer has seen me already, at the chapel yesterday."

"If so, he's seen me, too—I got there before you did, in case you've forgotten."

"Ah, *oui*, but you were there as a witness, not an investigator. In fact, it's good if he saw you there. You would be the logical person to have the bones, since Beauvoir no longer does. You, or perhaps Mademoiselle Lovelady."

"No!" I practically shouted. "Not Miranda. I can't let you put Miranda at risk." He raised his sunglasses and squinted at me. "I'm responsible for her."

"*Pourquoi?* She is an adult, yes? Twenty-five years? Thirty years?"

"Of course she's an adult. But she's my assistant. That makes me responsible."

"But didn't she come to Avignon to work for Beauvoir?"

He had me there. "Okay, technically, you're right. But most of the time, I'm her boss. Keep Miranda out of it. Please."

He shrugged. "I can try. But as I said yesterday, you are both involved. Perhaps you and I are not the only ones who have an interest in her."

My cell phone rang; the call was from Miranda. She was talking even before I finished saying hello. "Slow down," I said. "I can't understand you. Are you crying? What's wrong?"

"I've been robbed," she sobbed.

"*What?* Just now? On the street? Are you hurt?"

"No, I'm not hurt. It must have happened last night. My room—somebody broke into my room while I was sleeping there with you." She drew a few shuddering breaths. "When I got up this morning, I went for a long walk. Then I ate breakfast. I just got back to the hotel five minutes ago. My room had been trashed. They took my computer. My passport. My money. I'm scared, Dr. B."

TWENTY MINUTES LATER—spurred on by my fear for Miranda and my hope that if I did what Descartes asked, I could deflect danger from her to me—I signed my name to the message I would fax to each of Stefan's three fish. The wording Descartes and I had finally settled on was meant to be both tantalizing and threatening: *I am Stefan's partner. I know about your dealings with him. Now you must deal with me. Contact me within 24 hours, or I will go to the police. Brockton.*

Descartes reread the note and grunted his approval. "Okay," he said, "if they don't already have the bones, this will make them think that you have them. If they *do* have the bones, they will think you are blackmailing them. It might work. What do you think, Docteur?"

"I think it might get me killed," I said. "If they think I'm blackmailing them, what's to stop them from just shooting me—*bang!*—or crucifying me?"

"We'll be watching you," he said. "Besides, I don't think they have the bones. If they did, why break into mademoiselle's room?"

"And what do I do when they call our bluff and want me to deliver the bones—the bones I don't actually have?"

"Simple. You set the *hameçon*—the fishhook—and I reel in the line. You meet them, and we arrest them."

"Before or after they shoot me?"

He laughed. "Trust me, Docteur."

We took the note inside to Lumani's office, a tiny alcove just off the dining room—nothing more than a desk built into a recess in the wall. After Jean had made sure the machine would not transmit the inn's name or phone number, we sent the note to the three fax numbers.

Now, we waited for the fish to strike. To strike *me*.

* * *

"LATELY I FEEL like a time traveler," I said to Miranda. "Or like there are two of me. One me is here now, in the present, trying to help Descartes find Stefan's killer. The other me is somewhere back in the thirteen hundreds, trying to figure out how that box of bones ended up in the wall of the palace. And how in bloody hell the Shroud of Turin and this painter Simone Martini are connected to it."

We were back at the library again, once more on the trail of Martini and the Shroud. I nodded toward the immense reading room that had once been a vast banquet hall. Computers and steel shelves and halogen lights surrounded by frescoed walls and leaded windows and a coffered ceiling. "I feel as schizophrenic as this library." From somewhere below, an annoyed *sshh* floated up at me.

Miranda surveyed the space, the lavish architectural metaphor I'd just staked out for myself, then turned to me with a slight smile. "You could do worse," she whispered. "Pretty damn fancy, as psychoses go." I squelched a laugh and motioned her out into the stairwell so we could talk without disturbing everyone else. "We might as well hang out in the Middle Ages," she resumed with scarcely a pause. "Descartes himself said as much. He's busy bird-dogging those fax numbers, and you're waiting for the fish to bite. Meanwhile, why not keep plugging away on the bones and the Shroud?" Miranda had bounced back remarkably from her scare. It helped that the hotel had moved her to a new room, and that Descartes had agreed to post a guard outside her door at night. It also helped, I figured, to have something to occupy her mind.

"Sure," I said. "Maybe we can figure out the connection."

"Maybe we can even figure out where Stefan hid the bones," she said. "Wouldn't *that* be swell, if we could find them."

"I'm not so sure, Miranda. Maybe those bones aren't meant to be found. Maybe they're like the Hope Diamond—bad luck for anybody who tries to possess them."

"Oh, that's bullshit," she said.

"Stefan might disagree with you," I pointed out.

"I don't mean bullshit about the bones; I mean bullshit about the Hope Diamond. All that stuff about the curse—it's bogus. All those lurid tales of murder and madness and suicide? Hype conjured up to boost the diamond's mystique and jack up the market value."

"Remind me never to ask you about Santa Claus," I retorted. "But seriously, *none* of it's true? Nobody who owned it met a bad end?"

"Well, okay, there's King Louis the Sixteenth and Marie Antoinette; I guess the guillotine wasn't the greatest way to go." She winced. "But it does beats crucifixion."

"No kidding. So here's the thing I don't get. I thought I had the medieval mystery all figured out: This fourteenth-century monk, Meister Eckhart, pisses off people high in the theocracy. He's attracting a big following, the people love him, and the ruling priestly class feels threatened, so he's put to death. Sound familiar? Remind you of anybody else? Anybody from, oh, say, the first century?"

"There might be a parallel or three," she conceded.

"And somehow this painter, Simone Martini, sees Eckhart's body," I pressed on. "And *he* sees the parallels to Christ, so he creates this image, this pseudo burial shroud. Maybe he's moved by what he sees, or maybe he's just greedy, just cashing in on the trade in relics. Either way, the theory works. It fits the facts—or it *did* until the damn C-14 test said the bones are two thousand years old."

She studied my face. "Let me get this straight. You're disappointed about that?"

"Confused," I said. "Frustrated, I guess."

"How come?"

"I don't know. I liked the theory. Liked the story I was spinning."

She frowned. "Liked it better than the possibility that they really *are* the bones of Jesus?" I pondered that, and while I was pondering, she pounced. "I don't believe this. You're *jealous*, aren't you?"

I drew back; it felt almost as if she'd slapped me. "What on earth do you mean? Jealous of who?"

"Jealous of *Stefan*. You're afraid that he was right after all—that he really did make the greatest find ever." She shook her head, the disappointment in her eyes unmistakable. "He's dead, Dr. B; you're alive. You've got no reason to envy Stefan, and no need to be petty. If those *are* the bones of Christ, so what? It doesn't make you any less, and it doesn't make Stefan any *more*. It's pretty clear he was up to no good. But just think—what if he was up to

no good with the actual, for-real bones of Jesus
Christ? How totally amazing! Can't you *see* that?"

My mind reeled and raced, seeking how best to
defend myself. Then, almost as clearly as if they'd
been spoken aloud, I heard the words of Meister
Eckhart: *Do exactly what you would do if you felt most
secure.* But what would that mean, what would that
be? What *would* I do, if I were my best self right
now? I was so surprised at the answer that I laughed
out loud. "Thank you," I said. Her eyes narrowed,
and I saw her bracing for the next salvo of sarcasm.
"No, I mean it. Thank you. You're absolutely right."
Was this really me talking? "I cared more about my
pet theory than about the truth. That's wrong—
one of the cardinal sins in science. And yeah, I
probably wanted to look smarter than Stefan, be
righter than Stefan."

"Why?"

"Dunno. Maybe I wanted a little sip of schaden-
freude. Maybe I was desperate to impress you."

She shook her head again, but this time, as she
did, she began to smile. "Sometimes, for such a
smart, impressive guy, you can be *so* dumb," she
said. "But hey, that was good work you did just
then."

I took a deep breath, blew it out. "So. Let's re-
think this. If the bones really *are* first century, and
they're linked to the Shroud, does that mean the
Shroud's authentic after all? Was the carbon dating
of the Shroud botched?"

"What, three separate labs all got it wrong, and
all by thirteen hundred years? No way."

"What about the invisible-patch theory, then?

You think maybe the labs tested fabric from an invisible medieval patch?"

"Give me a break; the Shroudies are *so* grasping at straws there. Besides, I think Emily Craig's right about the image. I think it was created by a terrific artist in the Middle Ages using that dust-transfer technique she described. It's simple, and it's credible. And that pseudoshroud she did of her friend was pretty damn convincing. Emily's no Giotto or Simone Martini, but she proved her point."

"So, circling back to your snuff-film theory," I said. "How do you reconcile that with the idea that the bones are thirteen centuries older than the Shroud?"

"I don't. I can't." She shrugged. "But interesting symmetry, in an ironic way, don't you think? If the Shroud of Turin's a medieval fake, but the bones from the Palace of the Popes are the real deal?" Suddenly she grinned. "Hey, try this one. What if the Shroud's not the world's first snuff film but the world's first forensic facial reconstruction? What if your guy Martini saw the bones of Jesus and decided to put the flesh back on them? Maybe Master Simone was a thirteenth-century version of your NCMEC pal, Joe Mullins?"

My phone warbled, echoing loudly in the stairwell. The last call I'd gotten at the library had been the TBI agent's bad news about Rocky Stone, so I was already gun-shy; when I recognized Descartes's number on the display, I felt a tightening in my stomach. "Inspector?"

"Oui, Docteur."

"Does this mean the fish are biting? Has something come in on the fax machine at Lumani?"

"Ah, *non*, not yet. That is not why I am calling you. This is something else."

I felt my body relax, and only then did I realize how tightly I'd tensed when I saw who was calling. "What is it?"

"Where are you? Something interesting has just turned up."

"Again? This is a big day for interesting finds. Miranda and I are at the library."

"I am at Beauvoir's apartment. Not far away. I can be at the library in five minutes."

"Would it be easier if I came to the apartment?"

"It's probably better if you don't—one of the fish might be watching. It's okay if he sees us questioning you. But it's not good if it looks like you're part of our team."

"I understand, Inspector. I'll see you here."

"Meet me in the library courtyard. Without mademoiselle. Oh, and Docteur? Don't look happy to see me." Only after he hung up did I realize what he meant: One of the fish might be watching.

THERE WERE NO parking places beside the library, but Descartes didn't let that stop him. He pulled his car—a white Police Nationale sedan with lights and markings—onto the narrow sidewalk, practically scraping the passenger side against the wall of the adjoining building. It was the parking technique of choice—or necessity—in many of Avignon's narrow streets.

I'd been waiting for him on a bench in the library's courtyard. When he approached, I stood;

I was about to stretch out my hand when I remembered his sign-off, so instead of a handshake, I offered him a scowl. "What do you want now, Inspector?" He raised his eyebrows, as if to tell me I'd gone a bit overboard, so I backed off. "What's up?"

"This arrived at Beauvoir's apartment a little while ago," he said in a voice I felt sure could not be overheard. "Take a look." He handed me a padded FedEx envelope. The lettering on the airbill was faint and smudged; it was easy to tell that it had come from the United States but hard to tell much more than that. Finally I deciphered "Miami," and then—above that—two smeared words that looked like "Be Anal": words, I realized with a start, that were probably "Beta Analytic." The envelope was almost flat, but not quite, and I gave it an exploratory squeeze. Through the envelope's built-in padding, I felt something small and hard, like a pebble. Opening the envelope, I found, as the size and shape had suggested I would, a human tooth—a canine—its ancient enamel a dull grayish brown.

"I thought the carbon-14 testing would destroy the sample," Descartes said. "How can they send the whole tooth back?"

"Apparently they only used one of the teeth. We sent two," I said. I tipped the tooth out of the Ziploc bag and into my palm. "A molar, and this canine." I held it up for him to see, and suddenly an electric jolt shot through me. "My God," I breathed. "*Not* this canine."

"What do you mean?" Descartes leaned closer to inspect the tooth.

"This isn't the canine we sent." I raised my palm closer to his face. "At least, it's not the canine that I pulled from the skull."

"How can you tell?"

"Because when I pulled the tooth, it broke. The root snapped off in the jaw. Look—this one's perfect."

He plucked the tooth from my hand gently, as if it were a gem, or a ripe raspberry he didn't want to bruise. Holding it between thumb and forefinger, he turned it, scrutinizing it from every angle. "You are sure of this?"

"Absolutely."

"You think there is some mistake at this laboratory? A mix-up?"

"No," I said slowly, an idea dawning in my mind. An idea whose brilliance was matched only by its wickedness. "I think Stefan swapped the samples," I said. "I think he traded the teeth I pulled for teeth from another skull. A skull he *knew* was two thousand years old."

"But how is this possible? Where would he get such teeth?"

"Hell, he was an archaeologist," I said. "He could have gotten them anywhere. A dig in Greece or the Middle East—a site he knew dated from the first century. The catacombs of Rome, where there are thousands and thousands of skeletons that age. Maybe even the Museum of Natural History in Paris; there's a whole building there filled with fossils and bones." I snapped my fingers. "I just remembered—the first night I was here, we were talking about C-14 dating. He mentioned something about Turkish goat bones from the first century. He might have teeth from that same site."

"So he faked it? *Merde*, every case I get now involves a faker or a forger. Do you think he planned this *tout entièr*—the whole thing—a long time in advance?"

I opened my mouth to say yes, but I found myself shaking my head no. "No, actually I think it was a spur-of-the-moment idea," I said. "I think he really did find the bones in the palace—the wall collapsed first, Stefan was called second. I think the only thing he faked was the C-14 test, once he found that ossuary. I think the inscription—the cross and the lamb—put the idea into his head." A realization struck me: If Stefan had rigged the C-14 test, maybe the skeleton was medieval after all . . . and maybe the Shroud of Turin really was created in Avignon. "The skeleton Stefan found is significant," I added. "But he wanted it to be the most important—and most valuable—skeleton in the world. Unfortunately, his plan worked too well, and it backfired on him."

Descartes was staring off into space. I wasn't sure he was following me, or even hearing me. "Inspector?"

"Excuse me for one minute, please." He took out his cell phone and made a call. The only words I caught for sure were "*cherchez*" and "*appartement*." Descartes listened a long while, then murmured, "*Ah, oui? C'est bon.*" When he hung up, his face was a mask, but his eyes were gleaming. "As you were talking, I remembered. In his apartment were some small glass jars containing bits of metal, pieces of pottery, small bones. And—this is what I called to ask them to look for just now—two teeth. A *dent de sagesse*, the tooth of wisdom"—he pointed at one of his third molars—"and a dogtooth, a canine, broken at the root, *exactement* as you describe." He caught my gaze and held it. "Okay, I'm leaving now. We should finish with a small fight." He jabbed a finger in my chest. "You are not telling me everything, Docteur," he said loudly. "I think you know where are these bones. I am watching you. And I can make things very bad for you if you give me a reason."

He spun on his heel and walked toward the street. "Descartes," I called after him. He stopped and looked back at me. "We saved your butts in World War Two," I shouted. "If not for America, you'd be goose-stepping and eating sauerkraut."

He resumed walking, and he raised both arms, his middle fingers extended. Unless it had a radically different meaning in France, the gesture needed no translation.

And the man claimed to be a lousy actor.

CHAPTER 25

WHEN MIRANDA AND I left the library an hour later, we persuaded Philippe to let us out a back door. We took a long, meandering way back to her hotel, detouring through the Rue des Teinturiers—the street of the tinters, the dyers. For centuries this was Avignon's textile district, where the wools and silks for tapestries, vestments, courtiers' cloaks, and ladies' gowns took on hues of red, orange, gold, green, blue, violet, indigo. A small canal paralleled the street, and the buildings lining that side all had small bridges leading to their entrances. A smattering of ancient waterwheels, some still turning, offered picturesque reminders of the importance of waterpower to medieval industries. Miranda stopped to snap a waterwheel photo with her iPhone, then climbed the steps onto the small bridge beside it. Leaning on the stone balustrade, she peered down at the water. "Fancy a dip?" I called.

She shook her head. "Remember what Stefan said about the pollution in the Rhône? This looks a lot worse. The water's opaque."

"Urban runoff," I said. "Brake fluid, mop water, dog crap—not great for the water quality."

"Imagine, though, what this must have looked like in 1350. If all these buildings were dyers' shops? This water probably changed color every time somebody emptied a dye vat. Wouldn't that be fun? The canal running fuchsia one minute, burnt orange the next? Like something out of *The Wizard of Oz*."

"That's a pretty image," I said. "And Avignon did play the part of the Emerald City for most of a century."

"We're not in Kansas anymore, that's for sure."

A few blocks later, we wandered past the historic marker that mentioned the poet Petrarch and his unrequited love, Laura. Pointing it out to Miranda, I asked, "Do you know their story?"

"Petrarch and Laura? A little. He saw her at church and fell instantly in love. But it was doomed—she was married to someone else, I think—so he spent the rest of his life worshiping her from afar."

"They were never together?"

"Only in his dreams. Well, and his poems."

"DO YOU KNOW the story of Petrarch?" Elisabeth and Jean looked up from their wineglasses and nodded in unison.

I'd dropped Miranda at her hotel after an early dinner at a Middle Eastern restaurant near the clock tower—couscous, grape leaves, hummus, and eggplant; not my favorite fare, but Miranda liked it. The last of the daylight was fading as I entered the sanctuary of Lumani's garden, and Elisabeth and Jean were sharing a bottle of red wine. A candle burned on the small table between them, and the wine in their glasses glowed like liquid rubies.

"Petrarch, *oui*," she exclaimed. "A famous poet *pastoral*."

"Pastoral? Like a pastor, a priest?"

Her brow furrowed, then brightened. "Ah, *non*. Like sheeps. Shepherds and maidens. Petrarch loved the countryside."

"And Laura? What do you know about his lady love?"

"She was very young," said Jean, "and very beautiful. Almost as beautiful as Elisabeth." She reached out and laid a hand on his cheek. "She was married to a French nobleman. Petrarch loved her, but could not have her."

"*Une tragédie*," said Elisabeth. "For him. But very lucky for us. He wrote many poems about her. He invented the sonnet, the love poem, just for her." She pursed her lips, thinking, then held up a finger. "*Ah!* Wait here. I will come back." She hurried across the courtyard to their house; a moment later she returned, holding a small book aloft as if it were a prize. "I have a book of Petrarch's sonnets. A gift from Jean years ago." She leaned down and kissed the top of his balding head—a simple gesture that spoke volumes about the easy, entwined intimacy of their lives.

She flipped pages in the book; some, I noticed,

were dog-eared, including the page where she stopped. "Listen. This is the poem he wrote when Laura died. He had loved her for twenty years by this time. He wrote in Italian; this is in French, which I will try to put into English for you—sorry if the translation is not good." She scanned the page, mentally trying out a word here, a phrase there, then held up a hand theatrically and began to read.

The eyes I used to speak about with words of fire, the arms and hands and feet and beautiful face that took me away from myself for so long and set me apart from other men; the waving hair of pure gold that shone, the smile that beamed with angel rays that made this earth a paradise—now they are only a bit of dust, and all her feeling is gone. Yet I live on, with grief and disdain, left behind, here in darkness, where the light I cherished no longer ever shows, in my fragile little boat on the tempestuous sea. Here let my loving song come to its end. The vein of my art has run dry, and my song has turned at last to tears.

She stopped, then wiped a tear from each eye. "Such sweetness, and such sadness."

"You say he loved her for twenty years?"

"More than that. He loved her for twenty years while she was alive. But then she died, during the Black Death. Still he loved her, after she died. He kept loving her, and writing about her, for the rest of his life—twenty-five, thirty more years."

"But he never got to be with her?"

"*Non*, never. She was married. She refused all his

advances. We don't even know if they ever talked together."

"That seems foolish," I said. "He wasted his life sighing for a woman he could never have instead of looking for a love that he *could* have." I gestured at the two of them. "Like you and Jean."

"But he was pledged to the church," she pointed out. "He was not supposed to have *any* woman."

"He was doubly foolish, then, to obsess about her for his whole life."

She gave me an odd look then—a look both critical and pitying. "Ah, *monsieur scientifique*—does your heart always obey the orders of your head? Have you never been foolish in the thing you wanted or the person you loved? Have you never loved unwisely, never grieved too much for someone you lost?"

Her question blindsided me. I felt light-headed and reached out to steady myself on the trellis beside me. Years before, when my wife, Kathleen, died of cancer, I'd retreated from people for two years, burying myself in my work. Then, just as I felt myself beginning to come alive again—just as I started falling in love with Jess Carter, a beautiful medical examiner from Chattanooga—Jess was killed. Then there was Isabella, with whom I'd had a brief romantic encounter, and who'd died in Japan when the tsunami struck the coast where she was staying. And now? Now I was struggling with my feelings for Miranda, a young woman who, because of her age and position, should be as off-limits to me as Laura was to Petrarch.

Elisabeth reached out a hand and laid it on my

arm. "I spoke too strongly," she said. "I think I have reminded you of something painful. I am sorry. Please forgive me."

I shook my head. "No, it's all right. It's my fault. What do I know about what's foolish and what's wise, or what's the best way to cope with pain? When I'm in pain, I study a skeleton. When Petrarch is in pain, he writes a poem. Most people prefer his way to mine. And who can blame them?" I gave her a rueful smile; she returned it with one of warmth and kindness.

"You find poems and stories in the bones," she said, and Jean nodded. "Good night." She gave my cheek a quick kiss, took her husband's arm, and walked with him across the courtyard into the golden light spilling from the windows of their home.

I wondered if it was too late in life to take up writing sonnets.

CHAPTER 26

DESCARTES SETTLED INTO A chair. I'd expected his eyes to light up at the array of pastries and berries—Jean and Elisabeth had started doubling the portions for his sake—but he looked bleak and bleary. "I've been up all night," he said, in answer to the question in my eyes. "Fishing. We have some information on all three of the fishes."

Coffee sloshed from my cup as my hand began to shake, filling the saucer. When I set the saucer down, milky coffee sloshed onto the table and dripped through the wooden slats, splatting onto the stones of the courtyard. "Tell me."

"The one in London is a British art dealer."

"An art dealer?" I was surprised, though I swiftly realized I shouldn't have been. After all, if collectors and museums prized fractured Roman pottery and gem-encrusted Aztec skulls, why wouldn't someone covet the bones of Christ, arguably the most revered figure of all time? "What else do you know about him?"

"Not him. Her. A woman named Felicia Kensington. She's very shady. She's been on the watch list of New Scotland Yard and Interpol for years now."

"What for?"

"Buying and selling black-market art. Forgeries and fakes. Stolen antiquities. Her name has come up more than once in cases like this—"

"Murder cases?"

"No, nothing violent. Cases where a valuable piece of art—a painting, a sculpture, a precious document—disappeared, or mysteriously reappeared. Sometimes with fake papers, sometimes with no papers at all. But she's slippery. Someone else always takes the fall."

"She's never been convicted of anything?"

"She's never even been arrested."

"Sounds like she's lucky, or smart, or both," I said. "What's your take?"

"My take?" He looked startled, then he frowned. "Isn't that what you call a corrupt policeman's bribe—his take?"

"Ah. Not quite." No wonder he'd looked confused and unhappy. "We do say that a crooked cop is 'on the take,' yes. But the money that a cop gets when he's on the take is called his 'cut,' I think. 'What's your take?' means 'What's your impression, what's your intuition?' So, what's your take on this shady art dealer, Felicia Kensington—could she have killed Stefan?"

He studied the biggest of the strawberries, then plucked it from the platter and bit off the lower half. "My take is, she's a *morceau de merde*—a morsel of shit, you would say?"

I smiled at the translation. "Americans don't say 'morsel' a lot. We tend to say 'piece' instead."

"Okay, she's a piece of shit," he said, popping the rest of the strawberry in his mouth. "But I don't think she's the killer."

"Because?"

"Because she's a woman, for one thing. Women almost never kill. They only kill their husbands or lovers. Well, sometimes their kids, but that's rare. Besides, this woman has an alibi. She's been in Cairo for the past two weeks. Probably buying mummies or robbing tombs."

"Okay, so we can probably rule her out. Who's suspect number two?"

He crossed himself, then raised his eyebrows expectantly, waiting for some sort of response. I shook my head and shrugged. Looking disappointed that I'd not understood the clue, he said, "The pope."

"The *pope*? *The* pope? As in the Holy Father in Rome? Holy smokes." The inspector nodded, cheered up by my dramatic reaction. "Well, well. I'll say this for Stefan—he might have been stupid, but he wasn't guilty of thinking small, was he? That's a damn big fish."

Descartes wagged a finger of clarification. "Not the pope himself, I think. The fax number belongs to the Vatican, though. The Vatican Museum, to be precise."

"I've been to the Vatican Museum," I said. "Took me six hours to go through it, and I skipped a lot. I'm guessing it's not a one-man operation. Any idea who Stefan was negotiating with?"

"Not yet. The wheels of the Vatican roll slowly."

"Gosh, there's a revelation." He didn't seem to get the pun.

"They have two different police forces. The Swiss Guard is there to protect the pope."

"Like the Secret Service in the U.S.," I said. "They protect the president."

"*Exactement.* The other force is the Vatican police—they do everything else. But neither group will cooperate with me unless someone *très important* commands it. The Catholic Church has had too many scandals lately. They don't want bloody hands from a murder." His lips twitched in an ironic little smile. "*En particulier* a crucifixion."

"That wouldn't look so good," I agreed. "But do you think it's possible that someone at the Vatican Museum would want the bones enough to kill for them?"

He shrugged. "I'm no expert. There's plenty of blood on the hands of the Church. The Crusades. The Inquisition. Sexual abuse and cover-ups. But would the Vatican kill to possess the bones of Christ—or to destroy them? Only God knows."

I slathered cherry preserves on a croissant and took a bite; for some reason, I'd started imitating Descartes, who seemed unable to string together more than three sentences without refueling. "So what do you know about the third fish, the one in Charlotte? Is it the Institute for Biblical Science, the place that contacted me?"

"No, that is not the place, but maybe there is some connection. This is a church."

"Catholic?" He shook his head. "Protestant?

Why would a Protestant church in North Carolina want to buy the bones of Jesus?"

"It's not typical Protestant, I think. It's called the Church of Dominion and Prophecy. A church *gigantesque*—a megachurch, *oui*?—with twenty thousand people. Also radio and television stations. The preacher is named Jonah Ezekiel. Not his original name; he changed it. He calls himself 'Reverend Jonah, Apostle and Prophet of the Apocalypse.' He's—how do you say it?—on the fluffy edge of crazy."

"Lunatic fringe?"

"*Exactement*, lunatic fringe."

"Why do you say that, Inspector?"

"He thinks the world will end soon."

"I hate to say it, Inspector, but millions of Americans—like, forty percent—think the world is about to end. Almost half of Americans believe that the Second Coming of Christ and the end of the world will happen by the year 2050."

He held up a finger. "Ah, but this preacher—he says he knows *exactement* when these things will happen. God brought him to Heaven, he says, and gave him a special preview." I had to admit, this was starting to sound fringy. "Two years ago, he tells everyone, 'The Rapture happens in six months.' So his followers quit their jobs to help him warn everyone. When the Rapture does *not* happen, does he say, 'Sorry, I was wrong, I am an idiot'? *Non!* He says, 'God gave me more time to save souls, so give me more money.'" He spat out a strawberry cap. "*Morceau de merde*."

It was the same phrase—"piece of shit"—that

he'd used about Felicia Kensington, the black-market art dealer.

"That isn't all. He *wants* the world to end. Look, I'll show you." He pulled several folded pages from the inside pocket of his jacket and handed me the top one. It was a printout from the church's Web site, advertising a series of upcoming sermons by Reverend Jonah titled "Signs of the End Times." Most of the page was filled by an illustration in vivid color. The illustration was captioned by a quotation from the Gospel of Mark: "Seest thou these great buildings? there shall not be left one stone upon another, that shall not be thrown down . . . and there shall be earthquakes in divers places, and there shall be famines and troubles: these are the beginnings of sorrows . . . For in those days shall be affliction, such as was not from the beginning of the creation which God created unto this time . . . " At the center of the picture was an immense, shining cross rising from the smoldering ruins of shattered skyscrapers. In the smoky sky, winged angels hovered beneath the gates of Heaven, welcoming a handful of white-robed, haloed people streaming upward from the ruins. Underground, naked bodies writhed amid the flames of Hell; some were being tortured, and others were engaged in sexual acts that were graphic, degrading, and grotesque.

I handed the page back. "I don't know which is more disturbing," I said, "his eagerness for the world to end, or his fascination with pain and perversion."

"He isn't just waiting for the Apocalypse. He's trying to speed it up."

"Speed it up? How?"

Descartes took a sip of coffee. "For one thing, by creating red cows for Israel."

I paused, my own cup halfway to my lips. "Red cows for Israel?"

"*Oui, exactement.* Red cows. For Israel."

"I don't understand, Inspector. What on earth do red cows have to do with the end of time?"

"I don't understand it, either," he said. "It's very complicated. But some of these end-of-the-world people—not just this preacher, but also some fringe Jews, Messianic Jews—believe that Jesus, or the Messiah, will come again after the temple in Jerusalem is rebuilt."

"Rebuilt by red cows?"

"*Oui,* special cows, trained in architecture and construction." He laughed. "*Non,* of course not. Here is how the red cow fits in. Somebody important a long time ago—Moses or Solomon or God, whoever—said that the best way to clean up sins is to sacrifice a red cow. *Pure* red, with not one hair of any other color—no brown, no black, no white— anywhere on its body. Also, not just a cow, but a *génisse.* I don't know the word in English, but it means a female cow, one that is young. A virgin cow, you know?"

"Ah. The English word is 'heifer.' Yes, a sacrificial virgin. Female virgins always seem to take the sacrificial bullet for the team. But I still don't get it, Inspector. What does sacrificing a red heifer have to do with the end of the world?"

"*Pffffttt.*" Descartes blew out a puff of air, a versatile French expression of irritation or impatience or uncertainty. "I'm telling you, it sounds crazy to me. *But.* These people who want the Apocalypse, they think that when the perfect red cow is sacrificed, the Jews will be purified and inspired. They will unite to drive the infidels from Jerusalem and rebuild their holy temple. And when that happens, *voilà*—the Messiah comes again."

"So the eager preacher in Charlotte," I mused, "joins forces with the militant rabbi in Jerusalem in the quest for the perfect cow."

"*Oui.* But not just looking for the cow. Creating the cow. The preacher is paying farmers and scientists to breed red cows. They thought they had her, the perfect *génisse*, a few years ago. There was much excitement in Jerusalem and Charlotte, but then *poof!*—she sprouted some white hairs in her tail. There was much disappointment. But they keep trying."

I looked around me, taking in the loveliness: the blooming lavender, the splashing fountain, the mobile rotating beneath the plane tree as miraculously and gracefully as the planets circling the sun. It was surreal, this conversation about the destruction of the earth, the desirability of mass suffering, and the notion that a cow's pigmentation could flip the switch of the doomsday machine. "You're making this up, Descartes. You're just messing with my head."

"*Non, non, mon ami,* I cannot make up such crazy shit—I do not have such a big imagination. It's all true. *Incroyable,* but true. And there is more. More and more and more. This preacher, Reverend Jonah Ezekiel, he thinks your government—well, not the government *tout entier*, but the Democratic Party, for sure—is controlled by demons. He's making friends with Republicans who have the potential to become president. Can you imagine? If your president—the man with the nuclear launch codes—decides to launch the battle of Armageddon? Very scary, Docteur."

"Demons, you said? He thinks demons—actual demons from Hell—are running the government?"

"*Oui*. Also Hollywood. Also Wall Street. So to fight back, this preacher and his followers want to get power—'dominion,' they call it, that's why it's in the name of the church—over everything and everybody."

I rubbed my throbbing eyes; squeezed my aching temples. "Unbelievable."

"Here's what worries me most," Descartes said. "In one of his sermons, the preacher says that God is calling for martyrs—people ready to fight and die in the battle against evil."

"Martyrs? Did he really use that word?"

"Yes. 'Holy martyrs,' those were his exact words."

"Yikes. He sounds like Osama bin Laden."

"*Exactement*. Put him in robes and a turban, glue a long beard to the chin, change the name of the religion, *et voilà*—an American bin Laden. *La même chose*—the same thing. *Fou, fanatique, et dangereux*. Crazy, fanatical, and dangerous." He handed me the other folded pages he'd brought.

One was a close-up of Reverend Jonah preaching, his arms outstretched and lifted toward Heaven. One hand clutched a Bible; the other brandished a sword. The expression on his face was like nothing I'd ever seen before, an electric mixture of elation and rage. *This is what zealotry looks like*, I thought. *He'd like nothing better than to hack some unbeliever to pieces with that sword.*

The final two pages were grainy photos from a security camera. Despite the poor quality, I recognized the first photo as Reverend Jonah. The other picture showed a large, muscular man—he could have been a professional wrestler or football player—sporting a shaved head, wraparound sunglasses, and a black suit and shirt that strained to contain his chest and shoulders. "Who's the gorilla?" I asked Descartes.

"That is the preacher's chief of security. His name is Luther Talbot, but his *pseudo*—his nicked name, I think you say?—is Junior." The inspector's translation gave me a smile, but the time stamp on the photo quickly took it away. In the upper right-hand corner of each photo was a string of numerals indicating the date and time of the photo. The men had been photographed two minutes apart—Reverend Jonah Ezekiel at 9:11 A.M. and Junior at 9:13.

The pictures had been taken at Charles de Gaulle airport, in Paris, less than twenty-four hours before Stefan Beauvoir had been transformed into a human crucifix.

CHAPTER 27

SIMONE MARTINI. THE NAME was like a fly against the windowpane of my mind, buzzing incessantly—and with more insistence than Stefan's name buzzed—as I hurried to meet Miranda at the Avignon library again. Could Martini be the creator of the Shroud of Turin? If so, when, and why? Had he done what Emily Craig postulated had been done—copied a crumbling first-century original? Or had Miranda nailed it when she called the Shroud "the world's first snuff film," created by the murder of its main character?

My sense of having split-personality disorder—or, rather, split-century disorder, of being torn between the fourteenth and twenty-first centuries—hadn't gone away. If anything, it had intensified as I waited for Stefan's three "fishes" to nibble at the bait Descartes and I had dangled. If not for the mystery of the bones themselves, I'd have gone off the deep end during the wait.

Elisabeth had shown me a book on Italian artists of the early Renaissance, but Martini merited only a few pages in it. So Miranda and I were returning to the library once more.

In the *M* section of art books, we found a slim volume devoted to Martini. Scurrying upstairs to the mezzanine—which we had to ourselves today—we huddled over the plates of Martini's paintings.

One of his earliest works enchanted me. The image—a fresco in a chapel in Assisi, Italy—depicted Saint Martin being knighted by the Roman emperor. With a golden disk behind his head and his hands folded in prayer, Martin looked every bit the pious saint. But other figures in the scene looked like entertainers at a medieval party. Three singers had been captured in midnote, open-mouthed, forever singing in close harmony. Beside them, a dark-haired man in a colorful, bejeweled robe strummed a stringed instrument—a mandolin? a lute? Accompanying the strummer was a flute player, smiling slyly, and for good reason. I pointed him out to Miranda. "Look," I said, "he's playing two flutes at once."

"Cool," she marveled. Then—a slight variation on her favorite utterance—"How does he *do* that?"

One of Martini's final works—*The Holy Family*—was striking in its treatment of Mary, Joseph, and a youthful Jesus, age ten or twelve. "Wow, a family quarrel," I told Miranda. "Mary and Joseph are scolding Jesus—you don't see many pictures of *that*, huh?"

"And get a load of that pout Jesus is giving them," she said. "What a brat!"

But it was Martini's Avignon portrait *The Blessing Christ*—the red-ochre sinopia drawing I'd seen in the palace—that I kept flipping back to stare at again and again. The drawing had been made as a study for a fresco at the cathedral, one of four scenes tucked beneath the small roof of the front porch. The paintings themselves were gone, but the underlying sinopia of Jesus had been found and moved to the palace to preserve it, along with a companion drawing of Mary. The eyes of Jesus seemed to be looking right at me, as if to say, "You're right—the Shroud, the bones, and I: Martini's Holy Trinity."

Miranda translated the artist's biography for me; it didn't take long, since details of his life were sketchy. "His first known work was in Siena, Italy, in 1315," she said. "He worked in Siena, Padua, Naples, and Florence for twenty years. He moved to Avignon in 1335 or '36 to paint at the papal court. He died here in 1344."

"At the papal court? So he *might* have had a connection to the bones," I noted. "Might have had access."

"That's a mighty big *might*," she said. "Hey, this is interesting. He was friends with Petrarch, the sonnet-spinning chaplain who loved to hate the papacy. Martini painted a frontispiece for Petrarch's copy of the writings of Virgil. Oh, *cool*—he also painted a portrait of Laura, Petrarch's not-quite girlfriend."

"Let's see it," I said. "What page is that on?"

"None, alas—it's long lost. But we know it existed because Petrarch wrote two poems praising the picture, and praising Simone's artistic genius."

But was it possible that Martini had a dark side? Was it possible that he'd created a "snuff shroud," as Miranda had speculated in Turin—a work made expressly to document the murder of the man it depicted? The idea was horrifying but undeniably fascinating. Wouldn't it be ironic if the relic revered by millions was actually a piece of forensic evidence—the world's most sensational and incriminating piece of forensic evidence, one whose meaning had been misunderstood for centuries?

But was Martini capable of committing a cold-blooded murder for the sake of . . . what? Did he have both motive and opportunity, as my detective friends had taught me to wonder? What might drive a talented and prominent artist to commit and document such a crime, and then commit the sacrilege of passing off the evidence as a holy relic?

I took out a pocket-sized notebook and flattened it open. At the top of a left-hand page, I wrote "Motive?" and—on the facing page— "Opportunity?" I stared at the neatly lined pages awhile, feeling foolish and bereft of ideas. Finally, shaking my head in frustration, I forced myself to put pen to paper. Under "Motive?" I wrote "artistic rivalry?" Did Martini have a competitor in Avignon he felt jealous of, threatened by? I nudged Miranda. "Know of any artists who've killed other artists?"

She looked amused. "Dueling paintbrushes? Spray cans of Krylon at twenty paces?"

"Come on, be serious. I'm talking poison, a dagger, a bludgeon, whatever. Murder motivated by artistic jealousy?"

"I think character assassination is more common in cases like that," she said. "Premeditated bitchiness."

"What about romantic rivalry? See if you can find anything on Martini's love life."

"Like, self-portraits showing him in a jealous rage?"

"Hell, I don't know," I said. "But Petrarch left a boatload of poems about his love life."

She gave me a skeptical look, but she humored me by scanning the rest of the bio. "Sorry," she reported. "Looks like your man Martini was the model husband."

"What's your evidence for that?"

"Spotty," she conceded. "Just before he got married, he bought a house for his bride, Giovanna— Italian for 'Joanna'—from her dad. He also gave Giovanna two hundred twenty gold florins as a wedding present."

"That doesn't prove anything," I argued.

"Okay, try this," she said. "Martini died in Avignon in 1344; three years later, when Giovanna moved back to Siena, she was still wearing widow's weeds. He must not have been too scummy if she was still mourning. Of course, who knows what evil lurks in the heart, right? But from the little bit of bio there is, he seems like a stand-up guy."

"The flower of Avignon?"

She nodded. "The flower of Avignon."

CHAPTER 28

Avignon
1330

THE FLOWER OF AVIGNON is unfurling, bursting into full and glorious bloom. By now, twenty years after the papacy arrived for a "temporary" visit, Avignon has grown from a sleepy village of a few thousand souls to a bustling city ten times that size. The cobbled streets clatter with the wheels of carts bringing in wine, meats, cheeses, spices, silks. Every square inch of ground within the old perimeter has been claimed, and the noise of prosperity is deafening: carpenters' saws rasping through framing timbers; hammers pounding pegs into newly raised posts and lintels; tiles scraping and clattering onto new roofs, occasionally slithering off to shatter in the streets below. Most of the new buildings are modest—tenements, tanneries, bakeries, butchers' shops—but others are grand. Avignon and Ville-neuve, just across the Bénézet bridge, now boast a score of cardinals' palaces, many of which outshine the pontiff's own makeshift quarters, which are crammed into what had been the bishop's palace until the papacy arrived and took it over.

Pope John XXII has now worn the papal crown for fourteen years. During his reign, he has steadily refilled the papal coffers; under his watchful eye, the treasury has swelled from a paltry 70,000 florins to 17,500,000 florins—an increase of 250-fold, which must surely please our Lord. The profusion of florins is heaven-sent—"sent" in a manner of speaking, that is, for the tithes and rents and payments for offices and indulgences must always be collected, sometimes upon threat of excommunication, by God's tireless, toiling clergy. But never before has the machinery of collection been so well oiled; Pope John has been blessed with a genius for organization and administration, and that genius has yielded a rich harvest. Still, wealth can be a heavy burden, imposing the responsibility of sound stewardship, of protecting what God has entrusted to His humble servant for safekeeping.

And really, could there be any better steward than Pope John? A banker's son by birth, a lawyer by training, John has brought the church's administrative and banking systems into the modern era. By consolidating and centralizing his minions and their work, he can keep watch over his flocks of clerks and accountants, his vast expenditures and vaster revenues. His eagle-eyed oversight has brought unprecedented protection against embezzlement and fraud. But administrative protection isn't enough; the ever-richer prize of the treasury must be physically protected as well. The snake pit that is Rome, God knows, became a hotbed of assassins and thieves during the papacy's thousand years of residence there. Now, with the papacy's wealth and power centered here, Avignon's gravitational pull is strong, attracting some of Europe's finest painters, sculptors, musicians, and poets. And where money and artists converge, can thieves be far behind? No, the treasury must be secured.

Such are the cares that increasingly occupy the thoughts and prayers of John XXII. The pontiff is now eighty-six—an age prone to mistrust and fear—and lacks the strength to undertake the project needed to safeguard the Church's assets. That work must fall to his chosen successor, Jacques—Cardinal Fournier—who stands before him in the plain monk's robe he still insists on wearing. The robe suggests pious simplicity, but the pope happens to know—His Holiness has spies in every cardinal's palace—that Jacques owns no fewer than twenty such robes, so he will never lack for a spotless one.

"Jacques, you must begin planning," the pope tells him. "I will be gone very soon, and you must act swiftly once you succeed me."

Fournier clasps his plump fingers and bows deeply. "You do me great honor, Holiness, but no one knows the will of God. You might yet reign for many years." *Just to spite me*, he thinks, but does not say aloud. "And when the sad time of your passing does come, the College of Cardinals might feel led to elect someone else as your successor."

"Don't waste my time with false piety and hollow protestations," the old man snaps. "I am old. I was old when they elected me. Seventy-two. That's *why* they elected me—they thought I would return the favor by dying quickly. For fourteen years I have disappointed them by continuing to live, despite three attempts to poison me. They killed my dear nephew Jacopo, but they could not kill me. And in these recent years, I have prepared the way for you, Jacques. I have created two dozen cardinals, most from southern France, three from my own family. The Italian cardinals are now few and weak; we French are many and strong; and you, Jacques, have distinguished yourself by defending the faith. You shall wear the crown and carry the keys."

Fournier bows again, but this time less deeply, and with an eager glint in his eye. "Thy will be done, O Lord," he murmurs in a mellifluous voice— perhaps to God, perhaps to his powerful patron.

"But there is one thing that could yet stand between you and your hopes," the old man pipes in his thin, reedy voice. "And you know what it is." *Christ*, thinks Fournier, *will he never cease to cudgel me with this?* "It is Eckhart."

"Eckhart has been swept into the gutter, Holy Father. He is dead, and you have condemned his heretical teachings. Eckhart's followers have scattered like dust. No one cares that he is dead. In a hundred years, no one will know that he ever lived."

"I pray that you are right, Jacques. But you must take care, lest the Dominican friars make him out to be a martyr."

"It cannot happen, Holiness. I alone witnessed his death."

"But what of his remains? Your Cistercian brethren revere the head of Thomas Aquinas. What if the Dominicans find Eckhart and proclaim his head or his heart to be relics?"

"He will never be found. His bones are in a sealed ossuary in the treasury, and only you, I, and the chamberlain have keys to that room."

"Bah!" The old man waves a trembling hand at their surroundings. "The treasury could be plundered by a dozen Carmelite nuns. You must build a proper palace, Jacques. One that is worthy of the heir of Saint Peter. One that is strong enough to protect God's gold. God has given us sway over emperors and kings, yet we huddle here in a building built to house a bishop."

"I have given this much thought since we first discussed it," Fournier says. "I've taken the liberty of having an architect draw preliminary designs. And such designs they are!" Animated now, pacing and gesturing, he paints a word picture of the mighty towers and lofty battlements that will surround a central cloister—an exterior of formidable strength, an interior of tranquil beauty. "When I am pope—if I am pope—the work will begin immediately. Eckhart's death, and Eckhart's remains, will be sealed deep within the walls. And there they will stay until the glorious morning when the last trumpet sounds, and our Lord and Savior returns in all His glory to reward the faithful . . . and to unleash His righteous anger upon heathens, heretics, and all other enemies of the one true faith."

He ends his impassioned soliloquy with his hands and eyes raised toward Heaven. He holds the pose a moment, then turns and looks to the pope for approval.

The old man is slumped in his chair, sleeping, slack jawed and drooling on his sumptuous silk vestments.

CHAPTER 29

**Avignon
1335**

SIMONE GASPS WHEN THE boat rounds a bend in the Rhône and the city comes into view. Seven years earlier, he had thought that Avignon could not possibly grow bigger or more glorious, but the mighty stone towers rising from the dome of rock prove him spectacularly wrong. The cathedral, which once held pride of place atop the rock, is now dwarfed by a mighty tower, which looms so close to the nave that the two structures all but touch. Wooden scaffolds surround three other towers in various stages of construction. "*Bellissimo,*" Martini breathes, partly because the city truly is beautiful, but also because he feels such secret relief: His painful decision was surely the right one after all.

On his previous trip to Avignon, in the fall of 1328, Martini had come to scout the city, to see what prospects and commissions it might offer one of Italy's most talented and respected painters. Avignon was indeed thriving then, but as he made the rounds of potential patrons—mostly the flock of wealthy cardinals who were descending on the city, trailing clouds of architects and decorators behind them—he was frustrated to find that most of the cardinals, and therefore most of the commissions, were French. For an Italian artist to move to Avignon on the strength of mere talent and brio would have been a foolish gamble in 1329. But now, in the fall of 1335, Martini's been begged to come by a newly hatted Italian cardinal, and he knows now that his family won't starve.

He has already landed a most unusual commission: a secular painting, a small picture of a young married woman, commissioned not by her husband, but by a poet who's madly in love with her. A simple assignment, really—the face of a lady, nothing else in the picture—and yet Simone has never done such a painting before, nor, for that matter, has any painter he knows of. Oh, it's common, and even crucial, to shoehorn the faces of rich patrons into chapel frescoes—to give one of the Three Wise Men, for instance, the craggy good looks of Count Corsino, if Corsino's the one who's piously paying for the fresco. But a picture of a woman—a woman as her real, true self, not masquerading as some saint or martyr, some spectator at a miracle? It's unheard-of! Simone's not sure how much demand there might be for such paintings, but who knows? If he does an inspired rendering of this heartbreaking beauty, portraits might actually catch on.

The lady's heartbroken mad poet, needless to say, is Italian.

On his prior trip Martini had traveled light. Now he's ponderously laden, freighted with so many tools of his trade that even he—who packed everything himself—finds the sheer quantity incomprehensible: boxes and jars of pigments, oils, solvents; cases of brushes and chalks and charcoals and easels and palettes; rolls of canvas and huge folios of paper; parchment envelopes containing gold leaf beaten thin as a day's layer of dust; a carpenter's shop worth of woodworking tools, needed to saw boards and build frames. The working gear is only the half of it, because he's traveling with his beloved wife, Giovanna, and all their clothing and household goods. Rounding out the party is his brother, Donato, also a painter—a wonderful man but a mediocre artist, the meagerness of his talent exceeded only by the meagerness of his earnings.

It wasn't easy, pulling up roots and setting sail to Marseilles and then upriver to Avignon. Twenty years of hard work, judicious flattery, and crowd-pleasing paintings had forged a solid career and a sterling reputation for Simone in Siena and as far away as Naples, where he'd been handsomely paid for his work—and knighted, too—by Robert, King of Naples. Moving to Avignon would require proving himself again, which now, at age fifty-one, was a daunting prospect. The move also meant uprooting his wife from her close-knit family—a leave-taking nearly as painful for Simone as for Giovanna, for her family is like his own, only better.

The good fortune of his marriage still fills Simone with gratitude. At forty years of age— and a homely forty, his discerning artist's eye had forced him to admit—he'd given up on the idea of marriage. Then a miracle occurred. He and another Sienese painter, Lippo Memmi, worked together and became friends, and bit by bit, dinner by dinner, Lippo drew Simone into the circle of his family. Simone fit there as naturally as if he'd been born into it. Lippo's father, uncle, and brother were painters as well, and dinners at the family's table were lively, raucous, joyous occasions. The other family member, Lippo's young sister, Giovanna—eighteen years Simone's junior— astonished Simone with her glances, her smiles, her blushes, and—eventually, astonishingly—her love. They married and moved into a cozy house Simone bought from her father, and for ten years they were happy in it, except for their occasional spats and their dwindling hopes for children. But the work was slowing down, not through any lessening in Simone's skill or reputation, but simply because Siena's building boom—and therefore its fresco boom—had peaked. The paint on his last major commission there, an Annunciation scene for the cathedral, had been dry for two years now, with nothing much on the horizon. So when Simone had sighed and told Giovanna that Siena's sun was setting, and that the future of art lay not in Italy but in Avignon, she'd cried . . . and then dried her tears and started packing.

As the late-afternoon breeze begins to calm, the boat tacks lazily up the final river-mile to the wharf beside the bridge. The twenty-two arches of the monumental span are the crucial links joining southern France to the Holy Roman Empire, the Kingdom of Savoy, the papal territories, and the great Italian city-states. Above its nearer end, the turrets and spires of Avignon seem illuminated from within, glowing with a golden light that soon deepens to orange and then to rose as the sun sinks. The effect—stone set ablaze by light—is dazzling; Simone has never seen its equal in any painting, not by himself nor even by Master Giotto, one of the few painters he acknowledges as his better.

Standing there in the bow of the boat, he feels Giovanna nestle up behind him, her arms burrowing beneath his to wrap around his waist. "*Così bello*," she murmurs. "So beautiful. And you, Simone—you will make it even lovelier."

ASIDE FROM BEING mad with love, the young Italian poet Francesco Petrarch is a charming and intelligent fellow. A thirty-year-old wonder boy whose family was exiled from Florence and ended up here, Francesco is a cleric of some sort, but his chief duties seem to consist in being eloquent, indignant, intellectual, poetical, moody, or whatever suits his fancy at any given moment. He loves to rail against the city and the papacy—"the Whore of Babylon," he calls it, when he's not busy feeding at her breast. He's been posted at some godforsaken village in the dry, dull west of France for the past few years, but he's currently maneuvering to return to Avignon, or some loftier place nearby, from which he can keep closer watch on the city he hates and the woman he loves.

The story, which Francesco clearly loves to tell, is this: During a Mass on Good Friday, nine years ago, he glanced to one side of the church and saw a beautiful young woman, with whom he fell instantly and forever in love. Pursuing her after Mass, he learned that her name was Laura de Noves—and that although she was only seventeen, she was already married, and to a French nobleman, a count. She refused to listen to Francesco's words of love, and so he began writing them down instead, and publishing them: hundreds of love poems dedicated to a woman he spoke to for half a minute, nearly a decade ago. Now, he's commissioning Martini to paint a portrait of her—an image he can gaze at whenever he needs to rekindle the flame of his love.

But perhaps "love" is not the right word. Martini has a sneaking suspicion that Petrarch cultivates his pain—a child picking at a scab—because it pleases him in some perverse way to carry an unhealed wound on his heart. It is his own version of the stigmata, Martini realizes, the wounds that proclaim, "Behold how I suffer!" Martini has been married to Giovanna for nearly a dozen years now. The two have fought, they've made up; they've laughed, they've cried; they've cooked and cleaned and pulled weeds together; they've made tender love and half-hearted love and primal, grunting animal love. Martini's pretty sure that since Petrarch has done none of these things with Laura—has done nothing at all with her, in fact, and furthermore knows nothing about her except that he can't have her—what the poet's really in love with is not the woman, but in fact himself and his own sense of heartbreak. The man is writing a never-ending tragedy, and casting himself as the tragic hero. What's more, it's beginning to make him famous; other poets have started to copy and circulate Petrarch's verses; some are even imitating his writing and his heartbreak.

No, Martini's got no starry-eyed illusions about this goddess: She's doubtless a pretty and privileged Frenchwoman of twenty-five, a knight's daughter who married up and became a countess at age fifteen. She certainly wasn't the first pretty girl whose youth and beauty were sold for a title and a life of ease, and Martini doesn't begrudge her the good fortune. Martini's got no illusions about his own role, either. If Petrarch wants him to immortalize his muse in paint, and is willing to pay well for the job—fifty florins!—Simone's happy to unpack his paintbrushes and start mixing his reds and greens and golds. "I'll get started right away," he tells the poet. "When it's finished, you must write a poem immortalizing my picture of your lady." Petrarch nods gravely, as if he doesn't realize that Simone is just joking.

CHAPTER 30

IN ALL HIS THIRTY years of painting, Simone has never worked this way before; has never had to squint and strain and sneak to snatch furtive glimpses of the face or figure he's painting. Often, in fact, he's had the opposite problem: a model whose ripe lips or plump breasts were offered not just to his artistic eyes but to his strong hands; a woman—or occasionally a man—whom Simone had to push away, but gently, so as not to spoil the sitting and hinder the painting.

At first, he hated watching the young woman, hated following in Petrarch's pathetic shoes— lurking in doorways near her house on Sundays; trailing her to Mass, or lying in wait inside the church to snatch a glance at her forehead or eyes; lurking across the aisle or behind a column as he studied her profile; dashing to his studio after the benediction to sketch and paint before the details of her face fade from his memory for a week. Gradually, though, Simone has been forced to admit that he likes the challenge—painting someone he can scarcely see—and he looks forward to studying her each week.

One Sunday as she kneels, he sees her head slump and her shoulders slacken; then, with a jerk, she awakens, wide eyed, and suddenly he hears her laugh—in church!—when she realizes what she has done. The matron beside her gives her a sharp, reproving look, and she forces her face back into its mask of composed piety. But Martini has now seen something else behind the church-face mask, and his curiosity is aroused.

That night, as he lies beneath the covers before going to sleep, he plays a painter's game with himself, imagining how he might paint her face in various scenes, with various expressions and emotions: worry, gratitude, tranquility, terror, irritation, delight, lust. And then, when Giovanna rolls her body against his in the dark, and her fingers seek him out, stroke him to hardness, and guide his flesh into hers, it is Laura's face, and Laura's breasts, and Laura's moans that he imagines and that make him gasp and shudder with a fiery passion that Giovanna's simple honest love has never managed to ignite.

THE NEXT SUNDAY, she is not there. He checks her usual stations—the side chapels where she always pauses to light candles—scanning the congregation with confusion and growing dismay. Somehow, because she has always been here, he has taken it for granted that she always would be here.

His surprise gives way to another feeling, one he recognizes as fear—no, as panic! What if she's gone for good—moved away to Paris, or killed by a sudden fever? How can he possibly finish the portrait until every detail of her is etched in his mind? How will he explain his failure to Petrarch? And then: How will he fill his Sunday mornings, and the other hours of his days and nights that she has come to occupy? *Good God*, he thinks, *I am worse than the poet. I have a good wife, a sweet and faithful woman who loves me, and yet I am turning into a schoolboy over this woman—this girl—who is thrice forbidden to me: She is married, I am married, and she is beloved by my friend Petrarch.* In a state of consternation, he stumbles over the feet of the other worshipers in his pew, turns up the side aisle of the nave, and makes for the door.

Just before he reaches it, he feels a tug on his sleeve. He turns, and there—hidden by a pillar—is the woman herself, a sight so unexpected he almost cries out in surprise. She watches him regain control of himself, then says, "*Monsieur, vous me cherchez?*": Sir, are you looking for me? Working with French painters and seeking French patrons, he has mastered much of the language by now, but he is so taken aback by her sudden appearance and blunt question that he resorts to a well-worn ploy, shaking his head and shrugging to indicate that he does not understand her, and adding "*Sienese*" to make sure she gets the message.

"*Ah, Siena, una bella città*," she says, switching to his own language so fluently and effortlessly, she might have grown up next door to him. "A beautiful city," she repeats. "If you are Sienese, sir, I envy you." She glances down briefly, then looks up at him again, and when she does, the intensity with which her eyes probe his is almost palpable: as if she were a blind woman, exploring his very soul with her fingers. She lays a hand on his arm. "Come. There is a garden in the cloister. I would speak with you." She leads him out a side door, through an archway, and along a loggia to a far corner of the cloister, to a bench tucked into an alcove of boxwoods. She sits, and motions for him to sit beside her.

"Now, sir. Tell me why you were looking for me. Don't pretend you weren't." Again he shrugs—not, this time, to feign incomprehension; this time, to acknowledge that he's been caught, and has no defense. "I've noticed how you watch me. Not just today, but for weeks. Every Sunday I feel your eyes on me. Why?"

"You . . . you are a beautiful young woman, my lady. What man could resist looking at you?"

Slowly she shakes her head. "Many men look at me. Some with contempt, some with longing. But no one else looks at me the way you do. You study me; you examine me, as if I were a flower or an insect whose parts you wish to catalog. Why?"

He opens his mouth to speak, but he can find no words. If he lies, she will see through it; if he tells the truth, she will hate it. He looks away, fixes his eyes on a statue of the Blessed Virgin, and sighs. "Forgive me, my lady."

"Sienese." She says it slowly, musingly, turning it over in her mind as she turns it over in her mouth. She looks down, then she reaches down, taking his right hand in hers, lifting it, examining his rainbow-tipped fingers. "You are a painter. The Sienese painter. Simone of Siena." He bows slightly in awkward confirmation. "I have seen your frescoes in Siena. They are wonderful. I was glad to hear that you had come to Avignon." He bows again, more deeply, and when he straightens up, he meets her gaze frankly for the first time. Her eyes continue to bore into him, but there is no anger in them, only curiosity, as well as the glimmer of something else crystallizing in her mind. "Why do you study me with your painter's eyes, Simone of Siena?" How can he even begin to explain? He does not have to. "Do you paint me, Master Simone?" He hesitates, then nods slowly. She looks away, and when she looks at him again, her expression has changed. "Do you paint me for him— for the poet who puts me on a pedestal?" He nods again. She looks down, and when she looks up, tears are beading at the corners of her eyes: dewdrops on a gray autumn morning. "I did not ask to be his goddess, Master Simone. I do not want to be his goddess. Why do I not have a choice? He has pinned me to the pedestal, in view of everyone, and now, no matter what I do, I cannot get down. With his eloquent and unrelenting insistence, he has made me into what he imagines. I've heard a story, Master Simone, about a Greek sculptor long ago who managed to turn a statue into a woman. This poet is transforming me from a woman into a statue."

"Forgive me," he says again. "I did not know— did not consider—how his . . . attentions . . . might affect you. I should never have accepted the commission. I will destroy the picture this very day."

"No!" Her eyes widen, and she puts a hand to her throat. "No. Wait." Her breath is rapid now, her cheeks flushed. "First, you must tell me about this picture. How are you painting me, Master Simone? What scene am I in? What biblical figure do I portray?" The corners of her mouth twitch. "I cannot be the Virgin Mary. Am I the woman caught in the act of adultery?"

The question makes him blush; can she read his nighttime thoughts? "Of course not, my lady," he says, perhaps a bit too swiftly and loudly.

"Am I Elizabeth, the withered old wife of Abraham, who finally conceives at age ninety?" Her eyes twinkle, and he's both shocked and delighted by the boldness of her teasing.

"Old and withered? Far from it, my lady. In my painting, you are young and beautiful. In my painting, you are no one but your own true self."

She smiles. "I knew you were a fine painter, Master Simone. I did not know you were a skilled flatterer, too."

"No. I have no gift for words. Only my brush can speak, and it says you are lovely and luminous."

She pinks. "And in this secret picture, what does your brush say that I am wearing?"

"You are wearing your green silk gown with the collar embroidered in gold, the one you were wearing when Petrarch first saw you. The one you were wearing when I first saw you. Pearls—the choker, not the long strand—encircle your neck. Your hair is pinned up, as it is now, but it is the cloisonné

comb, not this tortoiseshell, just above your left ear.
Your head is turned a little to the right, which is
why we can see the comb, but your eyes are looking
straight at the viewer. Straight at me." As he says
the words, her eyes are indeed locked on him, just
as in the portrait; just as in his imaginings. He continues, "The irises are mostly green—almost emerald at their edges—but flecked with gold, especially
near the center, where the iris meets the pupil." He
is leaning closer now, staring at her eyes, talking
almost in a whisper, almost to himself. "I wish I
could paint the way the pupils pulsate in time with
your heartbeat: larger, smaller; larger, smaller. But
even at their smallest, they are large. I have never
seen pupils so large as yours. They are quite . . .
remarkable."

Her eyelids close, and her breath whistles slightly
across her lips as she breathes in deeply. Then her
eyes reopen, glazed for just a moment before they
refocus and fix on him again. "I do not wish for you
to destroy the picture, Master Simone. I want you
to finish it. But I want you to grant me one request
in return."

"What is your request, my lady?"

"I want to see it. When you have finished it—
before you give it to him—you must show it to me.
Will you?"

"Yes. Yes, of course. When? Where? Shall I
bring it to your house?"

"By all means—if you wish for both of us to be
killed!" She smiles. "Where is your studio, Master
Simone?"

"It's not much of a studio. More of a shed. Right

behind the Carmelite church—the one with the open bell tower. Follow the smell of turpentine."

"When do you expect to finish?"

"I had thought it was finished, my lady, but I was wrong. I need to fix your eyes."

"Fix them? What's wrong with them?"

"I have not made them luminous enough."

She laughs. "See, such a flatterer. The courtiers in Paris should take lessons from you."

He holds up a hand. "God's truth, my lady. I had them right, but then I doubted myself. 'Simone, you fool,' I told myself, 'eyes cannot possibly be so green and also so gold.' So I changed them, made them more ordinary. Now, I must put them back as they were. As they are. As they must be."

"I will bring my looking glass with me, Master Simone, so I can inspect your repair work," she says. "When may I see it?"

"Perhaps next Sunday morning? Before Mass? Or after Mass?"

"Instead of Mass," she says. "I will be there."

"My lady? I, too, have one request. So that I can be sure I have it right, is it possible for you to wear the green silk gown?"

She bows. "Yes, Master Simone. And the pearl choker. And the cloisonné comb."

CHAPTER 31

Avignon
The Present

ELISABETH BROUGHT DESCARTES'S COFFEE and my tea; by now, she and Jean considered the detective to be a regular fixture at breakfast—the rule rather than the exception—and I made a mental note to ask, when I settled my tab at the end of my stay, if they needed to add an item to my bill: "Descartes's breakfasts, 40 euros." It no longer startled me to see him tuck a croissant into his pocket; I halfway expected him to start showing up with a Thermos and a lunchbox so he could load up on coffee, fruit, cheese, and baguettes.

This morning Descartes was branching out. He loaded the grain mill with oats, bran, and sunflower seeds, pressed the button, and presto, out came fresh-ground muesli, which he topped with dried cherries and fresh yogurt. He sampled the concoction, smacked his lips, and nodded in approval.

"*Bon*. Healthy, too." He took a bigger bite. "So, I've been looking for connections between the church in Charlotte and the research place that contacted you."

"The Institute for Biblical Science?"

"*Exactement*. As we thought, it's no coincidence. The preacher, this Reverend Jonah, he's on the board of directors of the institute. And the scientist—"

"Newman, right? Dr. Adam Newman?"

"*Oui*, Newman. Guess what else he is doing?"

"Uh . . . calculating the exact moment when the Antichrist will appear?"

"Ha! Maybe that, too. But for sure he's working on—"

He was interrupted by a phone call—my phone, not his. I glanced at the display. *Tennessee Bureau of Investigation*. I felt a surge of dread. The last call I'd gotten from this number had brought word of Rocky Stone's death in Amsterdam. "Sorry, Inspector, I need to take this." He nodded as I answered.

"Doc? It's Steve Morgan at the TBI. I hope I'm not waking you up."

"Not at all. I'm just having breakfast with a French detective. But why aren't *you* sleeping? Isn't it two in the morning there?"

"Three," he said. "I had some news I thought you'd want to hear. We swooped down tonight—us, the DEA, and the FBI—and rounded up the outfit that killed Rocky and his undercover agent. We owed it to Rocky. The guy he had the shoot-out with in Amsterdam—"

"Morales?"

"Yeah, Morales. The feds recovered his cell phone. It was a gold mine: all his contacts. We picked up one of them in Tennessee, two in Atlanta, four in Miami."

"Is that everybody?"

"No, but good enough for now," he said. "The top guys are in Colombia; they're out of reach, at least for now. But we got everybody who had a direct connection to the Sevierville operation. You can quit looking over your shoulder now—at least on this account."

I drew a deep breath and let it out. "That's a relief. Have you told Rocky's wife yet?"

"I'll go see her at a decent hour. After she's had a chance to take the kids to school. She'll be glad we got these guys, but it'll be tough for her to hear, too. She's still a wreck."

"I'm sure," I said. "I'll go see her and the boys when I get back from France. If you get a chance, tell everybody I said 'good work.' I'll do my part at the trial."

"Thanks, Doc. Stay safe."

I laid the phone down and picked up my tea. The sun was bright and the day would get hot, but not for another hour or so, and the warm mug felt good cradled in my hands. I took another breath to reground myself in the garden, in Avignon, in the case at hand. "Sorry, where were we?"

"The Institute for Biblical Science. Newman, the scientist."

"Oh, right. Can you tell if he's an actual, for-real scientist? Not some charlatan who bought a Ph.D. online?"

Descartes shrugged. "I don't know where he got the Ph.D., or how good it is, but he's a molecular biologist. So he's trying to make the perfect red cow for Israel, using DNA from the cow that was almost perfect. He—"

"Wait. They're not just breeding cows, they're *cloning* cows?"

"*Oui*. Cloning. Trying, but they do not succeed yet."

Alarm bells were tolling like crazy in my head. "And he's working with this preacher, Reverend Jonah—the guy who wants to switch on the doomsday machine? And these guys want the bones from the Palace of the Popes? Why?" But I already knew the answer, even before I finished the question. "Good God, they're hoping to get DNA from the bones. They want to clone Jesus. The high-tech Second Coming of Christ."

"Sure," said Descartes. "If you can clone a cow, why not Jesus?"

I set down my cup and raised my arms. "Because it's crazy and impossible," I sputtered. "There can't possibly be undamaged DNA in those bones—not nuclear DNA, not the kind you'd need for cloning. Maybe, *maybe*, there's mitochondrial DNA, but that's just little pieces; it's not the whole set of blueprints."

"You are sure of this?"

"Very sure. Besides, it's not unique to individuals. It gets passed down from mother to child, generation after generation. Your mitochondrial DNA is identical to your mother's, Inspector. And to *her* mother's. And her mother's mother's."

Descartes considered this. "Jesus had the same mitochondrial DNA as his mother, *oui*?"

"*Oui*, Inspector."

"So: the same as the Virgin Mary." He raised his eyebrows. "Another virgin birth, then, *n'est-ce pas*?"

"But mitochondrial DNA can't be cloned into a human being," I practically shouted. "It's scientifically impossible."

He shrugged. "All it takes is another miracle, *et voilà*."

I wanted to take him by the collar and shake him. "Damn it, Descartes, these aren't even the bones of Jesus!"

"Ah, you are wrong, Docteur—they *are* the bones of Jesus. There is scientific proof, remember? The carbon-14 report from Miami. The bones are two thousand years old."

"That was total bullshit, Inspector. Stefan faked that. You know that."

"But the preacher, he does *not* know. He has faith in this report. If we tell him it is bullshit, he won't believe us. He will say *we* are controlled by demons."

Despair clutched at my heart, and I found myself thinking the unthinkable. *Is the crazy preacher right about the end of the world? Is it time?*

CHAPTER 32

**Avignon
1335**

IS IT TIME? **SIMONE** counts the strikes of the bell ringing in the Carmelite church—ten—and realizes with despair that he has another hour to wait. To wait for her.

He sets to work tidying the studio but quickly realizes that it's hopeless. The place is a mess; it is, after all, a workshop, crammed with brushes, boards, fabric, pigments, solvents, and a thousand other implements and ingredients. He uncovers the small portrait, then covers it again, so he can watch her face as he unveils it. Realizing he has no chair to offer her, he rakes brushes and tools off the worktable, shoves them underneath it, and drapes the rough boards with a clean drop cloth. He paces, then perches restlessly on the table, then paces again. Sixty minutes is an eternity.

Finally the bell begins to toll eleven, the hour

of Mass, through the iron latticework of the steeple. By the second peal, he knows that she will not come. She *should* not come, he realizes—it could compromise her, and he would not wish to add that to her troubles. But then there is a knock at the wooden door, which he has left slightly ajar, and his heart surges when she calls his name.

"Yes! Please come in! I feared you would not come."

"I feared you would not be here when I did." Laura de Noves smiles. "What a lot of worry we've both wasted, Master Simone." She is wearing a black shawl around her shoulders and a black scarf over her head; they mute her beauty and the elegance of her dress, but even so, she must surely have been the most striking woman in the streets of Avignon.

"Was it difficult for you to get here?"

"Not very. I only had to poison my husband and strangle my maid."

Again he is startled and delighted by her humor. He wishes he could spend hours learning her habits of conversation, of mind, of movement. But he knows this will likely be his only chance to indulge his curiosity.

She points a silk-gloved hand at the small covered rectangle on the easel. "Is that it? Is that me?" He nods. "And did you fix my eyes?"

"I think so. I hope so. And did you bring your looking glass?"

"Of course. I said I would, didn't I?" She pulls a small silver-handled mirror from some inner pocket, some secret fold of the dress.

"I didn't know if you really meant it."

"I don't always keep my promises, Master Simone, but I do try." She smiles, though the smile has sadness in it. He sees the poignancy in her expression at the same moment he hears the poignant chanting of the Carmelite nuns. She lays the mirror on the worktable, then unties the scarf and folds it, setting it on the table, too, followed by the shawl. Picking the mirror back up, she inspects her hair, adjusts the cloisonné comb in some infinitesimal way Simone can't detect, and then walks to the easel. "Show me, Master Simone. How did you describe what you've painted—my 'own true self'? Show me my own true self, Master Simone."

Nervously, as if unveiling his very first painting for the very first time, the grizzled artist takes the cloth by the upper corners and lifts it. As it slides slowly up the picture, the threads catch now and then on the textured paint; the slight rustle of the moving fabric is the only sound in the room. Then he hears her breathe—a quick intake, almost a gasp. He dares to breathe now, too, and risks a glance at her.

He is shocked by what he sees. He'd hoped she would smile, perhaps even laugh or clap her hands in delight. Instead, she looks like a mother who has just witnessed the death of her only child. Her eyes are filled with anguish; her right hand flutters across her lips and chin and neck; her left hand, still holding the mirror, drops to her side. She closes her eyes and hangs her head, and her shoulders begin to shake.

"Oh, my lady, I have displeased you. I . . . don't

know what to say. Forgive me. Oh, forgive me, please."

"You have deceived me, Master Simone," she whispers. "This is not . . . my own . . . true . . . self. Perhaps it once was. But not now. I am not that woman now. Perhaps I never was."

"What do you mean? Tell me, I beg you—I cannot bear this." Never in all his years of painting has his work inspired such hope followed by such despair, and never in these years has he been brought to tears by a critic. Yet Simone of Siena, Knight of Naples, is crying now, too, and the chanting nuns seem to give voice to his pain. "Where is the fault? What is untrue? How have I disappointed you so badly?"

"You've put flesh and blood on your canvas, Master Simone. You should have painted stone instead. Marble, covered with words. I am nothing but stone and verses now. Even my heart has turned to stone. My husband prefers his mistress; the man who claims to love me sings my praises to everyone but me." She turns away and steps behind the easel so she will not have to see the portrait any longer.

Simone does not speak for some time. Finally he shakes his head. "Oh, poor woman. Oh, foolish man—what has he done to you?"

He takes a step toward her, looks closely at her face. "Perhaps you are right; perhaps I have not portrayed you faithfully. It was difficult to see your features well in the dim light of the church, from so far away. I should take a closer look, in this light." He is an arm's length away now—closer than he has ever been to her, except for that brief conversation in the cloistered garden. He reaches out, tucks the stained knuckle of his index finger beneath her chin, and lifts her head slightly. He leans closer, adjusts his hand so that he holds her chin lightly between thumb and index finger, and then turns her head slowly from side to side, scrutinizing the planes and highlights and hollows of her face. "I did my best," he says at last, "but you are right, I must confess. I did not capture your true self. Here, for instance." Lifting his other hand, he brings his index finger to a spot just above the right corner of her mouth. "You have a little mole right here." He grazes it with his fingertip—perhaps he strokes it lightly, or perhaps his finger is simply trembling. "I failed to see this mole. I'm sorry. I should have included it—it punctuates the line of your mouth."

He leans back to glance at the portrait, but his hands do not leave her face, and now his finger traces her upper lip. "I am sure I have the bow of this lip right," he says, "but I fear that I have not given enough ripeness to your bottom lip." He slides the finger along her lower lip now, pressing slightly; the finger catches and tugs on the lip. She is quaking now, and her breath is fast and ragged. He takes the lip between his thumb and forefinger, squeezing and rolling it, and she gasps, then whimpers softly. "Your jawline," he murmurs, stroking its edge, "I know I did not get that wrong. But these wisps of hair on your neck, I could not see them in the gloom." Both his hands now float across the loose tendrils of hair; he does not touch the skin of her neck, only the down, and it feels to her as if a spring breeze is caressing her. His hand returns to her mouth, his fingers tugging and teasing the front of her lips, then grazing her teeth, then easing between their edges. "If only the Mass had made you smile," he whispers, "I could have shown your teeth." He presses the edge of his hand against them; they part slightly, taking in the meaty flesh and then clamping down, causing him to groan. Her face is flushed, her breath is ragged, and her pupils dilated almost to the outer edge of her irises. He slides his other hand down her arm and lifts it, raising the mirror. "Look in this glass again and tell me now: Is this a woman of stone, or of flesh and blood and fire?" She stares at the image she sees there; her breath catches, her knees buckle, and she sags against him. He lifts her with his paint-stained hands and sinewed arms, carries her to the table, and with exquisite tenderness begins to undress her.

HE MAKES TWO small changes in the portrait, painting bare chested as she cleans herself with a damp cloth he has handed her. Near the corner of her mouth, he adds the mole, and on the bodice of her dress, between her breasts, he adds a small tongue of flame. As he finishes the flame, she buttons her dress, smooths the silk, and repins her hair. She inspects herself once more in the mirror, comparing herself with the portrait. This time she smiles as she tucks the glass back into the hidden pocket. They do not speak. She takes the paintbrush from his hand and lays it on the ledge of the easel, then places his hand on her breastbone, exactly where he has portrayed the flame. Pressing his hand tightly against her, she kisses him on the mouth, and then on each cheek, and then she slips out the door and into the street that will carry her from him.

The final, fading notes of the Carmelite choir waft in through the open door, entwining with the dissipating scent of her perfume and their musk. He wanders to the table, picks up the cloth she has used, and presses it to his face, inhaling their scent. It is the scent, he thinks, of forbidden fruit. The fruit of the tree of the knowledge of good and evil.

The next day he bundles up the portrait and sends it to Petrarch. He puts no note in the package; nothing but the picture. Besides breaking faith with Giovanna, Simone has broken faith with the man who is both his client and his friend. He knows this, and he suspects there will be a price to be paid, a penance to be done. But it must be a private penance, he resolves, one that he must impose on himself; a burden he must carry alone, to spare the feelings of those he has wronged. Inextricably bound to his memory of how she caught fire beneath his touch, Simone will bear the burden of his secret guilt.

Two weeks later, a courier brings him a package from Petrarch. It contains twenty-five florins—the balance of the fee for the portrait—and a poem. Petrarch has actually done it: taken Simone's jest in earnest and penned a poem praising the portrait. Simone scans the poem's opening lines, which declare that if all the best painters competed for a thousand years, they could capture only a fraction of Laura's matchless beauty. The next lines proclaim, "Surely my Simone was in Heaven, the place my gracious lady comes from; there he saw her, and portrayed her on paper, to prove down here—where souls are veiled in bodies—that such a lovely face exists."

Martini reads it a second time, and then a third. "Where souls are veiled in bodies," he says aloud, shaking his head and adding, "foolish man." He crumples the page with the strong, stained hands that gripped her ardent flesh.

A FEW DAYS after receiving Petrarch's poem and money, Simone receives a new commission, for a project he hopes will distract him from his longing and guilt: frescoes in the papal palace—in the pope's own bedroom! The room is high in the Tower of Angels, the massive stone fortification that Pope Benedict's army of workers has created during the past year. Just fourteen months ago they notched the massive foundation blocks into bedrock; now, the masons are capping the tower with crenellated battlements. *Curious*, Martini thinks. *Siena's cathedral, dedicated to God, took fifty years to complete, but this immense structure dedicated to the pope—papal palace, fortress, and strongbox—has sprung up overnight.*

Simone identifies himself to a guard at the tower's entry portal. The guard inspects him, clearly finding him lacking or distasteful in some way—perhaps it's the odor of turpentine, or perhaps it's the scent of foreigner that the French guard detects. Nevertheless, the guard waves him in, pointing

to the back of the room. "Go see Monsieur Poisson. Architect and master of the works." Poisson
is hunched over a mountain of drawings, invoices,
receipts, and notes. He looks up, weary and bleary,
as Simone bows and announces himself in French.
"Simone Martini, painter of Siena, at your service."

"Martini? Ah, yes, Martini—you're here to help
the French painters in the pope's chamber."

Simone shrugs. "I prefer to think that the French
painters are helping me," he jokes, but Poisson
doesn't notice.

He leads Martini up two stories via a spiral staircase built into one corner of the tower. The pope's
chamber, the fourth floor of the square tower, measures some thirty feet square, with walls twenty
feet high: room for buckets and buckets of paint.
Martini counts two dozen workers—a third of
them masons and plasterers, a third of them painters, and a third of them spectators or bosses, he
can't tell which. Scaffolds scale every wall, from
floor to ceiling. At floor level, painters weave in
and out of the legs of the scaffolds, covering a blue
background with loops and swirls of golden vines,
their branches populated by legions of birds. A level
higher, a troop of plasterers has just finished applying a fresh coat of smooth plaster, and painters
elbow them out of the way, eager to apply the blue
background paint. They must work swiftly, applying not just the background but also the vines
and birds, before the damp plaster dries. On the
third and highest platforms, masons are applying
the base coat of rough plaster to the top courses of
bare stone. It is this level, the last five feet of wall

below the ceiling, that Martini has been hired to paint—this, plus the deep recesses where windows have been notched into the massive walls.

Simone can't help feeling disappointment. The best part of the room—the largest, lowest portion—has been given over to the French painters, and clearly it's being wasted on them, these daubers with their simple swirls of gold on blue. Child's play! Simone could paint vines and birds left-handed—with his eyes closed!

He clambers up the ladder to the top level of scaffolding—his level—and surveys the bustling room from there. He has not yet settled on the theme for his frescoes, but he knows it will be something far more challenging, far more impressive. Something with depth, detail, and drama; something that will move the pope to point to the scenes and say, "Bring us the painter who has done these, that we may reward him and exalt him above all other artists!"

His reverie is interrupted by a shout from below. "Martini!" He looks down; the chief of the contingent of French painters, Jean d'Albon, is waving to catch his eye. "We need to mix more tempera," d'Albon says. "Can you bring us more eggs? Twenty eggs?" Simone glances at the clay pots in which the powdered pigments of red, blue, green, and gold have been stirred with egg yolk to moisten them and glue the paint to the plaster; indeed, the pots are nearly empty. Simone considers refusing—is d'Albon assigning him this menial errand simply to establish the pecking order?—but, in fact, all the French painters appear to be busy, and d'Albon puts his hands together in prayer posture, bows slightly, and adds, "Soon, when you are hurrying to finish your magnificent frescoes, I will bring eggs to you." Simone can't resist smiling—d'Albon will almost certainly never play the errand boy; he has apprentices for that—but the good-humored offer acknowledges that Simone is d'Albon's equal, and the other painters cannot fail to have noticed the gesture.

Simone clambers down the ladder, calling, "And where will I find these twenty eggs, laid by twenty pious hens to glorify God, His Holiness Pope Benedict, and French fresco painters?"

D'Albon laughs and moves his index finger in a downward spiral. "All the way down, at the bottom of the tower, where it's nice and cool. Soon it will become the subtreasury, filled with gold, silver, and jewels. But for now, it's the egg cellar. Eggs and plaster and rags."

Simone ducks through the doorway into the spiral staircase and starts down, but then—on impulse—he stops and looks overhead. The stairs continue upward, apparently to the roof, and Simone decides to take a quick detour before fetching the eggs. He jogs up the first spiral, walks briskly up the second, and lumbers up the third, huffing by the time he steps onto the rooftop.

The view from the roof is dizzying and dazzling. To the west, the arches of Saint Bénézet's Bridge cascade across the Rhône to Villeneuve. At their far end is another square tower, this one built by the king of France to collect bridge tolls . . . and to remind the sometimes arrogant residents of

Avignon who holds the real reins of power in this part of God's world. From below, d'Albon's voice wafts upward; an apprentice is getting a scolding for his clumsy plasterwork, and Simone turns from the view and scurries for the cellar.

Spiraling down turn after turn, he feels his head begin to spin, and he stops near the bottom and leans on the wall to steady himself. It's cool and dark down here—there are no windows in the tower's lower levels, only narrow slits that provide stingy hints of light and air. In the chamber just below him, he hears a gritty, sliding sound, punctuated by grunts of exertion. Curious now, he descends the final few stairs and peeks into the chamber— the egg cellar that will soon brim with treasure. By the golden glow of a flickering lamp, he sees a portly workman shoving a heavy chest into a deep niche in the wall, then wedging a flat stone over the opening and slathering mortar around the edges. The man's troweling technique appears oddly awkward, and his work looks shoddy. Simone's puzzlement only increases when the man finishes sealing the stone in place; when he stands, Simone sees that the pale garment he'd taken for a workman's smock is instead a floor-length white robe. A Cistercian monk's robe. The kind of robe favored, as everyone knows, by Pope Benedict himself: the White Cardinal who has become the White Pope.

Suddenly Simone senses the vulnerability of his position: lurking in the stairwell spying on some furtive secret of the pope's. Edging back up the stairs one level, Simone ducks into a dark, vacant room and waits until he hears footsteps. From his hiding place, he sees the white-robed figure pass by like some stout, panting ghost. Once the footfalls and panting have faded, Simone hurries back to the cellar. He should collect the eggs and hurry upstairs with them—the French painters will be running out of tempera any minute now, if they haven't already—but his curiosity triumphs over his sense of responsibility. Crossing to the far wall, he squats beside the mortar bucket and studies the crude handiwork, as if close inspection of the wall's surface might reveal what's hidden inside. Hidden by the pope himself! But why? Why hide a treasure chest inside the wall, when the entire room, floor to ceiling, is meant to be heaped with riches? In any case, why not order a real mason to do the work?

Astonished by his own sudden boldness, Simone picks up the trowel and uses the tip to scrape out the line of mortar holding the flat stone in position. Then he pries the panel free, leans it against the wall, and tugs the chest from its niche. The chest, a stone box, is wired shut, and the wires are crimped together with lead seals—the seals of Benedict XII!—to protect the contents. Rubies and emeralds? Gold florins? Perhaps even the Holy Grail?

Throwing aside any last vestiges of caution or respect for authority, Simone cuts the wires with the edge of the trowel and pries the close-fitting lid loose. Even before he lifts it off and sets it aside, the smell of death wafts out, so he's not completely unprepared to see bones inside. Simone's not squeamish—given that so many artists' models are beggars and whores, a painter can't afford to be squeamish—so it's natural for him to take a closer look at the bones.

He starts with the skull. Cupping it carefully in both hands, he lifts it from its nest of ribs and raises it to eye level. The face is long and narrow, the cheekbones high and prominent, the forehead slightly lower than he would have expected. He rotates the skull in his hands, looking to see if there is damage—marks of a violent death—but there is none. As the skull comes full circle in his hands, Simone's visual memory tells him there is something familiar about its shape and proportions. He frowns, trying to place it, and suddenly lays the skull aside and roots in the box until he finds what he's looking for: the bones of a forearm, which are—as he knew they would be—slightly splintered at their lower ends, just above where they once joined the wrist. Just where a spike would have passed through them on its way into the wood of a cross.

He rummages in the box for the other arm, and then for the feet. All four extremities bear the ragged, splintery evidence of piercings. Martini lays the limbs on the shelf alongside the skull and stares at them, the bones that were within the flesh he studied and sketched so attentively.

His mind ranges back to that odd night seven years ago, when he spent hours drawing by flickering lamplight, capturing every detail of the fresh corpse laid out on the floor of the cell. He remembers the parting words of the jailer: "I do believe he was a holy man. . . . His only sin was his holiness."

He fits the lid back onto the box. Then, acting on an impulse he could not have put into words, he reaches for a pair of tools lying on the floor—a chisel and a hammer—and swiftly incises a broad cross on the stone lid of the box. Then, beneath the cross, using the pointed corner of the chisel's blade, he gouges the outline of a lamb. Working swiftly—for the mortar in the bucket will harden soon, and he is surely risking his life to tamper with the pope's sealed secret—he replaces the box in its niche, wedges the slab back into place, and trowels mortar into the joints, taking care to mimic the Holy Father's sloppy workmanship.

As he slathers the final bit of mortar into the gap between the stones, Simone wonders why God has put this dead man—this blameless man, if the jailer's report was true—in Simone's path not once, but twice now.

He rises, and starts up the steps. Only then does he remember and turn back. God might require penance of him soon, but d'Albon's painters needed twenty eggs half an hour ago.

CHAPTER 33

**Avignon
The Present**

ELISABETH SURVEYED THE LEFTOVER fruit and pastries with surprise when she came to collect the breakfast tray, then peered at the untouched cup of espresso. "What," she asked in astonishment, "no *Monsieur l'Inspecteur*?" She cast a glance at the cornflower-blue sky. "Did the sun fail to rise today? Is the world coming to the end?"

"I'm as amazed as you are."

Instead of taking away the tray, she sat down in Descartes's usual chair beside the fountain. "I am glad he is not here," she said.

"I don't blame you. He's been eating berries and croissants by the truckload." I didn't mention the takeaway treats he always tucked in his pockets.

Her brow furrowed for a moment, then she beamed. "*Ah, non*. I do not mean for that reason. I am glad because I wish to talk to you. I have something news to tell you. I think you will be happy to hear it."

"Have you been playing detective again, Elisabeth?" The last time she'd looked this excited was when she'd shared her theory about our "zhondo": that the unknown skeleton from the palace might be that of Meister Eckhart.

She clapped her hands with delight. "*Oui!* Remember what you told me?" She leaned closer and spoke in a low, conspiratorial voice. "That the man had a unique shape? Legs that came almost up to the neck?"

I laughed. "Maybe not quite *that* long. But yes, very long legs for a man his size. As long as mine, and I'm much taller than he was."

"Yes. So. Last week I got in touch with my cousin—I told you he is a Dominican, yes?" I nodded. "I do not tell him why I ask, so don't worry, I keep the secret. But I ask him, 'What do the Dominicans know about the appearance of Eckhart—his size, his shape?' *Mon Dieu*, my cousin thinks I am crazy, but he says, 'Okay, I will do some research.' And this morning, I have an e-mail from him. No one painted a picture of Eckhart until hundreds of years after he died, so we don't know what his face looked like. *But.* Sometimes, behind the back, the other friars called him *Ciconia Dei*." She leaned back, looking pleased with herself.

"Why did they call him that?"

Her eyes danced and her smug smile broadened. "It is Latin. It means 'the stork of God.'"

CHAPTER  34

Avignon
1337

MARTINI AVOIDS LAURA AS assiduously as Petrarch seeks her out. Whenever Petrarch is in Avignon, he dogs the poor woman's steps, carefully trailing twenty or thirty paces behind her, scrupulously praying a stone's throw away: close enough to see her, close enough to be seen—his melancholy face, his artfully downcast gaze—yet far enough that the distance is conspicuously chaste. For Simone, on the other hand, no distance would be chaste or ethereal if he were in her presence, so he steers clear altogether.

And yet there's no escaping her, or at least the reminders of her; in a way, she trails Simone as relentlessly as Petrarch trails her. Scarcely a day goes by without some count or marquis or emissary or lady seeking him out, taking him aside, and murmuring in his ear, as if it were a secret, "I know you painted the lady Laura's portrait for poor Petrarch. I have seen it—and such a likeness!" Apparently everyone in Avignon has seen the secret portrait . . . and yet he knows that is not so, for occasionally, to test the admirers, he poses trick questions, which nearly always trip them up: "And what did you think of the emerald necklace she wore?" he might ask, or perhaps, "Was the blue of her eyes perhaps too deep?"

Astonishing, how the small, secret portrait of Laura—seen by few but praised by many—has put Martini's name on the lips of all. Petrarch has now written not one, but two sonnets praising the picture. These have been copied and put into wide circulation, perhaps by other poets, but perhaps by Petrarch himself, not one for self-effacement. Martini had been appalled by the poems, but he'd be a fool to turn down the well-heeled clients that the poems have brought him. One of them, Cardinal Corsini—even more prone to self-admiration than Petrarch, if such a thing is possible—has commissioned a portrait of his own dearly beloved: himself.

Between the portraits and the frescoes in the pope's bedchamber, Simone is now laden with work, and gradually the death portrait of Christ seems less urgent. The pope's frescoes are nearly finished. The twenty-four panels that crown the bedroom's walls depict scenes from the four Gospels, although—high on the walls as they are—who will be able to see and appreciate their details? The frescoes in the window recesses depict architectural features—arches, columns, and coffers—that heighten the illusion of depth, making the walls appear not merely six feet thick, but ten or twelve, so His Holiness can sleep secure in the knowledge of the strength of his fortress.

Simone now employs two assistants to do the drudge work for him: painting backgrounds and draperies and inscriptions, freeing Simone to focus on what he does best, and prefers above all: the faces and bodies that everyone tells him are more lifelike than any other painter's—and it's true! He's buried in commissions, working harder than he has ever worked in his life.

His latest project is a set of four frescoes commissioned for the portico of the cathedral. One of them, *Andrea Corsini Healing a Blind Man*, is paying the bills for the other three scenes, in a manner of speaking. The painting depicts a miracle that—according to the Corsini family, at least—occurred only a few years earlier, right here on the cathedral's front porch, one morning before Mass. A wondrous event, if true, restoring sight to a blind man, yet Simone can't help suspecting that the painting isn't motivated purely by piety. The Corsinis have launched a vigorous campaign to have Andrea declared a saint, and the fresco is central to their strategy: "See," it seems to say, "the proof is right before your eyes. You'd have to be blind yourself not to see it."

The second fresco, the *Madonna of Humility*, is obligatory—the cathedral is, after all, dedicated to Mary. This one, too, Simone finds it hard to put his whole heart into. Perhaps he's grown skeptical about the miracle of the Virgin Birth, but more likely he's simply tired of painting mothers and babies year after year, especially as Giovanna grows sadder and sadder about her barren womb.

The third scene, by contrast—*The Blessing Christ*—is a source of satisfaction and deep pride to Simone. Jesus seems to float in the sky; his right hand is raised in benediction, and his left cradles an orb. Within the orb, Simone has represented the world in miniature: a landscape, rippling waters, and a starry sky, all artfully contained inside the sphere. The Savior's gaze is strong and direct, as if our Lord were locking eyes with each viewer, one by one. Such an intimate, powerful gaze is bold and without precedent—unlike any portrait of Jesus that Simone has ever done, or ever seen. Surely this homage to Christ will bless the man who painted it; surely this will wash away Simone's secret guilt.

The fourth of the portal frescoes shows Saint George slaying a dragon and rescuing a princess. Not surprisingly, this fresco is livelier than the other three. Simone is not the first painter to portray the heroic deed, but he is the first—of this he feels sure—to bring such vivid drama to it. The knight, on horseback, charges forward, his lance gripped in both hands, galloping over the bones of earlier knights who died fighting the beast. The dragon rears up to fight, its scaly back arched, its talons clawing for the horse. The eyes are glittering with reptilian hate, and the sharp-toothed mouth is open to unleash a blast of fire. But the creature is a split second too slow: Although the dragon's body has not yet had time to register it, the mortal blow has, at the very instant portrayed, been delivered.

With unerring aim, Saint George has thrust his lance straight into the beast's open mouth, with such force that it has pierced the throat completely and emerged at the back of the neck, its sharp tip drenched with blood.

But despite its brilliance and drama, the Saint George fresco proves to be Simone's undoing. In portraying the princess rescued from the dragon, Simon has impulsively given the princess the face of the lady Laura. To be sure, the face is small—only a few inches high—but the few people who have glimpsed the work in progress seem far more interested in the princess than in the miracle worker Corsini, the Virgin, the Christ, or the dragon-slaying saint. As he puts the final touches on the dragon, Simone considers altering the princess's face, but stubbornness or pride overrules the voice of caution, and he leaves it unchanged.

On the Sunday morning that the frescoes are unveiled, a huge throng gathers before Mass to file through the portico and view the paintings. On hand to bask in their admiration is Simone, standing just inside the door with Giovanna beaming beside him. A hundred people have already filed through to gawk and congratulate, and another two hundred still crowd the stairway and street outside. Simone leans out the doorway to see how the line is moving, and what he sees nearly drops him to his knees. She—the young countess herself, Laura de Noves—is at the top of the stairs, stepping onto the porch. Dressed in the green silk, she wears a pendant around her neck; the stone, which rests on her breastbone, is a large ruby, cut in the shape of a teardrop . . . or a flame. Inching along beside her, his hand resting possessively on the small of her back, is a thin, sallow man with sparse red hair and watery blue eyes. Trailing the couple is a nurse-maid, carrying a small child on her hip. The boy's hair, eyes, and skin are black, brown, and tan: the earthy tones of Siena; the earthy tones of Simone—his father!

Simone staggers backward into the nave, then flees to a side door, leaving behind hundreds of disappointed admirers. Just before stepping through the door, he turns and sees his wife staring at Laura and the baby, Madonna and child. Even in the dim light of the church, Simone can see recognition, shock, and betrayal dawning—no, flashing like lightning—across Giovanna's face as she takes in the pale woman and the dark boy who is so clearly Simone's.

Simone stumbles down the hill and hurries to his studio, where he sinks onto a stool and slumps forward onto the table. The cathedral frescoes were not his penance after all—if anything, he realizes, the foolish arrogance of the Saint George scene only added to his guilt, because Giovanna is now wounded by the knowledge that he has been unfaithful to her . . . and has even fathered the son that she has never been able to give him. Now, not only has Simone betrayed her trust, he has broken her heart, shattered her innocence. He groans and sobs as he comprehends the full extent of his shame. Then, with startling, piercing clarity, he suddenly understands the penance he must perform. Somehow, he thinks, I must find a way to portray the death of innocence—my innocence, Giovanna's innocence, the world's innocence. And how better to represent the death of innocence, he realizes, than a death portrait of the innocent Christ modeled on the blameless dead man God has sent his way again. What was it the jailer had said? "His sin, I think, was to be holy, to be free of sin"?

Clearing off his worktable and unrolling his dusty sketches of the dead monk, Eckhart, Simone finally begins the penance he has been avoiding these past two years. The penance for betraying Giovanna.

CHAPTER 35

SIMONE SNATCHES A RAG from his worktable and savagely wipes the tempera from the wooden panel. He has painted a dozen images of the dead man now and has destroyed them all, finding them bland and insipid—utterly lacking the force of that stark corpse laid on the floor of that stone cell; completely devoid even of the force of those charcoal sketches he made by flickering lamplight almost a decade before.

He returns, for the hundredth time, to the sketches. Unlike his polished attempts with paint, the charcoal images of the man are rough but powerful. Why can't he render in paint what he captured in charcoal? Because, he thinks, a painting is too artful, too refined: a glittering object to be admired from a distance, not a force to be experienced and shaken by. The power of that scene, and of those sketches, lies in their rawness and immediacy. In the moment back then, and even in the sketches now, there is no possibility of distance, of a safe retreat into studied appreciation of color and technique, of composition and balance, figure and background, gilded borders and halos. *The Death of Innocence* cannot be a painting, he realizes; it must be something stark, spare, and haunting.

But sketches are not enough. Simone grasps the power of these rough sketches on coarse paper. But ordinary eyes—seeing humble materials—might be misled into dismissing the images as trifles; might not take them into their minds and hearts. Simone must help people let down their guard and open their hearts. To do justice to a man who was as innocent as a dove, Martini must be as cunning as a wolf.

An image pops unbidden into his mind: *The Mourning of Christ*, painted by Master Giotto on the wall of the chapel in Padua. The limp body of Jesus is surrounded by weeping followers; grieving angels hover overhead, their hands outstretched or clasped or clapped to their faces in dismay and grief. Behind the mourning people, a low rock ledge angles from the picture's lower left to its upper right. But something about the rock ledge struck Simone as odd the first time he saw the fresco: The ledge's surface seemed fluid, almost as if it were draped with fabric, and Simone had briefly wondered, all those years ago, if perhaps a burial shroud had been laid on the ledge to receive the body of Christ.

Now, that remembered painting and his own sketches of the dead man combine, and he knows how to proceed.

* * *

AT A WEAVER'S shop on the Rue de Teinturiers, the street of dyers, he inspects and rejects half a dozen fabrics—too coarse, too shiny, too short— before finally settling on one: a long strip of pale linen woven with a herringbone pattern that adds heft and elegance without calling attention to itself.

He buys the entire roll and takes it back to the studio. Grinding one of his sinopia chalks into a fine dust, he mixes it with egg yolk to make a reddish-brown slurry of tempera. On a small corner of the fabric, he daubs a bit of the mixture, but he sees at once that the contrast is too jarring, the effect not at all mysterious or mystical. Frowning, he picks up another sinopia chalk and draws directly on the fabric with the dry crayon, sketching eyebrows and the bridge of a nose. It's better, he decides, but still too obvious. To create the haunting effect he's after, Simone must create a haunting face—the shadow of a face, the ghost of a face. Finally, doubtfully, he takes a sheet of parchment and shades the nose and eyebrows, followed by the rest of the face, but this time he deliberately makes the image dark and heavy. Then he lays another corner of linen atop the drawing. Using the blunt, curved end of the pestle with which he grinds pigments, he rubs gently from all directions, pressing the cloth against the image in dust. After several minutes of rubbing, he folds back the fabric.

Simone gasps. There on the linen, staring back at him, is the ghost of the murdered monk; the ghost of the crucified Christ; the ghost of innocence lost.

CHAPTER 36

Avignon
The Present

I GLANCED FOR THE twentieth time at the doorway of the library mezzanine, listening for the staccato cadence of Miranda's clogs as she jogged up the stairs. I'd been waiting for half an hour, and I was getting anxious. It wasn't like her to be this late, especially when she was the one who'd called the meeting. Our librarian friend, Philippe, who had by now taken an interest in *our* interests—Eckhart, Martini, and the Shroud—had phoned Miranda an hour before to say that he'd found something intriguing, and Miranda had wasted no time summoning me. Upon arriving at the library, I'd been surprised that Miranda wasn't already waiting. Now, thirty minutes and a dozen unanswered cell phone calls later, my surprise was turning to genuine worry.

Finally I heard footsteps on the stairs, but they weren't Miranda's. Philippe appeared in the doorway. "Ah, good—I *thought* that was you sitting up here."

"Yes, but we're still waiting for Miranda."

"Unfortunately, I cannot wait any longer," he said. "I'm taking a class—art history—and I have an examination this morning. If I show you what I found, will you share it with her?"

"Of course, Philippe. Please."

He pulled out a chair and sat across the table from me, laying a folder between us. "My art history professor is a curator at the Petit Palais—do you know it?"

"That's the museum that's in a former cardinal's palace, right?"

"Exactly. Specializing in medieval art from the time of the Avignon popes. There is one painting on display there by Simone Martini—a Madonna and Child, not very interesting to you, I think. But my professor showed me a drawing in the storage room—not on display—that she is certain was made by Martini. It's not signed, but it was found in the city archives, filed along with some very old records about Martini's house and studio. She let me make a photocopy of it." He slid the folder across the table to me. Slowly I opened it. The image inside was a charcoal sketch of a man's face—or, rather, parts of a face: a pair of eyes and a nose. The nose was long and broad and slightly crooked. It looked like a nose that had been broken in a fight.

It looked like the nose on the Shroud of Turin.

* * *

TWENTY MORE MINUTES crept by after Philippe left me with the Martini sketch of the Shroud nose, and still no sign of Miranda. Finally, unable to sit still any longer, I went to the window that overlooked the library's leafy courtyard. The window was open, and the late-morning air wafting from the street was getting steamy with heat and smells. Along with the mouthwatering aroma of onions and potatoes frying, I caught the sour tang of sewage—one of the signature perfumes of ancient cities, I'd decided. Down below, two kids scampered toward the children's wing; they were trailed by a mother who—at 11 A.M.—already looked weary. On the opposite end of the courtyard, a stout dowager waddled behind a fat, waddling dog, reminding me of Miranda's comments on dogs and gods.

Suddenly, floating up from below, I heard music—the angelic voices of a mighty choir, funneled through a puny speaker. To my surprise, I realized that the angels were singing in English: "Glory, glory hallelujah! Glory, glory, hallelujah!" Scanning for the source of the sound, I glimpsed movement across the street. A man stepped from a shadowy doorway, pulling a cell phone from a holster. As he raised the phone, the hymn swelled by a decibel or two, then ceased as abruptly as it had begun. The man put the phone to his ear, and I thought I heard him say, "Praise God." I leaned out the window for a better view, and when I did, his face swiveled toward me.

I'd seen that face before. I'd seen it framed by upraised hands—one of them clutching a Bible, the other waving a sword—and I'd seen it in a Paris airport security photo, taken after I'd arrived in Avignon. As I stared, frozen in the open window, Reverend Jonah Ezekiel smiled at me for what seemed an eternity, his smile and his gaze never wavering, until a car—a sleek black sedan with dark windows—screeched to a stop directly in front of him. It paused just long enough for the preacher to slip into the backseat. Then it spun forward, skidded around a corner, and was gone.

Inspector Descartes didn't answer until the fourth ring, and by then my throat had clamped shut in fear. As I fought and failed to form words, he snapped, *"Oui? Il y a quelqu'un? C'est quoi, ça?"* Hearing no response, he hung up. I forced myself to draw a deep breath, then another, and hit the redial button. *"Oui,* Descartes," he practically shouted when he answered.

"Inspector, it's Bill Brockton," I managed to choke out this time.

"Docteur? Is something wrong? Are you hurt?"

"No, I'm not hurt, but I'm afraid something's wrong. Terribly wrong. I'm afraid Reverend Jonah has Miranda."

"Merde," he cursed. "What has happened? Why do you think this?"

Haltingly, with frequent pauses to breathe and to tamp down my panic, I told him.

"Merde," he repeated. "What kind of car? Which way did it go?"

"I don't know. Black. Four doors. A Mercedes? A BMW? Something French? Hell, I don't know, Inspector. I only saw it for a second before it disappeared around the corner."

"Did you see the driver?"

"No. The windows—" Suddenly the phone vibrated in my hand; startled, I nearly dropped it out the window. When I saw the number of the incoming call, though, my heart soared. "Inspector, I have to go. I'm getting a call from Miranda." I pushed the "send" button. "Miranda? Thank God. I was worried sick."

"No need to worry," said a man's voice, smooth and sarcastic. "She's in very good hands. She's in God's hands." The floor seemed to drop away beneath me, and the vast, frescoed reading room spun. "But you can get her back if you do exactly as I say."

"Who is this? And what do you want?"

"Don't play dumb. You know who I am, and you know what I want. You yourself offered it to me by fax. Shall we discuss a trade?"

I was heartsick. Descartes and I had gambled that Stefan's killer would still want the bones, and we'd been right. I'd been willing to risk myself, but Reverend Jonah had outsmarted me: He'd guessed, correctly, that the highest trump card he could hold was Miranda. I opened my mouth to speak, but once more my throat had seized.

"Do you hear me?" The voice had grown less smooth and more menacing. "I have your precious pearl. Give me the bones, or she dies."

"If you kill her," I managed to force out, "you'll have twice as many police after you."

He gave a short, scornful laugh. "They have no jurisdiction."

"Not just the French police," I said. "Miranda's

an American citizen. If you kill her, the FBI will come after you, too." I didn't know if that was true, but I hoped it was true, or at least *sounded* true, sounded intimidating.

"You misunderstand me," he sneered. "This world's authorities have no dominion over me." The words, and the thinking behind them, sent a chill through me. "But why are you talking about her death? The girl goes free when you hand over the bones. Do you not intend to do that?"

"Of course I do," I hurried to assure him. "But how do I know you'll keep your word? You've already killed Stefan."

"Only because he didn't keep his word. He betrayed me. I hope you won't make the same mistake."

"I won't. But how do I even know you've got Miranda? How do I know she's all right? Let me talk to her."

"I'll call you in an hour with instructions. You can talk to her then. Don't call the police, and don't play games with me. Not if you want her back alive." The phone went dead.

NINETY-SEVEN ENDLESS, AGONIZING minutes later, he called back. The signal was weak and his voice was breaking up badly; I didn't know if that was because he was calling from someplace with poor signal, or because I was deep inside the concrete headquarters of the Police Nationale. " . . . attention," the voice crackled. "Here's . . . do if . . . girl back alive. . . ."

"First I need to talk to her," I said. "I won't do anything until I know she's okay." I heard an angry breath at the other end of the line, and I feared I'd pushed him too far, but then I heard shuffling noises as the phone changed hands. "Oh, Dr. B, . . . sorry." Even through all the dropouts, Miranda's voice sounded thin and quavery; if it had been a pulse, I'd have called it "thready" and taken it as a symptom of shock. But still, the thready, shocky voice was *her* voice—blessedly her voice. "One of them . . . my hotel . . . paged . . . said you . . . chest pains. He had a car . . . hospital . . . with him . . . known better. God, I fell for the same . . . pulled on you . . . so very . . ."

"Oh, Miranda, *I'm* the one who's sorry. I told Descartes I didn't want to involve you, and look what I've done."

" . . . not . . . fault. . . . Stefan's." Her voice shifted gears—got higher, faster, more urgent. Shaking my head in rage and pointing at the phone, I stood and jogged out of the inspector's office and down the hallway to the building's back door, inwardly cursing Descartes for bringing me into the concrete bunker. "Listen . . . Stefan . . . greedy . . . upted. Don't let that . . . be interruptible . . . B, understand? Interruptible . . . key . . . get the bones. Do you hear . . . ? . . . key . . . bones."

I shoved open the door and raced outside, Descartes a few steps behind me. "Miranda, you're breaking up really bad. Can you say that—"

"Wait, I'm not *finished*," I heard her protest. Then came the sounds of scuffling and grunting, followed by the sharp *smack* of flesh on flesh, and the word "*bastard*" in Miranda's low snarl.

"Miranda? *Miranda?*" I was shouting into the phone, spinning around in the parking lot, frantic with frustration and fear. Two uniformed officers, chatting beside a patrol car, stared and started toward me, but Descartes waved them off. *"Miranda?"*

"That's all you get," snapped the voice I assumed was Reverend Jonah's, "until I have the bones."

"Bring Miranda with you," I demanded. "You set her free first, and I watch her walk away safely, or no deal."

"Don't push me. You're playing games with her life, and her life means nothing to me."

"But the bones do," I reminded him. "You want those bones just as much as I want Miranda. Her safety is your only hope of getting them."

"Bring them to the Templar chapel tonight," he said. "Midnight."

"No!" The thought of walking into a trap—or of finding Miranda's body strung up the way Stefan's had been—terrified me. What's more, there was no hope of finding the bones that swiftly.

"What's the matter, Doctor, does that venue disturb you?" He chuckled, and my blood ran cold. "I didn't think a man in your line of work would be so squeamish. You disappoint me."

"The police are probably still watching the chapel," I said. "Anyhow, I can't get to the bones until day after tomorrow."

"*What?* What are you talking about?" His tone was sharp and suspicious. "What do you mean, you can't get to them? Why not? Where are they?"

"Stefan and I put them in a very secure place.

A Swiss bank vault. I have to go to Geneva to get them, and the bank's closed tomorrow. Sunday. The Sabbath, Reverend."

"You're lying." My heart nearly stopped when he said it. There was a pause; I thought I heard whispers. "Which bank?"

"Credit Suisse."

"What street is it on?"

"Give me a break, Reverend. I'm supposed to help you plan my own ambush? I might be from Tennessee, but I'm not that stupid."

"Stefan said the bones were here. He was supposed to bring them that night."

"But he *didn't* bring them," I countered. "Why wouldn't he have brought them if they were here?"

"I told you. Because he got greedy. We'd agreed on a million, but that night he said he'd gotten another bid, a higher bid. He said the new price was two million."

I was stunned by the figures, but didn't dare show it. "That's not the way I do business, Reverend. If Stefan agreed to a million, I'll honor that price."

There was a pause, then more whispers. "I don't think you understand the situation yet, Doctor." His voice sliced into me, as cold and sharp as a straight-edge razor on a winter morning. "The new price I'm offering—the *only* price I'm offering—is the safe return of your assistant." He paused to let that sink in. "If you don't actually care about her, I suppose we could talk money instead. But that means I'll have to kill her. And killing her would mean considerable inconvenience and risk for me. You yourself said the FBI would come after me. So if you'd rather have money than the girl, the new price is half a million."

"You know I don't want money," I said. "I just want her back safe."

"Then quit playing stupid games."

"I'm not playing games. I'll be back from Geneva with the bones Monday night."

"If you're not, she'll die—and she'll die a much worse death than Stefan did. And after she does, so will you. By God, you will." With that, he hung up.

"*Damn* it, Inspector, why'd you put me in a cell-phone-proof building for that phone call? I missed half of what she was saying."

"Sorry," he shrugged. "I never have a problem using my mobile in there. It must be something about your American phone."

"She was trying to tell me something important," I fumed. "Something about where the bones were hidden." Twice she'd said something about "key" and "the bones." Piecing together the two fragmentary versions, I suspected she'd said, "the key is to get the bones." By *key*, did she mean *crucial*, as in "it's crucial to get the bones"? That seemed absurdly obvious; of *course* it was crucial to get the bones. No, she must have been talking about an actual key. She seemed to be telling me that the bones were locked in a hiding place that the key would open. But what key, what hiding place, and where? Wherever it was, the Geneva ploy had bought us thirty-six hours to find it.

Geneva hadn't been a spur-of-the-moment improvisation. Descartes and I had discussed how to stall while we looked for the bones, and the Swiss bank was the most plausible delay we could invent. We had also set other wheels in motion—a contingency plan, in case we couldn't find the ossuary. We feared that Stefan had sent photos to the buyers, so Descartes had commissioned a local mason to create a replica of the stone ossuary; my role in the ruse was to arrange for Hugh Berryman, the anthropologist who was holding down the fort for me at UT, to overnight an old skeleton from Knoxville.

Hugh had plenty to choose from. Shelved deep beneath the university's football stadium were roughly five thousand human skeletons: more than one thousand modern donated skeletons, plus several thousand Arikara Indian skeletons from the eighteenth and nineteenth centuries—bones I'd excavated from the Great Plains many years before as the Army Corps of Engineers dammed rivers, creating new reservoirs and flooding Indian burial grounds. The Arikara bones certainly weren't two thousand years old, or even seven hundred years old—more like two hundred to three hundred—but they had a gray patina that made them look convincingly old, and they bore no dental fillings, orthopedic devices, or other traces of modernity. I'd given Hugh detailed specifications: The skeleton had to be an adult male, roughly five and a half feet tall, and free of obvious skeletal trauma—except for the gouges I instructed Hugh to inflict on the wrists, feet, and lower left ribs to simulate the wounds of Christ, or the wounds of our Jesus Doe. We were performing a bizarre sort of crucifixion—a postmortem, postdecomp crucifixion, surely the only one of its kind ever done.

With this counterfeit Christ, I realized, I was joining the ranks of forgers, taking up a new trade: the trade in fake relics. With luck, the decoy skeleton would arrive in thirty-six hours, and while it might not fool a forensic anthropologist, it might fool a crazed televangelist.

It was risky. But we needed time. We needed bones.

And we needed a miracle.

CHAPTER 37

I FLIPPED THROUGH THE pile of papers on the desk for the third time, but it still wasn't there. My panic and my blood pressure were skyrocketing. I'd been back at Lumani for only a couple of hours, and already I felt caged and crazy. Descartes had told me to sit tight while he and a search team combed the palace for the bones, but I couldn't bear the confines of my room any longer. I desperately needed to talk to someone, but Jean and Elisabeth were nowhere to be found, and I couldn't find the phone number I wanted.

Finally I thought to look under the desk, and sure enough, down by the baseboard, hidden by the desk's square leg, I found the card with the number scrawled on it. My hands shaking, I dialed it.

"Sorry I missed you," announced a cheerful Irish voice, "but leave me a wee message and I'll ring you back."

I cursed silently; after the beep, my words poured

out like water through a collapsing dike. "Father Mike. It's Bill Brockton. The American anthropologist. We met a few days ago at the library. I don't know if you're still in Avignon, but if you are, I'd appreciate a call. *Really* appreciate a call. I . . . something terrible has happened, and I don't know who else to call. I . . . So if you're still around, please call me." After I hung up, I realized I hadn't left my number, so I called back and left that.

I nearly jumped out of my skin when my phone rang. I stared at the display. The number looked familiar, but I was having trouble placing it; on the third ring, I realized that it was the very number I'd dialed only moments before. "Father Mike, is that you?"

"Hello, lad. Yes, it's me. And yes, I'm still here. I'd been planning to leave this morning, but I had a drop too much last night and I missed my train. So here I am, at your disposal. The Lord works in mysterious ways, and the serendipitous hangover is one of his most mysterious." His voice grew serious. "Do you want to tell me what's wrong, lad?"

"I do. But not over the phone. Could we meet somewhere? Talk in person?"

"Of course. There's a lovely little church two blocks east of the Palace of the Popes. It's Saint Peter's, but the Frenchies insist on calling it Saint Pierre."

"I don't know, Father Mike. It's been a long time since I've been in a church."

"You didn't let me finish, did you? Right in *front* of Saint Pierre's is a lovely outdoor restaurant with green umbrellas. L'Épicerie. It's French for 'grocery,' or so I'm told. Somewhere nearby, I suppose, is a greengrocer's called Le Restaurant. Could we meet at L'Épicerie? I'm starving, and to tell you the truth, lad, I could do with a little hair of the dog, too, if you wouldn't mind terribly."

"I don't mind. I don't even drink, and I'm tempted to have a few. How soon can you be there?"

A YOUNG COUPLE was just sitting down at the last of the umbrella-shaded outdoor tables when I arrived at L'Épicerie fifteen minutes later. In the restaurant's doorway, I noticed Father Mike talking earnestly with the headwaiter. The maître d' was shaking his head stubbornly, but suddenly he paused and seemed to listen more attentively. He leaned closer; he smiled; finally he nodded. Father Mike smiled, too, and shook the man's hand, and a moment later the young couple—now the indignant young couple—was being ejected from their table, and the waiter's profuse apologies did little to smooth their feathers. They glared at Father Mike, who shrugged, smiled sheepishly, and pointed heavenward before taking one of the vacated chairs for himself and offering the other to me.

"That was impressive," I said. "The power of the collar, or the gift of the gab?"

"Neither, lad," he grinned. "The allure of the euro. I slipped the bloke a twenty."

"You're very worldly, for a priest."

"I wasn't always a priest, remember. Besides, I'm just doing what the Lord told us to do."

"Jesus said something about bribing maître d's?"

"In a manner of speaking, lad. He said to be as crafty as serpents and as innocent as doves."

"I'd say you've got the first part down cold, Father Mike."

He laughed, but then his face turned solemn. "But we've got more serious things to talk about, haven't we, now? You've gotten more bad news, I'm thinking. Something more about that undercover fellow?"

It took a moment to realize that he wasn't talking about me. "No, no, it's not Rocky. Not at all. It's Miranda."

"Forgive me for being thick, but who's this Miranda?"

"She's my assistant. My graduate assistant. She's here for the same reason I am—the old bones I mentioned to you. But she's in terrible danger, Father Mike."

"What kind of danger?"

"She's been kidnapped."

"Kidnapped, is it? Are you sure? I'll bet she's just off on a lark with some French lad she's taken a fancy to."

"The kidnapper called me, Father Mike. And he let me talk to her. She sounded scared, and he's threatening to kill her."

"Dear Lord in Heaven. Have you gone to the police?"

"Yes, of course, but if this guy finds out, he'll kill her for sure."

"Well, let's pray he doesn't find out, then. How much ransom money is it he's wanting? Is it a huge lot? Can you get your hands on it?"

"It's not money. He doesn't want money."

There was a silence before he asked the obvious next question. "Then what does he want, Bill Brockton? You don't have to tell me if it's too personal. But I'm thinking you want to."

I considered keeping the secret, but the idea made me angry, I realized: It had been Stefan's secrecy—his damnable secrecy and lying—that had caused all this trouble in the first place. "The bones."

"Excuse me? I'm not quite following you, lad."

"He wants the bones. The goddamned, stupid, *sonofabitch* bones."

If he was shocked or offended, he didn't show it; all he said was, "These must be some mighty important bones, then."

"Yes. And no. People think they're important—one guy's already been killed over these bones—but they're not as important as Miranda is."

"Well, then, it's simple, isn't it? Just give him the bloody bones."

"I wish I could. It's not that simple, Father Mike."

"Ah, well, then. It usually isn't, is it? If it were, you wouldn't be sitting here with me, would you, now? So how can I help you, lad?"

I shook my head. "I don't even know. Just by listening, I guess. You do a lot of that, right?" He nodded and leaned forward, so I talked. I talked while the waiter brought beer for Father Mike and water for me; I talked while plates heaped with food appeared before us, and empty plates got cleared away. Starting with Miranda's unexpected invitation and sudden departure to Avignon, I told him almost everything that followed: my own hasty trip; Stefan's secrecy and paranoia; the facial reconstruction and its uncanny similarity to the Shroud of Turin; the carbon-14 results and the way Stefan had rigged those; finally, the murder of Stefan.

When I described the death scene, the priest gave a soft whistle. "Crucified? You're not feeding me shite here, are you, lad?"

"No shite. Honest truth. It was terrible."

"Jesus, Mary, and Joseph. I'm gobsmacked I didn't hear about it through the vine. Priests are terrible gossips—much worse than old women. Just shows how out of touch I've been while on me holliers." He took a long pull on his beer—his second beer, or maybe his third; he had a quick elbow, and I wasn't keeping track. "And you say this Stefan had three different folks on the string, all of 'em wanting to buy the bones? How do you know that?"

"Because the homicide detective found a fax that Stefan sent them. We don't know if all three were serious bidders. But we do know that one was. Deadly serious."

"Sounds like a bad business, Bill Brockton. Are the police making any headway tracking these folks down?"

I shook my head in frustration. "Not enough. They think we can rule out two of them. One's a shady art dealer, a woman who caters to rich buyers who want precious antiquities and don't care how they're obtained. The detective thinks she's a slimeball, but not a killer. And she has a solid alibi for the time of the murder. One is a distant colleague of yours, Father Mike—a curator or something, we don't know who—at the Vatican Museum."

He made a face. "Ah, the Vatican Museum—the Holy Father's lovely little art collection. One of the fringe benefits of the job. Art and altar boys. We have a lot to answer for someday."

"But the one we're pretty sure has Miranda is a Protestant fanatic. An end-timer. A preacher who sees himself as one of the Horsemen of the Apocalypse." The nearby church bell tolled, and I nearly jumped out of my seat. "He calls himself Reverend Jonah Ezekiel. And if I don't give him the bones in twenty-four hours, he'll kill her."

"So just do it. Why not? Because the police are telling you not to? Bugger the police; save the girl's life. Simple."

"It's not simple. We don't know where the bones are."

"What's that?"

"We think Stefan moved them, hid them, just before he was killed. We don't know where they are."

"So why did this crazy fellow kidnap the girl?"

I rubbed a hand across my weary eyes. "I let the detective talk me into pretending I had the bones. We were using them as bait. But we were just bluffing."

"And now this fanatic has called your bluff." I nodded miserably. "Raised the stakes a bit, too, I'm thinking."

"God, I didn't mean to involve Miranda, Father Mike. I thought I could keep her out of it, but I was wrong, and Descartes, the detective, was right. We're all involved, we're all implicated. One thing's for sure—if I can't find the bones in time, Miranda will die, and I'll be to blame."

"Well, then, there's only one thing to do, isn't there?" I looked up. "We have to find those bones, haven't we, lad? And right smartly, too." He laid a hand on his chest, studying me thoughtfully. "One more thing, lad. I know you're not a big believer in saints and relics, but would you think about wearing this?" He loosened his collar, reached inside his shirt, and fished out a large silver medallion on a leather cord. He took it off and offered it. "Look, it's a twofer," he said. "On this side, Saint Christopher, protector of travelers. On the other"—he flipped it—"Saint Anthony, patron saint of lost things."

"There's a special saint just for lost things?"

"Sure, lad. There's a patron saint for pretty much everything, and a prayer to go with it. There's a fancy prayer to Saint Anthony—you beg him for help, you tell him what you've lost, and then you grovel a bit, all polite and pious. But there's another version, a cheekier version, that I like a lot better. 'Tony, Tony, look around, something's lost and must be found.' Makes him seem like a friendly chap, a helpful bloke, you know?"

I took the medallion from him. The disk was big—it nearly filled my palm—and surprisingly heavy. I hefted it. "Jeez, this thing must weigh half a pound."

"That's the metal detector," he said. "It's built right in. It beeps when you get close to what you're looking for." Seeing my look of puzzled incredulity, he laughed and shook his head. "You're a trusting soul, Bill Brockton. I like that about you."

I studied the images of the two saints. "Travelers and lost things. Sounds like it's custom made for me. Okay, why not? I'll take all the help I can get." I slipped the cord over my head and tucked the medallion inside my shirt. The metal felt heavy and warm against my chest; also strangely comforting. "Thank you." He simply nodded.

As we were finishing up, the bells in the tower of Saint Pierre began to peal. "Ah, five o'clock Mass," said Father Mike. "I'd best be going in. I've been a bit lax this week." Without looking at me, he added casually, "You're welcome to come along, if you like. I find the music calms me nerves sometimes. But it's a good thing you've already eaten—the snack they serve is awfully skimpy." I nearly laughed in spite of myself . . . and then, to my surprise, I followed him into the church.

Saint Pierre wasn't big—closer in size to a chapel than a cathedral—but the design was ornate and complex. The doors and windows were framed by high, pointed arches. Above them, flanking the doorway, were two slender towers capped by steep, bristling stone spires.

The wooden doors—two sets of double doors— were immense: tall, thick, and elaborately carved with figures. The panels of the doors themselves featured saints, the Virgin Mary, and an angel. The most striking figure, though, was carved into a pillar that flanked one of the doors. Almost life-size, the figure was a stylized likeness of an American Indian or Aztec chief, complete with headdress. Although construction of the church had begun 150 years before Columbus stumbled upon America, the building wasn't finished until the 1550s.

The doors—a final touch—reflected Europeans' fascination with the exotic discoveries being made in the New World.

Inside, the high, fluted notes of a pipe organ echoed and faded as we slipped into the cool, dim interior. Father Mike dipped his finger in a basin of holy water just inside the door, then touched his forehead, bowed, and crossed himself before sliding into a pew near the back. I followed, feeling out of place yet glad of the distraction and the man's easy company.

Behind the priest, high above the altar, a large painting showed Jesus handing Peter the keys to the kingdom of heaven. Above the painting was a huge sunburst, easily ten feet in diameter, carved from wood but covered in gold. At its center was a stained-glass window depicting a dove, its wings spread, its beak stretching straight up, streaking toward heaven like a rocket.

The organ music was replaced by high, pure soprano voices chanting in close harmony. I'd long since stopped believing in angels, but the ethereal music that seemed to emanate from the stones themselves was almost enough to make me reconsider. The service itself alternated between French and Latin, which I couldn't have followed even if I'd tried. Yet despite being an outsider and a foreigner, on many different levels, I found solace in the sounds and sights and smells of the vaulted stone sanctuary, the gilded altar paintings, the drifting incense, and the ancient rituals.

But spiritual solace wouldn't help me save Miranda; for that, action was needed. What was it

Eckhart had said? "The price of inaction is far greater than the cost of making a mistake." I waved a slight good-bye to Father Mike and slipped from the pew. He started to rise and follow me, but I laid a hand on his shoulder and shook my head. His kind company and his attentive ear had helped, but now I needed to be alone again.

Pushing open the heavy wooden door, I emerged into the square. The sun had dropped below the rooftops by now, and every table at L'Épicerie was taken. My eye caught a flash of movement three stories overhead, and I looked up to see a cat, its fur the black-and-white hues of priests and nuns, tiptoeing along a ledge three stories above the restaurant. At the end of the ledge, where the wall of the building intersected the church, the cat crouched and then leaped up through an open window: a study in grace, agility, and fearlessness atop a perilous tightrope.

Wafting across the pavement, accompanied by the clanking of silverware and the clinking of wineglasses, came the distinctive scent of seared flesh. Unless I was mistaken, it was lamb.

My mind flashed to the image of the lamb chiseled on the ossuary. What was the story in the New Testament, the parable Jesus told about the shepherd who left his ninety-nine sheep in order to search for one other sheep, which was missing? What was the moral of that story? Something, I dimly recalled, about there being more rejoicing in Heaven when that one lost lamb was found than over the other ninety-nine, the ones that weren't in danger.

Where was the ossuary? And, far more urgent to me, where was Miranda—and could we save her?

CHAPTER 38

Avignon
1342

SIMONE HAS ALL BUT ceased to paint.

Cardinal Orsini, whose portrait Simone painted seven years ago, during the excitement of his arrival at the papal city, has been almost the only one able to pry any work out of him, and that's only because Simone's survival—his, and Giovanna's, and her talentless brother's, and the brother's family, too—depends on Cardinal Orsini's continued generosity. Simone is now putting the final fatigued flourishes on an altar polyptych, a folding wooden screen with eight hinged panels, each the size of a prayer book. Simone has sold the polyptych to Orsini as if it were a new commission, but the truth is, he painted the scenes themselves years ago—ten years ago; how can so much sand have slipped through the glass?— back in Siena, back when he was at his peak, he now realizes. Now Orsini is ill, probably dying, and the urgency of finishing the panels' decorative borders quickly, before the cardinal's purse is buried with him, is the only thing driving Simone to take up his brushes, punches, and gold leaf.

There is one other painting on his easel, also sold but not quite finished: a small Holy Family, not even two feet high, showing Mary, Joseph, and a boyish Christ—but such a Christ as has never been painted before. The scene portrays the parents reunited with Jesus after the boy has been missing for three days—days he has spent at the Temple, debating theology with the elders. Joseph scowls, and Mary, her cheeks splotchy with anger, scolds the boy—imagine, scolding the Son of God—while the young Christ stands defiant, arms folded coldly across his chest, a look of stubborn scorn directed at the Blessed Virgin. Simone can't quite say what has prompted him to paint such an irreverent scene. All he knows is that he feels an odd kinship with the stony-faced boy; having endured endless cajoling and scolding from people who want him to paint this or sketch that, Simone feels the urge to fold his arms across his chest and set his jaw just so.

Giovanna has forgiven his infidelity, perhaps because she sees that he scourges himself more savagely than she ever could. She understands self-inflicted wounds. Her deepest sadness in life is her inability to bear Simone a child, and knowing that another woman has done so is a bitter reminder of her own failure.

Simone still goes to his studio day after day, but he spends most of his hours staring at the ghost portrait on fabric, *The Death of Innocence*. He's lengthened his worktable to accommodate most of the strip of linen—nearly fifteen feet of it—and has applied a flat, smooth coat of plaster. Normally at this point he begins to paint, working swiftly so the paint bonds with the damp plaster. Not this time; this time, he needs a surface as dry and smooth as marble. Stopping often to consult the drawings he made by lamplight years before, he sketches the dead man lightly with a charcoal pencil—front and back, joining the images at the top of the head. Once he's satisfied with the faint sketch, he swaps the pencil for a thick piece of reddish-brown sinopia chalk and begins shading the features—heavily for the prominent ones, lightly for the hollows and recesses. It takes him three days to complete the figure itself, and another day to add the wounds. Finally, carefully, even tenderly—as tenderly as if he were undressing a beautiful woman—he unrolls the linen onto the image he has created. Once again using the rounded end of the wooden pestle, he rubs softly, stroking the linen from every direction to transfer a whisper of pigment from the tabletop to the fabric. The final step is to add the bloodstains—a watery tempera of red vermilion, brighter than the man's ochre image—to highlight the wounds.

He has just completed the trail of blood on the forehead—a meandering trickle that hints at furrows; a brilliant touch!—when someone knocks at the studio's door. He ignores it, as he ignores all knocks but Giovanna's distinctive, birdlike pecking at the wood, but it continues, growing more forceful with each *thump-thump-thump*. "Simone Martini, open the door," commands a voice that sounds accustomed to swift and unquestioning obedience.

"Leave me in peace," he calls out. "I'm working. I must not be disturbed."

"Open the door, Master Simone, or we will break it down."

Simone considers ignoring the command, but he lacks the energy to repair the door, so he pulls the bolt and opens it a crack. The commanding voice belongs to one of the papal guards, who pushes his way into the room, sees it empty except for Simone, and makes a beckoning gesture toward the open door. Half a dozen clerics file noiselessly into the room—two canons, a bishop, a pair of red-hatted cardinals, and lastly a monk. The monk is a large, white-robed Cistercian; it is, Simone gradually realizes, none other than Pope Benedict himself: an older, more dour version of the man he saw hiding the bones in the palace wall. Simone nods slightly in acknowledgment; he should, of course, kneel and kiss the pontiff's ring, but he continues to feel as petulant as the scowling young Christ on his easel.

"Master Simone, you are too stingy with your companionship and with your paints," says one of the cardinals, whom Simone does not recognize. "Cardinal Orsini—may God restore his health or ease his death—speaks so highly of your polyptych that we must see it."

"My friend and patron is very kind," says Simone, "but it is not yet finished, and I would be ashamed to show it."

"Nonsense, Master Simone," the cardinal counters. "You are much too modest." His voice is cheerful on the surface, but there is an undertone of malice: a verbal dagger enfolded within the voice of silk and velvet. His eyes fix upon the drape that covers the altar screen, and there is a sharp glitter in them. "Is this the piece?"

"Your Grace," Simone begins, but it is too late. With surprising quickness, the cardinal has stepped forward and flung aside the cloth that covers the panels. Simone hears "ahs" and words of admiration. The one cleric who does not seem to be impressed is the pope, but His Holiness is not known for his love of art—a shame, given that his palace has acres of barren walls still crying out for frescoes and tapestries to warm and soften them. Perhaps the next pope, Avignon's artists pray, will elevate art to its rightful place in the palace.

The pope turns aside from the screen and directs his gaze toward the Holy Family, propped on the easel. Walking closer, his sausage-fingers clasped behind his back, he leans close, studying the face of the young Jesus. The chatter in the room ceases as his entourage notices his frown. Finally he turns and faces Simone, his eyes narrow and cold. Without speaking, he approaches the painter, circles him, and then stands and stares. Finally he speaks. "Master Simone, how is your soul?"

"My soul? I am more accustomed to being asked about my paintings."

"I don't care about your paintings, except for what they illuminate about your soul, Simone Martini. I see a troubled soul in this picture."

The air in the studio crackles with tension now.

"There is much trouble in this world, Your Holiness," Simone slowly replies.

"But there is none in our Lord," the pope counters. "This painting is blasphemous. Possibly heretical." The papal entourage now murmurs its disapproval.

"I mean no blasphemy, Your Holiness. The scriptures teach us that God became flesh and dwelt among us."

"His Holiness needs no schooling on the scriptures from a painter," the officious cardinal exclaims.

"No, of course not," Simone replies. "But surely a mother's distress would show in Our Lady's face when her beloved son has been missing for three days? And surely our blameless Lord—even as a youth—would take offense at being chided?"

The pope trains inquisitorial eyes on Martini's face, gauging whether the artist is mocking him, then turns away. "What other blasphemies are you painting in here, Martini?" Simone makes no answer. The pope peers behind the large wooden screen at the long table, then squeezes through the opening for a closer look. The room falls silent. Suddenly the silence is broken by a gasp and a sharp cry. The pope staggers out from behind the screen, his face ashen, clutching his chest. He tries to speak, but he cannot. He stares at Simone in terror, as if he has seen a ghost: the ghost of a man he tortured and killed years before.

Half carried, half dragged, he is taken to the street and placed in a hastily commandeered cart that clatters to the palace. Three days later, the Inquisitor-turned-pontiff is dead, and a new pope—a great lover of art, a man who will open the papal purse strings like no one before him—is elected, taking the name Clement VI. He hosts a sumptuous coronation banquet to which he invites three thousand high-ranking clerics and nobles. "My predecessors," he tells his guests, "did not know how to be pope," and they agree. Avignon's greatest artistic and cultural boom is about to begin.

But it will begin and end with no further works by Simone Martini. His final sale, the day after Clement's banquet, is to an eager young cleric from Lirey who is the private chaplain to one of France's most illustrious knights, Lord Geoffrey de Charney.

The chaplain—part of the pope's entourage the day His Holiness was stricken—has returned to Simone's studio, curious to see the work that affected the pope so strongly. Far from being disturbed by the work, the chaplain finds the faint, haunting image quite intriguing . . . and most promising. Properly presented—not as a new work of art, but as an ancient relic, the actual winding-sheet of our Lord!—the image could inspire profound reverence, attract throngs of pilgrims . . . and unleash a torrent of donations from the devout.

The shrewd young priest from Lirey buys the shroud from Simone for thirty florins. Thirty pieces of gold.

Prices have gone up since the last time Christ was sold.

CHAPTER 39

**Avignon
The Present**

I CHECKED THE REARVIEW mirror, and sure enough, another car pulled from a parking space and fell in behind me. It looked like the car I'd seen the prior day, and this time I got a good enough look at the grille to tell that it was a black BMW. I even thought I recognized the driver's large, shaved head from the airport-security photo of Reverend Jonah's hulking bodyguard. Just as Descartes had predicted, Junior was tailing me to Geneva.

A quarter mile up the street, the wall was punctured by a gate, the Saint Joseph portal. I turned right, through the gate; behind me, a horn blared angrily. Checking the mirror again, I saw that a white panel truck—service vehicles look the same the world over—had run a stop sign and cut in front of the black sedan, tucking in almost on my bumper. When the light at the intersection turned green, I threaded the car through the narrow opening, then turned immediately right onto the three-lane road, Saint Lazarus Boulevard, which ringed the outside of the wall to my right. The road was like a modern-day moat of asphalt, swimming with cars rather than barracudas. Out my left window was the emerald-green Rhône, and as I checked my mirrors for the BMW, I caught a brief glimpse of Saint Bénézet's Bridge downstream. The banks of the river in this stretch were lined with barges and dredges, as well as old canal boats that had been transformed into luxurious houseboats. A small crane was bolted to the stern of one of these canal boats, and dangling from a cable, hoisted high above the reach of thieves, was an old-fashioned three-speed bicycle, much like the one gathering dust in my garage back home.

A quarter mile upstream the road branched; one lane continued to hug the wall, while the other dived into a tunnel. A road crew was working near the mouth of the tunnel, and a flagman was motioning cars slowly forward. As I approached, he stepped from the curb and began waving his flag. I braked, but he waved my car through, as well as the white panel truck behind me, before stopping the line of traffic. At the front of the line of stopped cars was the black BMW, and I smiled as I imagined Junior fuming at the delay.

Halfway through the tunnel I slammed the car to a stop, put the gearshift in neutral, and leaped out, leaving the engine running. Behind me, the side door of the white panel truck opened, and out sprang a gray-haired man who could have been my brother, wearing khaki pants and a blue shirt that mirrored my own outfit exactly. My look-alike nodded to me, tucked himself into the Peugeot, slammed the door, and took off. I hopped into the van, and the door slid shut. Inside, I could barely see Descartes in the dimness; he was just finishing a radio transmission, and as he did, I noticed a pair of headlights through the rear windows, rapidly closing the distance with our slow-moving van. "It won't take him long to catch up with the Peugeot," Descartes said. "That was *très bien fait*—very well done. Twenty-three seconds." In less than half a minute, the switch—taking me out of the Geneva-bound car and putting a double in my place—had bought us a day's delay. A day and a half in which to find the hidden bones or—failing that—to get the Native American skeleton that was en route from Knoxville. It was, I suddenly realized, another switcheroo: a look-alike, a stand-in—and it was standing in for another fake relic at that.

When we emerged from the tunnel, our driver turned right at the first intersection. The black BMW roared past, its speed and dark windows defeating my efforts to see the driver's features.

"The decoy—my doppelgänger; the fake me," I said to Descartes. "Who is he?"

"Just one of our inspectors; a guy who happens to look like you."

"Lucky him," I said. "How much danger do you think he's in?"

"On the way to Geneva, zero. On the way back, maybe more. They might try to ambush him and get the bones." The inspector shrugged. "He has military experience and tactical training. He's smart, a good driver, a good shot. He can take care of himself. But risk is part of the job."

The van lurched as the driver doubled back toward Avignon. "You think Junior will fall for it?"

"Let's hope so." He waved a finger at my clothes. "He saw you get into the car dressed like this, and he'll see your double get out of the car dressed like this. So unless something makes him suspicious, he'll assume it's you."

His "unless" dug into me, the way a splinter on a rough wooden railing can snag a passing finger. "What might make him suspicious?"

He shrugged. "If they had someone watching at the other end of the tunnel, maybe they noticed the extra twenty seconds it took for the car to go through. The police, we might notice that kind of thing. Your FBI might notice. But these guys aren't that good. They're fanatics, not cops or spies."

"Fanatics brought down the World Trade towers," I pointed out. "Never underestimate the power of fanatics."

"I don't underestimate their power," he said. "Just their capabilities. As far as we can tell, only the preacher and the big guy came to France for the bones of Jesus."

"The bones of *not*-Jesus," I corrected.

"True," he conceded, "but we can't tell that to them. If they learn the truth, they have no reason to keep mademoiselle alive. We must pray that they continue to have faith in our lies."

I wasn't much of a praying man, but there in the back of a lurching van bumping its way back to my hotel, I sent out a request to God, or to the universe:

Whatever it takes, truth or lies, help me get Miranda back safely. I thought of Meister Eckhart's criticism of the hypocrisy of praying *Thy will be done* but then complaining about the outcome. But I wasn't praying *Thy will be done;* I wasn't that virtuous or pious. I only wanted Miranda back, safe and sound.

The van turned again, entering the old city, and hugged the wall until it reached the tower that faced Lumani. The driver pulled onto the narrow sidewalk and stopped with the van's side door directly aligned with Lumani's wooden gate. "Stay here," Descartes reminded me, "until the decoy gets back from Geneva."

"Do I have to? This feels like house arrest, and it's gonna drive me crazy. I'd really rather help you look for the bones."

"It's too risky," he said. "If the preacher sees you, he knows you're not in that car. Then he kills mademoiselle. *Non,* you must stay out of sight. We will keep looking for the bones. Now go." He tapped the van's driver on the shoulder. The driver got out; luckily, he was skinny as a rail, or he'd never have managed to squeeze through the narrow gap between his door and the wall of the house. Stepping into the street, he checked carefully in both directions, then gave a quick, low whistle. Descartes slid open the van's side door, and without even having to lean out the opening, I put my key in the lock and opened the wooden gate. Then, in one step, I was inside the sheltering wall, latching the gate behind me. This maneuver took even less than the twenty-three seconds in the tunnel. *Très bien fait,* I thought. And *Please, bring her back.*

CHAPTER 40

A40 Motorway, Switzerland
The Present

IN A THREE-MILE STRETCH of tunnel carved through the mountains on the route from Geneva, Switzerland, back to Lyon, France, a black BMW whips to the left and surges forward, rapidly overtaking the old Peugeot that's chugging up the gradual grade. The German car rockets past the French one as swiftly as Hitler's tanks darted around France's Maginot Line back in 1940; it cuts in front and then brakes hard. The hulking bald driver, Junior—a name he hates, even though he, too, uses it for himself—checks his mirror, expecting to see the Peugeot's hood dip sharply, expecting to hear tires screeching in a panicky, reflexive stop—after all, the gray-haired guy in the piece-of-crap Peugeot is some kind of egghead professor, right?—but instead, the Peugeot darts to the right, wedging itself between the decelerating BMW and the wall of the tunnel.

Metal rasps and shrieks as the Peugeot rakes the entire passenger side of the BMW, clipping the outside mirror at the same moment it rips a warning sign off the right wall of the tunnel. The Peugeot driver's window is down and suddenly Junior sees what appears to be a pistol in the professor's hand: a pistol pointed out the open window; a pistol pointed—shit!—at him. Next thing Junior knows, the Beemer's passenger window is shattering and he's ducking for his life, and the Beemer is veering wildly to the left, where it slams into a concrete abutment, pushing the radiator back into the engine block and knocking the left front wheel off the frame. The steering-column airbag explodes, punching Junior in the face, breaking his nose, adding injury to insult. He's not sure which hurts worse, the broken nose or the knowledge that he's been outmaneuvered and outsmarted by an aging egghead in a piece-of-crap car.

CHAPTER 41

Avignon
The Present

EIGHT ENDLESS, NAIL-CHEWING, GARDEN-PACING hours after I'd climbed out of the van—as the afternoon sun was casting long shadows across Lumani's courtyard—my phone rang. "The preacher's muscleman just tried to ambush our decoy," said Descartes. I felt a jolt of fear, and sweat began beading on my forehead and trickling from my armpits. "Shit. What happened? Is our guy okay?"

"It's okay," he hurried on. "You got away. The muscleman's car is wrecked, so that's good; maybe he's hurt, maybe not. Our guy didn't stop—without backup, he couldn't take the risk, and besides, we didn't want to blow his cover. But you need to call the preacher right away, so he still thinks it's you on the highway."

I forced myself to breathe slowly—once, twice, three times—and then said, "Okay, tell me what happened. And tell me what I need to say."

"It was in the Chamois Tunnel, about fifty kilometers west of Geneva. An hour after you left the bank. The muscleman passed you in the tunnel and tried to force you to stop. You made a shot—"

"Good God, I *shot* someone?" I was shocked by the idea that I—even a counterfeit I—might shoot someone.

"We don't know if you hit him. All we know is that the muscleman's car ran into the wall in the tunnel. He's not following you anymore. You should call the preacher now, before he hears from his guy."

"THIS IS BROCKTON," I said when he answered. "That was really stupid, Reverend."

"What are you talking about?"

"I've got a good mind to turn this car around and go dump the bones in Lake Geneva. A spot so deep you'll never find them, no matter how long you look or how hard you pray."

"I swear I don't know what you're talking about, Brockton." His words said that, but his panicked undertone told me otherwise.

"You're lying, Reverend. Either that, or your goon's spinning out of control as badly as his car did just now."

There was a long pause on the other end of the line. "What car?"

"Don't insult my intelligence. The black BMW your bald-headed ape was driving. The one that just crashed into the wall in the Chamois Tunnel."

Another pause. "There was a wreck in a tunnel? Was anyone hurt? Are you okay?"

"Gee, thanks for your Christian concern, Reverend. I'm just fine, but I don't know about your muscle-bound friend—call me hard-hearted, but I didn't stop to play Good Samaritan. Maybe he's just shaken up, maybe he's dead—and if he is, frankly, I don't give a damn. I'm on my way back to Avignon with the bones, and if you actually want them, don't you dare mess with me again. God forgives, but I don't." I hung up the phone and, as Descartes had instructed, I switched it off so Reverend Jonah couldn't call me back—at least not until we'd made him sweat for a while.

Meanwhile, I was sweating, too. We'd gotten a break and gained an advantage over the end-timers, but I didn't want to put too much stock in it. If Junior had escaped unhurt and managed to get out of the tunnel and get another car quickly, our advantage might last only a few hours. And then what?

THE KNOCK WAS soft, but it nearly made me jump out of my skin anyway, and I gave a startled yelp of surprise. "*Excusez-moi, Docteur,*" said Elisabeth's voice. "Sorry you have fear when I knock." I yanked open the door, grateful for the distraction, cheered by the warmth in her face, and relieved by the sight of the immense package she cradled in her arms. "This just came for you."

The FedEx airbill confirmed what I'd expected and hoped: The package was from Knoxville, which meant that it contained the decoy skeleton overnighted by Hugh Berryman. I'd expected the airbill to be attached to one of our standard bone boxes, a foot square by three feet long, but what Elisabeth had lugged up the three flights of stairs was the size of a small footlocker. I thanked her, set the box on the bed, and ripped it open even before she'd started down the stairs. Inside the outer box, I found the long, narrow bone box I'd been expecting, along with a second box, a cube measuring about eighteen inches on each side.

Lifting out the bone box, I set it on the desk and raised the long, hinged lid. Hugh had chosen well. A forensic anthropologist would never mistake this Native American skeleton for the one we'd found in the Palace of the Popes—this skull was broader and flatter, and the front teeth were the shovel-shaped incisors characteristic of Native Americans and Asians—but apart from those differences, it closely resembled our missing man: Meister Eckhart or Jesus Christ or whoever the hell Stefan had been trying to sell for two million dollars. Hugh had also done a good job of simulating the wounds to the wrists and feet and ribs: Besides gouging the bones, he'd dabbed the splintered edges with a mixture of tea and coffee, a stain that mimicked the patina of time, making the fresh trauma look as ancient as the bones themselves.

Satisfied with the decoy skeleton, I turned my attention to the other box, the unexpected one. Taped to the top of it was a card, a pen-and-ink illustration of Don Quixote on horseback, his lance raised, windmills in the background. Underneath were these words in Hugh's handwriting: "Ephesians 6:11." Puzzled, I ripped open the box. What I found inside gave me a chill. I opened my computer and Googled the citation. It was a Bible verse from Saint Paul's letter to the fledgling Christian church at Ephesus. "Put on the whole armour of God," it read, "that ye may be able to stand against the wiles of the devil." Saint Paul, I decided—or maybe it was my own Saint Hugh—was a pretty smart guy.

THE PIECES OF our plan were coming together, though with maddening slowness. The decoy skeleton was the piece I'd been most worried about, and it had arrived on time and in excellent condition. The decoy ossuary should be coming soon—the stonemason had promised to deliver it no later than 10 P.M. And barring unforeseen problems, the decoy Brockton should make it back to Avignon before midnight.

Midnight was just four hours away—hours that I suspected would seem like centuries.

I SWITCHED MY phone back on—I'd left it off for two hours to keep Reverend Jonah twisting in the wind if he tried to call me again—and sure enough, the phone showed a missed call from his North Carolina cell number. I had a voice mail, too, and the instant the message began playing, I felt the instinctive revulsion that the televangelist's voice never failed to trigger in me. My revulsion swiftly gave way to panic, though, as his words floated up and their implications sank in. "If you're not with us, you're against us," he said. "You are not to be trusted. If you try any treachery when we meet, the girl dies. If I even think the police are watching, she dies. If you stall or bargain, she dies. And if the bones are not genuine, she dies." My heart skipped a beat when he said it. "I have photographs of the teeth," he went on, and I thought my heart would stop altogether. "Before I came to terms with your friend Stefan, I had him send pictures of them. I'm no big-shot forensic detective, but I swear by the blood of Christ, if the teeth don't match exactly, the girl will die, and so will you."

I stared at the phone in my hand, hoping it wasn't real, hoping this was a nightmare message, hoping that if I stared at the phone hard enough, clenched it tightly enough, I would awaken.

I did not awaken; the message was indeed a nightmare, but it was a waking nightmare. Flinging open the lid of the bone box, I lifted out the cranium and mandible, and grew dizzy with despair. I'd hoped and assumed the preacher wouldn't be tipped off by the decoy's shovel-shaped incisors, but I saw now that those were the least of the problem. The real problem was the number of teeth: the decoy had four more teeth than the missing skeleton had. Even a preacher inclined to have faith in miracles was not credulous enough to believe that the skull of Christ had sprouted four new teeth twenty centuries after his crucifixion.

Frantic now, I called Descartes, who was still searching the labyrinthine corridors and crannies of the Palace of the Popes. "You've got to find those bones, and find them fast," I said. I recounted Reverend Jonah's call, and his threat. "He's not going to fall for it," I said. "There's no way. Even a child could tell that these teeth aren't the same."

Descartes was silent. Finally he said, "We'll keep

trying, but we're running out of places to look. See if you can get more time."

"How do I do that, Inspector? We were pushing our luck with Geneva. He's getting suspicious. I'm afraid he's about to snap."

"I don't know. Try to think of something. We have two more towers to search. You probably won't be able to reach me—the only reason I got this call is because I stepped outside to call my office. I'll phone you back in an hour." He hung up, leaving me staring at the phone once more, my blood pressure soaring, my ears ringing, my heart racing. In a fury of frustration, I screamed—a wordless bellow of rage—and kicked savagely at the closest thing to me, the heavy wooden frame of my bed. It hurt—I wondered if I'd broken my big toe—but I didn't care; I hauled back the other foot and kicked the bed again. The bed scraped across the floorboards . . . and something clattered to the floor. Crap—had I broken the bed in my anger? Kneeling on the floor, I peered into the darkness, using my cell phone as a flashlight, the way Miranda had shown me.

The light glimmered off something made of metal: a bracket? a bolt from the bed? Lying prone, my head pressed against the nightstand, I fished it out. It was a key—an antique-looking silver key with a large oval head and several stubby ribs jutting from the spine. For a moment I thought it was Stefan's skeleton key to the palace, but it wasn't, not quite. The palace key had been ornate, practically a work of art, its head cut with intricate scrollwork and filigree; this one, on the other hand, was utterly unadorned—a blue-collar sort of key, more likely to be carried by some medieval janitor than a cardinal or chamberlain. It wasn't just the head that was simpler; so was the shaft—it had only three pairs of ribs jutting from the spine, not half a dozen. Suddenly it hit me, and I ripped open the desk drawer and rifled through the jumble of papers and receipts until I found the note Miranda had left on my nightstand after spooning up behind me in my bed the night after we'd found Stefan's body. "A souvenir," the note said. "Maybe it doesn't mean anything, but maybe it's important." When I'd awakened that morning and found the message, I'd thought that the note itself was the souvenir—an odd one, I'd thought, but then, Miranda's mind often worked more obliquely than mine. But the words, I now realized, made more sense if they referred to something else—something that had fallen off the edge of the nightstand, perhaps, and lodged behind the bed . . . until this moment. Was this a key Stefan had given her? Or had he lost it in her hotel room the night he tried to persuade her to come with him?

Suddenly I felt a chill as I remembered Miranda's barely intelligible words when Reverend Jonah had let me talk to her. "The key is to get the bones," she'd said. Twice. My God, she must have meant *this* key. But what door, what hiding place, did this key unlock? It must not be a door at the palace, because Stefan's master key—which Descartes and his men had a copy of—was different from this. What else had Miranda said during that important, frustrating, garbled call? She'd clearly been trying to tell me something else important, but much of the message had been mangled by the poor reception. She'd told me not to get greedy like Stefan, and then she'd said something about Stefan being interrupted. But then she'd added something odd, something I hadn't understood: She'd told *me* to "be interruptible." I'd been trying to ask her what that meant when Reverend Jonah had snatched the phone away from her and slapped her. "Be interruptible." Turning the key over and over in my hands, I stared absently at it and repeated the words slowly, as if they held some magic, some mantra. "Be interruptible. Be interruptible. Interruptible."

And then, tearing open my door, I raced down the stairs, flung open the wooden gate of the inn, and sprinted through the twisting streets, past the floodlit façade of the Palace of the Popes, beneath the outstretched arms of the cathedral's gilded virgin and oversized crucifix, and down a zigzag ramp to the northern edge of the city wall, toward the dark waters of the Rhône.

I'd just reached the base of the Bénézet bridge— the bridge of Incorruptible, Interruptible Saint Bénézet—when my phone rang. It was Reverend Jonah. "Now or never, Professor," he hissed.

"Now," I said. "Right now, by God. But you have to bring her to me. The bones and I are at Saint Bénézet's Bridge. Walk up the sidewalk from the south side of the bridge. If I see anyone with you but Miranda, I'll throw the bones off the bridge and into the river."

What bones? The rhetorical question posed by Descartes still applied. I didn't have the bones yet, didn't know for sure they were here. But they *had* to be here. There was no other explanation that fit . . . and no time to look anywhere else.

"And if I see anyone with you, I'll shoot the girl," he countered. "If you have any doubt about that, remember what happened to your colleague."

"What about the Sixth Commandment, Reverend? 'Thou shalt not kill'? Or did God say you could ignore that one, when he took you up to Heaven for your private sneak preview of the Apocalypse?"

"We're all sinners, Doctor. Some of us, by the grace of God, are forgiven sinners. That's the only difference. I've sinned many times in my life. I'll probably sin many more. But I am cleansed and made spotless by the blood of Jesus Christ. By the miracle of grace. And when the trumpet sounds—soon, very soon—I will stand with the righteous. Because I am the voice of one crying in the wilderness, 'Prepare ye the way of the Lord! Make straight his path!' Unworthy as I am, Doctor, I am God's chosen instrument."

His words—and his fervent, escalating intensity—filled me with dread, but I knew better than to show fear. "And so am I, Reverend," I said with as much conviction as I could muster, or could pretend to. Growing up, I'd been surrounded by fundamentalist Protestants—Southern Baptists, Primitive Baptists, even a few snake-handling Holy Rollers. I cast my mind back to that subculture and its language, hoping to speak to the preacher in words that would carry weight with him. "I'm the Lord's instrument, too. Listen to the Spirit, Reverend, and you'll know it's true. I found the bones. I escaped the snares you've set for me. And now I charge you—as Jesus charged the woman caught in the act of adultery—'Go and sin no more.' Forgiveness requires repentance, Reverend, and repentance isn't true—it's a lie—if you're already plotting the next sin. So bring her to me in ten minutes, and do it with a pure heart. I charge you in the name of Him you serve."

"Don't you dare presume—" he began, but I hung up. It was a risk, I knew, but then again, I was playing a high-stakes game of chicken with a madman. Doing *anything* was a big risk . . . but doing *nothing* would be a bigger risk. Seven hundred years after he'd said them, Meister Eckhart's words still rang true: "The price of inaction is far greater than the cost of making a mistake." In this case, I felt sure, the price of inaction would be Miranda's death.

I rang Descartes. The phone rang and rang, then finally rolled to voice mail. *Christ*, I thought, *he's in the basement of one of those thick stone towers. Those signal-proof towers.* After the voice-mail announcement finished—the only part I understood was the name, "René Descartes"—I blurted, "Inspector, it's Brockton. I know where the bones are. I'm meeting the preacher in ten minutes. Saint Bénézet's Bridge. Hurry. But whatever you do, don't spook him, or he'll kill Miranda."

A massive wooden door sealed the portal at the base of the tower that anchored the stone bridge to the rocky hillside. The door had an ancient-looking iron lock. By the light of my cell phone, I wiggled the key into place and turned. The lock resisted; I twisted harder, praying I didn't snap the ribs off the spine of the key. Still it resisted, so I applied more force, and more prayer . . . and the lock yielded. Hurling my weight against the door, I bulled it open and then raced up the stone stairs and out onto the top of the bridge. Fifty yards ahead was the crumbling little chapel where Bénézet's incorruptible remains had lain for hundreds of years, until the French Revolution dethroned the dual monarchies of king and church.

At the door of the chapel, I repeated the same sequence: light, key, prayer, force. Again, just as I was expecting the key to snap, the lock turned and the door opened.

The chapel's interior was pitch-black. The cell phone's display had offered plenty of light to see a keyhole, but it made a mighty feeble searchlight. On hands and knees, I searched the perimeter of the chapel. I found rat carcasses, pigeon droppings, and a few scraps of paper and plastic that the mistral had whirled through the window openings. But I did not find a stone ossuary.

I did, however, find another door, a small door set into one of the chapel's side walls. I stood up, found an iron handle, and opened the door. It opened onto a staircase that descended to a lower level: a low-ceilinged chamber that must have been the chapel's crypt. This must have been where Bénézet's body had lain until it was spirited away by nuns for safekeeping. Could this be where Stefan had hidden the ossuary—an ironic in-joke by the arrogant archaeologist?

On a simple stone altar in the center of the crypt was Stefan's last laugh: the ossuary, its inscribed cross and lamb plainly visible even by the faint light of my phone. Without even lifting the lid to make sure the bones were inside, I slid the box off the slab and staggered up the stairs to the top of the bridge.

CHAPTER 42

I REACHED THE EDGE of the bridge and balanced the ossuary on the narrow round railing just as Reverend Jonah emerged from the tower. Half a step in front of him was Miranda; with his left hand, he clutched her left arm; with his right, he pushed her ahead of him like a shield.

"Let her go, Reverend," I called. "Let go of her arm and keep walking toward me, with both hands where I can see them."

He brought his right hand from behind her back, and I saw it held a gun, which he pressed to Miranda's ribs. "Show me the bones."

My tongue felt glued to the roof of my mouth, but I knew I had to speak with apparent calmness and strength. "Let go of her first. And put down the gun."

"No, Doctor."

"That was our deal, Reverend. I get her; you get the bones."

"Our deal counts for nothing. My loyalty is to a far higher power than you. Now show me the bones, or by that power, I'll pull this trigger."

My mind was screaming, but I couldn't make out any of the words. "If you shoot her, the bones go into the river. And if you shoot me, the bones go into the river. You'll notice that they're balanced rather precariously here on the edge, Reverend. In fact, the only thing keeping them from falling right now is that I'm keeping a tight grip on them. But since you insist, I'll show you." I lifted the lid of the ossuary and set it down on the bridge, propping it against the knee-high lower railing. Keeping my eyes on him, I reached into the box and felt for a femur. Grasping it by the femoral head—the "ball" at the upper end of the thighbone—I lifted it from the box. "This is the left femur, Reverend. The left femur of the Son of the Most High. Now let her go." He shook his head and took a step toward me, pulling Miranda with him. I waved the femur at him warningly. "How will you explain this to your God, Reverend?" With that, I let the bone hang down alongside my leg, then I gave my wrist a quick snap. The bone flipped upward, tumbling end over end as it arced upward toward the far side of the bridge. Still spinning, it dropped below the railing and hit the dark water below with a faint splash.

Reverend Jonah gave a strangled cry and rushed to the railing. Then he whirled and leveled the gun at me. Anything could happen in the next instant, I knew, but at least Miranda was no longer in his grasp, with a gun to her ribs. "You . . . you . . ." His voice was shaking, and so was the gun.

"Remember, Reverend, if you shoot me, the rest of the bones fall into the water. And Reverend? This stone box is heavy, and my hand's getting tired." To underscore the point, I let the box wobble a bit on the railing. As it tilted farther toward the water, the bones shifted inside, grating slightly as they slid. "You probably know this, Reverend, but if you're looking for DNA in an old skeleton, the best places are the teeth and the long bones. They encapsulate the DNA better than the smaller bones do; they protect it from bacteria and pollutants and the ravages of time. The best of the long bones for what you hope to do is the femur." Reaching into the box again, I found the other femur and took it out, just as I had the first. "Unfortunately, by breaking your word, you've already lost one femur. It'd be a real shame to lose the other." I waved the end up and down, as if I were winding up to toss it.

"Don't," he gasped.

"Then put the gun down. I'm counting to three—the number of the Holy Trinity, Reverend. God the Father, God the Son, God the Holy Spirit. They're all watching, all wondering if you're about to fail them. If these bones go into the river, do you really think they're going to welcome you with open arms and say, 'Well done, thou good and faithful servant?' Somehow I doubt it, Reverend. But I guess your faith is stronger than mine. *One.*" I gave the bone an upward snap, but did not release it. "*Two.*" Another snap. "*Three.*" I dipped my arm lower this time, so I could put plenty of force in the toss.

"*Stop!* All right, all *right.*" He laid the gun on the cobblestones and held out both hands.

"That's better," I said. "Miranda, walk away."

"I'm not going without you," she said.

"Go on, Miranda. I'll be right behind you. As soon as you're off the bridge, I'll give the bones to the Reverend, and I'll be with you in sixty seconds. Now go."

"I can't, Dr. B." To my surprise, she was crying. "I can't leave you here with him."

"Yes you can. You have to." Surprised and moved by her vulnerability, I suddenly felt on the verge of coming undone myself. "Don't be afraid, Miranda. I'll be fine." I wasn't sure I believed that, but I needed *her* to believe it, at least long enough to walk out of harm's way. "I love you, Miranda. Now go."

"I love you, too, Dr. B." It came out as a whisper, but it bored into me more strongly than if she'd shouted it.

She began to walk, slowly at first, then faster, her heels clopping on the stones. Finally she broke into a run, her clattering footfalls echoing off the rock bluff from which the bridge seemed to grow. When she reached the tower and started down the stairs, I nodded to the preacher. "Okay, Reverend, come get your precious bones. But don't forget, they're still hanging in the balance here. It's not too late for me to let them go if I think you're trying anything."

He was ten feet away, walking slowly and stiffly, almost as if he were marching in a slow-motion procession; his eyes were gleaming, his breathing was fast, and his lips were forming whispered words that I couldn't hear. When he was two steps away, I said, "Stop." He stopped, swaying slightly as he stood. "Hold out your arms. I'm going to hand this to you. Brace yourself; it's heavy."

"Could you set it on the ground? I've got a bad back."

I wanted his hands occupied for a few seconds. "Have faith, Reverend. Remember the words of Isaiah: 'They that wait upon the Lord shall renew their strength. They shall mount up with wings as eagles. They shall run and not be weary. They shall walk and not faint.' Hold out your arms and get ready to take this, Reverend, because I'm about to lose my grip."

He took another step, and I swung the ossuary off the rail and into his outstretched arms. As he staggered under the weight, I darted across the bridge to the other side, snatched up the gun he'd laid down, and pointed it at him. "Liar," he hissed. "Deceiver. Son of Satan." He squatted and set down the ossuary with a thud.

"Not so, Reverend. I mean you no harm. I just want to make sure I get off this bridge alive." Keeping the gun and my gaze trained on him, I backed away from him, toward the tower and staircase at the end of the bridge. I'd made it halfway when a scream—Miranda's scream—split the night.

I turned and ran for the stairs, calling, "Miranda? *Miranda!*"

At that moment she emerged onto the bridge again, slung over the shoulder of Reverend Jonah's goon, who appeared like some twisted, evil version of Saint Christopher carrying the Christ child. How had he gotten back on the road so quickly, I wondered, after his crash in the mountain tunnel?

Had he flagged down a passing motorist? If so, what had become of the misguided Good Samaritan?

In person, Junior looked far bigger than the security-camera photo had suggested; he was a giant of a man, with a neck the diameter of a tree trunk and arms as thick as live-oak limbs. Miranda was writhing and struggling in his grip, with no more effectiveness than a toddler.

"Vengeance is mine," crowed Reverend Jonah behind me. "Thus sayeth the Lord." I turned to face him again. He was walking toward me, a second gun in his hand. He raised it, took aim at me, and I saw a flash from the muzzle, then felt myself flung backward as the fist of God slammed into my chest. I hit the wall of Saint Bénézet's Chapel with my back and head; my legs gave way and I slid down the rough wall and onto the stones of the bridge. "Vengeance is *mine*," I heard Reverend Jonah repeat. "Thanks be to God, which giveth us the victory." My vision was fading as he stepped toward me, but I could see him closing in, leveling the gun at my head. "Prepare to meet thy God." Dimly I heard a shot, and then another.

Clearly delirious now, I saw the preacher crumple to the stones directly in front of me, followed by Miranda and her burly captor. "Miranda, no," I groaned. But then, miraculously, Miranda pulled free and staggered to her feet. She stared down at Junior, whose head was lying in a pool of blood. "Dr. B, Dr. B," she was sobbing. "Oh, dear God, Dr. B." Behind her, striding toward me, I saw the angel of death coming to claim me. He was dressed in black, but instead of a scythe, he carried a rifle.

"Ah, lad, I'm sorry I didn't find you sooner," said the angel of death, whose features crystallized into the face of Father Mike.

"Take Miranda," I gasped. "Get her out of here."

"Let's see about you first, lad," he said. "Hurt bad, are you?"

"Not sure. Hard to breathe. How'd you find me?"

"Saint Anthony," he said. "Remember? 'Tony, Tony, look around'?" He took hold of my collar and ripped open the front of my shirt. He looked startled, and then he began to laugh. "I'll be damned. Maybe there's something to the hocus-pocus after all."

"What?" I looked down, expecting to see blood, but there was none. Then I remembered. "Oh, the vest." The gift Hugh Berryman had sent to accompany the Arikara Indian skeleton was a vest—a Kevlar vest, a bulletproof vest—and the Bible verse Hugh had referenced, Ephesians 6:11, admonished, "Put on the full armour of God." I'd recognized the vest right away; Hugh wore it whenever he worked a death scene, and I'd often teased him about it. But now I owed my life to it, and I vowed never to make fun of it again.

Before I could explain, Miranda reached to my chest, then held up the medallion Father Mike had given me to wear. The image of Saint Christopher had been obliterated; lodged in its place, at the center of the medallion, was a flattened lead slug. "My God," Miranda breathed. "Incredible. Absolutely incredible. What are the odds? So you're not even hurt?"

"Easy for you to say," I grunted. "Feels like I've

been kicked by a mule." But even as I said it, the pain was beginning to ease.

"You'll have a nasty bruise, I'm thinking," said Father Mike. "Maybe even a cracked sternum. But all things considered, you're one mighty lucky fella." He leaned closer, noticing the vest, inspecting it. "Takin' no chances, were you, Bill Brockton?" He smiled slightly. "This vest, by the by—it wouldn't have stopped that slug, lad. It'll stop a 9-millimeter, but not a .45, which is what the good reverend baptized you with."

Miranda stared at Father Mike, then looked again at the shattered medallion, turning it this way and that in the faint light. Jutting from one edge of the crater was a splintered bit of something green and gold, an incongruously synthetic material. "This thing has a circuit board in it," she said slowly. "Is this a tracking device? Have you been following Dr. Brockton?"

He shrugged. "Even Saint Anthony can use a bit of help."

She eyed him warily. "So who are you, really? You're clearly not a small-town Irish priest."

Other things began to crystallize in my mind. "It wasn't just coincidence that I met you that day in the library, was it? You'd been watching me, looking for an opening."

"I don't believe in coincidence, lad. It's true, I'd had my eye on you."

"That was you with the binoculars and camera," Miranda accused. "Watching us, taking pictures, the day we were up here on this bridge? You've been after the bones all along."

"And that whole story about the IRA and your brother," I added. "That was total bullshit."

"No, not total. I did lose a brother in the Troubles, but it wasn't the Brits killed him, it was me. A bomb I was rigging went off prematurely. So the penance part is true—I'll be doing penance for Jimmy till the day I die."

"But you're not really a priest."

He shrugged. "A priest, no. And if you ask the Holy Father about me, he'll say he's never heard of me. But I serve the church. I like to think of meself as a modern-day Knight Templar."

"So why do you want the bones?" Miranda asked. "Or why does the pope, or whoever the hell is your boss?"

"To cover the church's arse, Miss. If these *are* the bones of Christ, it buggers the story about the Resurrection and the ascension into Heaven. You can see the difficulty, can't you?"

"But they're not the bones of Christ," I said. "They're the bones of Meister Eckhart, a fourteenth-century theologian and preacher. I already told you that."

"Aye, so you did. You also told me that Eckhart was murdered—crucified, no less—by a cardinal who later became pope. And that Eckhart, not Christ, is the man on the Holy Shroud. Can't you see how *that* would bugger the Holy Father if word got around?"

I felt like such a fool. It was obvious—in the way he carried himself, in the ease with which he handled the weapon—that he was a soldier or cop. Was he one of the pope's Swiss Guards? Or part of some more secret agency—a Vatican version of the CIA? How could I have mistaken him for a simple village priest?

The rifle was slung loosely over his shoulder. It had a collapsible stock and a large-diameter scope that was designed either for low light or night vision. On top of the scope was a thin, cylindrical gadget that I guessed to be a targeting laser.

I felt an insane urge to laugh at the irony: Miranda and I had just escaped death at the hands of a Protestant fanatic, and now we were about to die at the hands of a Catholic assassin. I looked up at her, expecting to see sadness and fear in her face. Instead I saw stealth, cunning, and concentration. Almost imperceptibly she was edging behind Father Mike, edging toward the gun that had flown from my hand when Reverend Jonah's bullet had slammed into my chest. She was three feet from it, then two feet from it, and then she was there, directly behind him. I needed to distract Father Mike, or whoever this guy was. "So will you do penance for killing Miranda and me, too? What sort of penance will our deaths require?"

As I asked the question, Miranda reached for the gun. Without even looking, Father Mike swept a leg in a wide, swift arc, knocking her feet out from under her. She landed hard, with a thud and a grunt. She kept trying, though, going for the gun and managing to get a hand on it just as Father Mike's foot came down on her wrist. She cried out sharply in pain, and I struggled up to lunge for him. I was stopped short by the barrel of the rifle, jabbing into my throat two inches above the top of the Kevlar vest.

"I probably should kill you, lad, but I won't. If I wanted you dead, I'd've let the reverend do the bloody bit. I don't feel bad about shooting him and his ape—no penance needed for them two—but I don't need more innocent blood on my hands. It's asking for trouble, but I'll be letting you go. I hope you don't mind if I take a little souvenir with me, though." He took the pistol from Miranda's hand, then lifted his boot off her wrist. "Sorry to hurt you, miss. You strike me as a strong-headed lass, so I didn't figure you'd listen if I just said, 'Stop.' I hope I've not done any serious harm."

"I've got a bump on my head and maybe a sprained wrist, but I'll be okay," Miranda said. "Hurts a bit, but you saved me from the crazies, so if you promise not to kill me, I promise not to hold a grudge."

He smiled at that—a smile that reminded me of the kind, comforting fellow who'd offered a friendly ear on the staircase at the library a few days and a lifetime ago. Looking at me, he cocked his head at Miranda. "She's good in a pinch. I'd trust her with me back any day." He tossed the preacher's pistol over the railing, and it plunked into the water somewhere in the vicinity of the femur I'd lobbed a few minutes before. "Can I trust you two to sit here quiet-like till you can't hear me scooter any longer?" I nodded; he turned and looked at Miranda, and she nodded, too. "Fair enough. After that, you can scream bloody hell and sic the coppers on me. If they catch me, it means I've lost me knack."

He walked to the stone box sitting ten feet away, farther out on the bridge, where Reverend Jonah had left it. Lifting the lid from where I'd leaned it against the railing, he fitted it into place, but not before taking a quick look inside. Then he squatted and lifted the box, giving his right shoulder a shrug to keep the gun sling from slipping off.

"Those bones have brought bad luck to everybody that's tried to latch onto them," I said. "Are you sure you want them?"

He shrugged, and the box bobbed slightly. "It's not up to me, lad. I've got orders." He drew even with us, and as he did, he turned toward us. "Good luck to you both. I'd keep wearing that medal, lad— it seems to be working for you."

He turned away, and suddenly a bright mist of red sprayed from his back. Father Mike sank to his knees and set the ossuary down with a thud, as if taken by a sudden need to pray. Then he pitched forward across the top of it.

"Oh shit oh shit oh *shit*," gasped Miranda. She ran to him and laid a hand on Father Mike's shoulder as the life gurgled out of him. "Oh Jesus Mary and Joseph."

A man stepped from behind the corner of the tower at the end of the bridge and walked slowly toward us. "Hello, Docteur," he said. "*Bonsoir, mademoiselle.*" The man was Inspector René Descartes.

"Inspector? How long have you been here?"

"Five minutes, maybe." He shrugged. "In time to see the preacher and the muscleman die."

My mind was whirling, spun by a trinity of fear, sadness, and anger. "You didn't need to shoot the priest, Inspector," I said. "He wasn't going to hurt us."

"But I did," he said.

I was confused. "Did what?"

"I did need to shoot him."

"Why?"

"Because he was taking the bones."

"You could have just told him to put them down. He had his hands full. He was no threat."

"He was a big threat, Doctor. Or a big problem, at least. Just as you and mademoiselle are."

"I don't understand, Inspector."

"Do you know how much a French police inspector earns, Doctor?"

"No. Not enough, probably."

"Enough for a one-bedroom apartment and a ten-year-old car and one week at the beach every August," he said. "Do you know how much I can sell these bones for? Three million U.S. dollars."

"How? Who's left to sell them to, Inspector? The crazy Protestant and the commando Catholic are both dead now. The religious market would seem to have dried up rather suddenly."

"Ah, but you forget the art market," he said. He smiled ironically. "It seems the art dealer, Madame Kensington, has a very eager and very rich client, one who is happy to have another chance at the bones. It's a shame that you threw away one of them, but I think the blood on the box—along with the story of the crazy preacher and the soldier priest—will make up for the missing bone. A collector who will pay three million dollars for the bones of Christ is surely the kind of person who appreciates a good story. Imagine that you are a billionaire. Imagine that you have these bones, the most special bones in the world, and that you can take them out and show them off to your most trusted friends. Imagine how attentively they will listen as you tell how much money and how much blood it cost to get them. The story itself is worth a million, yes? Maybe I should raise the price, Doctor; what do you think?"

"I think you've forgotten something. A week ago you called Felicia Kensington a piece of shit."

"Ah, *oui*, she *is* a piece of shit. But she's a gold-plated piece of shit, filled with diamonds."

"So you're a faker, a forger, too," I said. "A counterfeit cop. You just pretend to care about truth and justice."

He shrugged, then wedged the toe of a boot under Father Mike's body and tipped him off the top of the ossuary. "Okay, let's go. My colleagues are slow, but even they will be arriving soon, after this many gunshots. Doctor, will you be so kind as to carry the bones?"

I squatted, then hoisted the box. "Father Mike was letting us go. Are you?"

"Ah, sorry, *non*, Doctor. The false priest gave you false hope. I give you the sad truth. *La triste vérité*. If you live, things will be very difficult for me. I wish I didn't have to kill you, but I do. Don't take it personally."

"I take it very personally, Inspector."

"*Quel dommage*. Too bad. But do as you wish."

Just ahead, something bright and orange caught my eye: the safety mesh spanning the gap in the railing. We were almost to the gap, and a desperate idea formed in my mind.

"Inspector, I need to shift my grip; I'm about to

drop this, and I doubt that your client will be happy if it gets broken. Let me just set it on the railing for a second."

"*Non*. Not on the railing," he said. "I saw how you balanced it on the railing to trick the preacher."

"Okay, okay, I'll set it on the ground," I said, "but I need to do it now. It's slipping." Without waiting for him to give permission—or deny it—I squatted and set down the ossuary, with the thunk of stone on stone. "Whew," I said, straightening up and bending backward to stretch. I interlaced my fingers, stretched my arms, and pushed my palms outward to crack my knuckles.

"That's enough," he said. "Come on."

"Okay. I'm ready. That helped." I squatted again and worked my fingers under the ends of the ossuary. "Miranda, can you give me a hand? Just till it's up?"

"Why don't you let me carry it awhile?" Miranda squatted on the other side of the box and wedged her fingers under as well. I felt her fingers graze mine on the underside of the box.

"No, I'll be fine," I said. "Just help me lift—that's the hardest part. Remember, lift with your legs, not your back." I tapped one of her fingers, a gesture I desperately hoped she'd interpret as a signal. Her eyes met mine, and when they did, I rolled mine upward as far as I could, raising my eyebrows at the same time. "Okay, on three," I said. "One. Two. *Three!*"

With all the strength I had, I straightened my legs and flung myself backward, shouting "*Push!*" as I did. Miranda shoved hard on the box, accelerating my backward fall. With my momentum, Miranda's push, and the ossuary's weight, I slammed into Descartes with the force of a linebacker. He grunted heavily and tumbled backward, my weight driving us both toward the gap in the railing. I felt momentary resistance as the orange safety mesh snagged us and stretched; we hung like that, suspended over the water, for an agonizing instant—the detective's arms windmilling for balance, grasping for anything solid—and then, with a crack as sharp as a gunshot, the plastic snapped and we fell: Descartes underneath, my body against his, and the stone box clutched to my chest. We did a backward flip in the air, and the centrifugal force of our spin sent pale bones cartwheeling into the black sky. We fell surrounded by them, as if we were inside some macabre snow globe of mortality.

Descartes hit the water flat on his back, and the double impact—first from hitting the water, then from being slammed by me—forced the air from his lungs like a punch in his gut. I'd braced myself as best I could, taking a deep breath and tensing my stomach muscles against the ossuary's weight.

The water closed swiftly over us, the momentum of our fall and the weight of the stone box driving us downward. Plunging through the cold blackness, the light fading fast above us, I felt Descartes struggling and clutching and scrabbling at me, as if I were a tree or a ladder he would climb to safety. I also felt the edges of the plastic webbing clawing at my hands and face as the loose ends fluttered and swirled around us.

I had no more than a few seconds of air in my

lungs, and I was plunging toward the river bottom, entwined with a drowning man and thirty pounds of stone. In desperation, I slammed my head backward, making solid contact with the inspector's face. His grip slackened long enough for me to twist free. I still had hold of the ossuary, clutching the edge of one end in my left hand. *Let it go*, a voice in my head screamed. *Let it go. Pull him to the surface.*

I ignored that voice. I redoubled my grip on the ossuary, and with my other hand I grabbed a fluttering end of plastic mesh and wrapped it around the box. Then, fumbling for the other end of the mesh, I cinched it around Descartes's foot. Only then, having trussed him to a stone anchor, did I push myself away and begin a desperate, breathless ascent. I felt his fingers clutch at my legs and then slip away as I kicked upward and he descended.

Only the faintest glimmer of light showed overhead, and as I flailed toward it, running out of air, the light began to dim. My last thought, as my mouth opened and my lungs filled with water, was for Miranda. *Keep her safe*, I thought—no, I prayed. Then: *It is finished. Now.*

And then there was blackness.

CHAPTER 43

SIRENS WAIL AND TIRES scream to a stop on the pavement at the base of the bridge. Eight men leap from the caravan of police cars, running toward the stairs, weapons in hand.

One of the officers cries out and points upward, and the others look just in time to see a figure—a young woman—climbing onto the railing of the bridge and scanning the water below for ripples, bubbles, anything. She balances there briefly, arms stretched wide, as if Jesus and Mary, Savior and Virgin, manifested at one and the same time. Then she sees something; she does not hesitate, but hurls herself headfirst, as heedless as a seabird that spies a flash of silver scales in the water. She cleaves the surface with scarcely a splash, and the policemen stand transfixed, staring at the widening circles that are the only evidence of what they have just witnessed. Long moments pass; one man clutches his partner's arm; another crosses himself.

At last the waters stir. The woman breaches, gasping and coughing and retching in the river. With one arm she pulls for the bank; with the other, she encircles the lifeless body she has harrowed from the depths.

She drags him onto the bank and presses water from his lungs, then—holding the shattered silver medallion he wears around his neck—she covers his mouth with hers and exhales, breathing into him the breath and prayer of life.

The man—Brockton—stirs, and groans, and lives again.

AUTHOR'S NOTE: ON FACT AND FICTION

Spoiler alert: This explanatory note refers to key details of the book's plot. If you haven't finished the book and don't want to risk spoiling the suspense, stop reading now . . . if you're strong enough to resist temptation.

Avignon—the city of the popes—is both faithfully and lovingly portrayed in this book. First settled by Celts several centuries before Christ, Avignon was forever changed in 1309 when Clement V, the first French pope, settled there with his court to avoid the perils of Rome, which was in the grip of a deadly feud between two powerful clans. Over the next seven decades, the Avignon papacy—called "the Babylonian captivity" by critics who believed that Rome was the only legitimate location for the papal palace—transformed Avignon from a small, sleepy town of some 5,000 to a booming, wealthy, and cosmopolitan city of 50,000. Avignon became the crossroads of money and power in medieval Europe. Kings, emperors, and other movers and shakers came to Avignon to seek papal favors, to apply political pressure, and to revel in luxuries that far surpassed those at the Parisian court of King Philip of France.

No surprise, then, that fourteenth-century Avignon was also a crossroads of artistic talent. Within Avignon's walls, popes, cardinals, and nobles rubbed shoulders with gifted painters and poets. Several famous figures from Avignon's glory days play prominent roles here in this book. Nothing here contradicts the historical record, though their actions in these pages do—admittedly, exuberantly and occasionally wickedly—go considerably beyond the bare-bones record history offers us.

Francesco Petrarch—the prolific poet and philosopher whom some historians call "the father of humanism"—bitterly criticized the Avignon papacy and the Babylonian captivity, even as he lived off the tithes and other proceeds collected by the "whore of Babylon." Petrarch's decades-long adoration of the unattainable young noblewoman, Laura—an infatuation that continued even after she died during the Black Death of 1348—is one of history's most famous unrequited romances. Petrarch wrote reams of sonnets to and about Laura; even at the time, though, some critics wondered if he was more in love with the idea of being in love— more smitten with himself as tragic hero—than with the actual, flesh-and-blood Laura: a woman whose lips he never even kissed.

Painter Simone Martini did, indisputably, paint

a small portrait of Laura for Petrarch. Alas, that portrait—the world's first commissioned portrait, say art historians—has been lost; if it could be found, it would surely fetch millions on the auction block at Sotheby's or Christie's. Little is known about Simone's personal life. He married into a family of Sienese painters; he and his wife, Giovanna, moved to Avignon in 1335 or 1336, and the couple had no children. When Simone died in Avignon in 1344, he left behind surprisingly few works from his time there, besides four frescoes (now undergoing restoration) in the portal of Avignon Cathedral and the sinopia studies for two of those frescoes: the powerful portraits of Mary and Jesus, that I—like Brockton and Miranda—found myself captivated by within the Palace of the Popes.

The Palace of the Popes, Europe's biggest Gothic palace, was begun in 1335 by Pope Benedict XII, who—prior to becoming pope in 1334 and taking the name Benedict XII—was named Jacques Fournier. In his six years as a cardinal in Avignon, Fournier was indeed known as le Cardinal Blanc, the White Cardinal, because of the white Dominican habit he always wore, even after he was entitled to far more sumptuous vestments. Fournier is a fascinating and (to me, at least) frightening study in contrasts. Immune to most of the temptations of luxury (except, apparently, food and drink), he built the fortress-like papal palace at least partly to safeguard the 17,500,000 gold florins amassed by his shrewd predecessor, Pope John XXII.

During Fournier's years as a cardinal in Avignon and, earlier, as a bishop and inquisitor in southwest

France, he was driven—I'd say obsessed, in fact—by the pursuit of heresy and the prosecution of heretics. Fournier became bishop of Pamiers in 1317; the following year he embarked on a systematic and thorough inquisition in the mountain village of Montaillou, whose entire population, astonishingly, had been arrested and charged with heresy a decade before, in 1308. Fournier reopened the matter and spent the next eight years interrogating villagers, shepherds, widows, and others whom he suspected of holding heretical views. He kept meticulous transcripts of his interrogations; Latin translations of those transcripts—called the "Fournier Register"—are bound in three immense volumes that are housed in the Vatican Library (Latin manuscript number 4030). Fournier judged many of Montaillou's inhabitants to be guilty of heresy, although he condemned "only" five to be burned at the stake. One of the five was Agnes Francou, the widow who is mentioned in chapter 17; Fournier interrogated Agnes repeatedly in 1319 and 1320, and eventually condemned her for refusing to swear an oath of truthfulness (despite the fact that Agnes pointed out to him, with some scriptural authority behind her, that "God has forbidden all swearing"). Several English-language translations of Fournier's interrogations—including his sessions with Agnes—can be found on the website of Professor Nancy Stork (http://www.sjsu.edu/people/nancy.stork/courses/c4/), a medievalist who teaches a course on Fournier at San Jose State University. A rich portrait of daily life and inquisitorial interrogation in Montaillou is presented in the book *Montaillou: The Promised Land of Error* by Emmanuel Le Roy Ladurie (what a great name, Emmanuel Le Roy: Emmanuel means "God With Us," and Le Roy means "The King"!). Ladurie's book, which is considered a pioneering ethnographic study, is based on the Fournier Register: the wealth of information Fournier gleaned from the "heretical" villagers of Montaillou. I feel an obligation to be crystal clear about a key difference between historical fact and this work of fiction: Although Jacques Fournier—the inquisitor who became a pope—was obsessed with heresy, and put at least five suspected heretics to death, the medieval murder attributed to him in these pages is purely speculative.

Many books and blogs have been written about the Shroud of Turin, Christianity's most revered relic. I won't attempt to summarize those here; suffice it to say that ever since its appearance in Lirey, France, in the middle of the fourteenth century, the Shroud has inspired both devotion and controversy. Those only intensified in 1898, when photographer Secondo Pia published the ghostly black-and-white photo negative he saw materialize in his photographic darkroom. That watershed moment marked the beginning of modern scientific scrutiny of the Shroud—scrutiny that culminated in 1988, when laboratories in Zurich, Oxford, and Tucson conducted independent C-14 tests to determine the age of the Shroud's fabric. The Tucson lab put the linen's age at 646 years, +/- 31 years; the Zurich lab, at 676 years, +/- 24 years; and the Oxford lab at 750 years, +/- 30. Averaging the three and taking the margins of uncertainty into account, the scientists responsible for the tests concluded—with

95 percent statistical confidence—that the Shroud of Turin was made sometime between 1262 and 1384. Almost immediately, die-hard believers in the Shroud's first-century authenticity—including scientific believers—began casting doubt on the findings. One theory that was offered claimed that a "bioplastic" coating on the fibers had skewed the results. Another, more creative theory claimed that the image had been formed by a burst of radiation at the moment of Jesus's resurrection, and that the radioactivity had skewed the quantity of C-14 level in the fabric. Still another claim held that the fabric samples had been snipped from an "invisible patch" woven into the Shroud during a sixteenth-century repair. One scientist who criticized the C-14 findings wrote, "It is simply not known how the ghostly image of a serene, bearded man was made." In a similar vein, other believers have claimed, countless times, that there is no technique known to artists—in medieval times or even modern times—that can produce an image with all the properties of the ghostly image on the Shroud of Turin. That assertion is simply not true, as Dr. Emily Craig demonstrated nearly two decades ago.

Emily—a medical illustrator turned forensic anthropologist—is lifted straight from life and transplanted into chapter 13 of our story. In 1994, while earning her Ph.D. at the University of Tennessee, Emily and UT textile scientist Randall Bresee published a peer-reviewed article in the *Journal of Imaging Science and Technology* (volume 34, number 1, 1994; available online at http://www.shroud.com/pdfs/craig.pdf) titled "Image Formation and the

Shroud of Turin." That article explained and demonstrated how a simple dust-transfer technique—using materials and techniques artists have used for thousands of years—could easily have been used by an artist to produce the image during the Middle Ages, the heyday of religious relics.

One other note on the Shroud of Turin: The passages in this book that discuss the Shroud figure's stature and proportions are, like Emily Craig, lifted from life. If the Shroud really were a direct, life-size imprint of Jesus' body, Christ—more than six feet tall—would have been a veritable giant back in the first century, when people were far shorter than they are today. If Jesus had been a head taller than his followers and his foes, it seems odd that none of the Gospel writers bothered to mention that detail. Also factual are the unusual, storklike proportions—the long legs and short, narrow trunk—that Dr. Brockton observes in the figure on the Shroud.

Last but not least, Eckhart, our "zhondo": Meister Johannes Eckhart—a prominent Dominican theologian and mystic—was indeed charged with heresy by the archbishop of Cologne around 1326. Eckhart appealed his case directly to Pope John XXII and walked 500 miles to Avignon to mount his defense. The pope put former inquisitor Jacques Fournier, le Cardinal Blanc, in charge of handling Eckhart's case. After journeying to Avignon, Eckhart seems to have dropped from sight; all we know is that he died sometime before March 1329, when Pope John issued a papal bull criticizing a number of Eckhart's teachings . . . and claiming that Eckhart repudiated his errors before dying.

The circumstances and date of Eckhart's death are shrouded in mystery. So are the location and fate of his remains. What's not in doubt is this: He was a renowned teacher and beloved preacher, but he was perceived as a threat by the high priests who held the reins of power; trumped-up charges were filed against him, and he died while trying to clear his name. As Miranda says, *Plus ça change, plus c'est la même chose:* The more things change, the more they stay the same.

—*Jon Jefferson*

ACKNOWLEDGMENTS

Many, many people contributed to the making of this book. Some of them—the larger-than-life historical characters who clamored to play parts in these pages—have been dead for centuries. Most, luckily, remain very much alive.

Anthropologists Angi Christensen, Norm Sauer, Richard Jantz, and Emily Craig all helped inform the sections on the Shroud of Turin. Richard, who co-created the University of Tennessee's ForDisc software, took measurements of the figure on the Shroud and noted the unusual, stork-like proportions. Emily, whose 1994 journal article on how the Shroud could have been created using materials and techniques readily available to medieval artists, examined our life-size, high-resolution photographic print of the entire Shroud and offered helpful insights; so did the co-author of her article, UT textile scientist Randy Bresee. Besides being smart scientists, Randy and Emily are also good sports (and brave people!), agreeing to make cameo appearances in these pages under their own names. Joe Mullins, a talented forensic facial reconstruction artist at the National Center for Missing and Exploited Children, likewise agreed to play himself in the book.

Researching Avignon was a writer's dream assignment, partly because the city is spectacular and partly because people there were lovely and helpful. Sylvie Joly, a press liaison at the Office of Tourism, provided background information, identified experts, and arranged interviews and tours. At the monumental and magnificent Palace of the Popes, conservator Sophie Biass-Fabiani—the keeper of the keys—graciously unlocked virtually every staircase, tower, nook, and cranny. And at Lumani, Avignon's loveliest guesthouse, Elisabeth and Jean Beraud-Hirschi (also portraying themselves in the book) went above and beyond the call of duty, offering not just hospitality but warmth, charm, and friendship.

Fr. Michael Demkovich—a Dominican friar, teacher, and author who has found inspiration in the life and teachings of Meister Eckhart—was generous with historical context and writerly encouragement. Fr. Michael (who bears *no* similarities to our story's Father Mike!) has likewise tackled the mystery surrounding Eckhart's death; his fictional take on it can be found in his novel, *The Death of Magister Aycardus.*

Art and artists figure prominently in the story. Stuart Riordan, a gifted Tallahassee artist, shared generously of her knowledge—and her books, and even her charcoal and paper, during a delightful but humbling drawing lesson. If the passages describing Simone Martini at work have any authenticity, Stuart deserves the credit.

This is the most complex of the seven Body Farm novels so far. Dennis McCarthy, Beth McPherson, and William McPherson all read the manuscript and shared a wealth of comments and encouragement. Jane McPherson—The Amazing Jane—was a co-conspirator from the beginning, hearing (and helping shape) the earliest, vaguest ideas; dashing to Turin; delving deeply into Avignon (ah, the food and wine research!); listening to a road-trip reading of a draft; and offering myriad suggestions that made this a better book. The swift, smart, and eagle-eyed Casey Whitworth signed on late in the project and made numerous eleventh-hour contributions to the manuscript itself, to www. JeffersonBass.com, to our Facebook pages, and to JonJeffersonAuthor.blogspot.com.

Turning an idea into a published book takes a lot of work. We appreciate all those at William Morrow who produce, promote, and sell our books, especially our editor, Lyssa Keusch; her able assistant, Wendy Lee (goodbye, and good luck with your own writing!); our production editor, Andrea Molitor; and our publicist, Danielle Bartlett. Hats off to them, and to our agent, Giles Anderson, who set the wheels in motion.

Putting a book into a reader's hands takes a surprising amount of work, too. Thanks to all the William Morrow sales people and booksellers who make that happen again and again, even in these lean times. A special thanks to Susan Seals and her tribe, of BoneZones.com, for putting our books out there always, and to Frank Murphy, Jennifer Alexander, and our longtime friends at WBIR's "Alive at Five" show.

Thanks, too, to our readers and fans. Without your interest and support, none of this would happen. What magic, to spin stories and characters out of the air and watch them take root in the minds and hearts of readers!

Finally—in the spirit of "first shall be last, and last shall be first"—our deepest appreciation to our families for their love and encouragement.

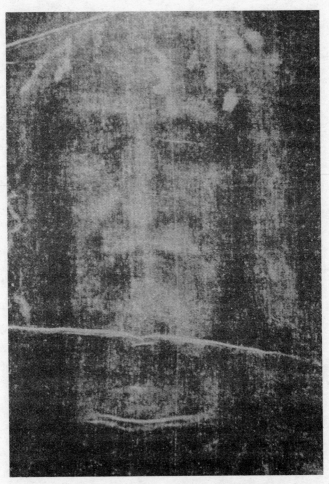

A black-and-white, photo-negative version of the face on the Shroud of Turin. The actual image on the Shroud is a faint reddish-brown. The dramatic negative was first seen in 1898, when Italian photographer Secondo Pia noticed the haunting, lifelike quality of the image he developed in his darkroom. Far more powerful than the positive image faintly visible on the fabric, the negative has arguably supplanted the Shroud itself as the main object of devotion.

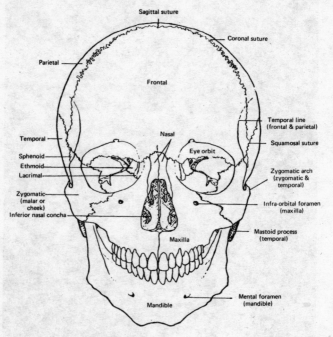

THE SKULL

BONES OF   PARTS OF

Sagittal suture

Coronal suture

Parietal

Frontal

Temporal line
(frontal & parietal)

Squamosal suture

Nasal

Temporal

Eye orbit

Sphenoid

Ethmoid

Zygomatic arch
(zygomatic &
temporal)

Lacrimal

Zygomatic
(malar or
cheek)

Infra-orbital foramen
(maxilla)

Inferior nasal concha

Mastoid process
(temporal)

Maxilla

Mental foramen
(mandible)

Mandible

THE SKULL

BONES OF

PARTS OF

Coronal suture

Sagittal suture

Frontal

Parietal

Temporal line

Lambdoidal suture

Squamosal suture

Nasal

Sphenoid

Temporal

Lacrimal

Ethmoid

Occipital

Zygomatic

External occipital protuberance

Maxilla

Mastoid process (temporal)

Ear (External auditory meatus) (temporal)

Tempero-mandibular joint

Mandible

Styloid process (temporal)

Mental foramen

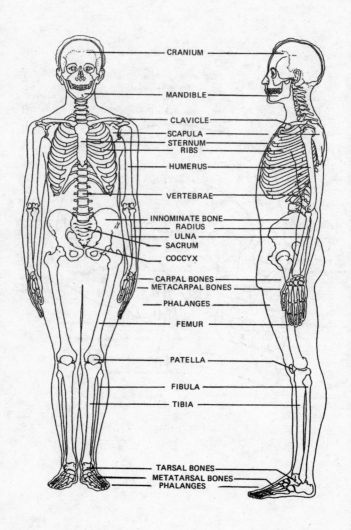

CRANIUM

MANDIBLE

CLAVICLE
SCAPULA
STERNUM
RIBS
HUMERUS

VERTEBRAE

INNOMINATE BONE
RADIUS
ULNA
SACRUM
COCCYX

CARPAL BONES
METACARPAL BONES

PHALANGES

FEMUR

PATELLA

FIBULA

TIBIA

TARSAL BONES
METATARSAL BONES
PHALANGES

Before Dr. Bill Brockton even considers hopping a plane to Avignon, France to follow the mystery of the bones in *The Inquisitor's Key*, Detective René Descartes has his hands full. He is a French detective in Avignon, who enjoys a hearty meal, a smooth wine, and an intriguing case. It seems the latter has just dropped into his lap. A bizarre break-in at Avignon's famed museum of medieval art plunges the detective into an elaborate, art-lined labyrinth: a labyrinth that leads him to a master forger's studio . . . and to a charred corpse. Just as he's finally closing the case, Descartes gets called to an even more bizarre death scene, where his path—and his fate—will collide with those of Dr. Bill Brockton and Miranda Lovelady, who find themselves far afield from Tennessee's famed Body Farm.

Continue reading to join the French sleuth as he delves into the high-stakes world of art theft and art forgery in "Madonna and Corpse," the mesmerizing prequel to *The Inquisitor's Key*.

CHAPTER ONE
Descartes

**The Petit Palais Museum
Avignon, France**

"TURN OFF THAT DAMNED alarm!" René Descartes—
Inspector René Descartes, of the French National
Police—waved his arm in a sweeping arc of annoyance that encompassed not just the bored police officers and the nervous museum staffers, but also the
museum itself, its collection of ancient paintings,
and possibly even their long-dead creators, as if the
artists themselves might bear some of the blame for
rousting him from sleep at one in the morning.

"We're working on it," croaked the museum's director, a withered crone named Madame Clergue.
Christ, how old is she? wondered Descartes, jotting
her name in a pocket-size notepad that he'd fished
from inside his jacket. *She probably bought these pictures from the guys who painted them.* Beneath her

hastily donned raincoat, Mme. Clergue appeared to be wearing only a thin cotton nightgown. Its embroidered collar was unraveling, sending tendrils of thread curling upward toward her wispy white hair.

Unlike Mme. Clergue, Descartes was fully decked out in his de facto professional uniform—dress pants, dress shirt, jacket and tie—not because he'd swiftly suited up when the dispatcher awoke him, but because he'd fallen asleep on the couch at eleven, still wearing the rumpled outfit he'd donned fifteen hours before. Somehow this had become his nightly ritual of late: nursing a few beers or a bottle of wine in front of the television until the news or soccer highlights lulled him to sleep. As a result, his dreams often hitched themselves to the sirens and shrieks emanating from the television, creating the odd sensation that he'd not actually fallen asleep, but had simply switched to a channel specializing in French surrealism. As the museum's alarm continued to jangle mercilessly, Descartes wondered if this, too, might simply be another of those dreams, conjured up to explain a particularly clamorous sound track.

Just as he could bear no more, the alarm ceased. Its clang echoed for several seconds in the stone corridors and stairwells of the vast structure. In the acoustic void left behind, the silence seemed as close and dense as fog until Descartes spoke, dispersing it. "And you're quite sure it's not a false alarm, Madame?"

Mme. Clergue nodded vigorously for a woman of her years. "Quite sure. Pascal"—she stretched a clawlike finger toward a uniformed guard hovering in a nearby doorway—"found the door propped open at the service entrance." At the mention of his name, Pascal, who managed to look as self-important as a key witness yet also as sheepish as a guard who's been robbed, approached the director and murmured in her ear. She blanched, then said to Descartes, "If you wish to see the security-camera footage of the thief, Pascal has it on the monitor."

"Sure, let's take a look." The inspector followed Pascal and Mme. Clergue through a doorway into a small, windowless room located just off the entry hall. Arrayed above a low, desklike counter that lined one wall, an appliance-store-worth of small televisions showed video feeds from a fleet of cameras. Three of the cameras monitored exterior doorways—the museum's main entrance, a large loading-dock door, and an emergency exit—and the others offered wide-angle views of the museum's galleries. At the center of the cluster, a larger monitor featured a zoomed-in view of the loading-dock door, propped open with a stone block. A man, frozen in midstep, was emerging from the building. Pascal stooped and snaked an arm between Descartes and Mme. Clergue to press a button on the console; on the screen, the door opened wide and the man exited the building.

Descartes leaned in for a closer look. As he did, he inadvertently collided with Mme. Clergue, who was likewise angling for a better view. "*Excuse* me," she squawked. It was an accusation, not an apology, and Descartes ignored it.

The man on the screen was wearing black: black shoes, black pants, black pullover, black cap. His head was bowed and as he emerged fully onto the loading dock, he wrapped one arm across his face and then turned away from the camera. "He knows where the camera is," Descartes said to Mme. Clergue. "Could he be one of your staff?" Using a wooden crate for a boost, the man scaled a gate and dropped into a quiet street on the other side. To Pascal, the detective said, "Back up. Let's watch that again."

Mme. Clergue pursed her lips and shrugged, then drew a deep breath and puffed it out, *pphhtt*, in answer to Descartes's question. "From this picture, who can tell? Nine men—ten, if you count the gardener—work at the museum. One is as fat as a pig, so it's not him." Descartes heard Pascal suppress a snicker. "One is tall enough to be an American basketball player; another could be a circus midget. I suppose it could be any of the others." She frowned at the screen as the man reemerged once more in playback, then turned and frowned at Descartes, her pale eyes raking him up and down. "But it could be anyone. It could be *you*, Inspector."

Descartes raised his eyebrows at her. "You missed your true calling, Madame Director," he said drily. "You should have been a detective." He gestured at the monitor. "So, with your keen powers of observation, what other helpful deductions can you share with us?"

His sarcasm brought a flush to her cheeks and a flash to her eyes, but she dutifully studied the screen once more. Finally, sighing, she said, "I deduce that we should hide our security cameras in the bushes, so the robbers won't know where they are."

Descartes laughed, his irritation unexpectedly dispersed by the dry, self-deprecating joke. "Touché, Madame." After a pause he added kindly, "Also, perhaps it's worth noting that the man's hands are empty?"

She drew a sharp breath, staring at the screen. "Then he's not stolen anything? Oh, thank God!" She breathed deeply in relief.

"Well, he hasn't stolen *everything*, at any rate," the detective hedged. "Does the collection include jewelry? Gold? Gems? Other small, precious things he might have put in his pockets?"

She pursed her lips, taking mental inventory, then shook her head. "Our specialty is medieval and Renaissance paintings. We do have some artifacts, but mostly sculptures and architectural fragments—the tops of columns, effigies from tombs, that sort of thing. Nothing of much value. Certainly nothing pocket-size."

Descartes tapped the figure frozen once more on the screen. "Could there be a painting under his shirt? Or rolled up in the leg of his pants? Something he's cut from the frame and tucked in his clothes?"

"Heavens, Inspector," she sighed, "just when I'm beginning to find you reassuring, you pull the rug out from under me again." She put a hand to her chin, a yellow, hornlike fingernail stroking thin lips as she pondered. "We have a number of small paintings. The only way to know is to check all the galleries. Shall I go and get started?"

"Not yet." Descartes turned to the security guard, who had rolled his chair away from the counter in search of more personal space. "Pascal, can you scroll through the footage from the galleries? Starting when the alarm sounded, and going backward?"

"Of course." The guard rolled toward the console again, parting the inspector and the director. "Starting with Gallery One?"

The inspector turned to Mme. Clergue. "Let's think like a thief, shall we? What's the most valuable painting in the museum, and how much is it worth?"

"Goodness, that's a difficult question, Inspector," she replied. "Most of our paintings were donated or loaned to us years ago, so it's hard to say what they might fetch these days. Take that piece, for instance." She turned and pointed through the security room's doorway at a picture suspended from the ceiling of the entry hall—a large portrait of a couple standing side by side. "Mary Magdalene and John the Baptist. That's just an enlargement, of course. We paid sixty thousand francs for the painting, thirty years ago. Earlier this year, a work not *nearly* that good fetched three million euros at auction."

"Three million, eh?" Descartes studied the painting with growing interest. The colors were vivid and vibrant, and the couple possessed moviestar good looks—sex appeal, even, he was surprised to notice. "But I thought you specialized in medieval art," he said. "Surely that's more modern?"

She gave him a tolerant smile. "Actually, it's six hundred years old," she said. "But it looks almost contemporary, doesn't it? Not the pinched, anemic figures you see in most medieval paintings."

"For a religious painting, that's pretty sexy,"

Descartes remarked. "Which gallery is that one in?"

"Six," the director said. Even before she said it, Pascal had switched the main monitor to the Gallery 6 camera. He scrolled backward rapidly, the minutes in the time-stamp box spinning down as fast as seconds.

"Stop," Descartes ordered. A shadow had flitted across the screen, so swiftly as to be almost invisible. "Go forward, Pascal. Not so fast." The guard reversed the direction of the playback. "There! Slow down, slow down!" A man entered the gallery, then turned toward the camera so that his face was clearly visible. "Damn," said Descartes.

"Sorry." Pascal shrugged. "Just me, making my rounds."

"Okay. Scroll back the rest of the way. All the way to closing time."

Pascal made two more cameo appearances onscreen, each time turning to face the camera. Otherwise the room remained empty except for the sundry saints and martyrs lining the walls.

Descartes turned to Mme. Clergue. "So what else might be especially tempting to an art thief?"

Pphhtt, she puffed again, shrugging. "We all have our own tastes."

He cocked his head quizzically. "And what's *your* taste? What would *you* steal, Madame?" She drew back, shocked, and searched his eyes for signs of accusation. He smiled and winked. "Me, I'd steal the sexy couple."

She flushed slightly, a faint pink suffusing the parchment of her cheeks, but her eyes twinkled. "Oh dear me," she fluttered. "Well, if I were shopping for my personal collection, I, too, might take the . . . the *couple* that you like. But if I were hoping to sell it on the black market, I'd go for name recognition and pinch the Botticelli."

Descartes's eyebrows shot up. "Botticelli? The guy who painted Venus on the half shell?"

"*Really*, Inspector, have you no respect?" She made a piping sound that might have been either a wheeze or a giggle. "Yes, Botticelli was the guy— the artist—who painted *The Birth of Venus*. We have—I *hope* we still have—a lovely *Madonna and Child* by Botticelli. In Gallery Eleven."

The guard was already on it. He'd barely begun to scroll backward when the screen flickered with motion. He stopped scrolling and reversed direction. For the fourth time, they watched as Pascal entered a gallery, faced the camera, and then strolled out of frame. Seconds later, though, he ran back in and—without slowing down or looking at the camera—sprinted out the doorway he'd originally entered. "That's when I heard the alarm," he explained. He pointed to the time stamp on the screen. "12:08 A.M."

Descartes consulted his notepad. "Yes, that's when we got the signal," he said. He chewed on his lower lip. "Do you have a floor plan of the museum?" Pascal tapped the counter; pressed beneath a glass top was a diagram of each level. The detective studied it, then pointed with the tip of his pen. "So when you heard the alarm, you were here. Where were you just before that?"

"Directly above, in Gallery Twelve," the guard answered. "The top floor. I came down the spiral

staircase"—he indicated the stairs on the map—
"and went through Gallery Eleven. When the
alarm sounded, I ran back to the stairs and came
down here, to see which alarm sensor had gone
off." He pointed to a bank of indicator lights—a
row of steady green LEDs, broken by one blinking
red diode.

Descartes nodded. "Okay. The video. Keep
scrolling backward, please." Pascal resumed, but
he'd barely gotten beyond his own 12:08 appearances before another shadowy figure began darting across the frame. Pascal twitched the knob on
the control panel. The video slowed, just in time
to show the black-clad man walking out of the gallery. He was carrying a painting, and for a moment,
as he passed through the wide doorway, the upper-
right corner of the picture was visible. It showed
the delicate face of a beautiful girl, who appeared to
be looking down at the man abducting her.

Mme. Clergue gasped and clutched Descartes's
sleeve. "Oh dear God," she whispered. "I think he's
got the Botticelli."

Descartes tapped Pascal on the shoulder. "Go
back. Play the whole thing in real time, start to
finish." The guard nodded and pressed a button.
After a few seconds, the black-clad man entered
the screen, moving in reverse, hugging the young
woman to his chest. "No, no," Descartes snapped.
"Forward, *forward*. Start at the beginning and go
forward."

"I *am* going forward," Pascal protested.

"Then why the hell is he moving backward?"

The guard shrugged. "I don't know why, but he
is," he insisted. He tapped the corner of the screen.

Sure enough, the time-stamp numbers were spinning up, second by second. "See?"

"I don't understand," Mme. Clergue fretted.

"He doesn't want to show his face," Descartes said. "Maybe he's teasing us, too, knowing we'll be watching. In any case, he knows where all the cameras are. He must be an insider." Mme. Clergue started to protest, but the inspector raised a hand for silence. They watched with growing puzzlement as the man stopped and leaned the painting against the wall, fished an implement of some sort from his pants, and struck the wall three times. Then, to their utter astonishment, he hoisted the painting from the floor, hung it, and strode from the gallery.

There was a moment of stunned silence, broken by a single bark of laughter from Descartes. "I'll be damned," he said. "He's not looting your collection; he's adding to it!"

"This is very . . ." Mme. Clergue began vaguely, but Descartes was already out the door, moving at a ponderous, middle-aged jog toward the spiral stairs. When Mme. Clergue caught up, he was in the middle of Gallery 11 staring at the wall. Hanging directly in front of him, where it had hung for years, was Botticelli's *Madonna and Child*. Hanging alongside it was . . . Botticelli's *Madonna and Child*.

"YOUR MYSTERY DONOR has a knack for copying," Descartes said finally, alternating his gaze between the museum's new acquisition and the original. The likeness was so perfect that the detective could not have said which was Botticelli's handiwork and which was the copy. And it wasn't just the images; even the frames—gilded wood with ornately carved borders—were twins. "A remarkable knack."

"Indeed," spat Mme. Clergue.

Descartes turned his attention from the Madonna's face to Mme. Clergue's. The inspector was intrigued; the director seemed furious. "What's wrong, Madame? You still have your Botticelli, and now you have a superb backup, if something happens to the original. Why the sour face?"

She glowered at the freshly hung painting. "But what's he *doing*?" she finally snapped. "Is he just having fun at our expense? What if he comes back and *does* take something valuable?"

"Madame, a word in private?" It was a command, not a request. She shot him a look, then spun and walked toward the doorway. "Very well," she said. "My office is just around the corner."

"Everyone out," Descartes ordered over his shoulder. The two uniformed police officers, Pascal, and another museum staffer whom Descartes had successfully ignored so far looked at him blankly. "Don't touch anything. Don't even look at anything. Everybody go back downstairs." They stared, unmoving, as rooted as Michelangelo's *Prisoners* in their blocks of marble. "Out," he barked. "*Now*." They scurried like shooed pigeons.

In her office, Madame Clergue sank into a high-backed chair behind the library table that served as her desk. Descartes drummed his fingers on the edge and studied her face, his eyes narrowed. Suddenly he demanded, "Who is 'he,' Madame?"

She blinked and shifted in the chair. "Who is *who*, Inspector?"

"Don't play games with me. A moment ago, in the gallery, you said, 'What's he doing? What if he comes back?' Who did you mean by 'he,' Madame?"

A deep crimson penetrated the chasmic depths of her wrinkles. "I . . . I meant . . . the thief."

"There was no theft," Descartes pointed out. "Therefore, no thief."

"Very well, the intruder, then," she snapped, "if you want to split hairs."

Descartes lunged forward in his chair, as if to hurdle the table and shake her by the throat. "I *don't* want to split hairs!" he roared, slapping the table with a sound like a rifle shot. The old woman gasped and shrank back, and her right eye began to twitch. "I want to know the truth, Madame. You were thinking of someone. Some particular 'he.' Tell me who."

"I was not," she quavered, slowly drawing herself up. They glared at each other. Finally, steeling her voice, she said, "Since, as you say, there was no theft, there is no need for an investigation. I do not wish to press charges for the break-in, Inspector."

Descartes's surprise gave way to suspicion. Only a fool—or someone with something to hide—would drop the matter here. "That's not how it works, Madame. If I suspect a crime—and I do, criminal trespass—I am obliged to investigate. And you are obliged to cooperate."

"I have no information that could possibly help."

"What are you keeping from me, Madame?"

"Nothing, Inspector."

"Then why is your eye twitching like that? And why are your hands shaking?"

She turned her face to the right, so he could no

longer see that eye, and folded her arms resolutely across the raincoat.

Descartes glowered. Finally he rose, anger emanating from him in waves. "Stay," he commanded sternly, shaking a finger at her as if she were a wayward spaniel. "If you move from that chair before I get back, I'll arrest you for obstructing an investigation." He spun and stalked from the room. Ninety seconds later he returned. "Now come," he said harshly. He led her back to the gallery.

Both paintings were gone.

She seized his arm with both hands, a pair of buzzard's claws clutching at a tree branch. "What have you done?" she gasped.

He pointed through the doorway to the adjoining gallery. The two paintings rested in the far corner, leaning against adjacent walls. Madame Clergue shuffled toward them, her feet—in slippers, Descartes noticed for the first time—rasping across the varnished floor.

"So, Madame Director," he said coldly. "Which is your original, and which is the copy?" Standing wide-eyed before them, she looked from one painting to the other, back and forth, back and forth, as if the Madonnas were engaged in a tennis match. "Well? Which is which?"

She opened her mouth to speak, but all that came out was a choked sob. Madame Madeleine Clergue wept, burying her face in her hands. When at last she looked up, her face had aged another ten years. "I don't know," she whispered. "God *damn* that son of a bitch."

CHAPTER TWO
Dubois

JACQUES DUBOIS DIPS A clean cloth in turpentine and drapes it across the painting, stretching and smoothing the fabric to remove all wrinkles. The white cloth—cut from an expensive linen bedsheet—is virtually transparent. Through the fine weave of fabric, as if behind a veil, a homely Virgin Mary cradles an even homelier Jesus. The baby's head is far too small for his body, his face more like a middle-aged man's than an infant's, his body bizarrely muscled like a miniature weight-lifter's. Dubois smiles at the pair and murmurs, "Soon you will be so much prettier. You'll thank me."

In his early years, Dubois felt guilty about taking solvents or a heat gun to ancient paintings simply so that he could recycle an old canvas or wooden panel for his own works. By now, though, he knows he's performing a service: ridding the world of mediocrities and replacing them with masterpieces. It's as if he's buying up dreadful shacks on spectacular lots, then knocking them down and erecting architectural gems in their stead.

After washing his hands in the paint-stained sink, he leaves the studio, crossing his backyard through clouds of blossoming plum and pear trees. In the kitchen of the old farmhouse, he assembles a simple lunch: fresh goat cheese, briny black olives, baby arugula drizzled with olive oil and lemon, a crusty baguette, and a glass—then another—of a delicate, apricot-hued rosé from a nearby vineyard. He eats slowly, savoring both the food and the latest auction catalog from Sotheby's of London, which includes one of his works, a "Gainsborough" landscape he painted two years ago. "A previously unknown work, this is a particularly fine example of the simple style Thomas Gainsborough favored in his later period," the catalog informs him. Once Dubois has finished with his modest portions of food, wine, and triumph, he washes, dries, and puts away the dishes before recrossing the backyard.

When Dubois bought the farm—*what was it, twenty years ago? no, my God, nearly thirty!*—the studio was a roofless set of walls, crammed with broken-down tractors, rusted plows, and God-knows-what-other ruined implements. The house was no prize, either, but Dubois focused solely on the barn for the first year, transforming the cavernous ruin into a bright, airy workspace.

For years now, every morning he's brought his coffee out here, gazing across the Rhône as the rooftops of Avignon catch fire in the rising sun. The light paints the grim gray towers of the Palace of the Popes a delicate shade of pink and sets the cathedral's towering gold statue of the Virgin blindingly ablaze. Dubois has tried to capture this magical morning alchemy of light and stone in paint on canvas, but even his prodigious skills are not up to the challenge.

Inside the studio, Dubois inspects the Madonna and the Christ-child. Their features have softened, as if the two glasses of wine are blurring Dubois's vision. Folding back one corner of the turpentine-soaked cloth, he presses a thumbnail to the paint and feels it yield. "Perfect," he purrs. He puts a CD into the Bose player and presses Play, and Mick Jagger laments, "I can't get no satisfaction." Nodding his head in time to the beat, Dubois begins to deconstruct the ancient painting.

Peeling off the veil of fabric, its fibers smeary with reds, blues, and golds from the painting, he lays it on the table and picks up a putty knife. Starting at the bottom-left corner of the panel, he scrapes upward and across in a series of short, swift strokes, taking care not to dig into the soft poplar wood beneath the paint. A moment's carelessness, a single gouge, and the panel, for which he paid half a year's income to a rapacious dealer in Rome, would be ruined, useless except as firewood or a tavern sign. The cost of Dubois's raw materials—mediocre medieval paintings exhumed from attics and junk shops; blank paper and vellum, sliced from the flyleaves of ancient volumes beneath the noses of dozing librarians; boards pilfered from unguarded old chapels and fortresses—has risen a hundredfold during his career. Luckily, his own prices have increased a thousandfold, at least for showpieces like the one he's about to create.

With each push of the putty knife, the paint glides another fraction of an inch up the blade, accumulating in thin, rippled ridges like multicolored cake frosting. Back and forth, left and right he works, pausing each time he reaches one side or the other to wipe the knife with a rag. After several hours of rhythmic strokes, he is approaching the base coat of white lead. He soaks another clean piece of linen in turpentine and lays it on the panel, then steps back to stretch. When he straightens up and arches backward, the ache in his back makes him groan. *Oh, shit, I'm too old for this,* he thinks, then, *Good thing I'm getting out.* Twisting his torso from side to side, he wrings a satisfying series of cracks from his spine and smiles slightly. *Not with a whimper, but some bangs,* he thinks. After a few more stretches, he removes the cloth and gently wipes off most of the white-lead primer, taking care not to rub all the way into the gesso, the underlying mixture of animal-hide glue and chalk dust used to fill the grain, smooth imperfections in the wood, and create a rigid, perfect surface on which to paint.

If he works quickly for the next few days, he'll be finished by the time François arrives from Marseilles, bringing Dubois the final piece of the puzzle. Dubois owes François for this—owes him both money and sex—but the investment will be well worth it.

CHAPTER THREE
Descartes

"THANK GOD I STUCK my chewing gum on the back of the copy." Descartes's proud announcement was not greeted with the outpouring of gratitude he'd expected.

The inspector, Mme. Clergue, and her chief conservator, Henri Devereaux—the museum functionary who'd been fluttering on the edge of Descartes's vision since one A.M.—were huddled blearily in the museum's workshop. They'd spent hours poring over the two paintings. They'd used their naked eyes, they'd used magnifying glasses, they'd even used ultraviolet light to search for the telltale fluorescence of modern pigments. They'd found innumerable minor differences—after all, each work was painted by hand—but absolutely nothing to indicate which painting was created in 1467 and which in 2012.

For a painting that was more than five hundred

years old, the Botticelli—whichever the hell the Botticelli was—looked damned good, Descartes thought. The inspector had been raised Catholic, so he'd seen enough Madonna-and-child paintings to last him an eternity. This one, though, was different. For one thing, it wasn't dark or gloomy; beneath a bright blue shawl, Mary wore a reddish-orange dress; the arched window opening that framed the mother and child was also a cheery blue. The Virgin—the mother—looked to be all of fifteen years old, Descartes thought; seventeen, tops. Her face was pale, with delicate, pretty features, large eyes, and a high, intelligent forehead. On her head she wore a sheer lace cap that allowed glimpses of golden hair; above the cap was a disk of gold filigree, so gossamer-fine as to be nearly invisible. Her neck was long, slender, and gracefully arched as she gazed down at the robust boy sprawled across her lap. Her right hand cradled his head; her left hand covered her right breast, and barely visible between the index and middle fingers was a nipple, all but concealed by the design of the dress and the modesty of the mother. Descartes had no children—he no longer even had a wife, not since that bitch Yvonne had dumped him for some German tourist she met in a bar—but somehow this painting evoked in him feelings of paternal protectiveness and tenderness he wished he could attach to a family.

After removing the paintings from the gallery wall, Descartes had kept the director twisting in the wind for hours, refusing to tell her about the telltale wad of chewing gum he stuck behind one corner of the copy's frame—not until he'd pried the truth, or at least some of it, grudgingly out of her. Three years before, the museum had hired a restoration expert, Jacques Dubois, to clean and restore the Botticelli, she'd finally told the inspector. "People think that paintings get dark over time," she said. "You've probably seen pictures like that—dingy old Rembrandts and Van Dycks that are almost black with age?" He'd nodded, though he couldn't quite recall if that was actually true. "But it's not the paint that's darkened, it's just the varnish. Strip that off, and a five-hundred-year-old painting is as bright as the day it dried on the easel." The Botticelli's varnish had dimmed the painting's vibrancy, so they'd hired Dubois—one of the best restorers in France, living right here in Avignon—to strip off the old varnish and put on a fresh coat.

"Why didn't you want to tell me this? And why did the appearance of the copy upset you so much?"

She'd looked down at her desk, unable to meet his gaze. "Against my better judgment, I allowed Dubois to do the restoration at his studio. With lesser works, we don't worry so much, but the Botticelli was a treasure. I was afraid it might be stolen. But Dubois was adamant. He insisted that the restoration wouldn't be as good if he had to work in our 'soul-sucking, fluorescent-lit circle of hell'—that's how he described the museum's conservation shop. I also knew there was bad blood between him and Monsieur Devereaux. So I agreed to let him take the painting. When I saw the copy, I felt . . . it seemed a betrayal of our trust. And the mocking way he hung the copy. It was a slap in the museum's face."

Descartes had felt sure there was more to the story than she was telling, but it was clear she was prepared to stonewall. He decided not to press the point—for now. But he would get to the bottom of it sooner or later. Was it possible that she and Dubois were in cahoots—colluding in some sort of scam—and that he was setting her up to take the fall? Descartes had good instincts—a good nose, he called it—and beneath the scent of the old lady's baby powder or face cream or whatever the hell it was, the detective caught a strong whiff of fear.

CHAPTER FOUR
Dubois

AS HE CHANGES THE CD in the Bose and begins squeezing white lead from a tube, Dubois laments the changing of the times. In the years since health agencies have banned lead-based paint in homes and offices, white lead—artists' favorite primer for millennia, a white so dazzling it makes paintings glow from within—has become virtually impossible to obtain. It remains perfectly legal, of course, for expendable artists like Dubois to risk lead poisoning, but alas—in dutiful obedience to the law of supply and demand—paint manufacturers no longer find it profitable to make the meager amounts of white lead required by artists, and so stockpiles go steadily down and prices go swiftly up. The single tube he'll use to reprime this one panel cost him a week's grocery money, and he had to grovel to get it at all. Soon he may be forced to make his own white lead, the same way the ancient

Greeks did, by suspending thin sheets of lead above a vat of vinegar (encased in fresh horse dung, for warmth!) until the lead is covered with white corrosion, then scraping off the corrosion, grinding it, and mixing it with linseed oil. *A damned nuisance*, he fumes, *and all because a few stupid babies ate too many paint chips.*

Once he begins applying the white lead to the panel, though, he forgets his irritation and, as always, falls under the spell of the work: the velvety feel and silky sound of the white lead gliding onto the panel. He turns and touches the Bose, and angelic voices fill the studio—a women's quartet singing an eleventh-century polyphonic chant, "10,000 Virgins." The soaring melodies infuse his studio and his paint and his *soul* with sublimity. At this moment, anything is possible; on this luminous, immaculate surface, he can be a Michelangelo, a Da Vinci, a Rembrandt, or any other genius of the ages. As it happens, he will be Botticelli, specifically, the Botticelli who painted the sweet *Madonna and Child.* This one, his third, will be his best yet—far better than the two that he's foisted off on the old bat at the Petit Palais—for this time, he has a buyer willing to pay a price worthy of the work.

It's taken three years to reel in the buyer, a British art dealer named Felicia Kensington. It began when she wrote to express her admiration of a Caravaggio painting—*Salome Receives the Head of John the Baptist*—that he'd cleaned and retouched for the National Gallery in London. "The painting now glows with Caravaggio's genius and your own,"

she said. Dubois responded with an equally effu-
sive thank-you note, and they passed a few more
flattering messages back and forth. Eventually he
mentioned, oh so casually, that occasionally he got
lucky enough to unearth a work by an old master—a
painting or drawing languishing, unsigned and un-
recognized, in some junk shop or attic.

"If," she'd swiftly responded, "you should
happen upon any unsigned works in the style of
Caravaggio—for instance, drawings or preliminary
studies of the *Salome* painting, or other scenes in a
similar vein—I should be most grateful for the opportunity to have them appraised, and to offer them
to certain clients of mine." Dubois, no fool, had instantly decoded the phrase "unsigned works in the
style of," and six months later, he wrote with the
happy news that he'd "discovered" three unsigned
studies "in the style of Caravaggio": one of Salome's
face, one of the Baptist's head on a trencher, and the
third of the old woman (Salome's mother, perhaps?)
lurking in the background. Kensington had paid a
thousand pounds apiece for them; a year later, he
read that a rare group of three Caravaggio studies
had been found and sold to a private collector, for
the rumored sum of a million pounds!

Not long after producing the "Caravaggios," he'd
dined with Kensington in Paris at the King George
V Hotel—a lovely, delicate piece of fish in white
truffle oil, he recalled fondly—and she'd asked him
to keep an eye out for other, similar finds. "My top
clients are especially keen on Rembrandt, Titian,
Michelangelo, and Botticelli," she'd gushed. In
that moment—the taste of the truffle oil vivid in

his memory—Dubois had glimpsed a remarkable opening.

He'd just been hired by Avignon's Petit Palais Museum to clean and restore their prized Botticelli, and it had occurred to him that the opportunity of a lifetime glittered before him, if he had the courage to seize it. "What do you think you could pay for a preliminary study of Botticelli's *Madonna and Child*?" he inquired in an offhand tone. "First quality, of course; verifiable fifteenth-century materials."

Her eyes took on a hungry gleam. "That would be quite a find," she said, struggling to keep the excitement out of her voice. "I imagine I'd be able to pay somewhere in the range of, say, fifty thousand pounds?"

Dubois had nodded noncommittally. Then—after a moment's pause—he delivered the coup de grâce: "And what if I told you that the museum that *thinks* it owns the finished painting has been deceived? That the painting hanging in Avignon is a modern fake . . . and that the actual, authentic painting might—*possibly*—be available, for the right price, to a very discreet buyer?"

She'd stared at him, openmouthed, all pretense of nonchalance gone. "You can't be serious." Then, leaning forward, laying a hand on his hand: "Can you? *Are* you? Is it really possible?"

He'd played it cool. "Notice, I said 'what if?' But I gather you find the idea intriguing. Do you have any clients with ambitions—and budgets—as lofty as that?"

She regained her poise swiftly. "I believe I do," she purred. "How soon do you need to know?"

"One month," he'd answered.

Two weeks later his phone rang. "I have a client who is extremely interested in . . . the painting you mentioned to me in Paris," she said. "Needless to say, he'd want assurances that the work is authentic."

"Of course," Dubois had responded, his voice smooth as fresh varnish. "And, I assume, he'd want proof that the other—the one on display—is not authentic."

"Yes. That, too."

"Neither of those conditions poses a problem," he went on. "*If.*"

"If what?"

"If the price is right. Bear in mind, only four paintings by Botticelli are in private hands. *Four.* For a true connoisseur, this would be the acquisition of a lifetime."

"I understand." She paused. "Did you have a figure in mind? A number I could relay to my client for consideration?"

"I like round numbers," Dubois had answered. "Do you recall the figure you mentioned for a preliminary study? Fifty thousand, I believe?"

"Yes, that's correct." Her voice was hungry.

"Multiply that by a hundred." He heard a soft gasp at the other end of the line. "It is," he reminded her, "one of Botticelli's finest early works. Simple. Sweet. Vibrant. I understand, of course, if it's more than your client can afford . . ."

"I didn't say that," she countered, perhaps more eagerly than she might have wished. "Let me run this past him, and I'll ring you back."

Two hours later, she'd called back. "If you can

conclusively demonstrate the authenticity of what you're offering, we're in."

Dubois was smiling as he hung up.

Now, months later, he smiles again as he finishes applying the white-lead primer, cleans his brush, and lays out the pigments with which he will paint the "authentic" Botticelli for Felicia Kensington and her wealthy, greedy, and gullible client. *Caveat emptor*, he thinks: *Let the buyer beware*.

CHAPTER FIVE
Descartes

DESCARTES'S STOMACH RUMBLINGS HAD been reverberating for hours in the museum's workshop. Still, before leaving for lunch, he dashed upstairs to Gallery 6 for a look at the portrait whose entry-hall enlargement had caught his fancy. The original was even more vivid and striking than the reproduction. Mary Magdalene's hair was long, wavy, and golden; her blue dress and red shawl were bright and cheery; her features, shown in three-quarter profile, were strong, anchored by a roman nose and eyes that were large, frank, and sensual. *No downcast, demure virgin, this one*, Descartes thought. John the Baptist was equally powerful. Over a furry animal pelt, he wore a full-length purple shawl trimmed in gold. His long hair and beard were dark brown and curly, and his sun-baked skin was a deep bronze verging on black, although the narrow, chiseled nose and cheekbones made it clear that he wasn't African. Staring at the painting, Descartes finds himself entertaining inappropriately larcenous fantasies. *Hell, as long as the guy was inside,* he thought, *why didn't he steal this one?*

Spiraling back down, he emerged, bleary-eyed, blinking, and famished, into the dazzling Provençal day, the sun nearly overhead. A leftover sandwich awaited him in the refrigerator at police headquarters, but he was far too hungry for that now. Swimming against a tide of tourists, he angled across Avignon's main square in search of a more satisfying lunch.

The museum was on the narrow, northern end of the long, thin plaza. Flanking the long eastern side was Avignon's main tourist attraction, the Palace of the Popes, an immense Gothic fortress where a series of pontiffs had reigned during the fourteenth century.

Descartes had lived in Avignon for nearly two decades—ever since graduating from the academy—but he'd never set foot in the palace. He regarded Old Avignon as a museum or a stage set—*mausoleum*, in fact, might be the word that best expressed his sentiments. The papal palace and the art museums were fine for the flocking tourists, but Descartes couldn't be bothered to care about power-hungry priests and self-indulgent artists who'd lived half a millennium ago. But now, the fact that a crime had occurred at the museum—not just spray-paint graffiti or rock-throwing vandalism, but something offbeat and baffling—suddenly made the museum itself intriguing. It was as if he'd discovered a youthful, racy photo of an elderly spinster aunt. Perhaps, he thought, there were similar mysteries, unknown depths to be plumbed, within the soaring walls and mighty towers of the papal palace.

Descartes's hunger pangs brought his mind back to the primal exigencies of the body. He needed to eat, he needed to take a dump, and he needed to take a nap. For need one and maybe need two, he angled toward a Moroccan couscous place a block beyond the Palace of the Popes. The food was simple but tasty, and the prices weren't bad, especially if you flashed your badge to remind the manager that you were a cop. Descartes's mouth began to water as he imagined the restaurant's chicken tagine, the succulent, tangy meat—seasoned with green olives and lemons and sweet, plump raisins— falling off the bone, the savory juices saturating the small pearls of couscous.

A few doors before he reached the restaurant, he passed Cinema Vox and paused to see what was playing. Leaning against the theater's large front window, he cupped his hands around his eyes to block the glare and peered in at the posters. *The Avengers*, *Battleship*, and *Best Exotic Marigold Hotel*. *Foreign crap*, he thought, conveniently overlooking the fact that he actually preferred foreign crap—especially American action thrillers—to the depressing, pretentious fare French filmmakers produced.

Just as he was pulling away from the window, something he'd glimpsed shifted from his subconscious, and he leaned back in for another look. For some reason, the cinema had a large print of Botticelli's *The Birth of Venus* hung over the refreshment stand, but the picture wasn't quite right. Descartes stared, then laughed out loud. Instead of

Venus, Marilyn Monroe perched on the clamshell, her feet in stiletto sandals, her pleated white dress swirling around the tops of her thighs, her mouth open in her signature vampish smile. It was an unprecedented experience for the detective: seeing a modern painting that was a playful riff on a classical masterpiece—one of the few classical masterpieces Descartes actually knew. With the force of an epiphany, he realized that art itself—like the museum he'd just left—was both more intriguing and more sexy than he'd ever dreamed.

AFTER CHASING HIS lunch with two strong hits of espresso, the inspector decided to forgo his nap and gut it out until bedtime, so as not to wreck his sleep cycle even more thoroughly. Instead, he spent several hours in Avignon's library—a spectacular old building, he noted with newly appreciative eyes, housed in what had been a cardinal's palace back in the fourteenth century, when the popes called Avignon home. Situated in the vast reading room, surrounded by ancient frescos, hand-glazed floor tiles, leaded windows, and an ornate coffered ceiling, Descartes scanned a stack of books about art restorers and art forgers. He learned, to his surprise, that the line between restoration and forgery was not as bright a line as he'd assumed, and that in practice, the two endeavors were often separated by only the narrowest and most slippery of slopes. A restorer hired to repair a flaked-off Virgin Mary here, a water-stained Jesus there, might eventually be asked to re-create entire scenes, repaint entire canvases . . . and might well be tempted to sell similar re-creations for more than the paltry wages museums paid for restorations. The more Descartes read, the more flooded with fakes the art world seemed—and the more gullible and foolish art "experts" appeared. One British forger, a cheeky Cockney named Tom Keating, had such scorn for the experts that he planted blatant clues in his fakes. He used modern materials, included modern images in his backgrounds, and even went so far as to scrawl the word *FAKE* in lead-based paint beneath the primer of his "masterpieces," so that any dealer, auction house, or museum that bothered to X-ray the work would see, instantly and beyond a doubt, that it was a modern counterfeit. Astonishingly, Keating managed to pass off some two thousand fakes before he was caught.

Another Brit, Eric Hebborn, became a one-man assembly line for "old master" drawings. Unlike Keating, Hebborn—a classically trained artist of considerable talent—was careful to use antique paper, centuries-old recipes for inks and paints and varnishes, and historically authentic techniques to create his pieces. By Hebborn's reckoning—he published a boastful memoir shortly before he died—he'd passed off hundreds of his drawings as the works of old masters before he was exposed . . . and hundreds more afterward, once unscrupulous dealers knew he was the go-to guy for high-quality forgeries.

Thus forearmed with knowledge of the wiles of fakers, Descartes felt prepared to take on Dubois. He would trick the artist, ensnare him in a trap from which there could be no escape. Leaving the library, which occupied a clogged artery in the ancient heart of Avignon, the detective threaded the Peugeot police sedan through the maze of streets, then out through a portal in the medieval city wall. He took the Daladier Bridge over the Rhône, then midway across, veered onto the exit ramp for Barthelasse Island—"the largest river island in France!" the Tourism Office liked to boast, though the competition was not particularly fierce, as best Descartes could tell. Still, the island—mostly public parks and private farms—was a pretty piece of pastoral land, with great views of Avignon's medieval skyline, and Descartes had had good luck bringing dates here on pleasant weekends. Take the water taxi over—*women love that shit*, he reflected with a smile—and pack a picnic lunch. Plenty of wine and a big blanket, those were the essentials.

The GPS was worthless out here—there wasn't a numerical street address for Dubois—and it took Descartes twenty minutes and a half-dozen map checks to find the artist's place. It was a renovated farmhouse in the northern, less developed part of the island, set a half mile down a narrow lane that led to a handful of other farmhouses. The lane was tightly hemmed in on both sides by stone walls, and while Descartes wasn't much prone to claustrophobia, he heaved a sigh of relief when the walls widened and Dubois's property hove into view on his right. A semicircular drive arced past a wooden fence with trellised gate, and Descartes parked behind a rusting Citroën that was pulled off the driveway just ahead of the gate. Descartes felt the car's hood and found it cool, but he noticed that the tires had left fresh tracks in the mud, which meant the car had been driven home and parked sometime after yesterday's rain shower.

Inside the fence, the property seemed more botanical garden than yard, with riotous red beds of poppies, dangling clusters of violet wisteria, and enough lavender to turn the whole yard purple-blue and supply the Chanel perfume factory, come midsummer. Somewhere behind all that foliage, he felt sure, was a house.

When he found it, he rapped the weathered brass knocker three times without getting an answer. He peered through a side window, saw no signs of movement, and cocked his head to listen. Rock-and-roll music—an English band, Dire Straits, if he wasn't mistaken—floated up from somewhere behind the house. Descartes followed the sound around to the back, through an orchard of blooming fruit trees, and up to the door of a building that was simultaneously rustic and sophisticated: rough stucco walls into which large, many paned windows had been set, the roof composed of clay tiles, supported by exposed rafters whose carved ends curved upward slightly: a French peasant of a barn that had acquired an aristocratic Japanese accent somewhere along the way.

Descartes held his police credentials in his left hand and rapped the door with his right—moderately at first, to no effect, then harder, so as to be heard over the throbbing bass and drums of the music. Putting on a stern face, he rehearsed the steps that would lead Dubois slowly but inexorably into his snare. Dubois beat him to the punch, though, flinging himself into the trap the moment he opened the door and saw Descartes's credentials. "Welcome, Inspector," he said with a smile that actually seemed genuine. "I've been expecting you for hours. Have you come to ask why I was crazy enough to sneak a fake Botticelli into the museum . . . or why I was stupid enough to return an original masterpiece I'd managed to make off with?"

Descartes was taken aback, but only for a moment. He gave a half smile, a compliment to an adversary whom he realized he'd been underestimating. "Which question *should* I be asking?"

Dubois shrugged. "If I knew that, it would mean I knew which painting was which. And the sad truth is, I don't."

"Excuse me? Don't *what*?"

"Don't know. Come in, Inspector. Take a look around my studio. Have a cup of tea, or a glass of wine. And hear my mortifying confession."

Two hours and two bottles of wine later, the inspector's head was spinning with pigments, fixatives, sizings, solvents, brushstrokes, and discourses on the unique, unmistakable, inimitable, yet easily aped techniques of Michelangelo, Rembrandt, Van Gogh, and—last but not least—Botticelli. "Botticelli was the Andy Warhol of his day," pronounced Dubois. "You've seen Warhol's posters of Marilyn Monroe's face, yes? He transforms her into a cartoon character with rainbow-colored skin. Look at Botticelli's *Birth of Venus*. The goddess is almost a cartoon. A beautiful, sexy cartoon, but a cartoon nonetheless. I tell you, Inspector, if Botticelli were alive today, he'd be making his art with cans of spray paint on city walls."

Descartes tried to recall the trap he'd designed for Dubois, but the vision was gone, dispersed by the painter's preemptive strike of erudition and wit—or erased by the second bottle of wine—a delicate rosé that packed a deceptive punch. "But wait," the detective said, raising an index finger to halt Dubois. "What about *Madonna and Child*? You said you had a confession."

"Ah, yes." Dubois looked chagrined. "The terrible truth, Inspector, is that I abused Madame Clergue's trust."

Descartes leaned forward eagerly, taking the notepad and pen from the inner pocket of his jacket. "In what way? Tell me everything."

"I talked her into letting me bring the painting here to do the restoration. I convinced her that I couldn't do as good a job there, in that horrid shop of theirs."

Descartes pounced triumphantly. "And that was a lie!"

"No, no, that was completely true. Have you seen the shop? Dreadful! Those fluorescent lights would have given me the shakes in a matter of minutes, Inspector. No, I did a beautiful job of restoration here, just as I said I would. I've brought at least a dozen of their paintings here to work on. But— *but*—once I finished restoring the Botticelli, I took the liberty of making a copy. As exact a copy as was humanly possible."

Descartes's eyes shone in bloodshot triumph. "And you gave the museum the copy and kept the original!"

"Here's the thing, Inspector. I just don't know."

"What do you mean, you don't know? One was

five centuries old; the other had a 'wet paint' sign on it. How could you not tell them apart?"

Dubois shrugged. "I'd just removed the old varnish from the original and put on a new coat, so it looked and smelled new. And I treated the copy to make it look older than it was. Then, disaster struck. The day before I was to return the Botticelli to the museum, the wind tore the roof off my studio. Remember how fierce the mistral was last March? It blew down buildings all along the Rhône Valley."

"I remember. It blew a tree onto my neighbor's car."

"You see? So when it started to rip the roof off, I scooped up all the paintings and put them in the cellar of the house. I was lucky nothing blew out of my hands when I was crossing the yard. But in the confusion, I didn't keep track of which was the Botticelli and which was the copy. So the next day, when Madame Clergue called and demanded the Botticelli back, I panicked. I couldn't tell the paintings apart. So you know what I did, Inspector?"

"No, but I suspect you're about to tell me."

"I flipped a coin. I literally flipped a coin. 'Heads, it's this one; tails, that one.' It landed on heads, so I took that one. When I delivered it, I was sure Madame Clergue and Devereaux, that smug, snobbish curator of hers, would denounce it as a fake. Instead, they went on and on about the brilliant restoration." Dubois shook his head sadly. "I shouldn't have given it another thought, but instead, Inspector, I became obsessed. What if I'd given them the wrong painting? Finally I couldn't stand it anymore. So, yesterday, when I was returning another painting I'd worked on—a piece-of-crap *Annuncia-*

tion that was starting to crack and flake—I hid the *Madonna and Child* in the same crate. I arrived when I knew Devereaux and Madame Clergue were out to lunch and I'd have the shop to myself. I uncrated both paintings, left the *Annunciation* for Devereaux to find, and hid in the furnace room until midnight. Then—as you know—I took the painting I'd smuggled in up to the gallery and hung it alongside the other, so the museum could sort it out."

"But they can't," said Descartes. "Madame Clergue and Devereaux are both tearing their hair out. They can't tell Botticelli's work from yours."

Dubois smiled. "Well, I'll take that as a compliment. A high compliment indeed. But yes, it's simple to tell the two apart."

"How?" Descartes held the pen poised above his notepad.

"Mine has the word *Dubois* in lead foil embedded under the gesso and the primer," Dubois said. "X-ray the two, and mine will be as plain as the nose on your face. I'm surprised they haven't already tried that. Still too cheap to buy an X-ray machine." Descartes made a note—"lead: cf. the Brit, Keating"—then looked up and lifted a bushy, inquiring eyebrow. "It was my way of keeping myself honest, Inspector," the painter explained. "Of making sure I couldn't fool the museum even if I were tempted to." He shrugged sheepishly. "It never occurred to me that I might accidentally fool myself."

Descartes smiled. "Well, if the camera never lies—the X-ray camera, in this case—I'm sure Madame Clergue and Monsieur Devereaux will be very relieved."

Dubois hesitated, then added, "Do you think they might be persuaded to return my copy to me?"

"I'll ask," said Descartes, "but that might be pushing your luck." The inspector glanced at the wall of windows in the nearer end of the building. Night had fallen, and instead of seeing outside, the inspector saw only reflections—his and the artist's, multiplied almost to infinity by the wall of windows at the opposite end of the studio. They were in a rustic version of the Hall of Mirrors at Versailles. "Shit, I'm late," said the detective, rising from the chair, a task that took more effort than it should have. "But can I ask you a question?"

"Isn't that why you came, Inspector? To ask me questions?"

"But this one's unofficial. It's personal."

"Now you've got me on pins and needles, Inspector." Dubois smiled slyly, and Descartes felt a moment of panic: *My god, is he gay? Does he think I'm hitting on him?*

"No, no, it's not about your sex life or anything," the inspector blurted. "It's about a painting I saw at the museum. It's six, seven hundred years old, but the faces looked modern. A man and a woman— John the Baptist and Mary Magdalene."

"Ah, yes. The Puccinelli. Puccinelli prefigures Botticelli in some important ways, you know," the painter went on, and Descartes nodded, though of course he *didn't* know, or hadn't known, until this moment. "Human figures in low relief. Not much depth or volume to them. Doesn't that painting remind you of a cinema poster?"

"That's it!" Descartes exclaimed. "I couldn't quite put my finger on it, but that's it." His mind makes a connection between the religious painting and the playful painting of Marilyn Monroe on the half shell.

"Puccinelli died half a century before Botticelli was born," Dubois went on, "but it's almost as if Botticelli apprenticed with him. Puccinelli worked in Siena and Florence, so Botticelli would have seen his works, of course." He smiled. "Sorry. You didn't ask for an art-history lecture. Did you have a specific question about the painting, Detective?"

Descartes suddenly looked self-conscious. "I was wondering . . . Obviously you have quite the knack for copying. Could you do a copy of that one?"

Dubois smiled, again almost flirtatiously. "Come." He led Descartes to a stack of paintings leaning against the studio's back wall. When he'd flipped halfway through the stack, he motioned for the inspector to look.

Descartes was stunned. The picture leaning so casually against a wall, in a jumble of other paintings, was a perfect likeness of the one in the museum. "Would you consider selling it to me? Not that I could afford it, I'm sure."

Dubois laughed. "Ah, Detective, this is my own personal copy. It has, shall we say, sentimental value to me." Seeing the detective's crestfallen expression, he added, "But I expect I could dash off another copy without much trouble. Maybe not quite this good, but close. I suspect you wouldn't be able to tell them apart."

"What would it cost?"

The artist smiled. "For you, Inspector? No charge. Consider it my initiation gift."

Descartes raised his eyebrows, puzzled. "Initiation?"

"Your initiation into a new addiction, Detective. Art. Its joys and its sorrows."

Descartes laughed. "I won't get addicted. I just happen to like this one painting."

"It always starts with one painting, Detective. That's the gateway drug. Soon you'll be coveting others. Other portraits of Mary Magdalene and John the Baptist. Other works by Puccinelli. Works by later artists he inspired. A *Madonna and Child* by Botticelli, for instance."

THE NEXT DAY at noon, the inspector, Mme. Clergue, and Devereaux took the two *Madonna and Child* paintings to the Radiology Department at Avignon Hospital for an X-ray examination, which the museum lacked the equipment to perform. One painting—the painting Dubois had hung on the wall thirty-six hours before; the painting the inspector had tagged with his used chewing gum—looked uniformly gray in the films. The second painting—the one the museum had displayed proudly for two years since its "restoration"—lit up, the word DUBOIS in white block letters. "I'll be damned," said Descartes. "You had the copy and he had the original. And he brought it back. He actually brought it back."

Once more Madame Clergue cried, with a mixture of humiliation and relief—humiliation at having been fooled, relief at having the lost masterpiece restored.

CHAPTER SIX
Dubois

A LESS SKILLED, LESS confident artist would have begun by sketching the Madonna's outlines in pencil, then painting over them meticulously. The result might have been close to the original in all its dimensions, yet it would have been patently inferior: clearly the work of a cautious, tentative copyist. From years of experience, Dubois knows that it's not enough to *imitate* Botticelli; no: he must boldly *become* Botticelli, just as a skilled actor temporarily loses himself in the character he's portraying.

So he begins by sketching a collage of disjointed, deconstructed images atop the brilliant white lead: A pair of downcast girlish eyes here, another pair there. A rosebud of a mouth, floating freely in one corner of the panel. A baby's pudgy arm and outstretched fingers, reaching for nothing but the edge of the panel. Dubois dashes off these images swiftly, with the bold strokes of a limbering-up exercise not meant for any eyes but the artist's alone. As he sketches, he moves in an almost balletic dance with the panel, accompanied once more by the intricately entwined voices of "10,000 Virgins." In his mind the trappings of the modern world blur and dissolve, like the paint he's scraped off the panel, and he travels back and back and back: back to a time when Lorenzo de Medici—*Il Magnifico*—ruled Florence with an iron hand and a golden purse; back to a time when Michelangelo and Leonardo and Botticelli blazed across the starry firmament like dazzling comets. The sketches are the perfect way to warm up. But more than that, they're also a brilliant part of his plan.

They take less than an hour. He steps back to survey his work. Although he's drawn them with a crayon of dull gray lead—he casts the crayons himself by melting down fishing weights—the images are bold and energetic. They're just the sort of studies, he feels sure, that a cocky twenty-two-year-old Botticelli might dash off, brimming with confidence after eight years of grueling apprenticeship.

Satisfied with the images, and with his own chameleon-like transformation from an aging Frenchman to a youthful Botticelli, Dubois exchanges the lead crayon for a broad brush. He dips it in white lead, and in minutes the sketches have vanished, covered by another silky coat of primer: the foundation for the painting itself. Thanks to a series of extensive, expensive experiments he performed years before in Rome, Dubois knows that if the finished painting is X-rayed—as he'll earnestly

suggest that it be, for everyone's peace of mind—
the London dealer and her American client will be
astonished. Beneath the lovely *Madonna and Child*,
their eyes will behold a hidden treasure: the ghostly
image of Botticelli's own preliminary study for the
finished work. The panel, they'll realize, is a miraculous two-for-one deal, easily worth ten times
the paltry five million pounds Dubois has settled
for! It's a *steal*, they'll congratulate each other. All
parties to the transaction will be delighted, including Dubois, who earmarked part of the five million
for a secure, climate-controlled vault in Switzerland, where the genuine Botticelli—the *genuine*
genuine Botticelli—awaits him, safe, sound, and
spectacular.

Only the final piece of his plan remains to be set
in motion.

CHAPTER SEVEN
Descartes

SIX WEEKS AFTER MADAME Clergue's "original" Botticelli was restored to its prominent spot in Gallery 11—six weeks after the lead-signed fake was consigned to an ignominious storage bin—Descartes received a call from Detective Sergeant Reginald Smythe of New Scotland Yard. According to the excruciatingly courteous Smythe, London's National Gallery was having serious doubts about the authenticity of one of its prize paintings. The painting was Caravaggio's *Salome Receives the Head of John the Baptist*, which had passed through the hands of an art restorer in Avignon, a Jacques Dubois, several years before. Before Smythe traveled all the way from London, he wondered, might Inspector Descartes be so very kind as to determine, by discreet observation, whether Dubois was, in fact, still in residence and available for interrogation? Of course, Descartes assured the British detective, he'd handle it immediately.

Descartes tried Dubois throughout that morning and afternoon—a dozen calls—with no answer. Finally, as darkness fell, he decided to take a drive out to Barthelasse Island. It was possible the artist was away, but it was equally possible that he was simply absorbed in painting.

The day had been gray and cool, and as he crossed the bridge to the island in the deepening dusk, Descartes noticed fog spooling down the river, blanketing the emerald-green waters, spilling onto the low-lying farmland, triggering—for some inexplicable reason—his lifelong fear of drowning. By the time he descended the exit ramp, the road was dark and blanketed in mist. If Descartes hadn't saved the GPS track from his prior visit, he'd never have found his way back to the narrow lane that led to Dubois's place.

Halfway up the narrow, walled lane—all the more claustrophobic in the darkness and fog—Descartes felt the hairs on his neck prickle. At first he could not attach the sensation to anything but the looming walls and blinding fog. As he approached the house, though, he realized that the mist ahead was glowing red-orange, the light flickering and throbbing, rapidly growing higher and brighter. He punched the throttle, heedless of danger, careening between the high, narrow walls. Suddenly, with a crack like a gunshot, his left mirror snapped against one wall. Reflexively he swerved slightly, and with another sharp crack, his right mirror shattered.

By the time he reached the house, the foggy glow had resolved into flames—soaring, roaring flames—and he saw that behind the house, the studio was ablaze, the inferno fueled by turpentine, oil, and God only knew what other flammables. Skidding to a stop behind Dubois's old Citroën—*he's home?* he wondered with a mixture of surprise and concern—he leaped from the car and raced through the gate, not even slowing to glance at the incongruous object propped against the fence.

The high clerestory windows in the shop burst just as he reached the building, raining bits of glass upon Descartes. Shielding his face in the crook of one arm, he ran to the door and tried it, but it was locked. Pushing through the lavender that hugged the wall, he reached a large window and peered inside. Even through the glass, the heat broiled his face and he wrapped both arms across it, leaving only a narrow slit through which he surveyed the interior. Through the dancing flames, his eyes locked on a shape. "Shit," he muttered. Slumped over the work table was Dubois. His right arm was splayed out on the table, and resting atop the hand, slightly askew, was what appeared to be a pistol. The left side of the artist's head was missing.

"Shit," Descartes repeated—"shit, shit, shit"—and stepped away from the window to call the dispatcher. He had not even begun to dial when the window exploded. Shards seethed past his head and tore across the yard, shredding the leaves of ornamental plants. Moments later, the window on the other side of the door blew, too. Arms of flame reached out from each window, enfolding the building in a deadly embrace, clawing at the roof. Small blooms of flame sprouted through the arches of the clay roof tiles. Then, in swift succession, the rafters burned through, and a hole in the roof opened like a maw, gaping wider and wider until it had swallowed the top of the studio entirely.

By the time the fire trucks arrived, the building had been reduced to smoldering embers.

THE AUTOPSY AND forensics report confirmed what Descartes already knew. The corpse was burned beyond recognition, but the coroner confirmed that it was a white male, somewhere in his fifties or sixties. Although the fingers had burned down to bare bone, and the artist had no dental records that Descartes could locate, DNA from the charred corpse was matched to DNA from a hairbrush in the house, so the dead man was positively identified as Dubois. His manner of death was a single gunshot wound to the head, and his death was ruled a suicide.

As he tucked the autopsy report into the case file, Descartes took one last look at the note Dubois had tacked to the gatepost at the entrance to his yard. "The police in London plan to arrest me, but they're too late. I cannot bear the thought of prison, and so I take the coward's exit. My life has been one long series of deceptions and evasions, so this sort of death is only fitting." Descartes replaced the note, closed the dossier, and filed it in the archive of closed cases. Then he signed out and headed home for lunch.

When he unlocked the deadbolt, Descartes stood in the apartment's open doorway, his face breaking into a smile as he surveyed the opposite wall. There, Mary Magdalene and John the Baptist—regal, serene, and sexy—basked in the glow of the halogen track lights Descartes had stayed up late last night installing. The painting looked infinitely better than the horrible Jackson Pollock print that had hung there for years. Thank God that bitch Yvonne had taken it with her when she left.

Perhaps he should have left Magdalene and the Baptist where he'd found them, propped against the fence at the Dubois place, beside the post where the artist had tacked his farewell note. But what business was the painting of the National Police? The painting was a parting gift—a personal gift—from the old faker. A second note, taped to the frame, made that clear: "Goodbye, Inspector. I enjoyed meeting you, and I hope this trifle brings you much pleasure. —R.D."

He'd driven home in the pale, watery light of midmorning, the second note tucked into his pocket, the painting tucked into the trunk of his car, the shattered mirrors dangling and flapping on either side of the car. He'd slammed the trunk only moments before the firemen and the forensic technicians had arrived to hose down the ruins, recover the charred body, and gather their evidence.

CHAPTER EIGHT
Dubois

JACK WOODS RAISES THE back of his chaise longue and takes a slow, appreciative swig of sangria. Woods is a grizzled sixty-year-old Englishman; until six days before, he was a grizzled sixty-year-old Frenchman, Jacques Dubois. He's working hard to inhabit the new name, but so far he still thinks of himself as Dubois.

His eyes shielded behind reflective sunglasses, he surveys the youthful bodies gleaming on the sand here at Cala del Home Mort—"Dead Man's Beach"—a speck of Spanish coastline whose very name seems tailor-made for Dubois. With a few pale, doughy exceptions, the nude young men on display here are as tautly sculpted and bronze as any casting by Donatello or Rodin, and despite the name of the beach, they seem very much alive.

Dubois's lover, François—one of the pale, doughy exceptions—dozes on a neighboring chaise. He's neither attractive nor interesting, but he deserves Dubois's undying gratitude. If not for the cadaver François spirited away from his Marseilles mortuary—a fifty-six-year-old heart-attack victim, whose body François replaced in the coffin with sandbags—Dubois could never have composed such an artful forgery of suicide: the charred body; the gunshot-shattered head; the pistol in the outstretched hand; even the new hairbrush, raked through the corpse's hair and then planted on the bathroom counter. Yes, Dubois chose François wisely, and he *does* feel deeply grateful.

Nevertheless, he's pondering how to rid himself of the pasty mortician, who, having served his purpose, begins to grow tiresome. Dubois needs to shed François without angering him—that is, without sending him running to the police—but it's a tricky business. *He has to think the breakup is his idea*, Dubois realizes.

A nearby sunbather coughs, and the germ of an idea begins to incubate in Dubois's mind. *Perhaps if I came down with an illness, some malady*, he muses. *Something debasing and repellent, yet not so grave as to inspire nobility and self-sacrifice. Lip cancer? Irritable bowel syndrome? Cadaverous breath?* Finally, in a flash of inspiration, it comes to Dubois: *Warts—genital warts!* Molded of silicone, they can be glued on, their ranks and size growing day by disgusting day. Best of all, Dubois can lay the blame at François's own . . . door, since François—in a moment of drunken remorse—has confessed to three recent infidelities. (Dubois could have consoled François by making a similar confession, but instead he wept, a study in wronged innocence.) Yes, warts will do nicely; in a week—two, at most—François will scurry back to Marseilles, brimming with guilt and compassion. After a day or so of public melancholy, Dubois will set up an easel on the beach, sketch beautiful young men, and swap art for idyllic interludes with one Adonis after another.

Dubois will soon need a more meaningful outlet for his prodigious energies. But he has a plan for that, too. Only yesterday, on a stroll through town, he spotted an ad in a realtor's window: "Private villa for lease." The property—perched on a rocky bluff, with stunning Mediterranean views—includes a gardener's cottage that would make a charming studio. Already, in a Barcelona warehouse an hour away, Dubois's materials—sheaves of ancient paper and parchment, handmade pigments and brushes, musty frames and panels, even a few dreadful, sacrificial old paintings—await their metamorphoses into masterpieces.

He wishes he'd had the nerve to bring the Puccinelli, too, but the risk seemed too great. Astonishing, to think that a policeman—a provincial dolt!—possesses an authentic medieval masterpiece. For the moment, Dubois can appreciate the mirror-image ironies: the blissful ignorance of the museum in Avignon, proudly displaying its "original" Botticelli, and the ignorant bliss of the policeman, adoring his free "copy" of Mary Magdalene and John the Baptist. Someday soon—perhaps with the help of some lithe, lock-picking Spaniard—Dubois will retrieve the original from the policeman, replacing it with an undetectable copy. The swap will be his third time to deceive the inspector, he realizes: first, with the pair of faked Botticellis; second, with the faked suicide (he smiles, recalling the daring ambiguity of the phrase "this sort of death"); soon, with the theft of a priceless painting from the policeman's own home. All in all, a delightful hat trick.

CHAPTER NINE
Descartes

DESCARTES WAS STILL SAVORING his lunch and his painting when his mobile jangled. He glanced at the display and frowned; the call was from his boss, the chief inspector. "What's up?" he asked, trying not to let his annoyance show.

"A new case for you. A homicide."

Shit, not a homicide, Descartes groaned inwardly. *Homicides are such a pain in the ass.* "Me?" he said, feigning surprise. "Isn't Pierre next in the rotation?"

"Pierre is sick. Jean-Paul leaves tomorrow for antiterrorist training. And Etienne is still on paternity leave. Besides, you have the best English, and the case involves two Americans. One . . ."—a pause, and Descartes heard papers rattling— "named William Brockton. The other, probably his girlfriend, Miranda Lovelady."

Hmm, Descartes thought, *a homicide involving*

foreign lovebirds. That might be interesting after all. "Okay," he said, as if he actually had a choice. To guilt the boss, he added, "But you owe me. Don't forget, I put in a shitload of overtime on the Dubois case. A weird one, eh?"

"Ha," the chief inspector scoffed. "This one is much more bizarre."

"Bullshit. What could be more bizarre?"

There was a silence—Descartes thought he'd lost the call, but it was just his boss letting him twist in the wind briefly. Then, with a mixture of smugness and horror, the chief inspector uttered a single word before hanging up: "Crucifixion."